THE
FIRST DAY OF
ETERNITY

**Pinnacle Westerns
by Spur Award–Winning Author**

CHARLES G. WEST

THE JOHN HAWK WESTERNS

Hell Hath No Fury

No Justice in Hell

Montana Territory

THE COLE BONNER WESTERNS

Massacre at Crow Creek Crossing

THE HUNTERS

To Hell and Gone

Published by Kensington Publishing Corp.

THE
FIRST DAY OF
ETERNITY

THE HUNTERS

CHARLES G.
WEST

PINNACLE BOOKS
Kensington Publishing Corp.
www.kensingtonbooks.com

PINNACLE BOOKS are published by

Kensington Publishing Corp.
119 West 40th Street
New York, NY 10018

Copyright © 2024 by Charles G. West

All Kensington titles, imprints, and distributed lines are available at special quantity discounts for bulk purchases for sales promotion, premiums, fund-raising, and educational or institutional use.

Special book excerpts or customized printings can also be created to fit specific needs. For details, write or phone the office of the Kensington Sales Manager: Kensington Publishing Corp., 119 West 40th Street, New York, NY 10018. Attn. Sales Department. Phone: 1-800-221-2647.

PINNACLE BOOKS and the Pinnacle logo Reg. U.S. Pat. & TM Off.

First Printing: January 2024
ISBN-13: 978-0-7860-5021-5
ISBN-13: 978-0-7860-5022-2 (eBook)

10 9 8 7 6 5 4 3 2 1

Printed in the United States of America

For Ronda

CHAPTER 1

Cody Hunter remained standing motionless for what seemed like many minutes, staring down at the engraved stone that seemed so out of place here in this wilderness. This was not the roughly carved names and dates left by emigrants and travelers so often found on these wagon roads. The persons responsible for memorializing this rugged-looking patch of scrubby weeds and bushes thought it worthy of a permanently engraved and polished gravestone. He was still in a mild state of shock as he read the gravestone again. The tragic attack had happened fifteen years ago, but the stone had obviously been left here at a more recent date, judging by the condition of it.

In loving memory of
Our Father and Mother, Robert and Rose Frasier
Our brothers, Tim and Bobby
And their friend, Cody Hunter

Fifteen years had passed since the attack on the three wagons traveling the Mullan Road to Washington Territory, and Cody had been only five years old at the time. So, his memory of the attack was vague at best. He remembered the sudden explosion of shooting and his parents telling him to run to the lead wagon. He remembered he had been walking with Bobby Frasier when the shots first rang out. He and Bobby ran until Bobby suddenly fell. After that, there was nothing until he awoke one morning in a Crow tipi to find an Indian woman smiling down at him. Her name was Morning Rain, wife of Spotted Pony. When Cody was well enough to understand, Morning Rain told him that Spotted Pony had found him under a bush after the attack on the three wagons. She told him about the wolf that was protecting him until he was found by the Crow hunters. She also told him that Spotted Pony had found the bodies of his father and his brothers.

Now, after so many years had passed, years that saw him accept Spotted Pony and Morning Rain as his parents, he is stunned to realize one of the bodies Spotted Pony found was not that of his father. He had said he found the body of a woman and a man. They were evidently Bobby Frasier's parents. The bodies of the two boys were those of Bobby and Tim Frasier. He remembered then that the Frasiers also had two daughters. Looking at the tombstone again, he guessed that the daughters were responsible for its existence. At the moment, he wished he had never seen the stone. He had grown into manhood thinking his real parents were dead and he was proud to be a Crow warrior. To learn now that his father and brothers might still be alive was more of a troubling nature to him. He could not deny a natural curiosity about them, but the contrast in their lives might be too much to overcome. Maybe best to leave things as they are, he decided, and push on westward. "Things happen for a reason, Storm," he announced to his big dun gelding as he climbed back up into the saddle. "And it seems to me that I was supposed to walk the path of the Crow. I've got no complaints." He wheeled his horse around to follow the trail out of the Mullan Pass.

* * *

Cody continued to follow the road down from the pass, just as his father had fifteen years ago. It was supposed to lead him to Clark's Fork River. Although only five at the time, he remembered that the river would take them up a valley to a place called Hellgate Village. He remembered that he and his brothers had laughed at the name. He could only assume he would know the river when he reached it, for he was now traveling where he had never been before. Since he was in no particular hurry to reach Hellgate Village, he was inclined to keep an eye alert for any signs of deer activity. He had already decided to stop and make his camp if he discovered a good hunting spot, and he came to an obvious one when he approached a healthy stream making its way down from a tree-covered ridge north of the trail.

When he reached the point where the road crossed the stream, he was gratified to discover a multitude of deer tracks going and coming on a path he assumed led to the river. There was no longer any decision to be made, he was ready to select a spot to camp for the night. If he had read the sign right, and he was confident that he had, then he should be able to take care of his needs for meat for quite a while. So he turned his attention toward the selection of a place to camp that would serve him for a few days while he butchered and smoked a quantity of deer meat to last him for some time. The camp he needed would have to provide grass and water for his horses for the few days he would spend there. So it only made sense to follow the stream to the river, camp beside the river, and hunt the game trail the deer followed to the river. That way, his camp would be far enough away from his hunting and not likely to scare the deer away.

He was pleased to find the river was closer than he thought. When he reached the point where the stream emptied into it, it appeared to be a popular crossing point for the deer. It seemed that he had happened upon the perfect hunting ground. He wasted no time in selecting the location for his camp and soon had his horses and packs taken care of. There was plenty of wood available for his campfire as well as his smoke-curing of the meat. He thought then of his Crow brother, Bloody Axe, and their many hunting trips together. Bloody Axe would have thought this a perfect setup.

By the time he had his base camp established, the sun was already setting and soon it would be dark and the deer would be coming out of the tree-covered hills above to go to water and graze. He planned to do most of his hunting in the morning, but he decided he might as well enjoy some fresh meat tonight. So as not to take the risk of scaring the game away from the trail, he decided to kill his deer tonight with his bow. With that possibility in mind earlier, he had made it a point to notice likely spots to ambush a deer on the path down to the stream. So he picked up his bow and started back up the slope on foot, walking through the trees parallel to the game trail. When he reached the last spot he had mentally noted, he cut over to the path and settled himself across the stream from it.

After a considerable wait, he was beginning to think he might not know the habits of the Montana mountain deer. Then he heard the soft padding of deer hooves on the path above and a large buck passed on his way to the river. Behind the buck, three does followed. Cody notched an arrow and drew it back. Aiming for a lung shot behind the front leg of the hindmost doe, he released the arrow. At that short distance, both his aim and his power were enough to cause her to stumble at once, then attempt to get up to run. But Cody was quickly on her to end her suffering before the other deer knew she was down. "I'm glad you weren't any bigger," he said when he strained to get her up on his shoulders. Once he got her settled, he very carefully retraced his tracks back down the slope to his camp.

As soon as he got back to his camp, he gutted and bled the deer. Then he hung the carcass from a tree limb, all this before he started his fire. The spot he had selected for his camp was at a sharp curve in the river, and he located his fire back against the elbow formed by the curve. With a thick stand of fir trees lining that side of the river, he figured his fire would be very hard to detect, especially from the road that continued north after crossing the stream, a considerable distance away. That was important to him since he planned to stay long enough to supply himself with meat enough to last him for a while. He built his fire then and while it was gaining life, he started butchering the deer, setting aside the cuts to be his supper that night and his breakfast in the morning. He then prepared cuts of meat for smoking, including some thin strips to be smoked and eaten later on as jerky. After his fresh meat was done, he went to work converting his fire to a smoking chamber, using green wood and leaves and branches to produce the smoke he needed to preserve the rest of the meat.

Still feeling no need to hurry, he remained there for a couple of days until he decided he could not reasonably carry any more on his two packhorses. It was with a fair amount of reluctance that he finally closed down his camp. Had it not been in the vicinity of a well-traveled road, he might have considered wintering there. As carefully as he hunted, he was convinced he would never interrupt the endless supply of meat that came down the stream. "Time to get movin' tomorrow," he told the dun gelding. "Another day or two in this camp and you'll be too fat to travel."

It crossed his mind that he would be traveling the same road his father and brothers traveled after the attack by the

Blackfoot party, thinking that he was dead. The thought of how they must have felt caused him to wonder if he should make any attempt to let them know he was alive. He had already decided it best to leave things as they were. Now, he wasn't sure if that was the right thing to do. Ultimately, he decided he would try to find his father and brothers if he could. Then he could decide whether to tell them the true story or not. That decision sat easier on his mind. After fifteen years, it was unlikely anyone in Hellgate Village would remember that one wagon, anyway.

He was awakened shortly before daybreak by the sound of gunshots. A hunter, he wondered, but still groggy after having been awakened by the shots, he wasn't certain exactly how many he had heard. They were not that far away and sounded as if they had come from the wagon road. He decided it in his best interest to see if he could find the source of the shots so he could avoid being shot at himself. In the darkness he might be mistaken for a deer. So he packed up his camp, figuring to cook his breakfast after he checked on the shots. He climbed on his horse and started back through the trees until he reached the wagon road again just as the first rays of light began to expand. After riding what he estimated to be a distance of about half a mile, he was approaching another stream crossing. He spotted a thin line of smoke wafting up through the trees a few dozen yards off the road. He decided it best to check it out, so he turned the dun gelding off the road and rode into the trees beside the stream, where he dismounted and pulled his rifle from the saddle sling. Leaving his horses there, he proceeded to make his way to the fire on foot. He had not gone far when he saw the campsite through the trees in a small clearing and what looked like a body lying several feet from the fire.

Immediately alert then, he crouched and advanced a little closer to the fire, holding his Henry rifle ready to fire. He hesitated and listened for a few moments. Hearing no sound other than the insects by the stream, he took another step forward in time to hear the snap of a bullet behind his head, followed at once by the report of the rifle that fired it. At the same time, he saw the muzzle flash directly across the campfire in the bushes on the other side. He reacted at once. Hearing no sound of another cartridge being chambered, he instinctively charged right across the fire and into the bushes on the other side. The collision with the shooter sent them both tumbling and both frantically fighting for possession of the shooter's rifle. Cody easily overpowered his opponent who turned out to be a woman who continued to struggle until she realized it was useless.

When he felt her relax her arms, he said, "I have not come to harm you. You have nothing to fear from me. Do you understand? The person lyin' beside the fire, is that your husband?"

"He is my brother," she answered. "They killed him. I thought you were them coming back to look for me." He released her arms then, feeling sure she was no longer a threat.

"You're sure he's dead?" Cody asked.

"Yes," she answered. "They shot him three times." She started crying then. "I ran into the bushes and they came after me, but I climbed up into a tree and they didn't see me in the dark. I waited a long time after they gave up before I went back to my brother. I'm sorry I shot at you, but I thought it was them."

"How many were there?"

"Two," she answered. "Two vile men. They took our horses and the little food we had. They said they wouldn't hurt us and then they shot my brother down and that's when I ran. I outran them and kept running till I got tired and hid in that tree. I heard them talking when they walked under that tree. I was so afraid they were going to look up and see me. One of them said I would come back to the fire to get anything I could use. So they went away to make another camp, then sneak back here when I came back."

"I'm surprised they left you a rifle to use against them," Cody said.

"They didn't see it," she said. "Tom propped it up against a tree when he went to get more wood for the fire. And that was why he didn't even have a chance to fight when they pulled their guns."

"I'm sorry about your brother," Cody told her, "but right now I expect we'd better get ready for their return so you can get your horses and whatever else they took from you. I've gotta go get my horses and move them down below your camp so they don't see them."

"Are you sure we shouldn't just run before they come back?" she asked. "These are two rough men."

"They need to answer for killin' your brother," Cody told her. "And we need your horses back. So you stay right here outta the clearin' and I'll be right back." She looked uneasy about it as if he just might leave and keep going rather than fight two killers. But she nodded her head vigorously. He went back toward the road to get Storm and his packhorse. In a few minutes, he was back, and when he led the two horses past her, he held out a piece of deer jerky. "You hungry?" Again, she nodded vigorously and took the jerky while he went to hide his horses.

CHAPTER 2

"Whaddaya reckon that shot was?" Elmo Cox asked. They had been gone for more than half an hour, but they hadn't ridden but a quarter of a mile at most. "I didn't see no rifle at their camp."

"I know it, but you know that feller musta had one. He just had it hid somewhere," Paul Pickett said. "So it had to be that woman firin' that shot."

"But whaddaya reckon she was shootin' at?" He pulled at his chin whiskers as he thought about the slender little woman. "She ran like a little doe through them bushes. You don't reckon that one shot we heard was her shootin' herself, do ya?"

"I hope to hell not," Pickett replied, "but you can't really blame her after she got a look at you. We better let me break her in first."

"The hell you say," Elmo replied. "We're gonna flip a coin to see who gets to saddle break her."

"I say we'd best get back down there and find out what that shot was about," Pickett insisted. "I've got a bad feelin' about that woman. She just mighta stuck that rifle under her chin and pulled the trigger. Maybe we shouldn'ta left her back there by herself. Hell, let's get the horses rounded up and get on back there." That was motivation enough to get both men hustling to get back to find the explanation for the one shot.

Aware now that the woman had a rifle and might know how to use it, the two outlaws approached the spot where the road crossed the stream. They decided it best to leave the horses there by the road, and they would go into the camp on foot. They left their rifles on their horses, but both had their handguns drawn in precaution as they carefully made their way back to the clearing. Just before reaching it, they both stopped upon seeing the woman sitting beside a tree on the opposite side of the fire from them. "There she is, Elmo. She's just settin' there waitin' for us."

"I don't see no rifle. Be careful," Pickett warned. "Wait a minute! Yonder it is. It's leanin' up against a tree on this side of the fire. Ain't no way she can get to it before I can put a bullet in her head. Hello there, Missy!" He called out to her. "Did you think we was gonna run off and leave you? We decided we was gonna take good care of you."

They headed straight for her then and still she did not move from her position by the tree. "Who you want first?" Elmo asked, advancing even closer. He was surprised when she answered him.

"I want you," she said and pulled her hand out from under her skirt with Cody's .44 Colt in it and pulled the trigger. At the same time, Pickett dropped to his knees when a shot from Cody's rifle slammed him in the chest. Elmo staggered backward, hit in the side by the woman's shot. He raised his pistol to fire as she dived behind the tree, but he crumpled to the ground from Cody's kill shot in the center of his back.

"It's over now," Cody called out to her. So she came out from behind the tree where he had positioned her with strict instructions that she was to take one shot, then dive behind the tree whether she hit or missed. "You did a good job," he said. "I think your brother would have been proud of you." She carefully handed his .44 back to him, and he removed the empty shell. He had been totally surprised when she requested that she be given the opportunity to personally avenge her brother's murder. He thought it too dangerous for her to try and only agreed to it because he was confident he could cut both men down before they could react to her shot. Now, seeing the satisfaction her vengeance had brought her, he was glad she managed to get the shot off.

"Thank you for letting me shoot one of Tom's murderers," she said. "I guess it's about time I thanked you for coming along when you did. I'm so grateful to you and I'm pleased to meet you, Mister. . . ." She paused and waited for him to fill in the blank.

He hesitated a second before saying, "Hunter, my name is Cody Hunter."

"I'm so glad to meet you, Cody. My name is Katie Cole. To tell you the truth, when you first found me I took that shot at you because I thought you were an Indian. I still thought you were one until you landed on top of me and I could see your face."

"I suppose I could have told you my name is Crazy Wolf, but my birth name is Cody Hunter. I was raised by the Crow Indians from the age of five."

"Well, we make quite a team, Cody and Katie," she said.

"I reckon so," Cody agreed. "But right now we've got some work to do. First, we need to take care of your brother. I don't even know what direction you are headin' in. Where were you and your brother headin'?" When she said Missoula, he hesitated, then said, "North?"

"That's right," she said, "north. We were on our way to our father's house. Which way are you going?" When he said he was going north, too, she said, "Then I guess we might as well travel together." She paused, then said, "If that's all right with you."

"That's all right with me, but what do you want me to do with your brother's body? Do you want me to bury him, or do you want to take him home to bury? I don't know how far that would be."

"Bury him," she said without hesitation. "It's gonna be hard enough to tell Pa that Tom's dead without showing up on the front porch with his stiff body."

"All right, you can pick the place and I'll dig him a grave. Before I do that, though, I'll drag those two off away from the stream somewhere for the buzzards to eat. Then I'll go out to the road and bring in all their horses and stuff."

"Or would you rather eat some breakfast first?" Katie suggested. "Have you got any more of that deer jerky?"

"I've got better than that," he said. "I've got fresh deer meat that I killed yesterday, that should still be fresh enough to eat this mornin'. If it isn't, I've got a load of smoked meat as well as jerky. I'll bring my packhorse up and you can take a look at the meat."

She was obviously thrilled to find he was so well supplied with food, and she volunteered to do the cooking while he removed Elmo and Paul from the clearing. She and her brother had used up the last of their money in Helena and were about ready to start cooking their shoelaces. But Cody was well supplied with coffee, flour, salt, and sugar, so that it was like a feast to Katie. When they finished, Cody found a short-handle shovel and a one-hand pickaxe on the outlaws' packhorses that he used to dig Tom's grave. Afterward, Katie said a few words of farewell over the grave. She helped him search through the belongings of the two outlaws, and Cody inspected the horses and saddles they had acquired. Although it took them into the early afternoon before they were finished, they packed up their camp and started moving farther along the road to Missoula.

They followed the river road for about twenty miles before stopping to make camp for the night. The spot Cody picked was a grassy clearing close to the edge of the river where there was ample grazing for the horses they had accumulated. And there was plenty of firewood in the trees that surrounded the clearing. Once the horses were taken care of, Cody returned to the fire and poured himself a cup of coffee while Katie cooked up some of the smoked venison. "How far do you think we are from Missoula?" Cody asked her.

"I'm not too good at guessing things like that," she answered. "But I'd guess we're another day or a day and a half away."

"I don't have any idea of the distance, myself," Cody told her. "The last time I was this far up this road I was just five years old and I'd never heard of Missoula. Where did you and your brother Tom start out from on this trip?"

"Near Great Falls," she answered. "Tom rode all the way from Missoula just to escort me back home." She paused then to try to prevent the birth of a tear in her eye. "And it ended up costing him his life."

"I'm sorry," Cody quickly apologized. "I shouldn't have asked you. It's none of my business, anyway."

"No, there's no need for you to apologize," she insisted. "After what you've done for me, I'll tell you anything you wanna know." She hesitated for a few moments to decide whether or not to make a confession. "I'm on my way home to tell my father I'm sorry for leaving after he tried to make me see how wrong I was. But he told me I was always welcome to come home. And no matter where I was, he'd send Tom to come get me."

"That was bad, what happened to your brother," Cody

said, "but it sounds like your father will be mighty glad to see you when you get home."

"I don't know if he will or not," she said, having decided to tell Cody the complete story, "especially when he finds out that Tom's dead." She continued her story while she formed up some pan bread to fry in the grease from the smoked venison. "I got tricked into a bad decision by a sweet-talking drifter who was passing through town. Troy King was his name, and he said he fell in love with me the first time he saw me. Said he'd been looking for me all his life, and now that he'd found me, he couldn't leave town without me. Pa and Tom both told me I was making a mistake if I believed Troy, but I was too dumb to listen to them." She paused then, realizing she was dragging out her life story and Cody might not want all the details. "Anyway, to make a long story short, I went with Troy after he promised we would get married when we got to Great Falls. But I found out right away that Pa and Tom were right, and Troy turned out to be an outlaw who rode with a gang that holed up outside of Great Falls. He had no plans to marry me, so when he went with his gang to rob a bank four days away from there, I went into town and telegraphed Pa, and he sent Tom to get me. So that's the innocent maiden you just saved from those two men."

He realized that, for some reason, she thought she owed him a confession for risking his life to save her, and he felt truly sorry for her. "I'm sorry that happened to you, Katie. But it wasn't your fault you were lied to. I believe you've already paid a terrible price for makin' a wrong decision, but there can't be any blame thrown your way for believin' what a liar told you. My advice to you is to start your life all over again in Missoula."

"You are truly an unusual man," she stated simply.

"I've got my faults," he replied.

* * *

They started out early the next morning after Cody saddled all the horses they were in possession of now. He decided to tie a packhorse to his and Katie's horses and let the rest of the horses follow on their own. "At least, I think they'll follow along, but if they don't, I'll tie 'em onto a rope." It turned out that the horses running loose were inclined to go with the lead horses, so Cody and Katie took to the road, planning to cook breakfast when they stopped to rest them.

Katie found herself in a great state of mind on this morning. She felt that she had confessed to the mistakes she had made and yet Cody showed no signs of condemning her for her poor decisions. And he continued to treat her like a lady. She told him that when she and Tom had first fled from the shabby cabin where Troy King had left her to wait for his return, she feared that he would immediately try to come after her. But once they reached Helena, she felt he would not care enough to follow their trail any farther.

However, if Katie had known Troy King a little better, she would have known that he would go to any means to punish anyone who rejected him, and she would have been in fear for her life. Pushing his horses hard, Troy King was confident that he would overtake her before she made it home. He didn't waste any time trying to track her because he knew she had only one place to run, and that was home to her father's house in Missoula. After taking care of Katie, he planned to quiet the old man as well if he didn't catch up to her before she made it home. Once he was on the wagon road that followed the Clark Fork River, he was surprised to discover a great many recently made hoofprints at a couple of stream crossings. He was curious enough to follow the tracks at one of the crossings, for there were many tracks following the creek as well as some fairly fresh droppings that indicated horses were left there by the road for a while. He decided to follow the tracks that led into the trees by the river.

When he reached the clearing where a campfire had been built, there were plenty of signs that something had gone on including some blood where it appeared a couple of bodies had lain. He decided then that there might be more to gain than just the settling with Katie Cole, and from that point on, he became more alert to any more tracks. He followed the tracks of what he decided was about a dozen horses. It was getting late in the day now, and he guessed that he was about forty miles from Missoula. The party he had been following would no doubt be going into camp soon. He had also decided that Katie Cole had likely joined the party and that there were probably three or four in that party. He was going to have to see if there were more than he could handle, but first, he had to see if Katie was with them.

As he expected, he soon came to the place where the tracks turned off the road and went through the trees, toward the river. With his rifle ready now, he followed the tracks in through the trees. When he was far enough in to hide his horses, he dismounted and tied the horses. Then he continued on until he saw the campfire, and Katie was kneeling beside it. He almost gave a yelp of surprise but contained it. He had been telling himself that she was with the party he had been following, but he realized he had been hoping and not really convinced that he was right. But there she was! He scanned the entire clearing then and saw no one else there. He looked at the horses standing around the clearing, five with saddles still on. Where were the riders? He listened. There was no sound of anyone anywhere close around. This made no sense. She could not have controlled all the horses by herself. Then she suddenly looked up and called out, "Cody." Troy raised his rifle to his shoulder and waited for the man she called to appear. When no one appeared in the little clearing, she stood up and called out again, "Cody, where are you?"

"That's right, darlin'," Troy mumbled to himself, "stand up nice and tall. I'll take care of Cody after I shoot you." He laid the front sight on Katie's breast, squeezed the trigger, and screamed in pain as the rifle sent a shot straight up in the air. The rifle was snatched from his hands as he staggered backward, grasping for the long skinning knife lodged in his gut. Cody cranked another cartridge into the chamber and ended Troy's agony with a shot in his forehead.

Near frantic now, Katie screamed out his name again, and Cody answered. "I'm right here, Katie. Everything's all right now. I don't think you have to worry about that fellow—what's his name—chasin' you anymore."

"Troy?" Katie exclaimed. "Is it Troy?" She started running into the trees toward him, now that he stepped out of the bushes.

"I don't know," Cody answered, "but he was fixin' to shoot you when you stood up."

"Oh, my Lord in Heaven," she gasped when she saw him lying there staring at the sky above him.

Cody wasn't sure what her emotions were, seeing him lying there with a black hole in his forehead and nothing but the handle of a skinning knife protruding from his gut. After all, she had thought enough of him to follow him to Great Falls. "I had to stop him. He was fixin' to shoot you."

"I know, Cody. Don't worry about my feelings for him. They died long ago. I'm just thankful that you were here to save my life again."

"Go on back to the fire now," Cody said, "and I'll take

care of his body." She nodded and turned to go back to the fire.

He waited until she was gone before he placed his foot on Troy's chest and yanked his knife out of his gut. Then he cleaned the blood from the blade on Troy's shirt and returned the knife to its sheath. He removed the gun belt and checked his pockets for anything of value before dragging the body deeper into the woods and leaving it for the scavengers to eat. Then he went back to find Troy's horses and led them to the spot where he had been checking Storm's hooves. "I reckon I owe you one," he said to the big dun gelding and stroked his face and neck. The horse had sensed the arrival of a strange horse and issued an inquiring whinny. If Troy King's horse hadn't answered Storm, Cody would not have known another horse was coming in from the road.

"How did you know he was there?" Katie asked when Cody returned to the fire.

"My horse told me," Cody replied. "You sure you're all right now?"

"Yes, I think I am," she said, "thanks to you. I don't know if it might not have been better if Troy had been able to kill me, though, after the mistakes I've made."

"That part of your life is done with," Cody said. "You can put it behind you and start out on a new road."

She smiled then. "I reckon I can do that. Anyway, I'll be home before dinnertime tomorrow. Pa's farm is almost ten miles south of Missoula." She shook her head before adding, "That is, if we don't have any more visitors. So I guess I'll lighten up the load on that packhorse of yours and cook us some supper now. I'm afraid I've used up a lot of your food supply already."

"That won't be a problem," Cody said, pulled a roll of paper money out of his pocket, and handed it to her. "Your late Mr. King was carryin' three hundred dollars. I figured he'd want you to have it. I took twenty dollars of it to pay for the supplies we've used up and since your pa has a farm, I figure he could always use some horses."

Almost stunned by his generosity, Katie didn't know what to say. She automatically assumed that he would claim everything since he was the one who had killed for it, protecting her in the process. "I didn't think about getting any of this," she said. "You are the one who's responsible for us having it."

"I don't need to be foolin' with a herd of horses where I'm headin'. I've got some guns I can sell and plenty of ammunition that I can always use. Besides since your brother ain't comin' back with you, you at least oughta be bringin' him some gifts." He could see that she was trying to think of some words to express her gratitude, so he said, "Enough talk, let's get something on the fire to eat."

"What the hell . . . ?" Thomas Cole blurted when he came out of the barn and saw a small herd of horses coming down the lane that led to the wagon road. They were led by two riders, and at that distance, one looked to be a boy and the other looked like an Indian. "Likely figurin' on drivin' their damn horses to the river to water 'em. They oughta have enough sense to know if there's a lane from the road, it's bound to be private property. Well, they can just turn 'em right around. I don't need to have a bunch of horses gallopin' through my cornfield." In case he might need it, he went back in the barn to get his shotgun, and in a minute he was back and walking down the middle of the lane to meet them. He stopped abruptly when they were close enough to see that one of the riders was not a boy. Katie yelled a loud hello then and kicked her horse into a lope to meet him. "Katie!" He yelled when he saw who it was and started to run to meet her. She jumped down from her horse and ran to hug him. "Thank the Lord you're all right! Where's Tom?"

"Pa, Tom's dead. He was killed by two men that stopped us on the way back home. They shot him before he could get to his gun."

"Oh, mercy me," her father groaned. "I shoulda gone to get you and let him stay here." He looked back at the horses still approaching. "Who's the Injun and what does he want?" He figured he was looking for a reward for bringing his daughter home.

"He's not an Indian, Pa. His name's Cody Hunter, and he saved my life twice. He doesn't want anything. In fact he wants to make you a gift of most of those horses." Her father released her from his embrace then and turned to meet Cody as he stepped down from the saddle. "Cody," Katie said, "this is my father, Thomas Cole."

"Pleased to make your acquaintance, Mr. Cole, and I'm sorry your son didn't make it back."

"I wanna thank you for the safe return of my daughter," Thomas said. "I don't know what I can do to repay you."

"Just take good care of her, I reckon. She's a fine woman," Cody replied. "And she's had a mighty tough time trying to get back home."

"I can promise you that," Thomas said. "You two must be hungry. I was just goin' to the house to fix something to eat for dinner."

"Why don't I do that?" Katie said. "I'll go in and see what I can find in the kitchen to eat." She looked at her father and grinned. "Pa's been living like a bachelor for a while now. I might have to borrow a little more of your smoked venison, Cody. You two can find something to do with those horses." She took the saddlebags off her horse and went to the house.

"We can put 'em in the corral," Thomas told Cody. "Keep 'em from wanderin' off while we eat."

"I was wonderin' if you might have some use for some extra horses," Cody said. "I don't really have a need to drive that many horses the way I travel."

"I could always use the horses," Thomas said, remembering Katie's remark about the gift. "But I'm afraid I'm not in a position to pay you what those horses are worth."

"I wasn't thinking about sellin' the horses," Cody said. "I was talking about givin' 'em to you if you could use 'em."

Thomas tried to act surprised. "Why, that would be a mighty generous thing to do. Of course I could use 'em, and I'm mighty grateful for the gift."

"You're more than welcome," Cody said. "I'll just keep my saddle horse and my packhorses and leave you the rest of 'em. We might as well go ahead and take the saddles off 'em." So they unsaddled all the horses, left Cody's saddle and packsaddles on the corral rail, and took the others inside the barn. It wasn't long after they had the horses taken care of that they heard Katie ringing the cowbell.

A long time was spent at the dinner table as Cody and Katie told her father all about the series of events they went through on their journey to bring Katie home. Katie had to tell him how her brother had been killed and how she was left alone in that wilderness until Cody came to take care of her. When dinner was over, both Katie and her father invited Cody to stay for a while, but he said it was time for him to go. And when they pressed to know why, he finally told them of his quest to find out what happened to his father and his two brothers. They understood then and wished him success in finding them.

Thomas discreetly remained at the kitchen table while Katie walked out to the corral with Cody to thank him once again for showing up when he did. "I wouldn't have missed it for the world," he said casually and gave her a big grin. "I would have been disappointed not to meet

Katie Cole. You take care of yourself and take care of your pa." He climbed up into the saddle.

"You take care of yourself, too," she told him. "And if you're ever back in this part of the country, you know how to find me." She stepped back away from his horse to give him room to wheel it away from the corral, feeling an intense ache in her heart to see him go.

CHAPTER 3

Cody figured he must be getting close to the upper end of the valley when he began to see cabins here and there along the river. The buildings of the town appeared shortly after, and he arrived in the little settlement at about suppertime. He planned to make camp as usual, but first, he decided to confirm his whereabouts as Hellgate. The place he picked to find out was a large general store that looked to be older than the other buildings. It had a sign that proclaimed it to be Conway's General Merchandise. Cody tied his horses out front and went inside.

"Yes, sir, can I help you?" Gilbert Conway greeted him when Cody approached the counter, and Gilbert determined that he was not an Indian but a white man dressed as one.

"Yes, sir, you sure can," Cody replied. "I'm needin' to buy some coffee and a sack of flour, if the price ain't too high."

"Roasted ground coffee, twenty-five cents a pound," Gilbert said, "ten and twenty-pound sacks. The twenty-pound sack will save you a penny a pound."

"I'll take the twenty-pound sack," Cody told him. "I

ain't ever been up this way before. I'm tryin' to get to Hellgate?"

Gilbert shook his head. "This is Missoula," he said. "There ain't no Hellgate anymore. The folks up there just moved down the river a little way and now they're all here."

"Seein' as how Missoula is built up, I reckon that happened quite a few years ago," Cody remarked. "So there ain't much use in askin' if you remember somebody who passed through here fifteen years ago."

"Nope," Gilbert answered. "I couldn't help you, but maybe somebody else can." He walked down to the end of the counter and opened a door to the back of the store. "Hey, Pa!" he yelled, then came back to Cody.

In a short time Arthur Conway came through the door. "What is it, Gilbert?" He asked while looking Cody up and down.

"Fellow, here, was wondering if you might remember a party of folks that came through here back when we were at Hellgate. I told him I doubt it, but it wouldn't hurt to ask."

"That's been a while back," his father said. "And I didn't meet everybody who came through."

"I know there ain't much chance of you remembering," Cody said, "because it was actually about fifteen years ago. So you'd have to have one helluva memory of everybody passin' through this valley on their way to Washington Territory."

"Fifteen years ago?" Conway asked. "I can tell you right off, there wasn't many folks headin' up that way, once they got here. That was when the Flathead Indians went on the warpath and closed that road up through the Bitterroot Mountains. That was about the time when settlers who made it this far decided to try their luck in the Bitterroot Valley. Who are you tryin' to find?"

"I was wonderin' if you mighta remembered meeting a man named Duncan Hunter," Cody answered. "He had two small boys with him."

"Duncan Hunter?" Conway repeated, somewhat in surprise. He hesitated, paused to exchange puzzled glances with Gilbert, then continued. "No, I didn't meet Duncan Hunter when he first came through here, but I know who he is, him and his sons Morgan and Holt. Gilbert could have told you that the Hunters own the biggest cattle operation in the Bitterroot Valley." He paused again when he read the complete shock reflected in Cody's eyes. "I used to do a fair amount of business with the Hunters until the town of Stevensville built up and Stevensville Supply took the business. So, are you tryin' to find the Triple-H ranch?"

"No," Cody answered. "I'm just on my way into the Bitterroots. I knew the two Hunter boys when I was just a little fellow, so I was just curious about whatever happened to them."

"Well, you don't have to wonder anymore," Conway remarked, "those two little boys turned out all right. Here's your coffee and your flour."

"You never said how much for the flour," Cody said.

"A dollar, eighty," Gilbert responded. Cody nodded and counted out the money. "'Preciate the business," Gilbert said, then asked, "Are you gonna ride down the Bitterroot Valley to visit the Hunters?"

"I don't think so," Cody said. "It's been so many years. They most likely don't remember me. But I thank you for the information." Actually, he was more interested than before. Maybe not to get in touch, but how could he not be interested to see for himself the success of his father and brothers? "In case I change my mind, how far down that valley is their ranch?"

"Stevensville is about thirty miles from here," Gilbert

replied. "And after you get a mile or two outta the other side of town, you're on Hunter's range."

"You mean they own the whole valley on the other side of Stevensville?" Cody responded.

"No," Gilbert chuckled. "They ain't that big. Nobody owns the valley or the river. There's settlers all the way down that valley. The Hunters just graze cattle all up and down the valley. From what I hear, they get along real fine with the small farmers." He watched as Cody picked up his two sacks and started for the door. "Well, stop in to see us if you're back this way again."

Cody tied his two purchases onto his packhorses and rode the main street out the other end of town where he came to a road leading in a southerly direction, following what he assumed was the Bitterroot River. With the mountains on his right, he started out along the valley road with the intention of stopping to make camp for the night at the first likely spot. He came to a place that suited him when he reached a narrow creek that emptied into the river about two miles after turning onto the valley road. After he took care of Storm and the packhorses, he built his fire and prepared to eat more of his venison. The night passed peacefully enough.

He awoke to the tranquil sound of the river waking up to a new day. It was a sound he always enjoyed, so he lay in his blanket a few minutes longer until Storm began to nudge his feet with his muzzle. "All right," Cody told him, "I'm awake." He saddled the dun and loaded the packhorses again, starting out on the road to Stevensville at the first light of day. He planned to ride about fifteen or more miles, then stop to rest the horses and cook some breakfast. He met a couple of people on their way to Missoula, even at that early hour. He also took notice of the many cultivated fields. At one point, he was surprised to come to an apple orchard across the road from the river. At least, they looked like apples on the trees from his position on the road. Seeing no sign of human life anywhere near, he decided to confirm the sighting. So he rode off the road and pulled up beneath the branches of one of the trees. He picked an apple off and took a bite. Pleased with the taste, he picked three more apples, one for each of his horses. Then he guided Storm back to the valley road. "If I owned a piece of this valley, I'd damn-sure plant me some apple trees," he told the dun. From what he could see so far, however, the land was already claimed by small farms with not much grazing land for cattle.

After riding a good fifteen miles, he stopped to rest his horses and gave each one of them an apple to eat. Then he built a fire and put his coffeepot on to try some of the coffee he just bought to have with his venison. After the breakfast stop, he reached the small town of Stevensville. It was not as big as Missoula, still it offered several shops and stores, as well as a hotel. He noticed the Stevensville Supply Store that Conway had referred to at the far end of the street, so he decided to ride on down there where he pulled his horses up before the hitching rail and dismounted. Just as he stepped down, a tall, fairly young-looking man walked out the door, followed by another man who wore the apron of a store clerk. Cody couldn't help thinking the tall man might be just what Morgan or Holt would look like today. "Take your time gettin' up that list of supplies, Hal," the tall man said. "I'm gonna go to the Valley Tavern and get a bite to eat and maybe a drink of liquor before I go back to the ranch."

"Yes, sir," the clerk responded. "I'll have it all ready for you. Enjoy your dinner."

Cody tried to remember how his father talked. It was easy to believe he might have sounded just like the tall

man. The odds were heavily against it, but he couldn't
resist the temptation to follow his hunch. He remained
standing there while he watched the man walk down the
street to what appeared to be a saloon. "I can afford to buy
some dinner," he muttered, "and they must have decent
food or he wouldn't be eatin' there." He took Storm's reins
and led his horses down to the Valley Tavern and tied
them at the rail. As a matter of habit, he pulled his rifle out
of the saddle sling and walked in the dimly lit room behind
the tall man in time to hear the bartender's greeting.

"Howdy, Claude," the bartender sang out cheerfully.
Then seeing Cody walking in behind him, he asked, "Is
that Injun with you?"

Surprised, since he wasn't aware of anyone with him,
Claude turned to discover Cody walking silently behind
him. He remembered then. "Nope, he ain't with me. He
was standing at the hitchin' rail when I came outta the
supply store. Musta followed me down here."

"Another one of them poor-devil Injuns lookin' for a
handout," the bartender said and he walked out from
behind the bar to intercept Cody. "Set down wherever you
want, Claude, and I'll tell Minnie you want dinner," he
said to the man Cody followed in. Then he turned to confront Cody. "Hold on there, Chief, we don't serve Injuns
no alcoholic beverages, so you can just turn around and
walk right back out again."

"I don't want any alcoholic beverages," Cody answered
him. He nodded toward Claude and said, "I heard him tell
the store clerk that he was coming here to eat dinner. So I
came in to see if I could buy some dinner, too."

The bartender had to pause a moment when he realized
his mistake. Standing up close to the tall man in buckskins,
he could now see that Cody was not an Indian. "I swear,
Mister," the bartender blurted, "the light ain't too good

between here and that door, and you dressed in them animal hides. I couldn't rightly tell."

"Can I buy some dinner and a cup of coffee?" Cody interrupted, not sure if he still wanted it or not, especially since he found out the man he followed in was named Claude.

"Why, of course you can," the bartender said, a little disappointed that Cody still wanted it. "Set down right over there and I'll tell Minnie to fix up a plate for you, twenty-five cents for the food and a nickel for the coffee."

Cody reached inside his pocket and pulled out some change. He gave it to the bartender, then went over and sat down at the table he had indicated. It was a little way apart from the other tables, which suited Cody as well as he suspected it did the other customers, if they all felt the same way about Indians. He propped his rifle against the wall behind his chair and waited. In a few seconds, Minnie came from the kitchen and took a plate of food and a cup of coffee to Claude. She looked around then as if trying to locate the other customer. When she spotted him sitting apart from the rest of the entire room, she walked over and said, "My stars, you almost went out the back door, didn't you?"

"This is where he told me to sit," Cody replied.

She shook her head and shrugged. "Well, I'll be right back." She was as good as her word and returned right away with his dinner and some coffee. She paused a second to watch his reaction upon sampling the combination of beans and rice on his plate. When he nodded his approval, she smiled broadly. "I ain't seen you in here before. You gonna be around for a while or are you just passin' through?"

"Never been here before," Cody said. "I expect I'll be passin' on through, though." He took a bite of the pork sausage on his plate. "I might decide to hang around to come back for supper, though."

His remark pleased her. "I'll be back to check on your coffee," she said and returned to the kitchen. Her attention to the stranger did not go unnoticed by a couple of the saloon's regular customers.

"This place is goin' to hell, looks like to me," Jim Crowder commented to his partner, Alvin Smith. "I reckon they'll let anybody in here." He held up his hand and yelled to the bartender. "Hey, Ed, bring me one of them big cigars you keep under the counter."

The bartender acknowledged Crowder's summons and reached under the counter to take one large hand-rolled cigar from a box. Ed's boss, the owner of the Valley Tavern, kept those cigars for special customers and he gave them as a gift. Everyone else was charged fifty cents for one of the cigars. Crowder was not among those who received a complimentary cigar, and it irritated Ed when he signaled for him to leave the bar to deliver drinks and cigars to his table. But he did it without complaining. "Here you go, Crowder," he said, "one hand-rolled fifty-cent cigar."

"You ought not charge me anything for it," Crowder complained as he took the cigar and rolled it back and forth in his fingers.

"Ain't up to me," Ed replied. "I just do what the boss says."

"He oughta spend more time in here," Crowder remarked as he licked the cigar, bit the end off, and spit it on the floor. "Don't you want one, Alvin?"

"Hell, no," Alvin replied, "not for no fifty cents, I don't."

"He oughta spend more time in here," Crowder repeated as he struck a match on his belt buckle and lit his cigar. He exhaled a great cloud of smoke before commenting, "It's got pretty damn bad when you start feedin' Injuns in here."

"We ain't feedin' no Injuns in here," Ed insisted.

"The hell you ain't," Crowder said. "I'm lookin' at one right now, and you sure as hell marched him in and sat him down right here with the rest of us civilized folks."

"Ah, see, that's where you're wrong," Ed told him. "I made the same mistake you're makin'. That's a white fellow. He's just wearin' deerskin. He's a trapper or some-thin'."

"I swear, Ed, you're gittin' as bad as Otis," Crowder said, referring to the owner of the saloon, Otis James. "You need to be thinkin' about your regular customers and how long you're gonna keep 'em if you keep lettin' trash come in here. Hell, he even brought his rifle with him. You know them damn Injuns go crazy after a couple of drinks of firewater. He's liable to start shootin' the place up."

"He ain't drinkin' no whiskey, Crowder," Ed patiently repeated. "He's just eatin' some dinner. And I told you, he ain't no Injun. He ain't botherin' nobody, so just forget about him and he'll most likely be on his way. You're just gittin' yourself all worked up over nothin'. I expect you're thinkin' about that drunk Flathead Injun that came in here last fall demandin' whiskey."

"Maybe I am," Crowder replied, "and I reckon we knew how to handle that one," he added, referring to the public hanging that had resulted.

"Well, this ain't the same," Ed repeated. "Like I said, this fellow ain't no problem. Look around you, ain't nobody noticed that fellow but you. Just enjoy your cigar and I'll pour you another drink. All right?" Crowder didn't say anything, so Ed went back to the bar, thinking to him-self, Otis don't pay me enough, unaware of the storm of resentment stirring up in Crowder's gut.

Back at the table, Alvin complained, "You're gonna go show that feller where the door is, ain't you?" He knew the simple fact that the stranger dressed like an Indian was thoroughly stuck in Crowder's craw.

"Well, somebody ought to," Crowder replied, "and I don't see nobody else gittin' up."

"I swear, Crowder, that's 'cause ain't nobody else paid him no mind, just like Ed said. He's settin' over there by hisself and ain't botherin' nobody in the whole place but you. So why don't you just set there and have another drink, finish that fine cigar, and let that feller alone?"

"That's where you and me are different, Alvin. I don't stand for nobody to spit in my face and live to tell about it." He got up from his chair then and started across the back of the room to the lone man quietly eating his dinner.

Cody was aware of the man approaching his table, but he made no outward show of it. He wasn't expecting any trouble, since the bartender had already confirmed that he was not an Indian. So he was taken a little by surprise when Crowder walked right up beside him and stated, "Time for you to go, Injun, and don't let me catch you in here again. This is where the white folks eat."

"Are you the owner of this place?" Cody asked in response.

"No, he ain't the owner," Minnie declared as she came out the kitchen door in time to hear Crowder ordering Cody to leave. "And he ain't got no right to tell any of our customers they ain't welcome." Turning the full force of her anger upon Crowder then, she said, "You're the kind of customer we don't need. We need more like him. Ed already told you he ain't an Indian, anyway."

"Is that so?" Crowder responded. "Well, look at the way he's dressed up just like an Injun. An Injun lover is worse than a damn Injun. Maybe you forgot we hung the last Injun that come in here wantin' whiskey."

"He's just eatin' dinner," she yelled at Crowder. "And

he's a white man. If he wanted whiskey, we'd sell him some!"

Tired of arguing with Minnie and realizing that their argument had caught the full attention of everyone else, Crowder sought to end it. "Hell, he's done eatin', anyway. Ain't you, chief?" With that, he drew one last puff from his cigar and stuffed the butt out in the middle of Cody's beans and rice. "See, he's done." What occurred next happened so fast that Crowder was only aware of the result. He suddenly found himself standing with his back forced flat against the wall, the point of Cody's long skinning knife pressed firmly up under his chin. The Colt Peacemaker he had reached for was lying on the floor at his feet and there was blood dripping from the wrist of the hand that had reached for it. When he opened his mouth to protest, Cody filled it with the cigar butt embedded in a clump of beans and rice.

Filled with the typical drone of a noisy barroom moments before, the room went suddenly silent as everyone became aware of the incident taking place at the back of the saloon. With Crowder rendered sufficiently helpless, Cody looked to see where the next threat might come from. But Crowder's drinking companion remained at the table and showed no signs of retaliation. He had already decided he was not going to take part in Crowder's intimidation of the buckskin stranger. Just to be sure, however, Cody suddenly snatched his knife away from Crowder's chin and returned it to his belt. Before Crowder's knees had a chance to sag as a result, Cody grabbed the rifle propped against the wall and cranked a cartridge into the chamber. Ready to respond to any attack, he looked toward the bar, but the bartender showed no indication of taking action. It appeared that Crowder had acted on his own and at this point there was no indication anyone else was set to rally to his cause, not even the friend he had been drinking with. So Cody reached down, picked up Crowder's pistol, and handed it to Minnie, who was still standing there, dumbfounded. "I reckon you're the only person I trust with this till I get outta here. I'd appreciate it if you'd let me get gone before you give it back to him. I'm sorry I didn't get a chance to finish my dinner. It was mighty good. I'm sorry for the mess."

"You don't have anything to apologize for," Minnie answered at once. "I hope you know that jackass was acting strictly on his own. If the owner was here, he'd tell you that. If you choose to come back, I'd be happy to serve you. And if somebody don't like the way you look, you can eat in the kitchen with me."

"That sounds more to my likin', anyway," he said. Then speaking directly to Crowder, he said, "I'm going to be on my way now. I've decided not to kill you unless you come after me. I warn you, though, if you come after me, I will kill you. Do you understand that?" When Crowder didn't respond at once, Cody repeated, "Do you understand that? It's important that you understand that, because I will shoot you on sight." Still in a state of shock after having been so powerfully slammed against the wall, Crowder could do nothing but try to spit the foul combination of food and cigar from his mouth. So Cody turned and went out the front door of the saloon. He wasted no time untying his horses and climbing into the saddle. His rifle still ready to fire, he watched the door as he backed away from the rail. It appeared that Crowder had taken his threat seriously, since no one followed after him, so he wheeled Storm and galloped away from the Village Tavern.

He couldn't help wondering if the whole town of Stevensville shared Crowder's opinion of people wearing animal skins. "Surely not," he decided when he recalled Minnie's attitude. Then another thought struck him. *I wonder if my father and Morgan and Holt share Crowder's opinion about Indians.* He realized then that he really had no idea of the character of his family. And that was another reason not to disclose his true identity. However, it was not enough to persuade him to forget about his white father and brothers and continue on toward the far west as he had originally intended. So he continued on out the south end of town, planning to camp that night on land where the Hunter ranch grazed their cattle. A thought crossed his mind then that he was still a little hungry. The food Minnie had prepared was very good, especially for food you expected to get in a saloon. And Minnie was extremely gracious in her treatment of him. Then his thoughts shifted to Katie Cole. He liked her and hoped that she would find someone to treat her like a lady.

CHAPTER 4

As Cody continued following the Bitterroot River, he came upon many small farms that backed up to the river, but he also came to natural grassy pastureland in the valley with cattle grazing idly. He remembered Arthur Conway's description of the Hunter ranch's operation in cooperation with the small farmers. "Looks like an open invitation to cattle rustlers to me," Cody commented to his horse. What, he wondered, would keep any one of the farmers along the river from cutting out a steer any time they wanted fresh meat? When these and other questions occurred to him, it made him even more curious about the Triple-H Ranch. He noticed that the number of seemingly isolated groups of cattle began to be larger, the farther south he rode. *Maybe I'm getting closer to the ranch,* he thought. With no intention to visit the ranch house, he decided it was a good time to find his campsite for the night.

The spot he picked was across the river and downstream a couple of dozen yards. He built his fire in a semicircle of trees that opened toward the river. Once he took care of his horses, he unwrapped a sizable piece of meat and propped it over the flames to roast. While the meat was cooking, he went down to the the water to fill his coffeepot. He had not quite filled it when he got the first notice of company to his camp. Storm inquired as to the identity of the horses approaching. Careful not to make any sudden moves that might cause a violent response, Cody walked casually back to his campfire, where he set the coffeepot on the edge of the fire to boil. Relying on his sharp sense of hearing, he guessed his visitors were two. "You fellows gonna come on up to the fire?" Cody called out.

There was no answer for a couple of minutes and then the two men suddenly stepped into the circle of firelight, one on each side, both holding rifles cradled in their arms. The one who spoke was a gruff-looking man, older than his young companion whose dark Spanish features were partially hidden by a wide sombrero. "Couldn't help smellin' that meat you're cookin' on the fire there," the older man said. "Makes your mouth water, don't it, Juan?"

"Si, señor," the younger man replied.

"Is that a fact?" Cody responded. "Well, I've got plenty of it, so you're welcome to join me in eatin' some of it."

"That's mighty sportin' of you to offer to share that fresh beef with us," the older man said. "But we got a law out here in the valley against helpin' yourself to another man's cattle. I was thinkin' about cuttin' you some slack, since you was an Injun and thinkin' any live critter is fair game. But when I get a closer look, I don't believe you're an Injun after all, and you oughta know better than to steal a cow."

"I hate to disappoint you," Cody said and got up from his knee to pull the coffeepot back from the fire. The move caused both visitors to react by pointing their rifles at him. "Damn," Cody said. "You boys are touchy. I don't want my coffee to boil over." He pulled the pot away from the flames. "Now, as I was about to say, I hate to disappoint you, since you had your heart set on fresh beef. But what I'm cookin' here is deer meat." He took his knife, cut off a chunk, and tossed it to the older man. While he sniffed it, Cody sliced off another piece and tossed it to Juan. "If you'll take a look in those packs over there, you'll see I'm packin' enough venison to get me off your range without taking a single head of your cattle."

"I swear," Ike Dance declared without looking at Cody's packs. "How do I know you won't decide to try out some beef before you leave our range?"

"'Cause it ain't my beef to take," Cody said. "That's why I'm loaded up with deer meat. Venison belongs to whoever wants to take it. Now if you two are gonna eat some of this deer meat, I expect I shoulda filled my coffee-pot up. I didn't know I might have company for supper."

Ike chuckled at the stranger's offer to share his food. "Thanks anyway," he said, "but me and Juan already had our supper." He chuckled again and added, "That deer meat does taste mighty good, though."

"Like I said," Cody repeated, "I've got plenty. Who do these cows belong to, anyway?"

"These cows belong to the Triple-H Ranch," Ike replied.

"Triple-H," Cody repeated. "Does the H stand for Hunter?"

"As a matter of fact," Ike answered, "Duncan Hunter and his two sons. You heard of 'em?"

"I've heard of 'em," Cody replied, "but I didn't think I was campin' on their range."

"Well, you ain't, really," Ike told him. "This is public land, but we graze a lot of our cattle on it. You won't be on Triple-H land unless you ride on down the valley another three miles."

"No wonder you're lookin' for cattle rustlers in this part of the valley," Cody remarked. "I expect you have quite a few cows wanderin' off to end up on one of these farms all along this river."

"Not as much as you'd think," Ike continued. "You see,

ole man Duncan and the boys get along just fine with the small farms. They give the farmers a free cow every other month. The farmers appreciate it, and they even help look after the cows. It's a helluva deal for the farmer and his family, and it don't count for much more than a normal loss of cattle for the Triple-H." He let Cody consider that for a moment, then asked, "Which way are you headin', up the valley, or down the valley? Maybe I can help you find what you're lookin' for."

"'Preciate it, but I ain't really lookin' for any place in particular. I'm plannin' to ride west. But when I got to Missoula, they told me that a lot of folks decided the Bitterroot Valley was the place to settle. So I decided to take a look down the valley to see for myself. A fellow back in Stevensville told me about the Triple-H, so I decided to ride down that far."

"Well, you're just about there," Ike said. "From right here, I'd say you're about three miles from the ranch headquarters. There's another ranch about seventeen miles past the Triple-H called the Double-K. Did that fellow in Stevensville tell you about that one?" Ike was not ruling out the possibility that this stranger might actually be heading for the new ranch that suddenly sprang up less than a year ago with undisguised intentions of vying with the Triple-H for control of the cattle business in the Bitterroot Valley.

"Nope," Cody answered, "didn't say anything about another ranch."

"Are you lookin' to hire on with a cattle outfit?" Ike asked then.

"Nope," Cody answered honestly. "I ain't lookin' to hire on anywhere. I don't know much about tendin' cows. I expect I'm just lookin' for some country that suits me, where I can hunt and raise a few horses, maybe do a little trappin'."

"Hope you find what you're lookin' for," Ike said. "Thanks for the deer meat." He turned toward his young companion then. "I reckon we'd best be gettin' on back, Juan. It's gonna be dark in a little bit."

Cody watched them depart, then returned to his place by the fire. He had been tempted to ask them more questions about the owners of the Triple-H, but he thought it best not to be too interested. At least he knew that his family had a competitor for the cattle business in the valley. He decided then, that as long as he had come this far, he might as well hang around the area for another day or two. He was curious enough to scout the Triple-H ranch house and maybe even get a glimpse of his brothers or his father. With that plan in mind, he banked his fire and crawled into his blanket.

The next morning, he resurrected his campfire and cooked his breakfast before moving on toward the headquarters of the Triple-H. He figured his visitors of the night before had gone straight back to the ranch, so he followed their trail away from his camp. He found Ike Dance's estimated distance to the ranch house was dead on, for he saw the house and the barn in the distance before he had ridden three miles. He found that the ranch buildings were close to the river, so he could use the trees along the river to hide his approach. He rode past the large ranch house, the barn, a bunkhouse, and a cookhouse. There was another house, not quite so big as the ranch house, positioned so that the main house stood between it and the outbuildings. Then he paused his horses and looked at the obvious symbols of apparent success. There was a strong feeling of pride for the accomplishments of his father and brothers. There was also a sense of deep disappointment with himself, however, when he thought of what he had accomplished in the same time period. He had become a Crow warrior and an army scout. With that sobering thought, he decided to leave Cody Hunter with the dead. But he stayed to watch a while longer, since it was no more than about seventy-five yards from the corner of the bunkhouse where two men stood, apparently waiting for someone.

In the next few moments, he felt his heartbeat increase, for the man who came from the back door of the house to join them was Duncan Hunter! There was no question about it. He recognized his father at once. Older, grayer, but without a doubt, it was Duncan Hunter. And when he walked over and took hold of the shoulder of one of the men who had been standing there waiting, Cody realized the man likely was his brother, Holt or Morgan. However, he was not sure. His heartbeat racing now, Cody could only stare. Then his father turned and went back to the house. The two young men went to the corral where two horses were tied, climbed on, and rode out of the barnyard.

"Why does the boss want us to ride down to that little creek again?" Johnny Becker asked as the two men rode south out of the barnyard, following a well-traveled trail. He was referring to a sometimes creek they called Switch Creek. It was so named because in dry weather, it would sometimes dry up. "Me and Shorty drove them cows outta that pocket last night."

"Pa wants to make sure there ain't some more cows in that pocket this mornin' already," Holt Hunter told him. "We're losin' some cows somewhere and it just might be that our friends down at the Double-K mighta discovered how our strays love to congregate in that little pocket by that creek."

"You think Double-K would rustle our cattle so close to our range?" Johnny asked.

"Let's just put it this way," Holt replied, "I ain't seen or heard anything about that bunch that would make me believe they would stop short of drivin' 'em right outta the barnyard if nobody was watchin'. If there's any more strays at that creek, we'll move 'em on over with the main herd north of the ranch."

They continued along the river trail for three-quarters of a mile before approaching the creek. Holt suddenly pulled his horse up to a stop when they were met with the first of eight stray cows coming up out of a narrow path from beside the creek. He signaled Johnny at once. They both secured their horses, drew their pistols, and waited until all eight cows came up from the creek. As they expected, the two riders driving the strays came up from the creek then. Holt signaled Johnny to stay put until the two rustlers came up on the river trail. Then at his signal, he and Johnny pushed through the bushes they had waited behind. "You boys are workin' a little bit outta your range, ain't you?" Holt asked.

Both Double-K riders were startled, finding themselves looking at two pistols aimed at them. "We're just roundin' up some of our strays," one of them, a tall thin man with dark black hair and mustache said.

"They wandered a long way from the Double-K," Holt said. "Kinda strange, too. I don't see no Double-K brand on any of 'em. Now, ain't you glad we came along in time to keep you from makin' a mistake like that? While I've got my .44 aimed at them, Johnny, why don't you relieve them of their handguns? We'll drive 'em back to the ranch with the cows and arrange a court for them."

"You can't hold no court for us," the black-haired man insisted.

"You come on our land and try to steal our cattle, we can do any damn thing we want to you," Holt informed him. He was startled then when he heard the shot from the creek and Johnny dropped to his knee.

"You get the next one in the chest, if you don't drop that six-gun," the shooter warned Holt as he rode up from the creek. Seeing the rider with his rifle already aimed at him, Holt saw no choice but to drop his weapon. "You heard him say we was roundin' up our strays. We ain't stealin' no cows."

"Damn, Reese, what the hell took you so long?" the black-haired man asked.

"That don't matter," Reese replied. "We sure made a mess of this little job of roundin' up our strays. Ain't nothin' to do but finish up the mess you made and get the hell outta here. And we'd best not leave any witnesses to go complainin' to the county sheriff." He cocked his rifle again and aimed it at Holt. At the sound of the shot, Holt felt nothing, but he dropped to his knees at the same time Reese keeled over on his horse's neck before sliding off onto the ground.

Stunned and totally confused, Holt, Johnny, as well as the two outlaws, all turned to see the lone individual wearing buckskins some fifty yards away, a complete stranger to them. Only one of the two outlaws saw fit to try to retaliate. The black-haired rustler turned to shoot Holt Hunter at point-blank range. The unidentified rifleman put a round into the rustler's chest before he could squeeze the trigger of his six-gun. When Holt looked again, the mysterious rifleman was gone. He looked at Johnny, who was straining to get to his feet, his arm hanging limp and useless.

Holt picked up his pistol and held it on the one surviving rustler. "There's been enough killin'. Get on your horse and go back to the Double-K. Take them with you and tell the Kincaid brothers this is the price of war with the Triple-H." He helped the shaken young man load the two bodies on their horses. Then when he rode away, Holt took a look at Johnny's wounded shoulder. "Can you ride well enough to help me drive these damn cows back to the main herd?"

Johnny said that he could and then he asked the question: "Holt, who was that feller with the rifle that shot those two men?"

"I swear, I don't know," Holt answered. "But I'm glad you saw him, too, 'cause I wasn't sure I wasn't seein' things."

"But where'd he go?" Johnny asked. "I think he saved your life."

"I know he did . . . twice," Holt said.

"What the hell happened, Holt?" Morgan Hunter called out as he hurried across the barnyard to the cookshack where Johnny Becker was sitting on a stool outside the shack while Sully Price was bandaging his wounded shoulder. "How bad's he hurt?"

Sully, the cook and doctor substitute, answered for Holt. "He's lucky he got it in the shoulder. Feller shot at him with a rifle at pretty close range. Bullet went in one side and out the other. It he'd been hit in the chest, we'd be diggin' a grave for him."

"Right now, it don't feel lucky," Johnny complained.

"What the hell happened?" Morgan repeated.

"I'll tell you what happened," Holt responded. "The Kincaids must have decided they're gonna take over our home range. Pa sent Johnny and me to check that little pocket by the creek to make sure there weren't any more strays there. We got there just in time to catch two Double-K hands drivin' our cows outta that creek. At least we thought there was just two of 'em. We got the jump on 'em, but we didn't know there was another one comin' along behind the first two. He's the one that shot Johnny."

"And he was fixin' to shoot Holt, too," Johnny said.

"But he got shot before he could get off another shot, himself."

"Who shot him?" Morgan asked, trying to set the picture in his mind.

"Don't know," Johnny said.

Confused by his answer, Morgan looked at Holt for clarification, but Holt merely shrugged in response. "Whaddaya mean, you don't know?" Morgan insisted. "You mean somebody was in hiding or something?"

"No," Holt tried to explain. "Johnny and I both saw the man who shot them. We just don't know who he was. He was about fifty yards away and mighta been an Indian. He was wearin' buckskins. But he was gone before there was time to get a good look at him."

"Gone?" Morgan questioned. He looked at Holt, then looked at Johnny before returning his gaze to Holt. "That doesn't make one bit of sense," he finally said. "Man you never seen before just shows up and cuts down somebody gettin' ready to shoot you. Then he just disappears? I'll let you explain that to Pa. Here he comes now."

Holt turned to see his father striding across the yard, heading in their direction. Some of the other men were heading their way, too, having heard that Johnny had gotten shot. Duncan Hunter, naturally concerned when he heard one of his men had been shot, was anxious to hear the story. So Holt and Johnny repeated their version of what had taken place by the creek earlier that day that resulted in the deaths of two Double-K riders and the wounding of Johnny Becker. There was still no logical explanation for the mysterious rifleman who appeared only long enough to prevent the death of Holt Hunter before vanishing.

"I think I might know where that rifleman came from," Ike Dance spoke up then. The brief description Holt gave of the shooter fit the one Ike had of the man he and Juan visited in his camp the night before. "Me and Juan slipped up on him when he was cookin' himself some supper. Thought he might be cookin' some Hunter beef. I reckon I oughta say I thought me and Juan slipped up on him. Truth is, he called out and invited us to come on in by the fire before we got close enough to get a good look at him. Come to find out, he was cookin' deer meat. His clothes was made outta animal hides, like the Injuns wear. He sounds kinda like the man you saw with the rifle."

"Did he tell you where he was headin'?" Duncan asked.

"No," Ike answered. "He said he was passin' through Missoula, headin' west, when somebody told him there were a lot of settlers in the Bitterroot Valley. So he decided to spend a couple of days here to take a look. I asked him if he was lookin' to hire on at one of the cattle ranches. He said he weren't. Said he didn't know nothin' about raisin' cattle."

"Sounds like he could be the same man you saw, Holt," Duncan declared. "But it still doesn't make any sense that he would just ride away without a word. I reckon I owe him a helluva lot for savin' the life of my son. I'd at least like the chance to thank him for that."

"Are you sure about that, Pa?" Morgan couldn't resist japing.

CHAPTER 5

"What tha hell . . . ?" Tater Duggan drew out slowly when he saw Willy Vick approaching the barn, leading two horses, each one with a body lying across the saddle. He didn't hesitate further. "Otto, go up to the house and get Emmett." When Otto failed to respond right away, Tater pointed toward the three horses approaching.

"Uh-oh," Otto reacted then. "Who's he leadin'?"

"I don't know," Tater answered. "Looks like Blackie's horse and maybe Reese. Go get Emmett." Otto hustled off to the ranch house to alert Emmett Kincaid, the working foreman of the Double-K and half owner with his brother, Ralph.

Otto knocked on the kitchen door, but when Sadie Springer opened the door, Otto didn't step inside. The news that two of their crew of cowhands had returned to the ranch lying belly-down across their saddles was enough to get an immediate response from the owners. Emmett came out the door immediately. "Where?" he wanted to know, and Otto pointed toward the barn where Willy Vick was just then arriving. "Son of a . . . ." he started. "So they finally made it a shootin' war. Well, we can damn sure play that game." He went down the back steps and hurried across to the barn. "What happened,

Willy? Ambush?" He took a quick look at the two corpses, shaking his head in regret when he saw Reese. Blackie was no big loss, but Reese was good with a gun and kept a cool head in a hot situation.

"No, sir, Boss," Willy answered him. "It weren't no ambush. You know that little hole where that creek empties in the river? Where we rounded up some of their strays before? Well, they caught us drivin' some more of their cows outta there." He went on to tell him exactly how it had actually happened. It was not a story that pleased Emmett.

"So you're tellin' me that Reese wounded one of their men in this gunbattle, but their sharpshootin' rifleman killed Reese and Blackie?" Emmett asked. "Why'd they let you get away?"

"They said that there was enough killin'," Willy replied, "and for me to take that message back to you."

"Right," Emmett remarked sarcastically, "they decided that after they killed Reese and Blackie."

"They acted like they didn't know who the fellow was that shot Reese and Blackie," Willy said. "They looked almost as surprised as I was."

"That don't make no sense," Emmett said. "They're just tryin' to keep you confused. They started the killin'. We'll see who's still standin' when we're done." He thought of the men of the Triple-H, old man Duncan Hunter and his two innocent sons, settlers from back east, family men. It was them against him and his brother Ralph and a gang of the roughest outlaws they had been able to put together. It had taken him and his brother two years to build a herd big enough to start their cattle operation. They started with a herd of eight hundred cows stolen in Mexico and added onto that total with cows from Texas ranches until they had increased their herd to about thirteen hundred. This was the initial herd they pushed down the length of the Bitterroot

Valley in spite of the fact that the Triple-H Ranch was already established in the valley. Comparing the men who rode for the Double-K to the cowboys who rode for the Triple-H, he liked the odds on who would eventually control the valley.

"All right, Willy," Emmett said, "get a couple of the boys to help you and go dig a grave for Reese and Blackie. It's about time for dinner, ain't it, Tater?" Tater said that it was, so Emmett told Willy he could eat first, if he wanted to.

"I druther," Willy said. "I'll bury 'em and I'll take Reese's boots. I always admired them boots."

"As far as the rest of his and Blackie's belongin's, split up the money," Emmett said. "Then I reckon you can bid on anything else they owned. This business today is gonna cost Hunter some cows."

An interested observer, Cody Hunter, knelt on the top of a high bank of the Bitterroot River at a distance he estimated to be one hundred and twenty-five yards from the Double-K barn. Thinking one of the two young men he had seen leave the Triple-H ranch earlier might be his brother, he decided to follow them. He had at first assumed the men driving the little bunch of cows out of the creek were part of the Triple-H crew, until the two he trailed drew their guns. So he was content to think the situation was under control. He didn't realize what was actually happening until another suddenly appeared behind them and shot one of the two he had followed. At that point, Cody had no choice. He had to save his brother. Holt or Morgan, he wasn't sure which brother he was, but he was pretty sure he was his brother. As soon as he knew that his brother was safe, he immediately withdrew, for he was still not certain whether it was best to let them know he was alive or to continue on west as he had first intended. When his brother let the third man take his two dead companions back to the Double-K, Cody had decided to trail him back to their ranch.

Kneeling now on the riverbank, he was attempting to determine what matter of men were operating this ranch competing with the Triple-H. The ranch buildings were roughly built, giving him the impression that they were put up as fast as they could be. There were even odd lengths of boards protruding from some of the corners of the bunk-house and the cookshack, evidence that no one cared enough to saw them off flush with the corner. To Cody, the ranch resembled a hideout more than a ranch. His main concern now was what the next move might be. He had no way of knowing if there had been other men killed, or if today was the first. If he was the first to draw blood, maybe he should come forward and admit it. He was still not convinced, however, if it was in his or his family's best interest to reveal the fact that he was not killed in the Mullan Pass fifteen years ago. It might be too long ago with lifestyles far too different to reconcile. So he made a decision. He would not contact his father or his brothers. But he decided it best to stay a while and keep an eye on the goings on at the Double-K Ranch, hopefully to prevent any surprise attacks on his father's ranch.

With that decision made, he needed to establish a base camp, one where he could go and come without the risk of having it discovered. Looking behind him at the steep Bitterroot Mountains, he felt there could be no better country for his needs. He had plenty of supplies, enough to last him for a couple of weeks before he would have to hunt. He had his bow in case there was a shot too good to pass up. He waited there a while longer, watching the ranch from a hundred and twenty-five yards distant. The men he could see seemed to be in no particular rush to get anything done, leaving the two horses carrying the bodies standing in the barnyard. It appeared to Cody that the men were more interested in eating than taking care of the dead. Finally, the man who brought the bodies back to the ranch returned with a couple more men with shovels. They led the horses down past the bunkhouse, then cut back up the slope of a steep ridge, obviously with the intention of burying the dead. There was definitely no sign of a war party forming to retaliate against the Triple-H, so he decided to go then and establish his camp.

He decided on a distance halfway between the two ranch headquarters, so when he figured he had ridden about that far back toward the Triple-H, he began to look for his spot. He didn't ride much farther before seeing it. High up a steep mountain slope on the other side of the river, he could see a strong stream being forced through a split in the rocky face of a cliff. The rushing stream disappeared almost immediately into the heavily forested slope below the cliff. Satisfied that was what he was looking for, he cut over into the trees along the river and followed the bank until he came to the point where the stream emptied into the river. Confident it was the stream he had spotted before, he rode up it and through the trees as the slope became steeper and steeper. When Storm and the other two horses began to have trouble getting solid footing, he decided that was high enough, and he guided Storm out of the stream.

"This oughta do," he declared as he stepped down from the saddle. The trees were large and dense enough to provide an almost solid cover from the sun. He had plenty of water and there was also plenty of small plants for the horses to graze on along the edges of the stream. He picked a place for his fire and a place to set up his hide sleeping tent. Then a good part of the afternoon was spent hanging his food supply on ropes from the tree limbs to

prevent his sharing it with the wildlife. Since this camp
was primarily a base for sleeping and hiding his existence,
he was concerned about his two packhorses. He planned
to be on the move during the daytime, so he would leave
the packhorses there in the camp. He had plenty of rope to
tie them while he was gone. His concern was the possibility that something might happen to him and he couldn't
get back to free them. He finally decided not to tie them in
the trees but to hobble them instead. He knew that would
keep them from wandering far away from the camp. But if
something happened to keep him from returning, they
could eventually leave the camp. With that settled, he
made some coffee and ate some deer jerky with it while he
decided what to do that night. Thanks to him, the Double-K
was definitely the injured party. Even though the men he
watched in the barnyard earlier that day had shown no
emotional outburst when their two dead riders had been
brought in belly-down in the saddle, surely there would be
retaliation. They were bound to react, he thought, and
probably tonight. Would it be a killing attack on the
Triple-H, or a large rustling attempt? He couldn't say, but
he decided it would be best for him to keep an eye on the
Double-K headquarters tonight.

"How do you want your steak, Bo?" Emmett Kincaid
asked Bo Dawson when Bo walked in the kitchen door for
supper.

"Any way will do, long as it ain't still quiverin' on the
plate," Bo answered. He was more interested in the reason
for his being invited to eat supper with Emmett and Ralph
instead of eating with the rest of the men at the cookshack.
He figured it had something to do with Reese and Blackie
getting killed, and he was not surprised when he had been
summoned. It confirmed his belief that he ranked second

behind Reese when it came to leading any dangerous undertakings. *Too bad about Reese,* he thought, *but I shoulda been number one to begin with.*

"Might as well tell Sadie how you want it," Emmett said, "and that's the way she'll cook it."

"Well, that bein' the case, how 'bout you leave it a little pink on the inside, Sadie? We don't get no choice from Tater. Just depends on how lucky you are," Bo declared.

"One medium rare comin' up," Sadie announced and went back to the stove while Bo sat down at the table with Ralph and Emmett.

"You probably already figured it out," Ralph said. "It looks like it's time to quit foolin' around with the Triple-H. It's time for the war to begin to see who's gonna rule the cattle business in this valley. They started it by killin' two good men, and we owe it to those two men to make sure the Hunters pay that debt."

"Yes, sir, we owe it to 'em," Bo agreed. Although the way Willy told it, Reese fired the first shot when he wounded one of the Triple-H men. That didn't matter, Bo decided. What mattered was who did the first killing.

"That's why we think it's important to strike back right away," Emmett said. "We can just tell all the men to saddle up and ride into their headquarters tonight and shoot the place up. Kill every son of a gun who tries to fight, then I expect the damn army would be in here after us. Or we can just wait till later tonight when there ain't nobody but the men ridin' night herd guardin' their cattle. Then we take out those unlucky men and drive that whole herd of around six hundred cows they're grazing outta that pasture south of the ranch. Me and Ralph are kinda leanin' that way 'cause that would take a big part of their total herd. That would hit 'em mighty hard. Then the Hunter brothers would have to decide how much they wanna risk to try to take their cattle back." He studied Bo's reactions while he talked to him and his enthusiastic nodding to his comments. "You see why me and Ralph hired fightin' men now, don'tcha Bo, instead of hog-sloppin' sodbusters?"

"I reckon so," Bo answered.

Sadie came to the table at that moment, carrying a platter with three big steaks on it. She served them to each man according to his preference. "You boys better eat every bit of this meat up. It sounds like you're gonna need all your strength."

"When we get through eatin'," Emmett told Bo, "you go on back and tell the men we'll be ridin' tonight. Tell 'em we'll come down to the bunkhouse and tell 'em what we're gonna do."

Cody guided his horse through the trees hugging the riverbank on his way to the spot where he had watched the Double-K ranch house from before. He purposefully guided Storm to the same spot, but he was careful not to follow the same path when he had approached it before. He was always careful not to break branches or leave other clues when riding through a wooded area. Still he avoided taking the same path twice, just in case he might create a sign for a tracker to find. When he reached his chosen lookout position, he could see that most of the men seemed to still be around the bunkhouse and the cookshack, even though the cook was already scrubbing pans in the small creek behind the house. While he watched, two men came from the back door of the house and went to the bunkhouse. "They're callin' a meetin'," Cody declared when all the other men hanging around outside followed them inside. He was pretty sure now that his suspicion of some form of retaliation was definitely in the works. It was too bad that he had no way of knowing what they were planning. All he could do was continue to watch the ranch and hope for an opportunity to warn his father and his brothers when he figured out what was going to happen. He couldn't avoid a feeling of being completely helpless, however.

The meeting in the bunkhouse lasted for what seemed a long time. When it was over, the men came outside, appearing to be in no particular hurry as they went about the process of saddling fresh horses from the corral. It was obvious that they were getting ready to ride, possibly on a full-scale attack against the Triple-H. But it was a four-hour ride from there to the Triple-H headquarters, he thought. And they would arrive on spent horses in the middle of the night. Most likely, Cody figured, they would stop to rest their horses when halfway there, planning their attack in the early-morning hours. That made more sense and would give him time to warn the Triple-H of the planned attack. With that in mind, he would have left to warn his family of the attack immediately, but he could not be sure he was one hundred percent right. So he decided to wait them out and follow them when they actually started.

It happened around midnight. Emmett Kincaid gave the signal to the men lounging around the bunkhouse and they went to their horses. Cody counted nine men who climbed up in the saddle and followed Emmett out of the Double-K barnyard, heading north up the river trail. Cody climbed aboard Storm and followed along behind. They held to a comfortable walking pace for what Cody guessed to be a little short of two hours, which put them on Triple-H range, but still less than halfway to the headquarters. Emmett called for a halt there to rest the horses. Maintaining his distance, Cody dismounted and let his horse drink from the edge of the river. The dun gelding was not even close to needing a rest, which caused Cody to wonder why the Double-K crew decided to stop there, instead of pushing on a little farther. In a few minutes, there was more to stir up his curiosity when Emmett, the man Cody identified as the leader, and another man came away from the other men and rode directly east, away from the river.

Confident that wherever Emmett went, the rest of the men were going to follow, Cody climbed back up into the saddle and followed the two men away from the river. They seemed to be following a trail toward a long ridge to the northeast about a mile away. As they neared the ridge, Cody could see there was a narrow canyon formed where a wide creek cut through the ridge. The two men went through the canyon. Cody cautiously followed. He found them sitting on their horses, gazing down the far side of the ridge at a herd of several hundred cattle peacefully passing the night.

It struck Cody at once that they were not going to fight the Triple-H. They were definitely going to steal their cattle! Having spent almost all his life as a Crow warrior, he naturally assumed the Double-K would seek revenge for the killing of their two men. He supposed the theft of this large portion of the Triple-H's herd would indeed be a severe blow for his family's ranch and certainly start a full-scale range war. The Kincaid brothers obviously were of the opinion that in that circumstance, they held the advantage. So the first thing Cody had to do was to prevent the rustling of that herd of cattle.

He moved up a little closer to the two men still sitting and watching. When he did, he saw what they were discussing. In the flat pasture beyond the ridge, he saw the flickering flames of a small fire. It was obviously built by the men riding night herd on this large number of cattle. Cody figured Emmett and the man with him were trying to determine how many men were riding night herd on this bunch of cattle. Cody was no cowhand, but he assumed that whatever the number watching the cattle, they would not likely all be sitting around the fire at the same time.

Finally, Emmett and Bo turned their horses around and started back through the small passage through the ridge. Evidently, they must have determined how many men were watching the herd, Cody figured and backed Storm up into the trees until they passed by him. Whatever the number of men they had determined, Cody had to believe they would try to kill them first, quietly if possible, and then move the cattle out of the pasture and up through the ridge.

Cody would have preferred a plan to prevent the loss of that many cattle, but he couldn't see that he had any time to come up with one. Maybe he could at least prevent the killing of those men on night herd. He rode on down the ridge to the fire beside the creek. There was no one by the fire when he got there, so he dismounted and waited for someone to show up. He didn't have to wait very long.

"Frank?" L.C. Pullen called out as he rode up to the figure standing beside his horse. "Who are you?" L.C. blurted when he got closer, realizing it was not Frank Strom.

"Someone who's come to tell you you've got trouble headin' your way if we don't act pretty quick," Cody answered.

L.C. backed his horse away from the fire. "Who the hell are you?" he demanded, and started to reach for his six-gun.

"Just hear me out," Cody said, his rifle already aimed at the startled man. "You'd be a fool to reach for that gun. If I wanted to kill you, you'd already be dead."

"What do you want?" L.C. asked, convinced that what he was just told was a fact.

"Right now, there's a gang of ten riders from the Double-K ranch restin' their horses about a mile on the other side of that long ridge. As soon as they're ready, they're fixin' to come down here to drive this whole herd of cattle out of here and dare you to come get 'em."

"Hell, they can't do that," L.C. objected. "This whole little valley here is on Triple-H range."

"That's what they're fixin' to do," Cody insisted, "and the first thing they're gonna do is kill you and whoever else is ridin' night herd. Then they can just drive the cattle back outta here with no trouble at all. And there'll be a range war if the Hunters try to come after their cattle. And they figure they've got more gunmen than you have."

Completely flustered and confused by now, L.C. didn't know how to react. "How do you know that? Who are you, anyway?"

Before Cody could answer, they heard another horse approaching. Cody took a step back out of the firelight. "Who is this?" he asked L.C. "Is he one of your men?"

"I don't know," L.C. answered, unable to identify the rider yet. Then when he saw it was Shorty Black, he felt a small sense of embodiment. "It's Shorty. He's one of our men."

"Who are you talkin' to, L.C.?" Shorty asked, since he had just passed Frank Strom on the far side of the herd.

"I don't know," L.C. answered, feeling bolder since he now had an ally. "A drunk Injun maybe. He's been tellin' me a wild story about the Double-K crew comin' after the cattle."

Cody was beginning to wonder if he wasn't just wasting his time, but he felt he had to make an attempt to save their lives if possible. "I'm tryin' to save you and your partner's lives if I can, and anybody else who's out here with you. And I ain't got much time left to do it." He repeated to Shorty the situation they were in, just as he had to L.C. "How many more men have you got out here, anyway?"

"One more," Shorty answered without thinking.

"Well, let me tell you what's gonna happen down here

in this pasture in a very short time now. There's gonna be about three men to take care of each one of you, to make sure you don't make a lotta noise. I expect they'll silence you permanently. They ain't got any reason not to. And then they'll start movin' this herd outta here nice and easy, all the way to the other side of the Double-K range. That's the plan." He paused to see if they were buying it or not. "Unless," he said then, "you believe what I'm tryin' to tell you. If you believe me, I think one of you oughta ride like hell back to the Triple-H right now and tell 'em they're being rustled. The three of us that are left can try to stampede those cows back toward the Triple-H. They are gonna have to try to drive that herd through that narrow pass in the ridge. I think it'll be easier to stampede 'em back toward your ranch." He looked at one of them and back to the other for their reaction. "That's my plan. Anybody got a better one?"

"I may be crazy," Shorty replied, "but I believe you." He looked at L.C. and said, "It wouldn't hurt to ride back to the ranch and tell 'em we're gittin' rustled, just in case."

"What's goin' on?" Frank Strom called out as he rode up. He listened to L.C. and Shorty's telling of the situation while watching Cody closely. "Who the hell are you?" he asked Cody. When Cody just shrugged in response, Frank asked, "Ain't you got a name?"

"I'm called Crazy Wolf," Cody replied.

Frank grunted in response. "Well, that clears it all up, don't it? If one of us goes ridin' hell for leather back to the ranch yellin' rustlers, it might just cost us our jobs."

"If Crazy Wolf's on the level and we don't do what he says, it might cost us our lives," Shorty said. "I believe him. One of us oughta ride back to the ranch and tell 'em." He looked at Frank and L.C. and they both shrugged in response. "Why don't we odd man out for it, since whoever stays here is gonna be in for some shootin'." Shorty won the job of riding for help, so he asked, "When should I get goin'?"

"Half an hour ago woulda been good," Cody said, so Shorty took off at once.

CHAPTER 6

Emmett had a set plan to take the Triple-H's cattle with the least amount of effort. He and Bo Dawson had scouted the herd until they were sure there were only three men riding night herd. They would move inside the ridge and set his three best ropers along the back of the herd. He explained to Bo that the ropers could wait in the dark for the three night herders to pass by and lasso the unsuspecting rider right off his horse. That way, there would be no gunfire to stir the cattle up, or to alert anyone else. They would simply slit the night herders' throats. Bo didn't react one way or another to his plan right away, so Emmett asked, "You see any problem with that?" Bo, just having been promoted to Emmett's number one man with the death of Reese Walsh, was reluctant to disagree with anything Emmett suggested. "Spit it out, man! What's wrong with that?"

"Ain't nothin' wrong with that idea a-tall," Bo countered. "It's just that I don't think any of our boys are really that good at ropin'. They do all right at brandin' time, runnin' down a steer, but I ain't so sure they'd be any good at runnin' out of the bushes and lassoin' a man off his horse. I'd be afraid he might miss."

His response didn't please Emmett a great deal, but he

paused to give it some thought, and he had to admit that his crew came with outlaw backgrounds, instead of herding cattle. "You understand the reason for ropin' is we need to cut down on gunshots, right? How else are we gonna do that?"

"If it was up to me," Bo replied, "I'd find a spot on their regular ride around the back of the herd where they rode between two good-sized trees. Then we'd just stretch a rope between the two trees, wait for 'em to come along, and rake 'em off their horses. Then we oughta be on 'em before they knew what happened."

Emmett nodded thoughtfully. It was a much better idea than the one he had suggested. "I like your idea better," he said. "That's the way we'll do it, and we might as well get to it." He called the men together and explained the plan to them. When he was satisfied they all understood the need for quiet in order for their plan to work smoothly, he selected two of the men to help him and Bo select the right place to set their snare. Then they all mounted up and rode to the ridge where six of them waited outside the tiny pass through the ridge while Emmett, Bo, and the two other men went through the pass. Once on the other side of the ridge, they remained on the slope above the herd of cattle and rode through the heavily forested slope. They continued until Emmett saw the ideal spot for their trap. Leaving their horses on the slope, they made their way down to the cattle and the obvious trail already created by the countless times a night herder had circled the cows. They hurriedly figured the ideal height for their rope, then cut notches in the trunks of the trees to use as guides when they stretched it across the path.

With their trap set, there was nothing left now but to wait for the first night herder to come around. They figured there would be ample time to permanently take care of the first rider before the next one came around. Emmett was quite pleased with the plan and figured he had chosen the right man to take Reese's place. Minutes passed with no sign of a cattle guard. More minutes passed. "Where the hell's the guard?" Otto Ross asked. "One of 'em shoulda made the rounds by now."

"They mighta all stopped on the other side by that fire to drink some coffee or somethin'," Bo suggested.

"Most likely," Emmett agreed. "They'll start up again. They was all split up before, makin' the rounds." Still, more time passed with no sign of a night herder watching the cattle. "I don't know what the hell is goin' on, but we can't sit here any longer. We need to move these cows outta this hole now if we're gonna drive 'em south of the ranch. Looks like we ain't gonna be able to get 'em movin' without firing some shots, though. Bo, you and Otto get on your horses and ride around that way." He pointed in one direction. "I'll ride around the other way. Be careful with your shots. Get close so you make 'em count. Slim," he said to the fourth man, "go get the rest of the men. We're gonna drive these cows outta here."

"I swear," Frank Strom uttered when he saw the cattle rustlers splitting up to head around the herd in opposite directions. "You were right on the money, Crazy Wolf." He looked over at L.C. and said, "Me and you was supposed to get yanked off our horses down there between those two trees. And now, they're goin' to look for us." They had watched the preparations the outlaws had performed from the trees halfway up the slope of the ridge, hardly able to believe what they witnessed.

"So now, there ain't nothin' stoppin' 'em from driving our cattle outta here," L.C. commented.

"Nothing but the three of us," Cody said, "if we wanna try to keep them from stealing the cows."

"You said there was ten of 'em," L.C. said. "They kinda got us outnumbered, ain't they?"

"That's a fact," Cody replied. "I'm plannin' to see if I can keep 'em from takin' the cows. I reckon you two have to decide for yourselves what you're gonna do."

"I'm still tryin' to figure out who you are and why you give a damn if our cattle get stolen or not," L.C. stated.

"I just don't wanna see that crew from the Double-K just walk right in and help themselves to somebody else's cattle," Cody said. "It's just not right."

"How the hell are you gonna fight ten of 'em by yourself?" Frank asked.

"I ain't figurin' on tryin' to fight all ten of 'em," Cody answered. "I'm hopin' the cows are gonna help me." When that resulted in an exchange of puzzled glances between L.C. and Frank, Cody proceeded to explain. "Those men are plannin' to ride down there and start the cattle back up the ridge and drive 'em right through that narrow gap where the creek flows between the slopes. I figure if I ride into the point of that herd, raisin' all the noise I can make with my rifle, I can turn 'em back and maybe even stampede 'em in the opposite direction. Once I get 'em started, it oughta be easy to keep 'em goin' in that direction."

"Until you get shot by one of those outlaws," L.C. saw fit to point out.

"Yeah," Cody admitted, "that is a risk. So I reckon I'll be ridin' low in the saddle and in the middle of the stampedin' cattle. I figure most of their men will be tryin' to get ahead of the cows to try to turn 'em back toward the ridge, and that ain't gonna be so easy."

"Look!" Frank said. "Here they come now!" He pointed back up toward the gap in the ridge as the outlaws rode down the slope to the pasture. "They're fixin' to find out we ain't down there no more."

"That's right," L.C. said, "and they'll already be on the

north side of the herd, so all they'll have to do is start drivin' 'em back up this way."

"I reckon it's time for me to see if I can't change those cows' minds," Cody said and cranked a shell into the chamber of his Henry rifle.

"Hell," L.C. uttered, "I'm goin' with you." He pulled his rifle out of his saddle scabbard and cocked it.

"I reckon I'll go, too," Frank said, pulling his rifle. "I'm afraid you two might not get killed and you'd tell everybody I chickened out on you."

"We oughta be able to make plenty of noise now," Cody said, grateful for their decisions to help. "Let's spread out a little and see if we can get 'em started." They rode down among the cows before they started shooting. The startled cattle reacted immediately and bolted down across the pasture toward the equally startled outlaws who were still puzzling over the missing night herders.

Suddenly confronted with the herd of six hundred cattle stampeding toward them, the rustlers' reaction was to pull their weapons and try to turn the lead cattle. "There ain't but three of 'em!" Emmett shouted, figuring it was the three missing night herders behind the stampede. "They're tryin' to drive 'em toward their ranch! We need to turn 'em and drive 'em back through that gap in the ridge!" They rode into the confused cattle, guns blazing, and created enough chaos to split the charging herd into two directions. With half the cattle turned, Bo Dawson, with three of the men, kept after them until they managed to drive them up the ridge to the passage through it. But L.C. dropped back to turn the cattle away from it. Seeing L.C. then, one of the men with Bo took dead aim at the unsuspecting L.C. Before he pulled the trigger, however, he was knocked out of the saddle by a shot from

Cody's Henry rifle. L.C. rode back into the confused herd when Cody yelled for him to disappear.

Bo's efforts had resulted in a secondary stampede up the slope by part of the herd, only to form a blockade before the tiny pass through the ridge. The thick cloud of dust created by the panic-stricken cattle added to the confusion of the riders caught in the midst of the boiling sea of bodies. When more of the crazed cattle were driven up behind those already stopped by the impasse at the pass, there was no place to go but back down the slope where Emmett and three of his men were planning to turn them back once again. The cattle were of a different opinion, however, and were encouraged by the constant harassment by Cody. Emmett and his men contributed by shooting at any vague form that might be riding a horse in the cloud of dust covering the pasture. When he finally realized that most of the herd was now halfway to the Triple-H headquarters, he called out to his men to let the cows go before they were drawn into a shooting gallery at the hands of the Triple-H crew.

"Frank, is that you?" L.C. called out cautiously, still straining to see through the dusty fog not yet settled.

"Yeah, L.C.," Frank returned. "Glad to see you made it."

"Looks like we saved the cattle," L.C. said. "Listen to that, you can still hear 'em bawling way down past the creek. Some of the boys might already have met 'em, dependin' on how fast Shorty got back to the ranch."

"Reckon where Crazy Wolf ended up?" Frank wondered.

"Right behind you," Cody answered, causing both of them to start.

"I swear, I believe you are an Injun," Frank said. "We surprised the hell outta that bunch of cattle rustlers, didn't we?"

"We sure did," Cody agreed.

"I reckon I owe you my thanks for savin' my life," L.C. said. "I got kinda careless. It almost cost me, if you hadn't cut that fellow down." Cody merely nodded in return. "Well, I reckon we'll ride on back to the ranch now. Ain't no need to hang around here no more. You gonna come on back with us? I know the boss will wanna thank you for what you done."

"Reckon not," Cody said. "I'll be ridin' along behind that gang of cattle thieves for a ways. I've got two horses I left hobbled in a camp up in the mountains about two miles back toward the Double-K. I've gotta go take care of them. I can't leave them like that all night."

"We'll go with you," Frank said. "Help you get your stuff together and you can come on back to the Triple-H. Boss is gonna wanna talk to you for sure."

"Frank's right," L.C. commented. "Hell, if it hadn't been for you, me and Frank and Shorty, too, would most likely be dead and all those cows would be on their way to the Double-K."

Cody hesitated, even though he was still not certain why. His practical side reminded him that he had shot up a big portion of his .44 cartridges just making noise. Maybe he might be compensated for them if he mentioned the fact. But when he was honest with himself, he found that he couldn't resist an opportunity to meet his father and his brothers face-to-face after all the years since he had been with them. "All right," he said, "but I can go get my horses, myself. No need for you two to have to ride back to my camp."

"I think we'd best go with you," Frank said. "Don't you think so, L.C.?"

"Yep, we'd best go help you," L.C. agreed.

"Suit yourself," Cody said.

* * *

"Yonder they are!" Shorty Black exclaimed and pointed toward the three riders approaching the barnyard in the early light of a new day. The three riders, one of them leading two packhorses, were making their way through the cattle that were scattered randomly around the Triple-H headquarters.

"Who's that with 'em?" Johnny Becker asked.

"Crazy Wolf," Shorty replied, "the feller I've been tellin' you about."

Ike Dance got up from the stool he had been sitting on and walked a couple of steps toward the barnyard for a better view. "I swear," he exclaimed, "that's him. That's that feller me and Juan came up on when he was cookin' some deer meat. He said he was gonna hang around for a couple of days." He turned back toward the other men standing around outside the cookshack. "Holt, I'll bet you a dollar he's the feller who shot those two Double-K men. He looked like he could handle a rifle."

Holt got up from the bench to get a better view of the riders, himself. "I didn't get much of a look at him then," he said. "He shot both of those fellows, and by the time I turned around, he was gone." He called to his brother, who was talking to some of the men at the bunkhouse door. "Morgan, L.C., and Frank are back. That mystery man is with 'em."

"I'll go get Pa," Morgan said. "I know he'd like to meet him, too." He hustled across the barnyard to the house, where he knew his father had gone to get a cup of coffee. The morning had started at an unusually early hour when Shorty came roaring into the ranch, firing his gun in the air and yelling that the cattle were being rustled. Every available ranch hand had rallied, only to find a peaceful herd of cattle, close in to the ranch and no sign of L.C., Frank, or Crazy Wolf.

Awakened with everyone else on the ranch, Pansy Hutto's first thought was to put a pot of coffee on to boil. So Duncan didn't wait for Sully to get the coffee started. When his eldest son opened the kitchen door and told him the mystery man was there, Duncan gulped the rest of his cup down and went out the door.

By this time, everyone on the Triple-H was curious about the man they now knew only as Crazy Wolf, so they all went to meet the three riders when they pulled up at the barn and dismounted. "Glad to see you two fellers back," Shorty called out. "Glad to see you brought Crazy Wolf with you."

"Yeah," L.C. yelled back to him. "Too bad you missed all the fun."

The men parted to let Duncan Hunter have a path to greet the stranger. He was followed by Morgan and Holt. "I'm glad to see you two made it back safely, too," Duncan said to L.C. and Frank. Then he extended his hand to Cody. "And I'd like to welcome you to the Triple-H, young fellow. I keep findin' out that I owe you a great deal of thanks for all your help. I'm Duncan Hunter. These are my sons, Morgan and Holt."

Duncan waited then for Crazy Wolf to give his name, but instead, he merely replied, "Sir." Then he looked at each brother closely and repeated their names. "Morgan . . . Holt." The young man's behavior struck Duncan as unusually strange. Dressed in all skins, much like an Indian, he wore no hat. His hair was long, but not as long as an Indian's, and his eyes were as blue as Morgan's and Holt's. Duncan was fascinated by the young man's willingness to step in and take sides in a war when he couldn't be sure who was right and who was wrong. "I was wonderin'," Cody started.

"Yes?" Duncan responded.

"I was wonderin' if it would be all right to unload my horses here by the bunkhouse, since I don't know how long I'm gonna be here," Cody said.

"Right," Duncan replied. "A man after my own heart, take care of your horses, and they'll take care of you. We can put those packs in the barn, your saddle, too. We're just about ready to eat a big breakfast that Sully's fixin' right now in the cookshack and we'd be glad to have you join us."

"That sounds pretty good to me, but I don't want to put you out none," Cody said.

"From what I've been told about how you stepped in and helped us, the least I could do is give you some breakfast," Duncan declared. He looked around at Holt and Shorty and the others standing close by. "Ain't that right, boys?" They all responded with a little cheer. "What is your name, anyway?"

"Crazy Wolf is the name I've been called since I was a little boy," Cody replied. "That is the Crow name I was given when I was adopted by a Crow village."

"You were obviously born of a white mother and father," Duncan continued. "Were you too young to remember what they had named you?"

He hesitated, afraid that his father was going to continue until he forced him to lie, for he was still not sure if he should confess or not. Finally he decided he still had his free will whether he told them the truth or lied. "No, I was not too young to remember. I was five years old when I went to live with the Crows."

"What was your Christian name?" Duncan asked.

"Cody," he replied. The smile on his father's face froze. Morgan and Holt turned to stare at each other in open-mouthed shock. The others standing close around them were struck dead silent. "Cody Hunter," he completed.

"What are you saying?" Duncan demanded when he could finally speak. "Where did you hear that name?"

"You asked my name and I told you my name," Cody answered. "I can see you are suspicious, but I do not come to ask you for anything. I am on my way to the far country, to Walla Walla maybe where I started out fifteen years ago with my father and my brothers. That was before we were attacked by the Blackfoot at the Mullan Pass. I ran for the wagon with Bobby Frasier, but we were both shot."

Unable to explain how he knew all this, Duncan insisted, "I came back to look for my boy. We buried all the dead, but Cody was not among them."

"I was found by a Crow hunting party right after the Blackfoot left. I was under a bush with a bullet in my back. My Crow father told me you and my brothers were dead."

Too stunned to speak up to that point, Morgan finally found his tongue. "What is our mother's name?" he asked in an effort to prove or disprove Cody's story.

"Louise," Cody answered him, then looked back to his father. "You have nothing to fear from me. I will be on my way from here today." He smiled and added, "After that breakfast you invited me to. If I have helped you since I have been here and you feel you owe me something, you might replace some of the .44 cartridges I used up stampeding your cattle."

Holt spoke up then because he was struck by the memory of a childhood incident. "I'm willin' to accept you as my brother on one condition. I see you're wearing moccasins. If there is no little toe on the foot in that left moccasin, I know you are my brother." His remarks brought a laugh from all four Hunters as they recalled an incident that involved Cody when he was four years old. He was not supposed to play with the axe, but he did and proceeded to chop his little toe off. Holt, who was playing with him, tried to tie the toe back on as tightly as he could with some tobacco twine. It was a masterful piece of repair and kept the severed toe in place for a week, but when Holt removed the twine, the toe fell off.

Cody suddenly felt the concentration of three sets of eyes focused upon his left moccasin. "You want me to take my moccasin off?" There was no verbal reply, but all six eyes continued to stare at his foot. Enjoying the humor of the situation now, he proposed one condition. "If I remove my moccasin and there are no missing toes, I still get to share the big breakfast your cook is preparing. Is that agreed?"

"That's agreed," Duncan quickly replied. "Shuck that moccasin!" They all stepped back to give Cody more room. He proceeded to untie the rawhide cords that bound his moccasin and unhurriedly pulled it off to reveal four toes and the tiniest bit of bone, long-since covered over with a callous sheath.

A joyful cheer erupted simultaneously. Holt stepped forward and gave Cody a hug. "Welcome home, brother." Morgan repeated the welcome as well. For their father, however, the moment was much too overwhelming. The many years of sorrowful regret and his failure to protect his youngest son had remained constant in his life. To have him suddenly reappear from the dead was almost too much to handle. Aware of it, Morgan stepped back beside him and took his elbow in support. Quick to pick up on his brother's signal, Holt grabbed Duncan's other elbow. "It's real, Pa," he spoke softly. "It's really Cody come home."

Suddenly, so many things that hadn't made sense now had logical answers—like a perfect stranger appearing to fire two shots that saved Holt's life—and the same stranger showing up to save Shorty, L.C., and Frank's lives, then start the stampede to save six hundred cattle. Duncan felt the strength returning to his legs and he strode forward to meet Cody, his arms reaching out to embrace him. "Welcome home, son." Morgan and Holt joined in the embrace and those who were close enough to have heard all that was said cheered lustily. The men standing farther away couldn't hear what the celebration was about, but seeing the four Hunter men embrace, they raised a cheer, as well. They somehow knew that Crazy Wolf was now part of the Triple-H crew.

"All right," Sully Price yelled out. "You better come and get it while it's hot!"

Duncan took Cody by the arm and walked up to the door of the cookshack before the line could be formed. He signaled for Holt and Morgan to come with them. "I just want to make an announcement real quick for those of you who ain't caught on yet. After fifteen years, my youngest son, Morgan and Holt's brother, finally found his way home. His name's Cody and some of you have already found out what kinda fellow he is. We'll get outta the way now and let you eat. I reckon you already know what you'll be doin' today." He received a polite chorus of chuckles for that remark, since the barnyard and ranch houses were alive with stray cows left by the stampede. Duncan stepped aside then to make a point of not being first in line for breakfast. His sons followed suit, until persuaded by their employees to go on through.

CHAPTER 7

"Why didn't you come right to the ranch and tell us when you found out where we were?" Morgan asked as the four Hunter men sat near the corner of the bunkhouse eating breakfast.

"I wasn't sure how you would take it if a stranger, a grown man, came knockin' on your door to tell you he'd come to live with you as part of your family," Cody answered honestly. "It'da been a different story if I coulda come with money to invest, or a sizable herd of cattle to combine with yours. Everything I own I'm carryin' on my two packhorses and my saddle horse. I know nothing about raisin' cattle, so I would have no experience to offer. I have been a Crow warrior ever since I was able to ride and use a gun or a bow. And until recently, I worked for the army as a Crow scout at Fort Keogh. I did not wish to live on a reservation for the rest of my life, so I decided to use my white man's name after I left Fort Keogh."

"What were you plannin' to do?" Morgan asked.

"The only thing I was ever taught to do," Cody replied. "I was goin' to the high mountains to hunt and trap, live like I've always lived."

"Damn," his father uttered in wonder. "It's an outright miracle that you stumbled over that tombstone up in the

Mullan Pass. I don't know how there could be a clearer sign that you were supposed to return to your family. And if you hadn't showed up on that little creek when you did, I mighta been short of another son today."

"I expect that's the most important thing you were born to do," Holt japed, "keepin' me from gettin' shot. So you know you're where you're supposed to be." He laughed, but he still remembered the feeling when he heard the rifle shot behind his back and thought it was meant for him.

"I was lucky to be in a position to take the shot," Cody commented. He didn't take it any further, but he was thinking that he knew what it was like to lose a brother, and he remembered the horrible feeling when Bloody Axe was shot down, struck by a bullet that was really meant for him.

"The important thing is that you finally found your way home," Duncan said. "I know your mother can finally rest now, knowing all her sons are safe and back together. When we get through here this mornin', and get these cows where they belong, we're gonna take you to meet the rest of the family. You can meet Morgan's wife, Edna. They got two young'uns, a boy named Mason, after your grandfather, God rest his soul. Mason's four. He's got a sister named Louise, after your mama. She's just had her second birthday." Cody nodded politely, although he was not really excited about the prospects. "Your brother, Holt, ain't talked his way into a marriage yet, but he's spendin' a lotta time sniffin' around the postmaster's daughter in Stevensville. You've got your own bedroom in the main house, same as Holt." He paused to shake his head slowly before continuing. "I always knew that bedroom would be needed. That smaller house on the other side is where Morgan's family lives."

"Somethin' botherin' you, Cody?" Morgan asked. He noticed that his young brother looked uncomfortable.

Cody looked at him and confessed. "I can't remember

when I slept inside a house, if I ever did. It would have to be before we left the farm in Minnesota."

"Uncle John's farm," Morgan asked, "you remember that farm? You were pretty young."

"That's about all I remember about it," Cody said. "Did we have bedrooms?"

"All three of us boys slept in a pantry we used as a bedroom," Morgan said. "But what Pa's talkin' about now is your own private bedroom, just like Holt sleeps in."

"That sounds like an awful lot of trouble for somebody," Cody said. "I think it would be a lot easier if I just make my camp like I always do."

"It won't cause anybody any trouble," Morgan said. "We pay a woman good money to take care of the house and cook the meals for Pa and Holt, and now you. Her name's Pansy Hutto. She'll be tickled pink when she finds out you've come home."

"I don't know if my horse won't go crazy if he ain't sleepin' close to me," Cody said.

Morgan strained to keep from laughing when he tried to reassure him. "He'll be all right. You can turn him out in the corral with the other horses. Your packhorses will be in there, too. If you'd rather, you can put him in a stall in the barn. He's been in a stable before hasn't he?"

"Yep, he's been in a stable," Cody said. "That might be better this first night, as long as my saddle and blanket are in there with him."

"He'll soon get used to the other horses on the ranch," Morgan said.

"Probably so," Cody agreed. *But I ain't sure I'll ever get used to it*, he thought.

When breakfast was over, Morgan called all the men together to decide who was going to do what after the unsuccessful attempt to rustle a good portion of the Triple-H's cattle. There was no way anyone could predict how the outlaws' utter defeat was going to affect the Kincaid brothers. As Duncan pointed out, the Kincaids would claim they had no part in the attempted theft and their main concern would be to protect their cattle from the same rustlers. "But Emmett Kincaid ain't likely to forget the loss of those two men down in that hole by Switch Creek."

"And he lost another one durin' that stampede," L.C. reminded him, "that one Crazy Wolf, I mean Cody, shot when he was fixin' to shoot me. He might claim that it was not one of his men, but he was sure fixin' to shoot me."

There was no doubt in Morgan's mind. This competition with the Kincaids had turned into a shooting war, and he was not sure how his cowboys could match up to Kincaid outlaws and gunmen. To make matters worse, there was no official law from which to seek help. At the present time, there was no sheriff of Ravilli County. The county seat, which had originally been Grantsdale, was now Hamilton, a small town with no resources to employ a town marshal, much less a county sheriff. *Well, there ain't no give-up in a Hunter,* he thought, *and we'll damn-sure fight for what's ours.* He looked over at Cody and thought, *and the Good Lord saw fit to send us a genuine Crow Indian warrior.* The timing couldn't be any better. So he concluded the meeting with reminders to everyone to keep their eyes open as they proceeded to move all those cows that were in the pasture below the ridge out of the headquarters yard where they now were. "We'll graze 'em in the north pasture," he said, "even if it makes it a little more inconvenient for Double-K men to steal 'em."

The morning was spent relocating the six-hundred cattle to grazing land north of the Triple-H. The noon meal was prepared by Sully again. Then Morgan and Holt spent the rest of the afternoon familiarizing Cody with the

Triple-H range. They showed him where their legal claim ended and the government's land beyond that where they grazed, as well. There wasn't time enough to see it all, but by the end of the day, Cody had a much better idea of what was Triple-H land. When it was suppertime, they returned to the ranch and Holt helped Cody feed his horse some grain, then put him in a stall. Storm looked a little uncertain but settled down when Cody threw his saddle and blanket in the corner of the stall. Then they went to the house for a "Welcome Cody" supper, a joint effort by Edna Hunter and Pansy Hutto. It was a supper that was eagerly anticipated by Cody's brothers, since they knew both women were great cooks. Edna and Pansy came to the door along with Morgan's two children to greet Cody and see if the image of the "wild Indian" brother they had formed in their minds was anywhere close to the young man carrying his personal estate in his saddlebags.

"Welcome home, Cody," Edna said. "I'm so glad to get to meet you. I'm Edna, Morgan's wife. And this is Mason and Louise," she said, introducing the children. They both gaped wide-eyed at the tall man in buckskins.

"Pleased to meet you, Ma'am," Cody said. "Mason, Louise," he acknowledged the two children.

"I'm Pansy Hutto," the other woman said. Older by more than a few years than Edna Hunter, Pansy was every bit as bright and lively. "I'll be taking care of you and your brother, Holt, and your father. Whatever you need, I'll be the one getting it done. So come with me and I'll show you your room and you can put that stuff away. Then we'll join them in the dining room. Your father's already waiting in there for you boys."

"Pleased to meet you, Ma'am," Cody repeated to her and followed her down a long hallway.

She identified the doors as they walked past. "Your father's room, Holt's room, and this next one is your room.

The last door is my room." She opened the door and stepped back to let him enter. He stuck his head in first and looked around the room. Seeing a window in the far wall, he walked over to look out of it. "I filled your pitcher with fresh water," she said and pointed to a pitcher and basin on a short table. When he looked back with a blank expression, she said, "That's in case you want to wash up or shave or something." He nodded and unconsciously stroked his chin to see if he needed to shave. "There's a chamber pot under the bed on the other side," she said.

"A what?" he asked.

"A chamber pot," she repeated. Seeing he was still baffled, she said, "A thunder mug." But he still didn't get it. "A pot to pee in so you don't have to go outside to the outhouse in the middle of the night."

"Ohhhh . . ." he drew out slowly, just catching on. "That's a good idea." He looked at the bed then, walked over, and sat down on it, letting his body bounce gently up and down on it. "Bed," he said, as if to show her that he knew what it was.

"I hope you find it comfortable," she said. "There's extra blankets in that cabinet there in case you need them." He nodded to confirm his understanding. "That's it," she concluded. "If you're ready to eat, supper's ready. I'm going to go along now and help Edna get the food on the table. You wanna follow me to the dining room?" He nodded, so she walked back up the hall and he followed. *This one is gonna be my favorite*, she said to herself. *It's gonna be like training a mountain lion.*

He couldn't help but wonder if every meal at the house was like the one prepared for this occasion. The food was very good, but there was so much prepared, it seemed an awful waste to him. Much like the few occasions when he decided to eat in a commercial eating place where there were other customers, he tried to be careful to use his knife and fork correctly. And like those places, he was aware of the eyes upon him as if waiting for him to grab everything up in his hands. Pansy busied herself all during the meal, making sure everyone had plenty. And although she had introduced herself as the cook and housekeeper, she ate at the table with the family. Cody wondered if she might, in fact, be taking the place of his mother. He was to find out later that his father had insisted that she join him and Holt at the table, just as an act of courtesy. There were questions, many from four-year-old Mason, all of them related to hunting. After supper, the four Hunter men retired to the study for a drink of whiskey and to discuss this final act of war by the Kincaid brothers and what they might expect to follow. Cody declined the glass of whiskey. His Crow father, Spotted Pony, had taught him and his Crow brother, Bloody Axe, that firewater was what turned the white man crazy and to avoid it at all costs. Cody didn't admit it, but he and Bloody Axe tried a drink of whiskey once, but the taste was so bad they never wanted any more.

When his father announced that he was ready to turn in for the night, Morgan was quick to follow suit. Holt said he was going to have one more shot of whiskey before he went to bed, so Cody said goodnight. "You remember which room is yours?" Holt japed. "We don't wanna hear Pansy screamin' later on tonight."

"If I go into the wrong room, you'll likely hear me scream," Cody told him as he left the room. When he reached his room, he could see a light coming from under the door. So he very carefully opened the door before stepping in to make sure it was the right room. He figured Pansy must have lit the lamp on the table. Inside, he closed the door and looked around him, recalling each thing Pansy had pointed out. He stared at the bed for a long time before going to the cabinet and getting a blanket from the stack inside.

* * *

"I reckon he ain't used to gettin' up early in the mornin'," Holt said to Pansy when she filled his coffee cup again."

"Maybe I didn't holler loud enough this morning," Pansy said.

"Well, he's damn-sure gonna have to learn that the day starts early on a cattle ranch," Duncan Hunter declared. "Pansy, go down to his room and wake him up."

She put her coffeepot back on the stove and walked down the hall to Cody's room. She wasn't gone long before she was back to announce, "He ain't in his room." Before they started asking questions, she said, "His bed ain't been slept in. Matter of fact, it doesn't look like anything's been touched. He's gone. I think he went out the window because I woulda heard him if he'd tried to open the outside door at the end of the hall. That door's locked and the key's in the drawer of that lamp table."

"Are his saddlebags gone?" Duncan asked, thinking about Cody having had thoughts regarding whether or not it would be best for him to stay.

"Yes, they're gone," Pansy said. "At least, I didn't see them anywhere."

"Well, I'll be damned," Duncan swore, disappointed.

They finished breakfast and went out the back door, heading for the barn. As usual, Morgan was already there, handing out jobs to be done that day. "Mornin'," he greeted his father and his brother. "I'm thinkin' it would be a good idea to put a couple of the boys extra to ride that southern edge of our range."

"I think that would be a smart thing to do," Duncan replied. That was the dividing line between Triple-H range and Double-K range. They didn't want any strays wandering anywhere close to Double-K's cattle. "I don't reckon you've seen anything of your brother, Cody, this mornin'."

"I saw him a while ago," Morgan said. "He went with Shorty and some of the other boys to help move the horse herd to some new grazin'."

"He was here?" Duncan responded, surprised. He turned his head to flash a quick grin in Holt's direction.

"Yeah," Morgan replied, surprised that his father asked. "He ate breakfast at the cookshack with the rest of the boys. Gus said when he opened the barn this mornin', he was surprised to find Cody sleepin' in a stall with that big dun he rides." He looked at his father, then his brother. "You didn't know he was gonna sleep with his horse, did you? We might as well get used to the idea that it's liable to take a helluva long time to turn that boy into a one hundred percent white man. The Indians had him fifteen years to turn him into what he is today."

"I'm just hopin' he wants to be Cody Hunter," Duncan said.

"You shouldn't worry about that, Pa," Morgan told him. "I think he does."

Unlike the crew at the Triple-H, there was no celebration at the Double-K after their ill-fated attempt to steal Hunter cattle. Sitting at the table in the cookshack, Ralph Kincaid asked his younger brother the same question once again, "What in the hell happened? You said you'd sent somebody to scout that herd of cattle two or three times and there weren't nobody watchin' 'em but a couple of night herders."

"I know what I said," Emmett responded in anger, having already gone over the unsuccessful attempt to steal Triple-H's cattle, "and there weren't nobody but a couple of night herders watchin' those cows most of the time. They were so close to the damn ranch house they figured nobody would have the guts to go after 'em. And when we got there, nobody was watchin' 'em. Then all of a sudden, all hell broke loose."

"And we lost one more man," Ralph complained. "That makes three of our men they've killed just in the last couple of days. I still don't understand how they shot Reese and Blackie."

"Willy said Reese shot one of their men, but he didn't kill him," Emmett said impatiently. He was weary of explaining the incident to Ralph. "Like he said, there weren't no shooting till Reese shot one of them. And then this feller popped up fifty yards or more behind 'em and cut Reese and Blackie down before they could get off a shot."

"That's the son of a bitch I want," Ralph said. "Who was he?"

"Hell, I don't know," Emmett declared. "Willy said the next minute he was gone. He was too far away to get a good look at him, anyway. Willy said he looked like an Injun."

"An Injun? Well, he oughta be easy to identify," Ralph responded. "Sounds like the Hunters went out and bought theirselves a sharpshooter. And I don't know about you, but the first thing I wanna do is to find that Injun and put him outta business. I can't think of no reason Duncan Hunter would hire an Injun sharpshooter except to start thinin' out our men."

That thought hadn't occurred to Emmett, but it made sense to him when his brother expressed it. The more he thought about it, the more he could picture a savage Indian constantly riding the extreme limits of the Double-K range on the lookout for a lone rider scouting for strays. "That sorry old son of a gun. I'll bet you're right. He ain't got nothin' but raw-butt farm boys and old men tendin' his cattle, so he went and bought himself a killer. Might be a good idea to let that Injun find out what kinda men the Double-K hires. Whaddaya reckon that Injun is worth?

You think an Injun's worth fifty dollars? Why don't we put a price on that Injun's head? Fifty dollars, that oughta be enough to interest our men. Oughta sharpen up their eyes when they're ridin' night herd, too."

"Sounds like a good idea to me," Ralph agreed. "We'll tell 'em this mornin'."

"You want any more of this coffee?" Tater Duggan asked when he saw them getting up from the table. When they both declined, he commented, "Don't neither one of you drink much coffee, do ya? You don't usually take but one cup, even when you eat with the rest of the men."

"That's mostly because we're pretty much floatin' in coffee by the time we get down here to the cookshack," Ralph explained. "Sadie always makes a big pot every mornin', whether we eat there or here."

Tater nodded his understanding. They had hired Sadie Springer to take care of the house, wash their clothes, and do the cooking. So he stuck his head out the door of the shack and yelled, "I'm fixin' to dump this coffee. If anybody wants some, they'd best get their butts up here." He had no takers. The coffee was that bad.

"I got a little announcement we thought might give you boys somethin' to think about while you're workin' the cattle today," Emmett declared. "It sounds to us like Duncan Hunter has hired himself a blame Injun to handle the jobs his tender cowhands ain't got the gumption for. He's already shot Reese and Blackie and mighta been the one that shot Andy in the middle of that stampede. So maybe if you keep a sharp eye, you might spot him before he sees you. Me and Ralph think it's worth fifty dollars bonus to the man who kills that Injun."

"Fifty dollars just to shoot an Injun?" Bo Dawson questioned. "I could use fifty dollars. Too bad there ain't but one of 'em to hunt." His remark caused a spattering of laughs and a few more questions about the fifty dollars and what kind of proof they needed to validate their claim.

"A dead Injun," Emmett answered, "but not just any dead Injun. Willy Vick will have to see him and verify he's the right one."

"You know I didn't get a real good look at him, Emmett," Willy at once declared. "It happened so fast after Reese shot that one feller. Pop, pop, and he was gone, and Reese and Blackie was both dead. Like I said, he looked Injun to me, but he weren't that close to begin with."

Emmett looked at Ralph and shrugged. Then back to Willy, he said, "There ain't no Injuns left around here for a while now, so if you see one ridin' with Hunters' men, he's the one we want. And he's worth fifty bucks. So now, let's get to it, we got cattle to tend to."

"I reckon that reward applies to everybody, don't it, Emmett?" Tater Duggan japed. "So I'm fixin' to shoot the first son of a gun comes riding into the ranch that looks like an Injun."

"Why waste a bullet, Tater?" Otto Ross cracked. "Just offer him a cup of that poison you call coffee."

"I'm gonna remember you said that, Otto," Tater threatened.

The Kincaid brothers were right. The prospect of collecting a fifty-dollar prize gave their men something to sharpen up their senses for as they scattered to report to their jobs for the day. The only men complaining were those who were assigned to work details at the barn or the ranch house.

CHAPTER 8

There was no more contact between the men of the two ranches in the valley for the next two days. It caused Duncan Hunter to wonder if the Double-K's loss of three men had been enough to discourage any grand plan the Kincaids might have had to overpower them. Both ranches were careful to patrol their boundaries, however, on the lookout for any strange riders trespassing on their ranges. On the second night, Cody turned Storm out in the pasture with the other horses and slept in the bed in his room. When asked at breakfast the next morning how he had slept, he answered, "Cautiously, but I think I'll be all right once I get used to it."

"Since things seem to be pretty quiet down the valley," Morgan said, "I'm drivin' a wagon into Stevensville this mornin' to pick up some supplies. I usually take one of the younger boys with me to help. But this mornin' I think it'd be a good idea if you went with me. You can meet Burt Rayford at Stevensville Supply. He needs to know who you are and that you can place orders there for the Triple-H." He paused and gave him half a looking over before he grinned and said, "I think we oughta be buyin' you some new clothes, too, something you'll be more comfortable to work in. Maybe a good pair of boots and some socks," he added.

Cody looked confused. "My clothes are in good shape. I have another shirt just like this one, in case I get a hole in it. I don't think I need boots. They don't look very comfortable to me. Besides, boots are no good if you're on foot and have to run."

"I hope that don't happen," Morgan replied with a chuckle. "It wouldn't hurt to get you a regular cowhand's outfit just in case you change your mind later on. You don't have to wear 'em right away."

"Reckon not," Cody said emphatically.

"It'd sure please Pa, though," Morgan remarked.

"The only thing I need is ammunition," Cody declared. "I shot up a lot of .44 cartridges durin' that stampede. I have some money, not a lot, but enough to buy some cartridges."

"We'll replace your cartridges for you," Morgan assured him. He paused and placed his hand on Cody's shoulder. "Cody, you're family. You're part owner of the Triple-H."

"Right," Cody responded. "It just don't feel like that."

"It will," Morgan assured him with a smile. "We'll drive a wagon into town, and while we're there, we'll eat dinner at a little place there where the cookin' is almost as good as Pansy's."

It was a two-hour drive to Stevensville in the wagon, and since they didn't leave the Triple-H until well after breakfast, it was approaching dinnertime when they rolled into town. "We can go ahead and leave the wagon here," Morgan said when he pulled in beside Stevensville Supply.

They hopped down from the wagon and walked into the store. Inside, Cody recognized the young man wearing an apron behind the front counter. He remembered the man named Claude, he had thought they could be brothers. Hea called the young man Hal. So when Hal greeted Morgan by name while sending a puzzled look his way, Cody said, "Mornin', Hal." He received a dumbfounded expression and a nod from Hal, plus a startled recoil of Morgan's head as he thought surely Cody didn't call Hal by name. Cody shrugged.

"Good morning, Mr. Hunter," Burt Rayford sang out as he came from the back part of the store. "What can I do for you this morning?" He cocked his eye at Hal then, trying to signal the confused young man to take charge of the Indian.

"Good mornin', Burt," Morgan returned. "I've got a list of things here that Miss Pansy needs, but first, I want you to meet my youngest brother." He expected the startled expression from Rayford, so he ignored it. "This is Cody Hunter. Cody, this is Burt Rayford, and that's Hal."

"Mr. Rayford," Cody acknowledged him.

Morgan went on to tell Rayford that due to a Blackfoot Indian attack, Cody had been lost from the Hunter family for fifteen years. But now that he was back, he would be taking part in the family's cattle business. So Rayford greeted Cody warmly and welcomed him home. "I'll just leave Pansy's list here with you while Cody and I step over to the Valley Tavern to get a bite to eat," Morgan said. "Pansy wrote the amounts she needs of all the items, so I don't think you'll have any problems with it."

"We never do," Burt replied. "She usually knows how everything is packaged. We'll have it ready for you when you get back."

Cody wasn't sure whether he flinched or not when Morgan said they were going to the Valley Tavern to eat. He was uncertain if he should mention to his brother that he had visited that particular saloon when he first hit town.

There would be little chance he wouldn't be recognized. He thought about the cook, Minnie, and what she told him when he left. *Maybe I'll just ask her if we can eat in the kitchen,* he thought. He thought about telling Morgan what had happened on his first visit to the saloon, but Morgan sounded as if eating there was a special treat for him. *Oh, hell,* he thought, *they won't do anything but ask us to leave.* It was good food, he remembered, at least that portion of it he had been allowed to eat. Maybe there would be no problem. At least they didn't tell him not to come back.

"Come on, Cody," Morgan said, "this place is right down the street. We'll take a little walk." He walked out the front door and Cody followed. "Yonder's the post office," Morgan said and pointed out the small building. "John Lawrence is the postmaster, and he's got a right handsome daughter that's got your brother, Holt, tied up in knots. Her name's Spring and she's well past marrying age. Edna and Pansy are wonderin' what Holt's waitin' for. What about you?" Morgan asked then. "You ever have a little Crow maiden you were sparkin'?"

"No, I reckon I never did," Cody answered. "I guess I never had much time to think about things like that. I was pretty young when I went to work for the army as a scout, so I didn't live in the Crow village for a good part of that time. I don't know what I woulda done with a wife, anyway."

"No, I reckon not," Morgan said and laughed.

They walked in the door of the Village Tavern and the bartender, Ed Bates, greeted Morgan. "Howdy, Mr. Hunter. Ain't seen you in a good while. You gonna eat some dinner, or you just want . . ." That was as far as he got before he saw Cody behind him and his jaw dropped open and he forgot what he was saying.

Morgan was anticipating a good meal and was oblivious to Ed's sudden loss of voice. "We're gonna see what

Minnie's cooked up today. She's the best doggone cook in the valley," he said, still unaware of Ed's focus on Cody.

"We?" Ed finally reacted. "Are you two together?"

"Yes," Morgan replied. "This is my brother, Cody. Cody, this is Ed Bates."

"Yeah, Ed, how ya doin'?" Cody responded while scanning the busy saloon in case there was anyone there that he'd met before.

"That table over near the kitchen door is cleaned up and ready," Ed suggested. "If you want, you can set down there and I'll go tell Minnie she's got a customer." He walked with them to the table, then disappeared into the kitchen while they sat down. Cody was tempted to tell Morgan that it was his usual table at the Tavern.

"One of your favorite customers is settin' right outside the kitchen door, and he's got one of your special customers with him," Ed informed Minnie. She gave him a puzzled look and waited for more information, but Ed promptly turned around and went back to the bar without another word of explanation.

Her interest keenly sharpened now, Minnie went out to wait on her customers. She took only a couple of steps out the door before she was stopped cold by the sight of the young man in the buckskins. "Well, I'll be . . ." she muttered softly to herself. Her first thought then was to quickly scan the barroom to see if Jim Crowder might possibly have come back. She didn't see him, but her gaze stopped on Alvin Smith, who had been with Crowder on that day. But Alvin had not participated in Crowder's attempt to throw Cody out, so she decided there was no threat from him this time either. Only then did she realize who Cody was sitting with. "Damn," she whispered, "Morgan Hunter." Anxious to hear the story behind those two opposites, she hurried over to the table then. "Afternoon, Mr. Hunter, are you gonna have coffee with your dinner?"

"Yes, I'd like coffee," Morgan replied, "and I'm not even gonna ask you what's for dinner 'cause I know it'll be good, whatever it is."

"Why, thank you, sir. That's a mighty nice thing to say." She looked at Cody then. "And how about you? You want coffee, too? Last time you were in here, you left in such a rush that I never caught your name."

"Cody Hunter," he said, "and I'll take coffee."

"Cody Hunter," she repeated. "Are you . . . ?"

"Morgan's brother," Cody finished for her.

"Why didn't you tell me that when you were in here?" Minnie asked.

"I don't know. Would it have made any difference?"

"I guess not," she said, then chuckled as she pictured that day in her mind. "Maybe if I coulda introduced you two, Crowder wouldn't have thought you were an Indian."

Baffled by the conversation between Cody and Minnie, Morgan held his silence as long as he could before demanding, "Will somebody tell me what the hell you two are talkin' about?"

Realizing then that she was wasting time right in the busiest part of her day, she said, "I'm sorry, Mr. Hunter, let me get you and your brother some coffee. Then I'll get you some food to get started on and we'll explain the whole thing." She started to go back for the coffee, but paused once more to say, "I can't believe your brother didn't tell you all about his last visit with me." She hurried off to the kitchen then.

As soon as she left, Morgan looked at Cody and asked, "Cody, what in the hell happened in here?"

"I stopped in here when I first hit town," Cody explained. "To tell you the truth, I followed a stranger in here because I thought he looked like you or Holt might look. I had a few words while I was here with a fellow who didn't like

Indians. But nobody got killed, or even hurt real bad, so no harm done, and that's about it."

At a table of five card players near the front of the saloon, Alvin Smith threw his cards in and pushed his chair back. "That's all my money you're gittin' today, boys. I can't draw a decent card." He got up from the table and another man immediately took his place. "If Lady Luck ain't the bitch she's made out to be, you oughta start gittin' some decent cards now," Alvin told his replacement. Then he headed for the front door.

Minnie returned to the table to place a plate of food before Cody and Morgan. "You could have knocked me over with a feather when you said you two were brothers," she declared. "Did he," she paused to make sure she heard it right, "Cody, tell you about the last time he was here?"

"Yep," Morgan answered. "He told me he had words with some fellow."

"He had words?" Minnie questioned and laughed. "They were mighty strong words. I'll tell you what he did. He got rid of the worst customer we had in here. Fellow name of Jim Crowder, a big-mouth bully, he ain't been back since Cody, here, slammed him up against the wall and made him eat his cigar."

Morgan paused with a loaded fork before his mouth. "Damn, brother, it sounds like you just stopped in town to build a reputation before you came out to the ranch." It was not an entirely casual remark. There was a considerable amount of honest concern as well. "I know how good you are with a rifle. Are you as good with that Colt you're wearin'? I mean are you as fast as greased lightnin' when it comes to drawin' it? How many men have you faced and killed?"

"You're paintin' a picture that ain't me, Morgan. I'm no fast gun like you're talkin' about. I've never called out a man or been called out to a duel in the street. I was raised a Crow warrior. My strong weapons are my bow and my Henry rifle. The Colt .44 I wear is handy for shootin' at snakes and varmints. If you leave me alone, you have nothing to fear from me. If you attack me, I will fight you with anything I can find to use as a weapon. This man Minnie told you about came from across the room to tell me to leave. When he destroyed my food, I knew he would have to be taught to leave a peaceful man alone. I wasn't sure how many friends he had, so I left after that."

Morgan looked at Minnie then, and she said, "It happened pretty much like he just said. He was just minding his own business."

"I'm sorry, Cody, I should have known better," Morgan said. He laughed then and said, "I reckon I knew it would break Mama's heart if her baby boy turned out to be a gunslinger. I don't know how she feels about a wild Indian, though. We're gonna have to get you some cow-hand clothes."

"I thought you'd be here," Alvin Smith said when he stepped up to the bar beside Jim Crowder at Bannerman's Saloon.

"Well, well, if it ain't my good friend, Alvin Smith," Crowder responded sarcastically. "What happened? Did they close the Village Tavern down?"

"Nope," Alvin replied, "it's still open. Matter of fact, I just came from there. I remember you told me you'd like to know if that wild Injun ever showed up in town again. You know, the one that shoved that cigar in your mouth?"

Crowder's face immediately screwed up into an angry scowl. "Whadda you lookin' for, Alvin, somebody to break your back for you?"

"I just came lookin' for you because I thought you'd wanna know that feller that looks like an Injun is settin' in the Village Tavern right now, eatin' dinner. And Minnie and Ed are waitin' on him like he was the governor come to town. Only this time, I noticed he ain't got that Henry rifle with him." Alvin's message had the effect on Crowder that he hoped for. Crowder became tense with rage. He tossed the whiskey back in the glass he was holding, then he tensed the muscles in his arms as he squeezed the shot glass in his hand. When he failed to break it, he threw it on the floor, causing the bartender to yell that he was gonna pay for the glass if it was broken. "Well, I just wanted to let you know that feller is back in town," Alvin continued. "I figured I owed you that." He turned away from the bar and walked back out the front door. He figured his mission was completed and if all Crowder's threats weren't just hot air, he might get to see a real show. He walked on across the street to the barbershop on the corner, figuring that was a good spot to see Crowder when he came out of Bannerman's. He could also see the front door of the Village Tavern, although it was a little farther up the street toward Stevensville Supply.

It was still a few minutes before Crowder finally walked out of the saloon, after a couple of drinks more, Alvin figured. He wondered if Crowder was just going to shoot the man on sight or if he was going to call him out to face him. Alvin hoped he would call him out. That would be more entertaining to watch. Crowder stood there for another few minutes, staring up the street toward the Tavern. Deciding, he went to one of the horses tied in front of Bannerman's and drew his rifle from the saddle scabbard. "Shoot," Alvin muttered, "he's just gonna hide somewhere and pick him off with the rifle."

As Alvin had surmised, Crowder had decided to take no risks with Cody. A simple execution was what he had in mind for the man who had humiliated him. So he cranked a cartridge into the cylinder of his rifle and walked up the street until reaching the post office. Then he walked around the little building to the other side to a rain barrel that John Lawrence kept there. Crowder figured the barrel could be used for cover, and it gave him a good view of the front door of the Village Tavern. As he watched the door, a thought crossed his mind that Alvin might just be havin' a little joke on him. "If he is, it'll be the last joke he ever pulls on anybody," he mumbled to himself. He brought his mind back to the Village Tavern then and thought about his retreat as soon as he fired the shot. There was nothing behind the post office but an open field of weeds and shrubs between the backs of the stores and the woods that hid the creek. He could disappear in those trees in a matter of minutes.

More minutes passed with no one matching the description of the man in buckskins going in or coming out of the saloon. He felt his temperature starting to boil, thinking that Alvin had the nerve to play a joke on him when another customer walked out of the saloon. Crowder froze when he saw the man in buckskins come out right behind the first man. They were together, for they were talking to each other as they stepped out on the boardwalk. *It was him!* He would never forget the look of the hunter in the man's face. He slapped his hand hard against his leg in an effort to stop its sudden trembling as he laid the Winchester rifle across the top of the water barrel. He squinted his eyes a little against the glare of the sun, which was almost directly overhead. It was a good angle. "I can't miss," he assured himself as his trembling finger began to tighten on the trigger.

Cody could not explain why he did what he did. He did not take the time to think about it before he lunged into his brother, knocking him off the boardwalk and onto the ground a split second before the .45 round from the Winchester rifle smacked the door frame behind them and the sound of the shot rang out. "Stay down!" Cody ordered. "The post office!" He pulled his six-gun and threw three quick shots at the barrel beside the building. One of them hit the barrel and served to flush Crowder out of his ambush and sent him running toward the woods. "My rifle's in the wagon," Cody announced as if admitting a failing. "Stay here, I'm goin' after him."

"I'll go with you," Morgan said.

"No," Cody said. "He's headin' for those trees. You stay here, so I'll know where you are." He didn't want to take the risk of them shooting each other if they were running around in the woods blindly looking for Crowder. He didn't wait for any further discussion but jumped to a full sprint across the street and into the field after the fleeing Crowder.

Watching from the cover of the boardwalk, Morgan was inspired to mumble, "You're right, I can't run that fast in my boots."

Cody had no reason to worry about losing him, for Crowder plowed through the weeds and bushes like a runaway bull. Cody easily overtook him and when Crowder ran out of wind and dropped down behind the bank of the creek in ambush, Cody cut deeper into the trees and circled around behind him. Then he moved silently up to the waiting assassin who was crouched behind the creek bank, watching his back trail. "I told you that if you came after me I would kill you," Cody declared. Shocked, Crowder turned around in panic, fumbling with his rifle in an effort to shoot. Cody took careful aim and put a bullet into Crowder's forehead, ending his panic.

Cody took the Winchester out of the dead man's hands, then relieved him of his gun belt and handgun. He searched his pockets for money or anything else of value, then he left the body where it was before he returned to the Village Tavern where he found Morgan and a small gathering of spectators waiting. They all stared at him with his spoils from the encounter. Especially wide-eyed was Burt Rayford's young clerk, Hal. "Come on," Morgan said to Cody. "Let's go get the wagon and get back to the ranch." Buying new clothes for Cody could wait. He felt pretty sure Cody didn't want to answer any questions. When they got back to Stevensville Supply, they found all their purchases were loaded and Burt had their bill figured up.

"We heard what sounded like a rifle shot that was followed by some shots from another weapon a little while ago," Burt said. "It wasn't too far away. Hal went down the street to see what it was. Glad to see it didn't have nothin' to do with you folks."

"Somebody havin' some problems, I reckon," Morgan remarked. "Let's see what you came up with." While Morgan went over Burt's figures with him, Cody dropped Crowder's weapons in the wagon, climbed up on the driver's seat and waited for his brother. "Was that the fellow you had the run-in with the first time you ate at the Tavern?" Morgan asked when he climbed up and took the reins.

"Yeah, that was him," Cody said.

Morgan didn't say anything else until they drove past the last building in the town, but he was thinking plenty. He thought that maybe he should tell their father that his youngest son had absolutely been effectively trained to be an Indian warrior. "I see you came back with a rifle and a sidearm, so I reckon that last shot was the one that done him in."

"Right," Cody answered.

Morgan hesitated but felt like he had to ask, "Did you take his scalp?"

Cody stared at him, puzzled. "What in the world would I want his scalp for?"

"Just askin'," Morgan replied with a smile of relief. There was one thing more that Morgan was curious about, however, so he asked, "When we walked out of that saloon, you knocked me off my feet."

"Yeah," Cody said, "sorry about that."

"Don't be," Morgan quickly replied. "I think you saved my life." He shrugged and said, "At least one of our lives, I expect. But how did you know that shot was coming?"

"I don't know," Cody answered honestly, "I just did." He was unaware that a tiny glint of the midday sun briefly flashing on the barrel of a Winchester rifle had triggered reflexes that were natural to him.

CHAPTER 9

The days that followed the attempt on Cody's life in town were spent in familiarizing himself with the boundaries of Triple-H property. He wanted to make sure he knew what was Hunter land and what was open prairie. Sometimes he worked with some of the other men on various jobs, getting to know them. For him, the jobs were generally learning experiences because he had no experience as a cattleman. He was aware that the men were always glad to have his help and appreciated the fact that he made no pretense of knowing what was best when it came to the cattle. It was on one of these days that he decided he wanted to ride alone. On this particular day, he told Morgan he wanted to ride down the valley to the southernmost boundary of Hunter land. Morgan told him that the actual boundary was a little creek that fed off the Bitterroot River and it was a natural place for cows to cross over to Kincaid land. With the recent escalation of the trouble between the Hunters and the Kincaids, Morgan had moved the portion of the herd that was grazing there away from that area. Cody said he would check to see if any of the cattle were drifting back to that creek. So he rode directly south until he had passed the last of the small groups of cows that had broken off from the larger herd.

According to landmarks Morgan had given him, he figured he must be somewhere in the neighborhood of a mile from the creek, so he continued in that direction.

Albert Bradshaw pulled the big bay gelding to a stop when he reached the creek that served as the northernmost boundary between Kincaid's land and Hunter's. They were still getting occasional Triple-H strays that found their way back to this creek, even though Hunter had pulled most of his cows back onto Hunter land. Albert had his mind set on the reward Emmett offered for that Indian sniper Duncan Hunter had hired. He knew it was going to be a real competition between a few of them to collect that fifty dollars. And the bragging rights would be worth more than the money. He figured he only had two competitors to worry about, Bo Dawson and Slick Wilson. They split up to go in search of the Indian, and both Slick and Bo had laughed when he picked the boundary creek. *Let them laugh,* he thought. *I got a feeling he's gonna be snooping around the boundary looking for a target.*

He crossed over the creek and guided the bay up the bank on the Hunter side and waited there for a few minutes in the trees that lined the creek. He looked a long time in one direction, then about the same time in the other, thinking the Indian might be riding that circuit. He decided to ride on over deeper into the Hunter range. Maybe Hunter had put the Indian to work tending cows. That might not be good, Albert thought, unless he could catch him off by himself after some strays because Emmett said he wanted to see a body for proof of the killing. "Let's just go see how good my hunch is," Albert said and gave the bay a kick with his heels, then immediately jerked the reins back hard, backing the horse into the trees again. There he was! The Indian! And he had almost ridden right out in front of him. Did he see him in the trees? If he did, he gave no sign of it as he loped on past, his attention on a little bunch of stray cattle on their way to the creek.

Shaken at first by the sudden appearance of the man in buckskins, he realized that his hunch had been dead on the money and he had been handed an easy fifty dollars. He drew his rifle from his saddle sling and gave his horse a kick of his heels again. He went after his target, keeping his horse in the cover of the trees. He hoped the Indian would stop before going into the creek after the cows but decided he would take the shot moving, if the Indian didn't stop. It would be a much easier target standing still. Everything seemed to be going the way he wanted, for his target pulled his horse to a stop before going into the trees after the cows.

Cody pulled his horse to a stop to see which way the strays he chased were going to head, upstream or downstream. In the next moment, however, his natural reactions took effect when he heard the distinct sound of a rifle chambering a cartridge. He didn't take time to think but dropped to the side of his horse and signaled him to go. He heard the snap of the bullet as it passed over Storm's back at about the height of a man seated in the saddle. He heard the sound of the second shot after Storm had charged into the trees beside the creek. Cody pulled himself back up in the saddle and guided the big dun down along the edge of the water, causing the group of five cows to scatter and charge up out of the creek to startle Albert. Not sure where his target was now, Albert turned his horse around to discover Cody behind him, waiting. Two quick shots from the Henry rifle slammed into Albert's chest, ending his chances in the fifty-dollar contest.

Cody could not be sure how his father, or brothers would prefer he treat the body of the man he had just killed. He could leave it where it lay, on Hunter property. So if his friends came looking for him, they would see he had been killed where he was not supposed to be. But what if his friends never came to look for him? He decided to load the body over the saddle with his weapons and everything else intact. Then he led the horse back across the creek to Kincaid property and gave him a smack of his hand. He wondered if the horse would find its way home as he watched it trot away. He would have led the horse back to the Kincaid ranch, but it would have been a long ride there and back to the Triple-H. And he would have been too late for supper. Since it was apparent that the man who had taken a shot at him had been alone, Cody turned his attention back to the five stray cows that were now standing and watching him. He rode over to check the brands they were wearing. And when he confirmed the brand was the Triple-H, he started herding them back toward the rest of the Hunter cattle.

When Cody returned to the ranch it was just about time for supper, so he thought he should tell Morgan what had happened on the south end of the range. He found him in the barn unsaddling his horse. "Did you ride all the way to the creek?" Morgan asked when he saw Cody come in.

"Yep, I rode to the creek," Cody answered. "Found five Triple-H cows there, so I drove them back with the others. I had to shoot another one of the Double-K riders, though." Morgan looked upset at once, so Cody quickly explained, "He took a shot at me and this was on our side of that creek, so I shot him."

"I swear, it looks like there ain't gonna be no end to this little war they've decided to have," Morgan complained. "But you're all right. How'd it happen? Did he call you out or just took a shot at you?"

"He just decided to shoot me," Cody replied. "I didn't

even know he was around until he shot at me. I figured I wouldn't give him another chance. He might notta missed the next time he tried."

"I expect we'd best tell Pa and Holt about it," Morgan said. "I hate to give Pa one more thing to worry about, but he needs to know. Supper's ready now, so I'll go to the house to eat, then I'll come to the main house and we'll talk about it. Maybe I'll have a cup of coffee and a piece of pie if Pansy's made one today. Can't nobody beat her when it comes to bakin' pies. Don't you ever tell Edna I said that."

Cody laughed. "I'm gonna keep that one in the bank in case I need it one day."

Cody ate supper that night in the kitchen with his father and brother Holt. Pansy filled a plate for herself and sat down at the table with them. They always ate in the kitchen except when Morgan and Edna and the kids joined them. On those occasions, they ate at the big table in the dining room. And Pansy ate with them in the dining room, too, but she was constantly up and down whenever a serving bowl became empty or someone needed coffee. Although Duncan Hunter hired Pansy as a cook and housekeeper, he saw no need to treat her like one. Consequently, she often commented on their discussions if she happened to find them interesting, or if she thought they were missing the point on the subject they were dissecting. On this particular night, she found the subject certainly interesting, but definitely disturbing as well. Cody had been shot at by a Double-K sniper. He, in turn, killed his would-be assassin, and they were all glad that Cody had prevailed. Duncan was naturally concerned for the safety of his three sons as well as that of the crew of men and boys who worked for the Triple-H. But all they talked about was the range war that they feared was coming and training their army to fight Double-K's army. It was at this point that Pansy felt obligated to comment.

"I know you boys don't really want the men to get ready to go to war with Double-K's crew, do ya?" she asked while she filled their coffee cups. "Most of the men workin' for Ralph and Emmett Kincaid were weaned on a Colt .45."

"What you say is true, Pansy," Duncan said. "But I don't see any way to avoid a fight with the Kincaids."

"I think you're missin' the main point here," Pansy insisted. All three Hunters paused to give her their attention as she took a kitchen knife and started slicing a freshly baked peach pie. Morgan glanced at Cody and shook his head to remind him not to tell Edna. "That fellow today went after Cody, 'cause he thinks Cody's an Indian," Pansy continued. "That makes three of their men killed by this same Indian. Maybe they heard about that fellow in town that went after the Indian, and the Indian got him, too."

"That may be so, Pansy," Morgan said, "but Kincaid won't know who killed that one today."

"But I betcha he's gonna guess that it was the Indian you hired to ride his range and pick off his men," she came back. "I expect he's gonna have some of his gunmen sneakin' around here lookin' for the Indian. If you get rid of the Indian, maybe Kincaid won't stalk our men out on the range."

"Damn if that ain't a good idea," Holt japed. "We can just hang Cody in the center of town and that'll take care of our problems."

"Buy Cody some new clothes," Pansy said, ignoring Holt's attempt at humor. "Then the Indian will go away."

"Maybe the Indian should just go away," Cody declared. "Seems like I ain't caused nothing but trouble ever since I hit this part of the country."

"I swear," Holt exclaimed, "do you really hate to wear white man's clothes so much that you'd rather leave home than take off those buckskins?"

"Almost," Cody declared. "I think a lot of what Pansy says is true. They could easily get the idea that I'm a sniper that we're payin' to scare some of their men off the range."

"You're still missin' the main thing here," Pansy insisted. "It they think you hired a special killer to start snipin' away at their men, then they're likely to hire themselves a special killer, too."

"Or just put a price on Cody's head," Morgan said, "and with that gang of outlaws they've got workin' their cattle, that oughta give their men something to do in their spare time." He looked at Cody and shook his head. "We need to go to town tomorrow, and not come back without those working clothes for you this time."

"What tha hell . . . ?" Otto Ross drew out slowly and pulled his horse to a stop when he saw the horse standing in the trail before them with a body draped across the saddle. He automatically looked all around him before moving forward again.

"That looks like Bradshaw's bay," Slick Wilson said when he pulled up beside Otto. Like Otto, he took a cautious look around, even though they could see there was no concealment for ambush anywhere close around. After a minute or two, they decided there was no danger in proceeding, so they rode slowly up beside the bay gelding in an effort not to cause it to run. Slick took hold of the bay's reins and looked at the head hanging down beside the stirrup. "It's Albert all right. Looks to me like he mighta found the Injun."

"I swear," Otto said. "He didn't scalp him or nothin'.

Didn't even take his weapons. Just threw him on his horse and sent him home."

"He almost made it back to the ranch house before he stopped here," Slick said. "I reckon that weren't all just braggin' when Albert said he knew where to look for that Injun. Too bad he found him."

"Sure is strange that Injun didn't take Bradshaw's rifle or his .45. Didn't take his cartridge belt or nothin' else. I don't reckon he took his money, if he had any," Otto said. "Maybe we oughta check to see if he was carryin' any." Then something else caught his attention. "Damn, Slick, look at his rifle."

Slick, who had already started to try to get to the dead man's pockets after Otto mentioned money, paused to look at the rifle in Bradshaw's saddle scabbard. "What about it?"

"It's turned around backward in the saddle sling," Otto answered. "Ain't that some kind of warnin' sign that some Injun tribes send their enemies? Means they're gonna be comin' after 'em or something."

"I don't know," Slick answered. "I ain't never heard of nothin' like that. Only thing I ever knew about Injuns is they'll take everything you got, includin' your hair."

"Well, I heard it somewhere," Otto insisted. "I didn't make it up."

They dismounted so they could try to get into Bradshaw's pockets without taking him off his horse. It proved to be somewhat difficult, even though his body had not started to stiffen up yet, but they persevered rather than go to the trouble to take him off and put him back on again. For their efforts, they were awarded one dollar and fifty cents each. "Well, let's take him on in and tell Emmett he's short another man," Slick said. "That'll tickle him."

Emmett Kincaid was walking across the yard on his way to the cookshack when he saw the two riders approaching the barn leading a third horse. He stopped when he saw the body lying across the saddle. "Who is it?" Emmett yelled, the muscles in his arms already tensing in anger at the thought of losing another man.

"Bradshaw," Slick yelled back. Emmett stood there and waited until they rode on in.

"What happened?" Emmett asked when they rode up to him.

"Don't know, Boss," Otto answered. "This is the way we found him, layin' across his saddle about three miles back. We don't know where he was coming from. When he left this mornin', he said you told him to pick up any strays he found around the boundary creek."

"Right," Emmett replied. "He thought it was about time we checked that creek again. Was he shot?"

"Yep, looks like two in the chest," Slick answered.

"About three miles from here?" Emmett asked. "Somebody shot him three miles from this ranch house?"

"I don't know how far from here he was when he got shot," Slick told him. "We found him about three miles away, but we found him just like that, layin' across his saddle. So whoever done it loaded him on his horse and that's where he ended up."

This was not news Emmett wanted to hear. He knew where Bradshaw had gone that morning. Albert had asked him to let him scout that area because he had a strong feeling the Indian rode along that creek when he was searching the ranch's southern pastures. He convinced Emmett that he had a better chance of spotting the Indian alone than if they sent a hunting party. Bradshaw had been right when he thought he knew where to find the Indian, but it looked like he was unlucky to have found him. "He was a good man," Emmett reminded himself to say for Slick's and Otto's benefit. But he obviously wasn't good enough to avoid being outsmarted by a savage Indian and resulting in the Double-K losing one more man. "Take him on into the barn and we'll dig him a grave after supper," Emmett said and went to the cookshack.

Slick and Otto continued on to the barn where they pulled Bradshaw off his horse and laid him on the wagon parked outside the door. "You know, he's startin' to stiffen up a little bit already," Otto said. "You reckon we oughta take some rope and tie him on the wagon to keep him straight?"

"Hell, he ain't gonna care if we did or not," Slick remarked. "I'm ready to get some grub. You can tie him up if you want to." So they unsaddled the horses and went to supper.

Half the crew was already in the shack eating when they walked inside, unaware of the latest killing by the Indian. Emmett had said nothing about it when he walked in a few minutes before Slick and Otto arrived. Bo Dawson came in and paused inside the doorway. "How come Albert Bradshaw is layin' in the wagon by the barn?" he asked.

"He better get his butt in here if he wants anything to eat," Tater Duggan answered Bo. "I wanna get my kitchen cleaned up sometime tonight."

"He didn't look like he was hungry," Bo said.

Willy Vick walked in behind Bo. "Hey, I just came by the barn and Albert Bradshaw's layin' up in the wagon, lookin' sick. I asked him if he was all right but he didn't say nothin'."

"He's dead," Emmett pronounced flatly, with a hint of irritation. "If you'da looked closer you mighta seen two bullet holes in his chest. We'll talk about it after supper. We'll have a meeting in the bunkhouse when we're through here."

He was frustrated because he had no real plan to fight the Hunters. He had thought his offering of a fifty-dollar reward for the Indian's life was going to solve his problems.

He thought he'd better wait till his brother Ralph could participate in the meeting. The conversation and speculation continued at a high pitch throughout the rest of the supper, with boastful proposals of outright hunting trips on Hunter property.

As soon as he finished his supper, Emmett walked up to the ranch house to talk to Ralph. He wanted to talk it over with his brother first, to make sure they were in agreement on anything they passed down to the men. Ralph was as upset when told of Bradshaw's death as Emmett had been. "Damn it, Emmett, we've pussyfooted around with that bunch long enough. It's a rotten shame we've waited around long enough to let them hire a common killer to pick our men off one by one. I think it's time we got a little bit rougher with them or we can just forget about taking over this whole valley."

"Whaddaya think we oughta do?" Emmett asked.

"Every time that Indian of theirs kills one of our men, we kill two of theirs," Ralph said. "There ain't enough grazing land in this whole valley for two cattle operations the size of Hunter and us. It's as simple as that. It don't make no difference if Hunter was already here when we moved in. It's time we started pushing Triple-H outta this valley."

"How are we gonna do that?" Emmett asked.

"They just showed us how," Ralph said. "They moved all their cattle outta that whole section just north of the boundary creek because they were afraid of losing 'em. So we'll move a couple hundred head of Double-K cattle into that section to graze."

"But that's their land, Ralph, we just can't take it over," Emmett objected.

"Why not? Who the hell's gonna stop us? They abandoned that section, so we'll claim it and hope like hell they'll wanna go to war over it. There ain't no legal help to save them. The army's already closed down that fort in Missoula. The soldiers are gone from there, and the US Marshal Service in Montana ain't got enough deputies to send up here in this part of the territory. So I say we move our cattle up into that section tomorrow mornin' with enough men to move the herd and a couple more to keep an eye out for that damn Indian."

"That suits the hell outta me," Emmett declared. "I'll get the men together and we'll move 'em right now."

CHAPTER 10

It was about an hour before dinnertime when Patch McGee loped a weary sorrel into the Triple-H barnyard, yelling for Morgan. L. C. Pullen came out of the barn. "Morgan ain't here, Patch. What's the trouble?"

"The Double-K!" Patch exclaimed as he peeled off his horse. "They drove a herd of cattle across the boundary creek onto Triple-H range! That whole section we moved our cows back from to keep 'em from crossin' over the creek to Double-K is full of Double-K cattle this mornin'."

"Well, that ain't the first time we've run a lot of their strays outta there," L.C. said.

"I ain't talkin' about no strays crossin' the creek," Patch declared. "I'm talkin' about two hundred or two hundred and fifty cows. Somebody had to drive that many cows over on our range. We got to do something, I don't know what, but we got to do something. Where's Morgan?"

"He went into town this mornin' with Cody to buy Cody some cowhand clothes," L.C. said. "I know what they're thinkin'. They think the Kincaids are spooked over that Injun they think Mr. Hunter hired." He turned and spat. "If it was up to me, I'd let him wear those skins he's so comfortable in and let the Kincaids go crazy worryin' about him. I think Cody would rather live in the woods by hisself, anyway."

"Well, I need to tell somebody about them cows," Patch said. "Reckon I oughta go up to the house and tell Mr. Hunter? How 'bout Holt? He'll know what to do. Is he here?"

"I think he's with Shorty and the boys cuttin' some timber for firewood," L.C. replied. "It's less than an hour before dinnertime. They'll all be showin' up pretty soon. Might as well just wait till then."

"I reckon," Patch agreed. "Too bad I dang-near wore that little sorrel out gettin' here."

It so happened that Morgan and Cody returned from town shortly after Patch McGee brought the news of the Double-K's decision to expand their range. Sully Duggan was the only one who made mention of the fact that when Morgan made those little, short trips to town he always ate dinner in town. This time, Morgan and Cody got back to the ranch in time to eat in the cookshack with the men. Sully took pride in his cooking, so he never suspected the cooking was better in the Village Tavern. He just figured Morgan had a little something going with Minnie Mills that went beyond her cooking. Had he known, Morgan would have reacted with a hearty chuckle. The reason he didn't eat at the Tavern on this day was because he was somewhat superstitious, and this would have been Cody's third time at the saloon. Thinking what had happened on the first two visits, he remembered the old superstition that the third time was the charm. So he thought, why push it? It might not be a lucky charm.

When Morgan and Cody arrived back at the ranch, Morgan went straight on to the cookshack while Cody stopped at the house to put his packages of new clothes in his room. Pansy saw him come in the back door, so she called out to him. "Is that your new clothes?" He said it was and she replied, "Good. I can't wait to see you in 'em. Get a chance to see what you really look like."

"I wouldn't get my hopes up," he said. He walked down the hall to his room and put his packages on the bed. Then he went out the front door to avoid any remarks Pansy had waiting for him on his way out.

When Cody reached the cookshack, Morgan had already been told about the Double-K cattle grazing on Triple-H range. Holt was back as well, and he and Morgan appeared to be arguing over the best thing to do right away. "We should have never moved the first one of our cows out of that section," Holt complained. "We shoulda known it would lead to this."

"It was the only way we could keep them from stealin' our cows when they supposedly came to get their strays," Morgan explained.

"Question is, what are we gonna do now that they have showed us they don't intend to respect our boundaries?" Cody asked. "It looks to me like they have declared war on the Triple-H and have already invaded our land."

"You're right, Cody," Morgan said. "But we can't go to war against that gang of outlaws. They would wipe us out in a shoot-out. Maybe we can come to some kind of peace with them, even if we have to give up some of our range."

"Listen to yourself," Cody pleaded, "listen to what you're saying. You're ready to concede to a bunch of robbers and killers what took you this long to build?"

"Damn it, Cody, I don't see that we have a lot of choice in the matter. If we don't make some kind of agreement with them, they're going to wipe us out. Maybe we're jumpin' the gun a little bit. Maybe they don't want a war any more than we do. They're losing in their effort to keep all their men from gettin' killed by the 'Indian.'"

"That don't make no sense," Cody said. "Every man they lost was shot on Triple-H land. If they don't wanna lose any more men, keep 'em off Triple-H range. It's as simple as that."

"He's right, Morgan," Holt said, "it's as simple as that. They're plannin' on takin' over everything we've built."

Morgan didn't say anything for a few moments. When he did speak again, he said, "You're both right. I reckon I let my hopes get in the way of my common sense." He took a long pause, then said, "I think we'd best ride up to the boundary creek to see if it's as bad as Patch says it is. If they're really taking a step as aggressive as it sounds, they might have somebody on hand to back it up."

"That's a good idea," Holt said, "we'll all three go."

"No," Morgan was quick to say, "just you and me. Cody still looks like that Indian they're sure we hired to take 'em all out. If there's a human being there intelligent enough to talk, I want to tell him that the Indian is gone for good. No offense to you, Cody. I just think it would be best if the Indian wasn't there."

"Well, hell, he just bought some new clothes," Holt said. "He could run over to the house and put 'em on."

"He'd look conspicuous as hell riding up to the boundary wearing brand-new clothes and boots," Morgan replied. "Wouldn't take 'em long to figure that out, and the shooting might start right away. Best he stay here. Besides, we'd better get up there right away. I want them to know that we are aware of what they've done."

Standing apart from the discussion, but listening in, Sully interrupted. "Is anybody gonna eat this chuck I fixed, or am I gonna have to throw it all out to the hogs?"

"I reckon we can grab a quick bite to eat, if we don't take too long," Morgan answered him. Then he caught

Cody by the elbow and said, "Don't get riled over this. I just can't take a chance on the sight of you settin' some maniac off before we even try to talk."

"No offense, Morgan," Cody assured him. "I'd rather eat, anyway." He walked into the cookshack behind his brothers.

One of the other men who had managed to hear much of the conversation the brothers were having about riding up to the boundary creek right away was Chris Scott. He stepped up beside Morgan and said, "There ain't no tellin' what you're liable to run into up there without no witnesses, Boss. Might be a good idea to take another good gun hand along with you." Morgan was not surprised. Chris came to them, looking for a job four years back. He was a big man, around Holt's age, and he seemed to have a special way with horses. He did his work with a quiet confidence that Morgan appreciated, and as he had implied, he was a better than average gun hand.

"I'd be glad to have you join us, Chris, especially since I don't think it's a good idea for Cody to go with us," Morgan told him. "But I just want you to realize I don't know what we're gonna find when we get to those cattle."

"That's what I figured," Chris said.

"All right," Morgan said, "grab yourself something to eat real quick and we'll head up range." He turned to find Holt and told him, "Chris is gonna go with us."

"Good," Holt replied. Chris was a solid man to have as a backup. It occurred to him, too, that Kincaid's men would probably think he was the third brother.

Cody was still close enough to hear Chris Scott's addition to the useless delegation. *That's good,* he thought. He hadn't been home long enough to know Chris well, but what he had seen impressed him. He understood his older brother's reasoning; he just didn't agree with it. So he decided it was better if all three of the Hunter brothers were there to negotiate with any Kincaid men who were tending the cattle. He intended to be there, and he intended to invite his rifle to join him. There were plenty of places ideal for concealment near that little creek for an expert in camouflage like Crazy Wolf. If at all possible, he would try to get himself in position to prevent Morgan's delegation to a pack of hungry wolves from becoming a suicide mission. That is, if Morgan's party was met by anyone but a herd of about two hundred misplaced cows.

Cody knew when his brothers' peace party actually left the ranch, so in an effort to reach the section where the Double-K cattle were supposed to be before them, he called for a little extra effort on Storm's part. The dun gelding was willing. He had taken an unhurried two-hour ride into town that morning with rest and water before taking the two-hour ride back to the ranch. The horse had a short rest, so it was not too much to ask of him. Cody would have saddled a fresh horse, but Storm was so accustomed to working with him on scouting and war missions that he almost seemed to know what Cody wanted before he asked.

When he was close enough to hear the bawling cattle ahead of him, he left the common trail and took to the tree-covered slope that formed one side of the valley. Weaving his way between the pine trees along the base of the slope, he stayed hidden until he came upon the herd grazing on the Hunter side of the creek. "Well, he was right about that," he said to himself, referring to Patch McGee's report. Sighting nothing but cows so far, he continued on, scanning the hillsides as well as the little valley, proceeding cautiously whenever he approached what he considered perfect ambush sites for someone entering the valley on the trail. Almost to the creek now, he was about to conclude that cows were the only occupants of the little valley at the present. But then he saw the smoke drifting up from the bank of the creek. He guided his horse up a little higher on the slope to get an angle looking down on the creek.

There were four of them, and they had built a fire in a pocket formed where the creek took a sharp turn around a stand of cottonwoods. "There they are," Cody muttered, not surprised that the outlaws were waiting for his brothers to show up. Their camp had been well chosen, for in the event any meeting with Triple-H turned violent, they had excellent protection behind the creek bank. "Except for a sniper with a Henry rifle who found himself a firing position high enough on the slope to get a few clear shots," he murmured. He had to consider that they might have snipers, too. But looking at the camp where they waited for Morgan to approach them, he decided they had none. The three Triple-H men would be out in the open with no protection. The outlaws didn't need snipers. Cody was immediately alarmed, for it appeared they were just waiting to execute Morgan, Holt, and Chris when they rode up to the creek. He was not sure he could be quick enough to kill all four before one of the four killed his brothers.

There was nothing he could do but wait for Morgan and the others to approach the camp. He considered executing the Kincaid party now. He had clear shots at two of the four men, but the other two were sitting with their backs up against the bank. And he really had no clear shot at anything but their lower legs. While he was still in the process of deciding, Morgan, Holt, and Chris Scott arrived on the scene, parting the cows as they rode straight toward the creek. Cody got ready to fire, but he hesitated when one of the Kincaid men climbed up out of the creek and signaled the Hunter men. "Well, I'll be . . ." Cody started. "They really came to talk." He lowered his rifle halfway.

Morgan saw Emmett Kincaid when he climbed up from

the creek and stood out in the open. "He wants to talk," Morgan said to Holt. "This was the right thing to do."

"Maybe, Boss," Chris muttered, "but I wouldn't trust 'em."

"Cody wouldn't believe this," Holt remarked.

They continued on up to the creek as Slick Wilson, Bo Dawson, and Leon Ritter, all heavily armed, climbed up from the creek bank and formed a line on either side of Emmett. "We ain't never talked real serious," Emmett said when the Triple-H men pulled up before them. "You'd be Morgan Hunter, right?"

"That's right," Morgan said, "and who might you be?"

"I'm Emmett Kincaid," he answered.

"Well, Mr. Kincaid, I'm glad to finally get a chance to meet you. And I appreciate the fact that you've come to talk about all these Double-K cattle on Triple-H range."

"Now, that right there is what we've come to talk about," Emmett responded. "This little valley here is Double-K range and we wanted to make sure you understood that. I know you used to graze some cattle in this valley, but when you moved them all outta here, you abandoned your claim on it. So we moved in and took over your claim, simple as that, you don't use it no more, and we can put it to good use."

The three men from Triple-H were dumbfounded by his response, and Morgan was left almost speechless. When he gathered his wits again, it was to say, "I can see that you're not very familiar with the law when it comes to squattin' on another man's property. I'd advise you to take a little trip up to Missoula and take a look at the Bitterroot Valley map in the land office there. You can find this little valley on that map and it'll tell you the number of this section. Then you ask the clerk there who owns that section, and he'll tell you Duncan Hunter. Now we rode up here this afternoon like any good neighbor would to offer our help, if you need it, to drive your cattle back onto Double-K land. You're gonna have to move 'em pretty quick because we need to give the grass in this valley time to recover."

"That's a mighty fine speech, Hunter, but there ain't a nickel's worth of truth in it. The whole valley between the Bitterroots and the Sapphire Mountains ain't in the state of Montana, 'cause there ain't no state of Montana. There ain't nothin' but Montana Territory and like all the territories, you take the land you need as long as you can hold it. You abandoned this land in this little valley and I'm claimin' it and I intend to hold it."

Morgan could not believe the man could be so insane as to really think he was within his rights to simply invade another ranch's range. He found himself with no way to negotiate a truce, so he said the only thing he was left with. "I hear what you're sayin' and you're leavin' me with no choice. The Triple-H will defend this land, and I'll expect you to move these cattle back below the boundary creek, starting first thing in the mornin'. We will meet all acts of aggression on your part."

Emmett smiled. "So you're ready to go to war, instead of givin' up a little piece of your range, right?"

"That's right," Morgan said, for he knew this little valley was just the first. Kincaid would keep taking little pieces until he ended up in the Triple-H ranch house.

"So be it," Emmett crowed triumphantly. "And tell that Injun sniper of yours that we're closin' in on all his hidin' places."

"The Indian is gone," Morgan replied.

Oh, damn, Holt thought, *maybe you shouldn't have told him that.* Looking at the four of them standing there holding their rifles, their six-guns riding handy in their fast-draw holsters, he thought, *Now the buzzards don't have anything to worry about.*

"Well, now, that is too bad," Emmett replied. "I was lookin' forward to hangin' that sneakin' devil. He musta been smarter than we thought he was."

The two war parties stood watching each other for several minutes since there was nothing left to be said. The question now for Morgan, Holt, and Chris was whether or not they would be permitted to leave peacefully, since war had been declared. Above, at his position on the slope, Cody brought his rifle to his shoulder and took dead aim at Emmett. At the first wrong move on his part, he was going to be sure Emmett Kincaid died. He was inclined to open up and cut a couple of them down while they were standing in the open. But he knew it was unlikely all three of his people would escape harm if he did. So he waited while the three cautiously backed their horses into the herd of cows behind them.

Cody lingered at his position while the four Double-K men talked about the wisdom of letting them ride away unharmed, instead of taking out the leaders of the Hunter family while they had the chance. They assumed that they had been talking to all of the brothers. "I reckon old man Duncan Hunter is gittin' too feeble to ride out here with his boys," Bo commented. "The one done the talkin', what was his name? Morgan? I expect he'll go cryin' back to his daddy. Daddy, those mean ol' men are gonna kill us." It was good for a chuckle.

"We shoulda shot 'em down while we had the chance," Emmett lamented. "Most likely the only chance we'll ever have again. And the rest of those cowboys would be runnin' around like chickens with their heads cut off." He looked at Bo and shook his head, then he smiled. "I reckon I wanted them to have a little time to think about us comin' after 'em." He shrugged. "Leon, go bring the horses up. Let's put out this fire. I don't wanna start a forest fire on this new section of land we just got. We'll go on back to the ranch. I know Ralph's wantin' to know how the meetin' went. I ain't worried about leaving these cows unprotected here. I can't think of a safer place for them."

"You don't reckon Triple-H will show up here in a little while to try to move these cows off their range?" Bo Dawson asked.

"Not today, I don't," Emmett replied. "I expect it's gonna take 'em the rest of the day to go back and decide what they're gonna do. And if they decide they're gonna come back and move this herd back to our range, it'll be in the mornin'. And we'll have a crew waitin' for 'em."

"Wouldn't hurt to leave one of us here just in case they come before mornin'," Bo said. "Hell, I'll stay."

Emmett gave it a couple seconds thought before he reconsidered. "Maybe you're right. Hard to say what they're thinkin' right now. I expect Morgan Hunter is gonna be spendin' the rest of this day tryin' to find out if his crew of cow punchers are willing to go to war for him. You're probably right, it wouldn't hurt to leave one man here, just in case. I want you with me, though, we've got to get the rest of the men ready to fight in the mornin'."

"I'll stay here," Leon Ritter volunteered. "I'm already ready to fight. And I've got some jerky I can eat."

"All right, then," Emmett declared. "I reckon we're ready to head back to the ranch. Leon will stay to make sure they ain't got no gang of men hidin' back behind the hill, waiting to move our cattle back. Sorry you're gonna miss your supper."

Cody was able to piece together most of the conversation between the four men as Emmett and the other two got on their horses and prepared to leave. He was ready to move from the place where he lay on the slope above their camp in the creek bank. And since it was close enough to hear what was going on, he had to be especially careful when he withdrew back toward his horse. He paused to watch Emmett and the other two get on their horses and head back toward the Double-K headquarters. As he watched, he was in the process of deciding what his plan of action should be. He supposed it was an honorable approach to the situation when his brother Morgan insisted on attempting a civilized settlement between the two combating cattle operations. But it was obvious to Cody that Morgan was not dealing with civilized men. The Kincaid brothers didn't hesitate to take what they wanted without regard to right or wrong but simply by the rule of whoever was the most powerful.

Cody worried about the men who worked for the Triple-H. They were honest, hardworking men. Young and old, they knew how to take care of cattle and endure the hard life that came with it. But they had never robbed a bank or a train. They had never killed a stagecoach guard or taken money for murdering someone. And these were the men they were now going to go to war against. In fact, he didn't know how many of the Triple-H men would agree to fight for the cause. He decided that he could not stand with Morgan and Holt to fight the Kincaids. He would fight his own war against the Kincaids, Crazy Wolf's war, a war of offense instead of defense. He knew that he would be more effective alone than he would be standing with his brothers. He also knew that it was going to be a difficult concept to explain to Morgan and Holt, and especially his father. So he decided it best not to try. As soon as he got back to the ranch, he intended to try to talk Morgan and Holt into another stampede while there was no one watching the herd. He was not confident he could stampede the cattle by himself.

At the present time, however, there was the matter of

the one guard that Emmett had left behind to watch the cattle. He would have to be taken care of and it would have to wait until Emmett and the other two were far enough away so a gunshot would not be heard. That might take a while, so he decided on another method. He went back to the thicket where he had left his horse. He rode along the slope until he was past the creek and on Kincaid range. Then he dropped back down to the valley floor, so he could approach the guard from the Double-K range.

He could see the man Emmett had called Leon leaning over the fire built in the curve of the creek bank. His back was toward Cody and he looked to be roasting a piece of jerky. "Hey, the camp," Cody called out when he was within ten yards of the fire. It had the effect he expected.

Leon Ritter jumped as if he'd been shot, almost dropping his jerky in the fire. He spun around, and upon seeing Cody, he exclaimed, "Judas priest, the Injun!" He reached for his rifle, but it was propped against a log out of his reach.

"Didn't mean to startle you," Cody said, his Henry rifle already pointed conveniently at Leon. "I'da called a little farther out, but I didn't see where you were till I almost stumbled on you. What did you call me, Judas priest, the Indian? Well, friend, Judas wasn't no Indian and neither am I. I'm just lookin' for a little information, and I'm wonderin' if you can help me. Whose property are these cows on?"

"Triple-H," Leon answered before he caught himself.

"So those are Triple-H cows, right?"

"No, they're Double-K cattle," Leon replied, confused by the stranger's questions.

"Oh," Cody responded. "So they're Double-K cattle grazin' on Triple-H range. So whaddaya say we cross on over this creek and kill us one of those cows. I'm damn-near hungry enough to eat one by myself. Triple-H ain't gonna care. They ain't their cows and there ain't nobody from the Double-K watchin' 'em either. So, whaddaya say?"

"No, man, we can't do that," Leon blurted. "I'm watchin' 'em. I ride for the Double-K." He took a couple of steps closer to his rifle and started to reach for it. "Best thing for you to do, friend, is to just keep ridin' the way you was headin'."

"You think you can get to that rifle before I pull the trigger on this one?" Cody asked.

Leon stopped cold. "No, but maybe I can reach this one," he said as he suddenly spun around with his drawn six-gun in hand. He was fast, but it was still a little slower than Cody's bullet.

Cody took the Colt Navy revolver out of the dying man's hand and stuck it in his belt. "Sorry," he told him, "but I had to leave a sign for Emmett to let him know his war with Triple-H ain't gonna be as easy as he thinks. I reckon this just ain't your lucky day."

Leon looked up at him with eyes threatening for good. "You are the Injun, ain't you?"

"That's right," Cody said. "I am Crazy Wolf." He pulled the six-gun from his belt and hurried Leon's passing with the bullet meant for him. He dragged Leon around and propped his back against the riverbank so that he appeared to be sitting by the fire. Then he put the fire out and left Leon to be discovered by whoever got there first, Triple-H if they stampeded the herd back where they came from tonight, or the Double-K when they realized Leon didn't come home. As for him, he figured he'd left his message for Emmett and his boys that it wasn't going to be as easy as he no doubt expected it to be. He had one more thing he hoped to accomplish and that was to hurry back to the ranch and hopefully persuade Morgan to stampede that Double-K herd back to their own range tonight. In Cody's mind, that would be another sign that the Triple-H was capable of war. Morgan's decision would also determine Cody's own decision regarding his performance in this range war.

CHAPTER 11

Cody returned to the ranch with little time to spare before supper. He wasn't worried, however, since he ate supper at the main house with his father and Holt. And he knew Pansy would make sure he got supper, no matter how late he arrived. So he took Storm to the barn, unsaddled him, and fed him a portion of grain before turning him into the corral. Just in case, he put one of his two packhorses in the corral, too. He made it to the house while his father and brother were still eating. "I was beginning to think you mighta decided you liked Sully's cookin' better than mine," Pansy greeted him when he walked in.

"You know better than that," Cody answered her.

"When are you gonna get out of those animal skins and let us get a look at you in your new clothes?" Pansy asked.

"I reckon there was so much important stuff happenin' all of a sudden that I just forgot about the new clothes," Cody said.

"I was wonderin' what happened to you, myself," Holt said. "Figured you'd wanna know what happened when Morgan and Chris and me rode out to see all our new cattle."

"I didn't know how long you would be gone, so I had to find something to occupy my mind till you got back. I piddled around here for a little while, then I rode on up to the northern pastures just to make sure we weren't gettin' raided from every direction. It took me a little longer to get back than I figured." He paused a moment, waiting for Holt to take over. When he didn't, Cody asked, "So what did you find? Was it as bad as Patch said?"

"It was worse," Duncan Hunter answered for his son. "The damn bandits just helped themselves to part of our range and told Morgan they were plannin' on keepin' it. I wish to hell I could still ride. I'd wanna be in this fight for sure." Cody could see that his father was feeling helpless in his aging body.

"What did you decide to do?" Cody asked Holt.

"Well, for sure, we're gonna ride down there in the mornin' with the intention of movin' those cows back where they came from," Holt replied. "Morgan will be back here after supper to talk some more about it."

"If you ask me," Cody stated, "instead of waitin' around here to talk about it tonight, we ought to ride down and stampede those cattle all the way back to Kincaid's ranch. That would show 'em pretty quick that Triple-H ain't got the time or the patience to put up with Emmett Kincaid's games."

"That sounds like the way to go to me," his father said.

"Me and Morgan talked about doin' something like that to show 'em we mean business when we say we ain't backin' down," Holt said. "Like Morgan said, the trouble is we don't know if our men are really ready to hang in there when the real killin' starts."

"I don't think any man knows if he'll stand the test until he faces it the first time," Cody said. "But I also think that most men who are willing to put themselves to the test will find out that he can fight the fight. The ones who don't want to put themselves to the test to even find out if they fail or fight are the problem. Those men are the ones who will desert you when the first shot is fired." He paused to look Holt in the eye. "Have you had any desertions since you got back from the boundary creek this afternoon?"

"No," Holt answered. "We told the men that we'd be ridin' back up there in the mornin' to move Double-K's cattle back off our range. We told 'em we'd be back to talk after supper tonight, but nobody said anything about not goin'."

A silent witness to the discussion, Pansy Hutto was more than a little bit interested. She was especially aware of Cody's passion to take the fight to the gang of outlaws who threatened all that Duncan Hunter and his sons had built. This, even though he had no claim to having had any part in the building of it, himself. She agreed with his father, they should do as Cody suggested and run those cows outta there tonight. When Morgan showed up a few minutes later, however, he was not very receptive to the idea.

"I understand how you feel, Cody. I felt the same way when I first heard about those cattle on our range. I think if you hadda been with Holt and me this afternoon and seen the four men waitin' for us to show up, you'd understand why it's important for at least one side in this dispute to act responsibly. Did Holt tell you? Emmett Kincaid and three of his men were waitin' there on that creek, armed to the teeth and ready to battle. Just like a band of wild Indians." He paused quickly and smiled, "No offense to your Crow family."

"None taken," Cody replied, returning the smile.

"Holt and I are going down to the bunkhouse to get the men ready to ride in the mornin' about three o'clock. Looks like you're still eating, so just come on when you're finished."

"I'm finished," Cody said. "I'll go with you."

"No, you're not," Pansy stepped in, "you ain't finished

but half of that plate. You're gonna need your strength if you're fixin' to go fight those outlaws."

Cody couldn't suppress a chuckle. "You heard the boss, boys. I'll be down there in a few minutes." They all laughed then, and his father and brothers left for the bunkhouse.

After they had gone, Pansy filled Cody's coffee cup once more, then sat down at the table while he finished eating. "I know you think you should be going after those cows tonight, instead of waitin' till mornin'."

"I'm sure Morgan knows what he's doin' with what he's got to work with," Cody said, "and he knows a lot more about runnin' a ranch than I do." He finished his supper and left to join the meeting at the bunkhouse.

"Come on in, Cody," Ike Dance said when he saw the tall warrior at the door. He appeared to be glad to see him. Cody nodded and walked on inside. Morgan was answering a question L. C. Pullen had asked. It had evidently been in regard to what their reaction should be if Kincaid's men refused to drive their cattle off the Triple-H range. Cody sat down on a bunk next to Johnny Becker who was no longer wearing a sling on his arm to support the gunshot in his shoulder.

"You reckon that shoulder's healed enough for some hard use?" Cody asked him.

"I reckon it better be," Johnny answered, "'cause it sounds like we might be gettin' some first thing in the mornin'."

"You don't think it might be better to rest that shoulder up a little more before you test it again?" Cody asked. "Somebody's gonna have to stay and watch the ranch while most of the men are gone."

"Shoot, no," Johnny replied. "There's gonna be a show-down between them and us, and I don't wanna miss it. Let some of the older fellows stay here and mind the ranch. Besides, the wound's in my left shoulder, anyway, it ain't

gonna bother me none." Cody was reminded of a young
Crazy Wolf about half a dozen years ago, anxious to prove
himself in battle and to earn the status of a warrior. Now,
at the advanced age of twenty summers, he was aware of the
risk of combat as well as its rewards. He had to think that
Johnny's attitude was the frame of mind that Morgan hoped
for in his men. Unfortunately, it was the same attitude that
Emmett Kincaid hoped to find in Morgan's men, as well,
eager to charge recklessly to prove themselves. It was
going to be up to the older hands to keep Kincaid's outlaws
from defying Morgan's defense of the Triple-H's range.

Morgan and Holt finished up their meeting, and
Duncan gave a little speech in which he told the men how
proud they made him feel, then urged them to get some
sleep. They were going to move out at three o'clock in the
morning in order to start the cattle moving by four-thirty.
When Morgan left his father and brothers at the front steps
of the main house, he said he'd see them at three. "And
Cody, I told Kincaid that the Indian was gone, so don't
forget to wear your new clothes."

"That's right, Cody," Holt japed. "You'll be like the only
one to have some new clothes for the dance."

"Right," Cody said, "I won't forget."

When they walked back in the house, they found Pansy
waiting for them. "Are you still plannin' to leave here at
three o'clock in the mornin'?" she asked. Holt said they
were, so she said, "I don't see why you're startin' those
cows out so early in the mornin'. You ain't gotta move
'em that far to put 'em back on Kincaid range." No one
had any answer for her. "Well, I'll be up to have something for you to eat. I don't want you to go off hungry."
She turned to look at their father. "And there ain't no
reason for you to get up in the middle of the night, so I
don't wanna see you at three o'clock." No one of the three

men had any argument with what she said, so they all went off to their rooms to get what sleep they could.

A little before three o'clock the next morning, Pansy went down the hall and knocked on Holt's and Cody's doors. She smiled when she heard a growl of profanity in response to her knock on Holt's door, but nothing from inside Cody's room. She didn't expect any from him. So she went back to the kitchen and the large cake of cornbread she had pulled from the oven minutes before. In a few minutes, Holt walked in, but Cody hadn't shown up. "Did you wake Cody?" Holt asked after he took a huge bite of cornbread and washed it down with hot coffee.

"I knocked on his door, same as I did on yours," Pansy replied. "Maybe I didn't knock as hard as I thought. I'll go back and get him up."

"Tell him to hustle up," Holt said as she hurried out into the hall. "We ain't got a lotta time."

She was not gone long before she appeared in the door to the hallway. "He ain't here," she said.

"Whaddaya mean, he ain't here?" Holt asked. "Where is he?"

"He ain't here," she repeated. "He's gone."

"Gone where?" Holt demanded, pushed past her, and ran down the hallway to Cody's room to discover what she said was true. "What tha . . ." he started, then stopped when it struck him. "He went out the window again. Musta woke up early and didn't wanna wake anybody else."

"I ain't so sure," Pansy said. "I think he's gone for good." She nodded toward the bed and the package of new clothes, still tied with string, never having been opened.

Frantic now, Holt quickly started looking around the whole room. "He didn't leave anything in the room!

He took off! He's gone back Injun." He looked at Pansy helplessly. "Right now when we need everybody who can fight, he deserts the family. I don't wanna tell Pa and Morgan about this. It'll break Pa's heart."

Pansy was listening to Holt's disappointment in his brother's act of desertion, but she could not bring herself to believe Cody was capable of such an act. "Before you totally condemn your brother for running out on you, think of who and what he is. Maybe he knows he can be more useful in a war between the Triple-H and the Double-K on horseback, by himself, like the Indian he was before he found us."

Holt wasn't sure about that; he didn't know what to think. "I don't know, Pansy, it just looks to me like he suddenly decided he didn't wanna fight in a range war. So he just put his Indian face back on and took off for wherever he was headin' when he stumbled on us. What's Morgan gonna think when I tell him Cody decided he didn't wanna go fight the Kincaids?" He threw his hands up in the air. "I've gotta go, before Morgan thinks we both decided to sit this one out." He grabbed another large piece of cornbread and went out the door.

"Where's Cody?" Morgan asked when he saw Holt hurrying to join him.

"He's gone," Holt answered.

"Gone?" Morgan responded. "What the hell does that mean? Gone where?"

"He's just gone," Holt answered, then went on to tell Morgan how he and Pansy had discovered that Cody was no longer in the house. "I reckon he decided he'd just get on his pony and head for the other side of the Rockies, like he started out to do in the first place."

Morgan was stunned at first, then deeply disappointed in their younger brother's choice to back out of the confrontation with Emmett Kincaid and his men. "And after all that talk about stampedin' those cows last night, instead of waitin' till mornin'," he said. Then another thought struck him. "You don't suppose he just decided to saddle up and scout that valley before we rode into an ambush or something?"

"You'da thought he mighta said something about it, if that was what he decided to do," Holt said. "Anyway, we're wastin' time standin' here talkin' about it. I've gotta go saddle my horse." He headed for the barn.

Still thinking about the possibility that Cody might have decided to scout on ahead of them, Morgan said, "I'll go with you." While Holt picked up his saddle and went to the corral to saddle his horse, Morgan went back behind the tack room where Cody had unloaded his packhorses. Other than some of the great supply of smoked venison he had been carrying, everything else was gone, including his cooking utensils and his standard cooking supplies. "Damn," Morgan uttered softly, "he's gone for good." He went back out of the barn to tell Holt what he had found, and more important, what was missing. "Well, that's too bad, ain't it?" He summed it up by saying, "I reckon we're gonna have to try to get by without him, like we did the last fifteen years. Right now, we've got more important things to take care of. Mount up, boys, we've got a herd to move," he ordered as he walked out of the barn. The five men he had picked to accompany him and Holt dutifully climbed on their horses, and he led them out toward the southernmost part of the Triple-H range.

Watching from the kitchen window in the main house, Pansy Hutto found herself wondering how many of those honest, working cowhands would make it back that night.

CHAPTER 12

"How many are you thinkin' about takin' with you?" Ralph Kincaid asked his brother.

"Three," Emmett replied, "and Leon's already down there. I'm takin' three good shots with me, Bo and Slick and Leo Blake. That'll give us five who know how to use a gun, and I think that'll be more than enough against those cowboys. I don't care how many show up to drive those cows. Nobody showed up durin' the night, 'cause Leon didn't come by to tell us. You shoulda seen 'em yesterday when they pulled up to that creek and saw me and Bo and Slick and Leon standin' there. They were shakin' so bad it felt like an earthquake gittin' ready to start up." He chuckled at the memory. "I don't know what was wrong with me. I should have just shot 'em down right there. Then, instead of ridin' back to that creek, we'd be ridin' into that ranch this mornin' to let 'em know the war was over."

"You sure you ain't underestimatin' those Hunter men?" Ralph asked. "The old man and his two sons started with nothin' and built that ranch into what it is today."

"Oh, I don't disagree with you there, brother. They're hard workers, and I gotta hand it to 'em for what they've built. But when you put honest, hardworkin' men up against dishonest gunmen with no conscience, I'm gonna put my money on the gunslingers. And I see my gun- slingers are in the saddle and waitin' for me." He walked out and climbed on the horse Bo Dawson was holding for him. He had no way to guess how early the riders from Triple-H might show up, but he wasn't worried about it. If they arrived really early, he expected they would meet Leon on his way back to warn him. When they were near enough to hear, Emmett was glad to find the cattle quiet, which meant the delegation from the Triple-H had not arrived.

They rode on up to the creek, and they could see Leon sitting with his back to the edge of the creek bank. "Well, I'll be damned." Slick Wilson chuckled. "He's asleep. He don't even know we're here."

"He let his fire go out," Bo said. "Let's wake him up." He pulled his six-gun out, but Emmett stopped him before he could fire a shot.

"Don't fire that gun!" Emmett exclaimed. "We don't know if that bunch from Triple-H is close enough to hear it or not." He got down from his horse and slipped quietly up behind Leon. Then he suddenly gave him a swat with his open hand, sending Leon's hat flying, the result of which caused Leon's body to slide over sideways to settle on the ground. Emmett jumped backward in shock, and the three men with him came off their horses, looking for any attack that might come from the darkness around them. "Take it easy," Emmett said, "he's been dead for a long time." He reached in his pocket and pulled out a match, struck it on his belt buckle, and held it down close to Leon's face. "He was shot," Emmett said, "one in the chest and another'n in the head."

"They came back yesterday after we left and jumped him," Bo said. "What would they do that for, if they were comin' back here this mornin', like they said?"

Bo was right, Emmett thought, it didn't make any sense. They would only do something like this if they had decided not to show up here this morning. But if they show up like they said they would, that might indicate that they don't know anything about Leon's death. And to Emmett, that could mean only one thing. This was the work of the Injun! Morgan Hunter had said that the Indian had gone and if he believed that, he wouldn't know that Leon had been killed. In that case, Hunter and his crew would show up here at the creek to drive the Double-K herd back to Double-K land as they had threatened. He tried to explain it to the three men with him, but they found it too complicated to understand. So he told them they were just going to wait for Hunter to show up, and they would do what had to be done to make sure those cows stayed right where they were. "Let's drag him outta here," Emmett said then. "This little crook in the creek makes a good place for cover when the shootin' starts. Drag Leon down there by those berry bushes, and if we get time, we'll put him in the ground later."

Bo and Leo each grabbed one of Leon's boots and dragged the stiffened corpse out of the makeshift camp and down to a bank crowded with service berry bushes. They dropped the body in front of the bushes. "There you go, Leon, just enjoy the fresh night air," Leo Blake said as he and Bo went back to the camp. "If we get a chance later on, maybe we'll put you in the ground."

Behind them, the branches of the largest berry bush parted far enough for Cody to look down at the body. He had left his horse about fifty yards upstream and made his way through the trees bordering the creek on foot to this patch of berry bushes about fifteen yards from the Double-K campfire. He had wanted to see how many men Emmett Kincaid brought back with him to deter Morgan's intentions to move the Double-K cattle back to the Double-K range. The fact that Kincaid had brought only three men back with him this morning told Cody exactly how seriously Emmett took Morgan's threat. With Leon Ritter's death, it left Emmett with three men, the same as the day before. Evidently, he was confident that was all that was necessary. Cody withdrew from the berry patch and retraced his steps back upstream to get his horse.

He walked Storm back toward the Triple-H until he saw the group of riders coming toward him. He stepped off the trail and pulled Storm to a stop behind a couple of pines. It was not yet first light of morning, but he could see that Morgan and Holt had five of the men with them. In the poor light, he could make out Frank Strom and Shorty Black, Chris Scott, and Johnny Becker. He wasn't sure, but he guessed the other man was John Bostic, one of the older hands. It was hard not to compare the two opposing sides and give the odds to the ones with the most notches in their gun handles. Morgan and Holt were going to need some help to survive this day. He turned the patient dun gelding back the way he had come. His intention was to find a position on the heavily forested slope of the ridge bordering the little canyon where he could help his brothers.

"Are you thinkin' about ridin' up to that creek to see if they're there?" Holt asked Morgan when they reached the cattle on the north side of the herd.

"What for?" Morgan responded.

"To tell 'em we've come to move these cows off our range," Holt answered.

"I told 'em yesterday what we were gonna do this mornin'," Morgan said. "I don't see no use in tellin' 'em again. If they're here, they'll find out when their cows start comin' home." He stood up in his stirrups then and looked back at the men. "All right, boys, here they are. Let's get 'em started back toward that creek. I'll ride point, Holt you and Chris ride swing, Shorty and John ride flank. Frank, you and Johnny ride drag, and I don't want a single cow left on our range. All right, let's round up those strays and get 'em started south."

It wasn't long before Bo Dawson announced, "I reckon they're comin'."

"Yeah, I reckon so," Emmett replied, unconcerned. The cries of encouragement from the other side of the herd were becoming a little louder now as the Triple-H hands started to get the cattle moving. There was beginning to be some movement in the cattle closest to the creek, as well. "I expect it's about time to let them cowboys know that the herd has already got where it's goin' today." He picked up his rifle and fired three shots into the air.

In a matter of minutes, the cows in the middle of the herd parted as Morgan Hunter approached to a point where he could be heard. "Kincaid!" Morgan shouted. "I gave you warning, if you don't move your cattle off Hunter land, then I would do it for you. That's all that's happenin' here today, we're doin' you a favor."

"Now, I'm gonna do you one, Hunter," Emmett shouted back. "That land you're settin' on right now is Kincaid property. If you turn around and you and your men get off my land, I won't shoot you for trespassin'. If you don't, we're gonna start pickin' you off one by one. How's that for a favor?"

"Kincaid," Morgan tried again, "you know I've got the law on my side. So I'm driving these cattle off Triple-H range."

"The only law this far down in the valley is six-gun law, and that decides who the land belongs to," Emmett shouted back. Then he looked over at Slick and said, "See if you can hit that son of a gun from here."

"It'd be my pleasure," Slick replied. He brought his

Winchester up to his shoulder and fired a shot at Morgan that missed by inches. "Damn, he moved." He cranked in another cartridge as they heard what sounded like an echo of his first shot.

Confused, Emmett turned to ask him what happened but was shocked to see Slick drop his rifle and collapse. "Take cover!" Emmett yelled. The three of them dived for the cover of the creek bank. "They got around us somewhere! Anybody see where that shot came from?"

"They got him in the left side," Bo answered, looking back at Slick lying on the open bank above them, "so it musta come from that direction." He pointed at the trees on the creek upstream. Looking back at Slick then, he said, "He's tryin' to move. It looks like he's hurt pretty bad."

"Reckon we oughta try to pull him down here?" Leo asked.

"And give that feller somebody else to shoot?" Emmett responded. "Let's see if we can see where that bush-whacker is first." He raised his voice and called out, "Just lay still up there, Slick, and we'll come help you directly. Bo, you come with me and we'll slip down beside the creek and see if we can't spot him. Leo, you stay here and watch those cows. If that damn Hunter is crazy enough to keep comin', shoot him down."

Not waiting for them to come looking for him, Cody had already left the position he had taken the shot from. He ran back to his horse, circled back on Double-K land to the opposite side of the creek bank. He hoped Slick's near miss had persuaded Morgan to drop back in the herd.

"You tryin' to get yourself killed?" Holt yelled at his brother. "You know, Cody was right, these vultures we're dealin' with here ain't gonna sit down and talk no peace talks with us. And there sure as hell ain't gonna be no peace talks now that we shot that one that took a shot at you."

"I know that," Morgan said, "and after I told 'em not to shoot till I said to. Who was it?"

"I don't know," Holt replied, "wasn't anybody near me. But you better be glad they did. That fellow's next shot might notta missed. So whadda we tell the men now?"

"The time for negotiatin' a truce is over," Morgan said. "The war's on, and I don't know if they've got any men hidin' in the bushes or not, but I didn't see but three men run down to that hole they dug in the creek bank. Tell me if I'm wrong, but it looks like to me Emmett Kincaid thought he could turn us back with just four men. And now there ain't but three of 'em. So you go to that side of the herd and I'll go to the other. We're gonna drive these damn cows right back over that hole in the creek bank. And fire at will!"

"Now we're talkin'," Holt said as he wheeled his horse to make his way back through the herd. "Cody woulda been proud of us." *That might be so,* Morgan thought, *and it looks like we're doing it without his help.*

As far as Cody was concerned, he saw that the Triple-H men were now moving the cattle, and they were shooting at the three men in the creek. Kincaid and his two men were well protected from their shots, and Cody was afraid that if they stayed there, the tide would turn in Kincaid's favor. Because when Morgan's men reached the clearing before the creek, they would have no protection. So Cody returned to the spot on the slope of the ridge where he had first been able to get an angle that would give him the possibility of a clear shot. There was still the same problem as there had been before, however. If all three men were crouched up tightly against the bank in positions to fire, he couldn't see enough of them to have a lethal target. And they were all sitting tightly against that bank now, waiting for the Triple-H men to suddenly find themselves charging across an open meadow. With no protection from the three rifles behind the bank, it might turn into a turkey shoot for Kincaid's men.

Cody looked frantically around him, trying to spot a better location to fire from. But unfortunately, there was no spot as good as the one he was already in. He evaluated his choices. He had a clear shot at one of the three men's boots, a couple of shots at a hand or elbow, if the target reached for a canteen. He even had a chance at a head shot if one of them raised his head up high enough to see over the edge of the bank. Unfortunately, all three had the good sense to dig out a trench to lay their rifles in, so they wouldn't have to raise their heads above the edge. Maybe, he thought, when Morgan and Holt get to that open meadow, he could throw enough lead in that hole to distract Kincaid and his two men. Nothing to do but wait.

"Emmett," Slick began to moan pitifully. "Emmett, I'm hurt bad. I think I'm dyin'."

"Just hold still," Emmett called out. He was not willing to risk leaving the cover of their dirt fortress. He was pretty sure that Slick was done for, anyway, so why bother? "You'll be all right if you just lay quiet."

That settled the dying man again, but this time for only a few minutes before his painful voice came again. "Leo," Slick pleaded this time. "I'm so thirsty. Give me some water, Leo. Please, Leo."

"He's dyin'," Emmett said. "Put him outta his misery, Leo."

Leo cocked his .44 and raised up to receive a shot in the side of his head. Bo and Emmett threw desperate shots in the direction the kill shot had come with enough rapidity to pin Cody down until they both scrambled out of the hole and ran down the bank where their horses were tied. Cody considered a chase but decided the mission was accomplished with the routing of Emmett Kincaid and his one surviving man. It was time for him to go, as well. Morgan and Holt were getting closer to the creek now. And with the stray bullets flying around from the Triple-H brigade, it might not be a safe area to be in. He didn't care to end this battle as the only casualty shot by the Triple-H. There was one thing he thought he should do before leaving, however. So he scrambled down the slope to the creek bank, drew his six-gun, and ended Slick Wilson's misery. Then he started back along the ridge at a trot to the thicket where he had left Storm. He climbed on his back and started out following the same trail Emmett and Bo had fled on. It had turned out to be a pretty good morning. The most important part being the survival of both his brothers. And without some revision of brother Morgan's plan, that outcome had been far from a certainty. The return of the Double-K's cattle to their home range was accomplished, as Morgan had vowed, and the land Kincaid had invaded had been reclaimed. It would all be satisfactory if the Kincaids had been taught a lasting lesson. However, since there were two Kincaids left standing, Cody figured it was just a matter of time before another assault upon the Triple-H's land or cattle. It would be necessary to keep an eye on their activities. But for now, he was hungry and he needed sleep, so he cut back toward the west and his camp in the mountains.

"What in the hell happened here?" Morgan wondered aloud as he and Holt looked at the hole that had been dug out of the bank of the creek to serve as Emmett Kincaid's fort. There was a body lying on the ground outside the hole, and another body lying partway out of the hole. "I recognize that one," Morgan said, pointing to Slick Wilson's body. "He's the one who shot at me when I told them we were gonna move the cattle. Who shot him, anyway?"

"Nobody's claimin' it," Holt said. "Musta been a stray shot from somewhere."

"It would have been a helluva shot from that distance if it was one of us," Morgan said, "'cause at that point I was quite a ways out in front of you men."

"Hey, Boss," Shorty Blake called out from down near a patch of berry bushes. "There's another dead one down here, but he looks like he's been dead for a while."

Morgan looked at Holt and shook his head. "There's a lot of this killin' that doesn't make sense, especially this," he said and pointed to the bodies of Slick and Leo. "And not one of our men claims he knows for sure he hit anybody. We know for sure that Kincaid was in this hole, but him and another man took off before anybody fired the first shot from this damn fort they dug in the bank."

Holt shrugged and they stared at each other for a long moment. "Cody." They both uttered at the same time.

"Nah," Holt said immediately after. "He took off, headed west."

"It sure looks like there had to be somebody else raising all that hell on this creek while we were wanderin' around in that herd of cows," Morgan said.

"Maybe it was the Indian," Holt said and grinned.

"Maybe so," Morgan replied. "Let's move those cows a little farther down this valley, so they'll really feel at home. Then let's get the hell outta here."

"I thought you knew what you were doin'," Ralph Kincaid yelled at Emmett. "How the hell can you come runnin' back here with your tail between your legs and expect me to believe that bunch of cowboys and sodbusters ran you off? Emmett, you lost three good men. What about those cows we drove up there? What happened to them?

You didn't stick around to see. We're probably gonna have to steal 'em back now."

Emmett sat there and let him rave until he got it out of his system. And when he finally paused to catch a breath, he said, "Are you through pitchin' your little fit now? Because we need to talk some sense about what happened on that creek this mornin' while you was settin' at the kitchen table havin' your coffee." He let that barb sting for a moment before continuing. "While that little ragtag bunch of cowhands were still tryin' to get our cows to move, they already had snipers set up on both sides of that place we fixed up to fight 'em from. In the first place, I left Leon there to keep an eye on things, and we found him dead when we got there this mornin'." He went on to relate the deaths of Slick and Leo, and his and Bo's narrow escape. "We had no choice," he concluded, "they had gotten men in positions all around us. And I hate it if it spoiled your mornin', but me and Bo were damn lucky to make it outta there alive."

"All right," Ralph said, "you're right, you made your point, I weren't there. It's just hard for me to imagine that crew workin' for Triple-H gittin' up enough salt to come after our cattle." Arguments like this between the two brothers were not uncommon, since it was Emmett's role to lead their men in the actual work that had to be done. Ralph's part, on the other hand, was in the planning of the job, especially after they decided to go into the cattle business. It was not always this way, for in their early years they made a living from stagecoach and train robberies to bank holdups. They shared the work and the danger until a shotgun blast at close range tore part of Ralph's right shoulder and most of the muscles of his right arm apart. Emmett beat the stagecoach guard to death with the barrel of his rifle. After a long battle to save the arm and a longer period of recovery, Ralph was left with a withered right arm, useless for most purposes.

"That's the mistake I made," Emmett said. "I didn't think they had enough salt to come back at us, either. They had to have come back there and killed Leon right after we left yesterday, else they couldn'ta got their men in positions on both sides of our camp."

"I know Hunter told you that Injun was gone, but I can't help thinkin' that mighta been something the Injun coulda done," Ralph said.

"I gave that a thought, myself," Emmett said. "Because that bunch with Morgan Hunter was still ridin' around on the backside of that herd, tryin' to get 'em started toward us. Oh, they was doin' some shootin' in our direction, and Hunter rode up close enough to tell us they had come to move the cattle. But they weren't close enough to do anything. That's when Slick stood up and took a shot at him. Hunter was too far away, so Slick missed him. And right then, somebody shot Slick from the side, and at close range. That's when we dived in that hole for cover. A little while later, when Slick started moanin', Leo stuck his head up and somebody shot him from the other side. Hunter's crew wasn't nowhere near us when that happened." He paused then and waited for Ralph's reaction.

Ralph didn't respond at once as if reluctant to say it. "It sounds like it coulda been the work of that damn Injun. Reckon Hunter was lyin' about him being gone?"

"If he really ain't workin' for the Triple-H, then what's he comin' after our men for?" Emmett forced a laugh. "Hell, I ain't shot an Injun since we was workin' Oklahoma Territory."

Sadie Springer walked into the study. "You gonna eat with us?"

"It is about that time, ain't it?" Emmett replied. "Yeah,

I'll eat with you, if you've fixed enough. If you ain't, I can go eat with the men. Tater usually cooks plenty."

"I cooked plenty," Sadie said. "It'll be ready in about five minutes." She did an about-face and left the room.

"After I get somethin' to eat, I'll take some of the boys and ride back up to the boundary creek and see where our cattle are," Emmett said. "Whaddaya think we oughta do now? Drive 'em back up on their range again, or leave 'em be for a while?"

"I ain't sure what's best right now after what happened this mornin'," Ralph answered. "I'd like to find out for sure if we're in a war with Triple-H or in a war with that Injun. If he don't work for Triple-H, then what is his war with us about?"

"That fifty-dollar price we put on his head didn't help a helluva lot, did it?" Emmett cracked. "And we lost another man in the process. Maybe we oughta back off the Triple-H a little while and go huntin' for that damn Injun, but nobody by hisself. Everybody take a partner, and when you find that sneakin' Injun, you both get a fifty-dollar bonus."

"That sounds like a good idea to me," Ralph said. "Let's talk to the men after we eat."

"Ya comin'?" Sadie yelled from the kitchen at that moment.

Ralph looked at his brother and grunted. "Hard to resist when a woman sweet-talks you like that, ain't it?"

"It is a little better than when she yells Sooowheee pigs!" Emmett remarked.

CHAPTER 13

Cody returned to the camp he had made before. It was high up a mountain by a stream that gushed through a split in the rocky face of a cliff before winding its way down to the river below. He had not quite reached the small clearing that held his camp when he heard the greeting from his packhorse. Storm returned it and they found the sorrel horse, his front legs hobbled, coming to meet them. It was a relief to Cody to see the packhorse, for he was a problem on occasions like today. He knew he was going to have to move often and fast when he left to go to the boundary creek the night before. He expected to hide Storm when he made his way on foot to move to closer lookout spots. Having his packhorse along would have been far too much trouble to deal with. Knowing he would be gone for a long time, however, he could not leave the sorrel tied to a tree with no way to escape should a bear or a mountain lion approach. He couldn't leave the horse free to gallop because it would wander away from his camp, or worse, follow him. So he chose to hobble the horse. He could move if he had to, but he would not be inclined to wander far. He needed his packhorse and that was why he was relieved to see him safe and sound and happy that a bear or mountain lion had not found him hobbled. There was nothing he could think of to protect the horse in that event. It would take too much time to teach the horse to use a gun.

As a precaution, he scouted around the little clearing to see if there was any sign that his camp had been visited— by man or animal. This he did in spite of the fact that none of his cooking utensils or supplies had been disturbed. He unsaddled Storm then and gathered some wood for a fire. Before long he had his coffeepot working up some coffee to go with his jerky and hardtack. That was enough to take the edge off his hunger, so he could go to sleep. Maybe he would hunt for some small game with his bow for supper. Even though it was in the middle of the after- noon, the cloak of tree branches covering his camp gave him a sense of darkness. So he fell asleep immediately and slept for what he estimated to be about two hours. When he woke, he walked over to a fallen tree where he could see the sky through the hole left in the branches and saw that the sun was still high in the sky. Good, he thought, because he wanted to see the aftermath of the morning's activities.

When he rode out again, he decided to first find out what happened to the cattle that Morgan drove off Triple- H range. That question was answered for him when he came upon the herd of cows quite some distance down the Double-K range. He was glad to see that Morgan hadn't stopped at the boundary creek. There were no Double-K hands watching the cows, so he decided to cut back toward the river and return to the spot where he had watched their headquarters before. Keeping a sharp eye out to avoid any Double-K riders, he rode to the same spot on the river, about one hundred and twenty-five yards from the ranch house. Like the last time he watched from here, there seemed to be no frantic activity taking place. If they were planning a counterattack, there was no sign of it. He re- mained there for quite some time, until suppertime, he realized, and still there was no sign anybody was planning to go anywhere. He decided that nothing was going to happen for the rest of this day, evidently, so he might as well retreat to his camp again. He felt the need to find something more substantial to eat than what he had for his dinner. *Maybe I'll scare up a rabbit or a squirrel,* he thought, as he turned Storm's head away from the river. "I'll be back to keep an eye on you boys tomorrow," he said in parting. It would have been of profound interest to him if he had known that he was the subject of a special meeting at the Double-K shortly after he rode away.

Ralph and Emmett called the men together in the bunkhouse after supper to let them know what their thinking was after the ill-fated encounter at the boundary creek. "Sounds to me like you mighta took them cowboys a little too lightly, Boss," Earl Mathers, one of the older hands, said. He and another of the older men in the gang, Smoke Davis, had commented that Emmett would have been wise to take a few more of the men to meet the Triple-H cowhands.

"I know," Emmett replied, "it mighta looked that way. But we had enough with the four of us to handle the Triple-H crew. What we didn't know was that Injun that was supposed to be long gone was still here. He's the one that cost us the men we lost. So the reason for this meetin' is to let you know it's time to send that Injun to the 'Happy Huntin' Grounds' for sure this time. Ralph and I will still pay fifty dollars for his scalp, but we want you to partner up, so there are two of you to watch each other's back. If you nail the Injun, you and your partner both get fifty dollars. Don't matter who pulls the trigger."

"I ain't sure I know what you're tellin' us to do," Ben Clark interrupted. "When we go out in the mornin', are we gonna go tend the cows like we do every day? Or are we just gonna ride the outer limits of our range on the lookout for that Injun, and never mind the lost strays and the calves?"

"No," Emmett was quick to reply. "What we're sayin, Ben, is that if you see fresh hoofprints from a horse, where there ain't supposed to be any, that's what you and your partner take care of first. We want you to keep your mind on what you're doin' out there. Anything don't look right, find out what don't make it look right. We've got us a weasel slippin' around our henhouse, and we're gonna have to catch him before we can get back to the job of takin' over the cattle business in the Bitterroot Valley." He let that sink in for a few moments before he continued. "Now, is there anybody who don't feel right about knockin' a stranger outta the saddle, just because he's wearin' buckskins? Then I'll tell you to think about Reese and Blackie, and Slick and Leon, and Albert and Leo. What I'm tellin' you is that was all the dirty work of one damn sneakin' Injun. After we nail this Injun, then we're gonna go to war on the outfit that'll hire somebody like that. So pick a partner you wanna hunt with and good huntin'!"

There was no cheering or clapping of hands after his inspirational message, but both Kincaid brothers were satisfied to see the serious expressions on the simple faces and the nodding to acknowledge important points in Emmett's talk. Afterward, when they returned to the ranch house and a cup of decent coffee from Sadie's coffeepot, they discussed it. "I swear, Emmett, I think you made a helluva speech down there," Ralph declared. "Bo Dawson looked like we was gittin' ready to go fight the Holy Wars. And they almost looked shocked when you said that stuff about not feelin' bad for shootin' a man just because he's wearin' buckskins." He paused to chuckle. "Especially since every man we hired is ridin' with us because he'd put a bullet in the back of the preacher's head for a price."

Listening to their assessment of the motivational talk Emmett gave the men, Sadie commented as was her habit. "That sorry bunch of loafers is liable to forget what you was talking about by the time they wake up in the mornin'. Whaddaya gonna do if don't none of 'em ever find that Injun?"

"I don't know, Sadie," Ralph answered her. "Reckon we'll just have to send you out there to find him. But I'll swear, that don't hardly seem fair to the Injun, does it, Emmett?"

Unaware that he was now the focus of all the men who rode for the Double-K, the "Injun" returned to his camp high up on the mountain. He had no notion regarding when or what Emmett Kincaid's next move would be. He planned to keep on the lookout for any apparent aggressive moves on the part of the Double-K. But that would be tomorrow. For tonight, he felt a need for some fresh meat. For the purpose, he took his bow and several small game arrows and went for a walk along the stream. He didn't really care what kind of critter he killed, rabbit, muskrat, raccoon. He wasn't looking for a deer because he did not want to skin it, butcher it, and smoke most of it tonight. He just wanted a meal. It turned out to be raccoon. He used up most of his flour to form cakes to fry in the grease from the raccoon and washed it all down with coffee. It satisfied him. He looked around him and decided he had picked a good camp. *Anyone stumbling on this camp will probably be looking for me,* he thought, because it wasn't on a trail going east to west, or north to south. He decided he would scout some of the Double-K range in the morning just to make sure they weren't mounting up another foray into

Triple-H territory. Then he would ride along the fringes
of Triple-H, just to see if everything looked peaceful there.
That settled, he decided it had been a full day; he crawled
into his blanket and went to sleep.

"You know, we came outta this thing today in a lot
better shape than we should have," Holt commented to
Morgan and their father. They sat at the kitchen table, finishing off the pot of coffee Pansy had made when Morgan
came over after supper.

"I don't know why you keep sayin' that," Morgan
replied. "We moved their cattle off our range, just like we
told 'em we would. We moved right across that creek
without losing a man. Then we herded those cows at least
three miles deep on their range. And we ain't seen hide nor
hair of any of their men tryin' to stop us."

"It sure sounds to me like you boys won the day," Duncan
Hunter commented.

"Yeah, but Pa, it wasn't exactly like we went charging
across that clearin' with guns a-blazin', and the Double-K
men took off runnin'," Holt insisted. He looked at Morgan
then and said, "We talked about this when we got up to
that creek and found dead bodies that none of our men
could claim." He looked his father in the eye and said, "I
think Cody was up at that creek, and Morgan did, too. If
those men hadn't been killed and the other two weren't
forced to run for their lives, they coulda sat right there in
that hole and cleaned us out. Like shootin' fish in a barrel."

Morgan was still not completely convinced. "We did
talk about that possibility, and I was thinkin' like you for
a while. But if Cody came back to fight with us, why didn't
he show up while we were in the middle of that herd of
cattle? Better yet, if he decided to come back, where is he?

He oughta be sittin' here with us right now, if he didn't run off for good."

"Hell, I don't know," Holt pleaded and threw up his hands. "Maybe he just can't give up the habit of sleepin' in the woods."

"He has to fight like he learned how to fight," Pansy said. "Excuse me, I know ladies ain't supposed to interrupt when the menfolk are talkin'. But I don't rightly remember anybody ever callin' me a lady. I told you this before when Cody left. He knows he can do you more good if he fights like he knows how, like a Crow warrior."

"He could have told us that," Morgan protested. "We would have let him fight any way he wanted to."

"I reckon he didn't know that for sure," Pansy said, "so he just decided not to waste time arguing the point."

"It still doesn't seem right," Morgan said. "He oughta be here with his family. This was just the first day of this war we've gotten into with Ralph and Emmett Kincaid. We need to decide how we're gonna protect our ranch. Is he gonna be here to stand side by side with me and Holt. I think we need to know that. We need to know if we can count on him."

Pansy just looked at Morgan and shook her head. "I believe those dead bodies you said you found after the other two deserted, oughta be a pretty good sign that you can count on him."

"You know," Holt remarked, "I believe you're right, Pansy. We oughta be thankin' the Lord we've got somebody we can count on—even if he is an Injun."

"I'd still like it a whole lot better if he would come on home, so we would have some idea what he's gonna do," Morgan complained.

"We need to be thinkin' about what Double-K's next move is gonna be," Duncan said. "I can't believe those crooks are gonna take that beating and just back off."

"No, sir, I'm sure they ain't," Morgan replied. "There ain't much we can do until they make another move against us. I've told the men that they've all got to stay sharp and keep an eye out for anything out of the ordinary. Other than that, we still have to take care of our cattle just like we do every other day."

"I reckon that's right," Duncan said. "So you boys better get to bed now and we'll see what tomorrow brings." Morgan and Holt both took their father's advice and said goodnight.

The morning began in typical fashion with both Holt and Morgan eating breakfast with the men. And after the crew got their assignments for the day's work, Morgan told Holt he was going to ride down to the boundary creek. "I want to make sure that herd of Double-K cattle ain't right back in that little valley again."

"What are you gonna do if they are?" Holt asked.

"I reckon we'll just have to do the same thing we did yesterday," Morgan said, "and try to drive 'em outta there again."

"You be damn careful," Holt said. "If they're back, it'll be with a sight more men than they sent the first time. Maybe I better go with you."

"No, I'll be all right," Morgan said. "I'm just goin' to be real careful and take a look to make sure we don't have to mount up our army again." He stepped up into the saddle. "Don't worry, if there's anybody there, I ain't plannin' on lettin' 'em see me. I ain't gonna order 'em off our land till I have you and the rest of the crew with me." He chuckled and rode away at a trot.

By the time Morgan crossed over the high ridge north of the little valley, the sun was already high in the sky. Listening hard in an effort to pick up any sounds of cattle bawling as he approached the open meadow of the valley that led up to the creek, he slowed his horse to a stop. There were no cattle in the meadow. Still he was reluctant to ride out in the open, so he rode along under the cover of the trees that skirted the meadow. No point in riding out in the middle of that open meadow and get shot by somebody watching from the creek, he reasoned.

You just made a smart decision, the man watching from the creek thought. "I had an idea somebody might show up back here this morning. I ain't surprised that it's you, Morgan." He debated the prospect of remaining where he was, so he could tell his brother that the Double-K cattle were well down on the Double-K range and he didn't have to worry about them for a while, anyway. But he wasn't ready to let his brothers know that he was still here. There was so much more that he could do when no one knew he existed. So he sat there in the saddle and watched as Morgan continued to circle around the meadow. Then when he was sure his brother was heading toward him, he turned Storm around and disappeared into the dark forest on the slope behind him. He went no farther than the spot from which he had fired down into the creek to kill Leo Blake. As soon as he left the creek, the buzzards returned to continue the banquet he had interrupted on the two bodies still lying there. He waited on the slope because he suspected that Morgan would come to examine the defensive bunker dug out of a corner of the creek once again.

When Morgan saw the gathering of the greedy birds, fighting and screaming over the remains of Slick Wilson and Leo Blake, he hesitated to advance any closer. He had thought to take a closer look at the bodies in an effort to see if they could have possibly been hit from his men coming toward them. If so, it would defuse the thinking that led him and Holt to conclude that Cody could have done it. Facing the raucous feeding frenzy taking place now, and the dislocation of the two bodies from their original positions, he decided his efforts would be wasted. He turned his horse away from the boundary creek and headed out across the meadow, straight for the Triple-H.

"Good," Cody mumbled to himself as he watched from the slope of the ridge. He continued to watch until Morgan disappeared into the trees on the far side of the meadow. Even though he was unaware of it, he had felt a sense of responsibility for his brother's safety. So he had remained there to watch Morgan until he looked to be heading safely home. Only then, did he climb on Storm again and head back down the valley. He wanted to see what was going on at the Double-K. If there were any signs of another attack being prepared, he wanted to pick them up before the mission was underway. So far, on his way to scout the ranch house, he had seen no sign of any riders working with any of the cattle. Also, he did not have to avoid any groups of riders heading to some work project. It seemed strange, but not so much that it caused him concern. Neither he nor the Kincaid brothers were aware of the fact that they were now all scouting on each other. While Cody was interested in any trouble Kincaid might be brewing to take over the Triple-H, the sole purpose for the Double-K scouts was the death of the Indian. As the morning drew closer to noontime, Cody decided he would rest his horse and eat some jerky before pushing on to his lookout post at the Double-K.

"Yonder!" John Simon exclaimed in a loud whisper. "Look yonder!"

"What? Where?" Jesse Grissom responded, trying to look in the direction Simon was pointing.

"Yonder!" Simon repeated frantically. "It's him! It's the Injun! Wearin' buckskins, just like Willy Vick said!"

Jesse pulled his horse over closer to Simon's. "I see him!" he exclaimed. "It's him, all right! Settin' there eatin' a rabbit or somethin'. This close to the ranch, too. That's fifty bucks a-piece settin' there."

"How you reckon we oughta do this?" Simon asked. "Willy said he was fast as lightnin' with a rifle."

"I ain't wantin' to see how fast he is," Jesse said. "Let's leave the horses here and slip down through them trees. We oughta be able to get down to about thirty yards from where he's settin'. Can't miss from that close with our rifles. We'll count to three and both of us shoot at the same time. We'll see how fast he is after that."

"That suits me," Simon said. "Crank a cartridge in your rifle right now, so we don't take no chance on him hearin' it when we get close."

They left their horses there and made their way down through the trees that shaded the little stream where their target was casually eating the meat from a rabbit he had killed and cooked. Jesse and Simon managed to make it to the point they had decided upon for their shots. There was no indication from their intended victim that he was aware of their presence. They took dead aim with their rifles and when Jesse whispered, "Three," both rifles fired and both bullets struck dead center.

They galloped into the barnyard at the Double-K headquarters, whooping like the wild Indian they had just killed. They each led a horse behind them, one carrying a packsaddle, the other a body draped across the saddle. Their entrance was loud enough to pull spectators from the house and barn. Seeing Emmett Kincaid as one of the excited spectators, Jesse sang out, "We got your Injun right here, Boss, me and John! He weren't more'n a mile from here, just settin' there eatin' a rabbit, pretty as you please." He jumped down from his horse, ran back, and pulled the dead man off to land on the ground.

Emmett walked over to the corpse and rolled it face up. He was at once skeptical. The dead man was wearing a buckskin shirt that went almost to his knees, which were inside woolen trousers that were tucked into a pair of worn-out boots. The fact that the man's unshaven face was covered with gray whiskers to match his unruly gray hair, was enough to cause Emmett to strain to hold his temper. He turned to address Jesse's proud grin. "You damn fool," he said as quietly as he could manage. He looked at John Simon then and pointed to the dead man. "Does he look like a damn Injun to you? You've just shot somebody's grandpa."

The grins on Jesse and Simon's faces shattered when their jaws dropped open. "You know the light's kinda bad back down in those trees," Jesse started, but Emmett cut him off.

"It's my fault," Emmett said. "I shoulda made a rule that said one of the two bounty hunters had to have a little bit of sense." Seeing Willy Vick standing there, with a grin on his face, like all the other spectators now, he decided to make sure. Although it had been a quick look, Willy was the only one who had gotten a look at the Injun. "How 'bout it, Willy? Is that the Injun?"

"No, sir," Willy answered. "I know for sure that ain't the man who shot Reese and Blackie."

"All right, Jesse," Emmett said, "you and Simon drag that unlucky drifter way the hell away from here and bury him. Turn his horses in with the herd and get rid of that junk he's haulin'. Wait a minute. Let's make sure he ain't got anything valuable on him. Damned if I want you two to cash in on a mistake as dumb as the one you just made." All the spectators hung around until all the dead man's clothes and possessions had been searched.

About one hundred and twenty-five yards away from the Double-K headquarters, Cody was straining to see what the little commotion had been in the barnyard. It was a little too far away to tell with the naked eye. But it had to do with what looked to be a body that was pulled off a horse. Earlier, he had heard two rifle shots fired at almost the same time, so it was logical to assume they had something to do with the body dragged off the horse. After a little while, the two men who brought the body into the barnyard put it on a horse, and rode away from the barnyard. All that activity was just something to occupy his thoughts for a little while, but then his interest was aroused anew. For the two men seemed to be heading in a straight line toward his position on the riverbank.

"Damn," he uttered, thinking he'd best prepare to retreat. Thinking surely they weren't going to throw the body in the river, he lingered a bit longer. In the meantime, he pulled his horse up close beside him. And he picked out a stand of trees about fifty yards from the place he now stood. "If they don't stop to bury that devil by the time they reach those trees, I'm leaving."

He dropped Storm's reins to the ground again when the two men pulled up at the stand of trees he had based his decision to leave on. He moved to another position on the riverbank, one from which he could get a better look at the gravediggers' activities. With pick and shovel, which they had evidently picked up at the barn, they dug a shallow hole for some unlucky soul wearing a long buckskin shirt. He waited until they finished their chore and went back to the barnyard where everything had already returned to the inactivity of before. Cody decided there was no counterattack underway at the present. So he got on his horse and left to scout the ranges farther away from the Double-K headquarters.

CHAPTER 14

Cody spent the rest of the afternoon riding the outmost Double-K grazing areas and was forced to avoid contact on two separate occasions. In both sightings, there were two riders who showed very little interest in any cows they happened upon. It seemed an especially careless attitude demonstrated by all four of the Double-K riders. And once, when two of them ignored a calf that had managed to get itself trapped in a hole at the edge of the river that was too deep to escape without help, Cody was tempted to call them on it. The cowhands seemed more interested in the conversation between them than anything to do with the cattle they were supposed to be keeping safe. They appeared to be heading in a general direction that, if maintained, should cause them to end up at the Double-K ranch house. And pretty close to suppertime, Cody speculated. It occurred to him then that both pairs of Double-K hands had appeared to be riding as lookouts for any Triple-H riders. Evidently, since they had made the initial invasion into Triple-H territory, they were now on watch for any sign of the same from the Hunters. So he decided there was no call for him to take any action, with the exception of saving the calf, who was neutral in the war between the two ranches.

So when the two riders passed on by that hole with the struggling calf in it, Cody felt sure they were on their way to the ranch for supper. So he rode down to the edge of the river and fashioned a noose in his rope and threw it over the calf's head. Then Storm pulled the frightened calf out of the hole and up on the bank. Cody shook his noose free and rewound his rope while the rescued calf went in search of its mother. "You're right," Cody told the calf, "it's time to go find something to eat. I'm gonna do the same thing." He didn't know if there was going to be any more fighting between the Hunters and the Kincaids. But for the time being, it appeared that each side was just on the lookout for any sign of trespassing. So he went on across the river and headed back toward his camp high up the mountain.

"Ben! Ben!" Clyde Peterson gasped frantically and pointed back down toward the river.

Ben Clark looked in the direction Clyde was pointing, jabbing his finger in the air for emphasis. "Sweet mother of Satan! It's him! It's the Injun and he's crossin' over to the other side of the river!"

"You reckon he saw us and that's the reason he crossed the river?" Clyde blurted.

"Hell, no," Ben said, "he ain't seen us. More'n likely, if he had seen us, he'da took a couple of shots at us."

"That's fifty dollars a-piece crossin' the river right now," Clyde said. "But it's a helluva long shot from here and it's gittin' longer every second. We try to make that shot from here and we're liable to blow any chance to get another'n at him."

"You're right about that and right now I don't think he knows we're even here," Ben said. "I think he's doin' the same thing we are right now, and that's the reason he crossed the river, instead of stayin' on the trail on this side. He's headin' back to a camp he's got up in those mountains somewhere. I'm of a mind to follow that devil up to his camp and make sure we get a good shot at him. Maybe we'll get a good shot at him before he gets to his camp, but what I'm saying is we don't wanna try any shots we ain't sure we can make. So whaddaya say? You agree on that? Follow him till we get the sure shot?"

"That suits me just fine, so we'd best cross the river and get on his trail before he gets too far. It'd be pretty easy to lose somebody in them mountains, if you knew they were on your tail."

Since they could still see Cody in the river, they waited where they were, afraid he might see them coming back down to the river. So they watched him until he climbed the bank on the other side, waiting to see which way he went when he left the river. But he didn't leave the river. Instead, he continued to follow it, so they waited to give him more lead, then they galloped back down to the river and started across. When they reached the other side, they could see his trail on the riverbank, so they set out to follow it. They soon caught sight of him in the trees beside the river, so they backed off again, afraid he might look back and see them. They continued on for a short distance more, following too far behind him to get a clear shot through all the trees. Both assassins were becoming impatient, but too cautious to close the gap between them.

For no reason he could explain, Cody had an uneasy feeling as he rode along the riverbank. So when he reached the spot where the stream his camp was on emptied into the river, Storm automatically started to turn to follow the stream up the mountain. But Cody held his reins firm and gave him a little kick to keep him going along the riverbank.

The little move was not wasted on Ben Clark. "Something's wrong," he said. "Something bothered him. He mighta figured out we're tailin' him. Be ready, Clyde." They unconsciously increased their pace a little.

Up ahead, Cody could feel something wrong, and when Storm's ears flicked back, he knew the horse had picked up the presence of another horse. Cody didn't hesitate then. He wheeled Storm into the heavy woods at the base of the mountain and pushed the big dun as fast as he could through the thick growth of trees.

Behind him, Ben galloped along the riverbank and plunged his horse into the brush, determined not to lose the Indian. Now, he could clearly see Cody ahead of him darting back and forth to dodge the trees. He felt it was worth a try, if he could time the shot to catch Cody when his horse moved right or left to avoid a tree. He would take the shot with his pistol because he couldn't use both hands on his rifle. Then suddenly, Cody reached a little clearing where there were no trees, Ben got his chance. He fired a shot but missed, fired a second and Cody straightened up, then slid off the side of his horse. He raced up to finish him off, only to find Cody lying on his back, waiting for him, his Henry rifle aimed at him. Too late, Ben realized he'd been played and he tried to come out of one of his stirrups and drop down on the opposite stirrup to put his horse between himself and Cody. It was not soon enough to avoid the .44 shot that caught him in the chest while he still had one foot in the stirrup and the other in the air over his horse's back.

Aware now that there were two of them, Cody came up on one knee in time to see the other one coming along behind the first rider. Seeing Ben go down, Clyde didn't think twice about what to do. He turned his horse around and fled back toward the river. Cody took his time to lay the front sight of the Henry on the middle of Clyde's back before he calmly squeezed the trigger. With an assist from a tree limb, Clyde was swept off his horse.

Cody cranked another round into his rifle as he hurried to make sure his assailants were finished. When he reached the first one, he found him mortally wounded and struggling to find the pistol he had dropped. Cody drew his six-gun and ended Ben's search. Then he continued on to the second body, finding it in like condition to that of his partner's, so he ended his misery, as well. He knelt there beside the dead man and searched for any movement in the trees between him and the river. Satisfied after a minute or so that there was no one else but the two he had just killed, his next thought was to move the horses and the bodies. They were too close to his camp near the top of that mountain. He decided the best thing to do was to take them back to Double-K as he had done with the first assassin who came after him.

So he caught the two horses before they took a notion to wander off somewhere and tied them to a tree. Then he searched the two bodies as well as their saddlebags for anything of value that he might trade, along with their weapons and ammunition. He was especially impressed when he pulled a Winchester 73 out of Ben Clark's saddle sling. When he examined it, he found it to be in excellent condition, almost like new. His ammunition and supplies were running low and he would soon have to find some place to trade for replacements. A rifle like that Winchester would be an easy sell. It was too bad he couldn't sell their horses, too, he thought. But there was no way he could take care of any extra horses. His one packhorse created enough of a problem as it was. It was also important to let the Kincaid brothers know that it was costing them, if in fact they were sending their men out to kill him. The thought occurred to him then that it might explain why he had seen their men riding in pairs and seeming to have little interest in their cattle. Maybe they were looking for him. Even though it was a sobering thought, at least it distracted the Kincaids from stealing Triple-H cattle.

He knew he couldn't chance having them found this

close to his camp, so he loaded the bodies onto their horses and led them back to the river. He followed the river back toward the Double-K range until he came to a shallow place to cross it. At that point, he was on Double-K land, so he released the two horses and sat there until they started to wander. And when he was sure they would not try to follow him, he wheeled Storm and went back the way he had come.

When he got back to the place where his little stream emptied into the river, he rode up the stream to his camp. But this time, he was a little more cautious as he approached the camp, having just had thoughts that he might be the target of an all-out hunt. So he was once again relieved to hear his sorrel packhorse's greeting. His thoughts returned to supper and his plan to hunt for some small game before he had been distracted by the visit from the two Double-K riders. He found himself thinking about the table Pansy Hutto would have set for his father and Holt's supper. "I swear," he uttered, "I believe I'm startin' to get homesick."

"There's still plenty of this stew left," Tater Duggan announced when he walked outside the cookshack where most of the men were eating. "What's the matter? Ain't you boys hungry tonight?"

"I'll take some more of it," Bo Dawson spoke up. "It ain't bad. Hell, Tater, it's almost fit to eat."

Bo's remark raised a couple of chuckles from those close enough to have heard it. "Maybe I'll just give it to the hogs, instead," Tater threatened as he plopped a heaping serving on Bo's plate. "Where's Ben Clark? He always likes it when I make this stew."

"You better save him some of it," Earl Mathers said.

"'Cause I don't think he's ate yet. Least, I ain't seen him. Is he in the cookshack?"

"No," Tater said. "Don't ya think I'da seen him if he was? Anybody seen him?" No one spoke up. "Who was ridin' with him?"

"Clyde Peterson," Bo answered him. They all looked around them to see if Clyde was there. When they saw that Clyde was missing, too, Bo stated the obvious. "They ain't come back yet."

"I'll keep this pot on the stove for a while," Tater said, "and see if they don't show up pretty soon. Anybody want more coffee?" Nobody did.

After almost an hour had passed with still no sign of Ben and Clyde, Tater announced to the few men still sitting around there, "I'm gonna give this stew to the hogs. I've got to get my kitchen cleaned up."

"I reckon I'd better go up to the house and tell Emmett that Ben and Clyde ain't back yet," Bo said. "Then I expect I'm gonna have to take a couple of the boys and go see if we can find 'em." Even as he said it, he knew there wasn't any logical place to begin a search, since he had no idea where they had headed when they left the ranch. With the way things had been going at the Double-K lately, he dreaded having to give Emmett any negative news. He told Tater as much.

"I know what you mean," Tater replied. "Maybe you could tell him in a positive way. Tell him you think Ben and Clyde mighta found the Injun."

"Damn, Tater, that ain't funny," Bo replied. "Ben and Clyde are two good men."

"Is that so?" Tater responded. "What are they good at? Stealin' cattle and anything else that strikes their fancy? Killin' a man for the money? They was just like the rest of us that ride for this outfit, just waitin' for their number to come up."

Bo wasn't quite sure how to respond to Tater's unexpected discourse on the sins of the Double-K crew. He couldn't deny anything the crusty old cook said, so he just settled for "Well, be that as it may, I reckon I better go tell Boss they're missin'."

"You don't have to," Tater said.

"Why not?" Bo asked.

"'Cause they ain't missin' no more," Tater said while staring past Bo's shoulder.

Bo turned to look in the same direction and saw the two horses standing beyond the bunkhouse, each with a body draped belly-down across the saddle. "Well, I'll be dipped in . . ." he started to mutter under his breath.

Otto Ross, who was one of the men still sitting outside the cookshack, jumped to his feet and exclaimed, "I know what that is." Thinking about the time when he and Slick Wilson found Albert Bradshaw's body returned to the ranch the same way, he jumped up and started toward the horses.

"Well, take it easy, Otto, don't spook them horses," Bo called out after him. "I'll go get Emmett!"

Bo ran up to the back door and knocked, and when Sadie opened it, she took one look at Bo's concerned expression and said, "I hope it ain't as bad as you look. He ain't in a very good mood tonight as it is." She could have told him that Emmett and Ralph had been arguing ever since they sat down to eat supper.

"This ain't gonna help it any," Bo said, "but I gotta tell him."

She looked back over her shoulder and yelled, "Emmett! Bo wants to tell you something."

A few moments later, Emmett came to the kitchen door

to address Bo, who was standing on the steps outside. A moment later Ralph followed his brother to the door. "Sorry to bother you, Boss," Bo started right away. "We had two of the men that didn't come back to supper tonight, Ben Clark and Clyde Peterson. I was fixin' to go look for 'em, but they just showed up right now, both of 'em layin' across their saddles. I figured you'd wanna know right away." Emmett didn't say anything immediately, but Bo heard Ralph swear behind him.

"Was it the Injun?" Emmett asked patiently, knowing it could hardly be anyone else.

"I ain't seen 'em yet," Bo answered, "but I expect so. They was workin' together as one of the pairs lookin' for him. I reckon they found him."

"All right, Bo, I'll be down there in a minute." He closed the door and turned back to face his brother.

"Well, our new plan to hunt that savage in pairs has definitely made a difference," Ralph declared, continuing the argument already underway. "Now, he's killin' our men two at a time. Damn it, Emmett, we're runnin' outta men! How many is that now? And how many has the Triple-H lost? Zero?"

"I ain't got no idea how many Triple-H has lost," Emmett answered him. "If you can believe Morgan Hunter, that Injun is gone from there and he ain't workin' for the Triple-H at all. The last three men he's killed have been men who went lookin' to kill him. If we hadn't sent men to find him, maybe he wouldn't have any reason to kill our men. I've been thinkin' about this thing a lot and I believe one thing is certain. For whatever reason, that Indian was a friend to Triple-H. So if we're fightin' with Triple-H, he's gonna fight on their side and against us. If we quit the fight and don't try to move in on Triple-H, quit tryin' to track him down, then he's got no reason to come after our men, right? Everybody's peaceful and there ain't no need for him to hang around. After a little while, he can go back to wherever he came from."

"That's a nice cozy little picture you painted for yourself, brother. So you're ready to let Triple-H take over the whole valley and maybe we'll just scale back and operate a little farm. Well, it ain't what I had in mind."

"What I'm sayin' is we draw back for a short while, just long enough for Duncan Hunter and his Injun friend to think we're no longer in competition with them. We'll be at peace with them while we're pickin' up the men to replace those we've lost. Then when we're ready, I say we declare war. We move against them and wipe them out before they know what hit 'em. No more stealing bunches of their cattle or pushing some of our cattle onto their grazin' land, tryin' to pinch off a little here and there. Instead, we go to war over grazing rights. It wouldn't be the first range war between two big outfits where there was a lot of casualties. And when the smoke cleared, we'd be the gracious winners and provide for the families of the deceased."

Ralph just stood there with his mouth gaping open while his brother shared his thoughts on a new and deceptive plan to ultimately crush Triple-H. The result of which would establish the Kincaid brothers as the kings of the cattle business in the Bitterroot Valley. "Do you really think something like that is possible?"

"I do," Emmett answered. "I still have the same opinion of the Triple-H crew as I did before, a starry-eyed bunch of cowboys. But I think we'd just have to play pretty for a little while. Then when the time was right, we'd crush 'em. Nobody would know for sure what happened. We might even convince the authorities the government might send to investigate that they were the ones who attacked us." He shrugged indifferently. "People get in range wars all the time, people get killed, but in most cases, nobody goes to jail. At least nobody who's pullin' the strings."

"You might be crazy as hell," Ralph declared, "but damned if I don't believe we'll have a better chance of gettin' what we're after if we do it that way. Why don't we tell the men that the bounty is off for the Injun's scalp. We're just gonna take care of our cattle for a while."

"I'll go down to the bunkhouse and talk to the men now. We'll bury these last two and tell the men we don't wanna endanger their lives anymore chasin' after that savage." He went out the kitchen door and walked down to join the men gathered around the two horses.

"I swear, Boss," Jesse Grissom declared, "it's Ben and Clyde. Both of 'em shot twice, once in the chest and once in the head."

"That's some sorry news," Emmett responded. "They were two good men and I'm tired of losin' good men. So as of right now, the deal is off. I'm not gonna pay anybody a dime to kill that Injun. I'm tired of wastin' our time tryin' to kill one man when we've got a range full of cattle to take care of. Me and Ralph are convinced that if we stop tryin' to kill him, he'll get tired of hangin' around or he'll get careless and get hisself shot. So startin' in the mornin', we're going back to raisin' cattle. We've got strays roamin' all over the valley. Let's get 'em back where they belong and we'll worry about Triple-H later on. Some of you grab some shovels and find a place to put Ben and Clyde in the ground. Take 'em over there where you and Simon buried that drifter, Jesse. Tomorrow's the start of a new day for the Double-K to get ourselves raisin' cattle again."

He left them after a talk he intended to be motivational but served to leave them asking each other what he was telling them. He and his brother weren't going to pay fifty dollars for the Injun's scalp anymore. They got that.

"I swear," Jesse commented when Emmett was out of earshot, "ain't it kinda funny how me and you always wind up diggin' graves for everybody who gets shot?" He and his partner, John Simon, were still stinging from the dressing down they received from Emmett for killing that innocent drifter.

"You got that right," Simon replied. "And now, he ain't even gonna pay the fifty dollars he promised for killin' that Injun. Said we was gonna go back to raisin' cattle. I don't know 'bout you, but I'm sick and tired of tendin' cattle. When I hired on with him and his brother, it was to steal cattle. I never thought about them turnin' me into a permanent cowhand."

"You sound like me," Jesse said. "I was doin' all right, me and a couple of my cousins, holdin' up a stagecoach here and there. Then Emmett came along and told me how he was gonna make us all rich men in the cattle business. I shoulda listened to my cousins and I'da still been holding up stagecoaches, instead of diggin' graves."

"I ain't never said anything to nobody else about this, but I've been thinkin' about cuttin' outta here and goin' back to makin' it on my own."

"I've been thinkin' about doin' the same thing," Jesse said. "There ain't nothin' keepin' me here no more." He paused for a moment, then asked, "Whaddaya say? You ready to cut outta here?"

"I reckon I am," Simon answered. "I s'pose we oughta take care of poor ol' Ben and Clyde like Mr. Kincaid told us to. We can take 'em over there short of the river where we buried that other feller."

"I don't leave nothin' in the bunkhouse, so I don't need to go back there," Jesse said. Simon said the same. "I'll go to the barn and grab a couple of shovels," Jesse decided then.

"What for?" Simon asked.

"So anybody watchin' will think we're ~~gonna bury~~ 'em," Jesse explained. "We might as well head straight for Stevensville and see if we can't raise a little cash to get us started."

Jesse made a big show of going to the barn for a couple of shovels. On the way back to the horses, he met Otto coming his way, having just left Simon and the two bodies. "Gotta go dig a couple of graves for poor ol' Ben and Clyde," he said to Otto. "You wanna come lend a hand?"

"I reckon not," Otto said, "Boss gave me a job to do in the barn."

Jesse chuckled. "I didn't think so." He handed Simon one of the shovels, then he climbed on his horse, and they led the two horses with the bodies out of the barnyard. When they reached the little clearing short of the stand of trees where they had buried the drifter, they pulled the bodies off the horses and searched them thoroughly for any hidden pockets. Any money or trinkets of value they found went into the saddlebags on their horses. They had been fortunate in that Otto was the only one left in the barnyard when they left with the bodies. And he didn't think to suggest the searching of the bodies before they were taken for burial, thinking more about avoiding the manual labor of grave digging. "All them that walked away are gonna be mad when they find out nobody said anything about splitting their possessions."

With no intention of digging graves for the deceased, they pulled the bodies over next to a large tree and placed a shovel beside each one. "We might coulda got a little somethin' in trade for them shovels," Simon speculated. "But we wouldn't want whoever finds 'em to have to dig the graves without a good shovel." They left the Double-K, short on cash, but with plenty to trade, including two good horses and saddles. And they knew the place to do their trading, a man named Harvey Tate, who had a business he called Tate's Store, a half mile shy of Stevensville. They would be there fairly early the next day, if they rode until after dark on the present day. By the time they were ready to make their camp, they were on Triple-H rangeland. And since they had no supplies, they decided it would be a proper parting gesture to butcher one of the Triple-H cows to have for supper and breakfast.

CHAPTER 15

The new truce in the valley was not recognized by all parties involved for a couple of days. Perhaps the first to notice was Cody, for on the day after the two Double-K assassins came after him, he noticed a difference. The Double-K men returned to the job of tending cattle and there were no more two-man scouting teams searching for him. In the days that followed, he continued to scout the Double-K range to confirm their returning to the business of raising cattle. It was difficult for him to accept the new peace at face value after his short history with the Kincaid brothers.

It took a couple of days before Morgan and Holt were forced to acknowledge the new peace with the Kincaid brothers. But it finally dawned on them one day while they were overseeing the erection of a fence around a cave-in of a small section of the riverbank. Several cows had fallen victim to the cave-in. One of them suffered broken legs from the fall, resulting in fresh beef steaks at supper that night. Holt was the first to broach the subject. "You know, we were talking about this yesterday at the cookshack. Nobody's seen any of those Double-K two-man patrols ridin' around the fringes of our range for the last couple of days. Whaddaya reckon that was all about, anyway? Think they were just trying to keep an eye on us?"

"I reckon," Morgan replied, "either that or they were lookin' for Cody. I'm sure they don't believe he's really gone."

"I didn't wanna say anything about it," Holt said, "but is it just me, or has Double-K backed off a little bit? I mean, it looks to me like they're keepin' their strays off our land. And in general, it almost looks like they're just mindin' their own business. After all the crap they've tried to pull on us, I can't believe they'd just give up. Can you?"

"No, that is hard to believe, but they have backed off a little bit. They got hurt pretty bad when they decided to move right in on our land. And Emmett Kincaid made a lot of big talk about taking over that valley of ours by the boundary creek. I expect he's still got a pretty sore throat from havin' to eat all those words." He shook his head slowly as he thought about the confrontation at the creek. "I hope this peace we're enjoyin' right now is because he's finally convinced we ain't gonna let him walk all over us."

"I hope you're right," Holt said. "I'm going into town in the mornin' to pick up some supplies. I've been puttin' it off for a few days because I didn't know if we might have some trouble with Double-K. And I was afraid to leave the ranch for half a day."

Morgan grinned. "Well, if you're still worried about it, we can always send one of the men in to get the supplies." He was pretty sure Holt was planning to pay a call on Spring Lawrence, the postmaster's daughter, while he was in town.

"I wouldn't wanna take one of the men from his work," Holt said, also with a grin.

"When are you gonna make up your mind to do something about that girl?" Morgan asked. "What is she, about seventeen? She ain't gonna waste much more time waitin' for you to work up your nerve to ask her."

"She's eighteen," Holt said.

"Eighteen?" Morgan responded. "Why, she's almost an old maid. Whaddaya waitin' for? Her to ask you? You keep waitin' and one of those store clerks in town will step up and take her to the preacher."

"I just don't know if I'm ready to settle down as a married man," Holt said. "I ain't got a house for her, like you built for Edna."

"Pa and Pansy are hopin' you'd bring her to live in the main house," Morgan said. "I know for a fact that's so. Pa gets lonely, and Pansy can't wait to help Spring raise all those kids you're gonna have."

"Shoot, Morgan, I don't even know if she thinks about me like that," Holt declared.

"Well, my advice to you is to find out, and the best way to do that is to ask her. But if you keep puttin' it off, somebody else is gonna ask her. She might be sweet on you, but she ain't gonna wait forever for you to ask her. Hell, man, she's eighteen years old."

"I'll ask her tomorrow," Holt decided. "Then if she says no, I won't have to worry about it no more."

"Now you're talkin'," Morgan said. "Good luck."

Pansy paused to take another look at him when he walked into the kitchen for breakfast the following morning. "What are you fixin' to do this morning?" she was moved to ask since he had put on a clean shirt and trousers.

"I'm goin' into town this mornin'," Holt answered, then scowled at her when her face immediately lit up with a grin. "Those clothes I had on yesterday got pretty messed up workin' on that fence around the cave-in. I don't wanna go into town lookin' like a drifter."

"It probably wouldn't matter to anybody in town, as long as you stayed outta the post office," Pansy said with a giggle.

"I hadn't even thought about that," Holt lied, "but I always check by the post office to see if we've got any mail."

"Well, you tell Miss Spring Lawrence that everybody back here at the Triple-H says howdy."

"She ain't always at the post office, but if I see her, I'll tell her you said hello." He poured himself a cup of coffee. "Anything else you think of that you might need that you ain't wrote down on that list in the pantry?" He hoped to get her mind off Spring Lawrence.

"Nope," she said. "If you got that list, you got everything I need. Looks like you shaved this mornin', too."

"I expect I needed one pretty bad," he replied impatiently. "I usually shave when I start feelin' the whiskers in the corner of my mouth when I'm eatin' breakfast, which I hope I can get here pretty soon."

She chuckled, knowing she had gotten his goat. That was something that was hard to do normally. Ever since Morgan had told her Holt was sweet on the postmaster's daughter, however, she had waited for an opportunity to tease him about it. She filled a plate with fried potatoes, bacon, and cornbread and placed it before him. "You know, I don't get to go to town very often," she said. "Spring Lawrence, I ain't sure I know her by sight. Is she that skinny little cross-eyed girl with the buck teeth that hangs around the post office?"

"Yep," Holt responded, "that's the one! I'll tell her you asked about her. Now, can I eat?"

She chuckled. "Yeah, I'll leave you alone. I can see you ain't in the mood for nonsense this morning. Got important things on your mind, I reckon. I hope they all go the way you want 'em to."

"Ah, I'm sorry," he said then. "I didn't mean to be so

grumpy to you. I guess I musta shaved too close this mornin'."

"No need to apologize," she insisted. "I always run my mouth a lot more than I should. I need to try to keep my mouth shut."

"Nope," he said at once. "You need to stay just like you are. I'm the one who's wrong. Don't you change. Me and Pa need you to keep us straight."

"Then you got it," she said. "And good luck today."

"Thanks," he said simply, but he was thinking that surely she didn't know what he had in mind to do in town that day.

"How much longer we gonna hang around this town?" John Simon asked. "'Cause if we keep this up we're gonna be broke pretty soon." He and Jesse didn't profit as much from their trading with Harvey Tate as they had anticipated. He traded in horses, but he had claimed he had too many on hand now that he was trying to sell. "I swear, Jesse, we oughta go back and shoot that cheatin' son of a bitch. Them was two good horses we tried to sell him and he wouldn't go but thirty dollars for each one of 'em. A good saddle horse like either one of them would cost about a hundred and fifty dollars." He banged his empty glass down on the bar and paused while Mutt Carlin poured him another shot before he continued ranting. "And ten dollars a-piece for them saddles, and then wanted ten dollars for that wore-out pack saddle he sold us for the horse we kept."

"At least we didn't let him steal both of those horses," Jesse allowed. "We shoulda just gone on to Missoula, but we didn't have a pot or a pan."

"You're right, we should have," Simon said. "It ain't but about thirty miles or so."

"Well, we wasted the time we spent hangin' around

here. There ain't nothin' in this town," Jesse complained. "We could hold up ol' Mutt here and make about twenty dollars."

"I wouldn't advise it," Mutt said. "I'd just blow a hole in the bar with my twelve gauge under here. And Mae Belle would plug the other one in the back with her pocket pistol."

"That's a fact," Mae Belle said, causing Jesse to jump when she slipped up behind him and nudged him in his back.

"I swear," Jesse said when he turned around to face the buxom woman. "Would you do that? Last night I thought you was in love with me. I reckon we'll have to think of somethin' else, John."

"I expect we've hung around this town too long," Simon said. "You ready?" Jessie said that he was, so they paid their bar bill and walked out the door and started to get on their horses.

"Look!" Jesse suddenly blurted.

"What?" Simon reacted.

Jesse pointed up the street. "Wells Fargo," he said. It was a Wells Fargo stagecoach stopped in front of the post office, and they were carrying several large boxes into the post office.

"What about it?" Simon asked.

"I wonder what's in them boxes," Jesse said. "There ain't no bank in this town. I bet if somebody had to send money here, it would have to be mailed." He looked at Simon and waited for him to understand, but Simon returned nothing but a blank expression. So Jesse spelled it out for him. "It's just settin' there waiting for us to come get it."

"Rob the post office?" Simon asked.

"Hell, yes," Jesse replied. "The post office ain't got no guards like a bank has. There won't be more'n one or two people workin' in the post office. And they sure ain't gonna be expectin' no hold up. There's bound to be some money in a lot of those packages."

Simon's eyes lit up when he pictured it. "They won't know what hit 'em!" Then he frowned. "How we gonna carry it? We can't stay around while we open all the envelopes. We need some bags."

"We've got bags," Jesse said. "We've got those sacks Tate sold us with our packsaddle." He opened his saddlebag and pulled out the two large sacks that Harvey Tate had included with the packsaddle. He tossed one of them to Simon. "This is the best idea we ever had. We'll just wait till that stage pulls away from there, then we'll walk our horses over there and tie 'em. Then we'll walk in and see if we've got any mail."

In a short while, the driver and the guard came out of the post office, climbed on the stage, and drove out the end of the street. There were a couple of people still inside, so the two robbers waited until they left before they went in with guns drawn.

Johnny Becker was at the barn so he helped Holt hitch a team of horses to the wagon. He knew that Holt usually took one of the younger boys into town with him to help out. But Holt told him he didn't need any help on this trip, and he wasn't sure that he wouldn't be late getting back. "Next time, you can go with me, and we'll eat dinner at the Village Tavern. You can remind me that I promised."

After the usual two-hour ride, Holt pulled the wagon in beside Stevensville Supply and went inside where he found Burt Rayford standing near the front of the store giving his clerk, Hal, instructions on how he wanted some boxes arranged on the shelf behind the counter. "Well, howdy,

Holt," Burt greeted him cheerfully. "How's everything at the Triple-H?"

"Howdy, Burt, Hal," Holt greeted them both. "Everything's all right for the last two or three days. Okay if I leave my wagon beside the store for a little while? I need to buy some things from you, but I've got a couple of things I need to check on while I'm in town. I've got a list of things that Pansy needs, and I need a new crosscut saw and a keg of nails."

"No problem a-tall," Burt said. "Leave it there as long as you want."

"'Preciate it, Burt. Here, I'll leave you Pansy's list in case you wanna go ahead and get it ready. I've gotta check by the post office for the mail. I might as well do that first." He hoped Burt and Hal hadn't noticed how nervous he was. He was afraid he was going to start to sweat for no other reason than nerves.

He walked down the street to the post office. There were two saddled horses and another horse wearing a packsaddle but no packs. He didn't give it a lot of thought until he heard what sounded like loud voices inside. Curious, he started to open the door but it wouldn't open. It wasn't locked, the knob turned but there seemed to be something blocking it. Really curious then, he put his shoulder to the door and gave it a good shove. A small chair that had been placed against the door toppled over as he lunged into the room.

"By Ned, you had to get in here, didn't you?" Jesse Grissom spat. "If you don't want a hole in your head, you just back up in that corner by the door and don't you move."

Holt was completely stunned. He wasn't wearing a gun, so he backed into the corner Jesse indicated. He was trying to make sense of the scene he had stumbled into. There were two men with bandannas tied over their faces, both with pistols drawn, both holding large sacks they were evidently stuffing mail into. There were several broken boxes and mail strewn all over the floor. *The two men were robbing the post office!* He couldn't believe it. He saw John Lawrence, the postmaster, seated on a stool with his hands tied behind his back, a bloody gash forming on his forehead. There was another man seated on the floor, his back against the wall. Holt recognized him as an employee of the post office. Then he saw Spring. She was standing with her back against the wall where the second robber could watch her while he stuffed his sack with mail. She looked frantic with fright.

"All right," the man beside Spring blurted. "That's all I can handle." His bag was nearly full.

"All right," his partner answered him. "It's time to go." He pointed his gun at Holt and said, "We're walkin' outta here now and you or the old man over there make one wrong move and I'll shoot you down." Holt didn't say anything, but he nodded that he understood. "Let's go, partner," Jesse said. "Bring the girl with you. We'll take her with us in case somebody tries somethin'." Simon grabbed Spring by the arm and pulled her with him in spite of her desperate efforts to resist.

Jesse dropped his sack of mail long enough to open the door while still holding his pistol on Holt. Then he held the door open with his foot for Simon to drag Spring through while he picked up his sack of mail again. But Holt stepped up in front of Simon. "The girl stays here," he said.

"She what?" Jesse blurted.

"I said the girl stays here," Holt repeated. "You and your partner get oughta here, but the girl stays here."

Jesse couldn't believe what he was hearing. "Why, you dumb son of a . . ." was as far as he got before Holt lunged against the door, pinning his gun hand inside the post office while the rest of him was outside. When the door slammed so hard on his wrist, he automatically released the pistol, causing it to drop to the floor. Holt snatched it up and fired one round that struck Jesse in the chest when he lunged back in the door. Caught flat-footed by Holt's unexpected reaction, Simon shoved Spring out of his way but not quick enough to beat Holt's second shot that dropped him to the floor.

Time suddenly stood still in the small lobby of the post office with not a sound for a long moment. And then it began again all at once as they realized what had happened and they were still alive. John Lawrence was the first to express his thankfulness for Holt's unexpected appearance that morning while Spring rushed to see how serious the gash on his forehead was. Lawrence's clerk, Stanley Thomas, got up from the floor and untied the postmaster's hands. He got up from the stool and looked around him at the mail scattered all over the floor. He stared at the two bodies, one of them lying halfway out the front door, both with mortal wounds to the chest. Now, more people arrived, attracted by the two gunshots. One of them was the town marshal, Tom Gordon. He immediately took charge of the scene, keeping the spectators outside while he questioned John Lawrence.

Lawrence told the marshal about the attempted robbery and potential kidnapping of his daughter. He then told him how Holt Hunter showed up and single-handedly took the two robbers down and saved his daughter as well as the US mail. "Lucky thing you were in town today," the marshal said to Holt. "How'd you happen to come to the post office when you did?"

Holt, still stunned to some degree, himself, answered, "I just came in to see if Spring was here. And if she was, I was gonna ask her to marry me."

His simple statement created another total silence while

an expression of surprise registered on Spring's face and expressions of shock were displayed on her father's and his clerk's. With the only amused expression, Marshal Gordon asked Holt, "Did you ask her yet?"

"No, sir, I haven't," Holt answered. "I was going to when I first got here, but things got kinda busy."

The marshal couldn't help enjoying the situation, so he continued. "Were you gonna ask her father's permission to ask her first?"

"Well, no," Holt replied. "To tell you the truth, I hadn't even thought about that."

"I see," Gordon pressed. "What would you have thought about that, if he had asked your permission, Mr. Lawrence?"

At this point, Lawrence was enjoying the situation as much as the marshal. "Well, I don't know," he replied. "I had kinda hoped Spring might marry a man who could take care of her and protect her. I reckon I'd had to think about whether Holt could do that or not."

Thinking the farce had gone on long enough, Spring interrupted. "If he ever gets around to asking, the answer is yes." She walked over to him, took Jesse's pistol out of his hand, and gave it to the marshal. Then she took both of Holt's hands in hers and asked, "Was there something you wanted to ask me?"

"Yes, ma'am," he replied with a smile. "Will you marry me?"

"Yes, I will, Holt Hunter. I will marry you and take care of you for the rest of our lives."

They received a warm round of applause from the few that witnessed the moment. It would be remembered for a long time and retold often, especially about there being two silent witnesses. Holt offered to help clean up the mess the post office had been left with, but John Lawrence insisted that the two young people should leave that for him and Stanley to take care of. They were going to have to sort out all the mail the two robbers had stuffed in their sacks, anyway. So Holt and Spring decided to go to the hotel dining room for dinner, and they could talk about planning the wedding. This was something that Holt hadn't thought about, the fact that Spring and her mother would want to plan the wedding. Holt had thought no further than going to the preacher and tying the knot, then driving Spring and her suitcase out to the ranch. By the time he headed back to the Triple-H that afternoon, however, he was sure of only one thing, he was going to get married. But he wasn't sure where or when. Spring and her mother were in charge of that.

When he got back to the ranch, he drove the wagon to the house to unload Pansy's supplies. The two of them carried all the packages inside to the pantry, then he left her to put them away. He was surprised when she didn't mention the subject of Spring Lawrence. He should have known that she preferred to wait until supper when she would have him trapped. It was just as well, he figured, since he was going to have to tell his father, anyway. He was glad that Pansy hadn't pressed him for information because he had really wanted to tell Morgan about it first. He trusted Morgan. He might tease him a little, but he would also give him good advice. After all, that was what big brothers were for.

Morgan saw Holt when he was unhitching the horses from the wagon, so he rode over to get his report. Grinning broadly, he asked, "Did you do it?"

"Did I do what?" Holt asked, playing coy.

"You know what," Morgan came back, "what you said you were gonna do."

"I did," Holt declared, unable to hold it inside.

"And?" Morgan pressed.

"And whaddaya think?" Holt answered. "Of course she

said she'd be honored to be the wife of a fine gentleman like myself."

"Hot damn!" Morgan chuckled. "Good for you. I was afraid you'd lose your nerve when the time came. When are you gonna tie the knot?"

"I don't know," Holt confessed. "Whenever Spring and her mother decide to do it, I reckon."

"Uh-oh, that don't sound good," Morgan japed. "Her and her mother might just be holding your offer for a while in case they get a better one. What did the postmaster have to say about you wantin' to ride off with his daughter? If he's anything like Edna's daddy, he'll have to be brought out to the ranch to live, too."

"Tell you the truth, I didn't really talk that much to Spring's father about the weddin'. They had a couple of fellows that tried to hold up the post office today. So Mr. Lawrence was busy tryin' to clean up a mess they left. Spring and I went to the hotel for dinner."

"What would anybody wanna hold up the post office for?" Morgan wondered. "Did they get away with anything?"

"Nope."

"I reckon you're gonna give Pa the news at supper tonight," Morgan went on. "And that's gonna get Pansy on your back for sure."

"She's already on me about it," Holt said. "She like to drove me crazy this mornin' at breakfast because she noticed I was wearin' clean clothes."

Morgan laughed. "I ain't surprised. It's hard to slip anything by that woman."

Just as Morgan had said, Pansy paused when she saw Holt come in the back door for supper. She didn't say anything at first, just stared at him as if reading his thoughts. To break the silence, he asked, "Is supper ready?"

"It will be in about five minutes," she finally spoke. "If you need to wash up go ahead and do it. You did it, didn't you?" He didn't answer. "I thought so," she said. "Go wash your hands. I'll go tell Mr. Hunter supper's ready. He's gonna want to hear all about it." He just shook his head and walked on through the kitchen to the pump on the back porch. When he came back into the kitchen, she had poured a cup of coffee for him and set it at his usual place at the table. "Your father's on his way. I told him you were gettin' married, and he's wantin' to hear all about it."

"Pansy, what if I told you I didn't ask her to marry me?"

"You'd be lyin'," she said, "and that ain't like you to lie."

"All right," he conceded, "I asked her, but she said no."

"There you go lyin' again. Why do you do that? You ain't no good at it. You asked her and she said yes, so when's the wedding?"

"That's what I wanna know," Duncan Hunter said as he walked into the kitchen. "I declare, Pansy and I were beginning to be afraid you were gonna end up a lonely life as a bachelor. We were afraid you were gonna let that little Lawrence girl get away 'cause there ain't many girls around Stevensville as pretty as she is. So when's the wedding?"

"I don't know, Pa. She wants to plan it with her mother. We'll be talkin' about all that stuff in the next week, I reckon. I wanna bring her out here to meet everybody. She might change her mind after that, though."

"I wouldn't blame her," Pansy said, then immediately started talking about her ideas for rearranging the rooms down the hall to best accommodate the newlyweds. Holt was beginning to foresee a nightmare in the making. He had a new appreciation for Morgan's insistence upon building a separate house.

CHAPTER 16

He sat beside the fire next to the busy stream that gushed from the cliff above him, eating freshly roasted venison from a deer he had killed that morning. A small doe, he had killed her with his bow for a couple of reasons. He needed to conserve the .44 cartridges for his Henry rifle and he also preferred not to have the sound of a rifle shot anywhere near his camp. He had allowed himself the time to hunt for fresh meat because there had been no sign of any harmful activity on the part of the Double-K for days now. And yet, he had no way of knowing if the war between the Hunters and the Kincaids was at a truce or not. With nothing better to do, however, he would continue to keep watch on the two ranches, even though he was going to have to ride into town soon. He was down to nothing as far as supplies were concerned. He had been out of coffee for a couple of days and that was beginning to bother him. He had things to trade, weapons and ammunition mostly, ammunition for a .45 caliber weapon. The more he thought about it, the more he was leaning on going into town. Finally, he decided he would do it as soon as he finished smoking the last of the deer meat. He would take one more look around the Kincaid headquarters, then go into town.

Finding nothing out of the ordinary happening at the Double-K headquarters, he went back to his camp to load his packhorse with the articles he was planning to trade. It would be close to suppertime before he got to Stevensville, so he held Storm to a pretty steady pace. He only knew of one place in the town where he could sell the weapons and such that he had accumulated from his encounters with Emmett Kincaid's men. He had never been to Tate's Store, himself, but his brother Holt had told him about it. Holt had also told him that Harvey Tate would cheat his dying mother out of her burial dress if he thought he could sell it.

He found Tate's Store about half a mile short of town. It actually consisted of the store itself, a barn with a corral, and a few outbuildings. When he pulled up in front of the store, Harvey Tate walked out the door to meet him. Cody figured that Tate had seen him coming down off the road and thinking him an Indian with nothing of value to trade, he would quickly send him on his way. "How do?" Tate greeted him.

"Howdy," Cody returned and stepped down from the saddle. "I was told that you would pay cash money for quality weapons and ammunition. So I decided to come see for myself if that's true or not."

"I swear, I thought you was an Injun when you rode up," Tate said. "I do some tradin' and pay cash sometimes when I've got cash on hand. Unfortunately, this is one of those times when I ain't got much cash."

"I was told you'd probably say something like that, too," Cody replied. "I don't care how much cash you've got on hand. I didn't come here to rob you. I came to see if you would pay a decent price for rifles and handguns in good repair, gun belts, and .45 cartridges. If you will, it'll save me a trip to Missoula where I know what I can get for 'em." He actually had no knowledge of such a place in Missoula, but he figured that Tate didn't know, either.

It was enough to tickle Tate's curiosity. "Well, I reckon it wouldn't hurt to see what you're tryin' to sell."

Cody untied the Winchester 73 rifle he had acquired when Ben Clark and Clyde Peterson attacked him on his way back to his camp. He handed the rifle to Tate to inspect, knowing it was in like new condition. Tate looked it over carefully and could find nothing to complain about it. "When the 73 model came out, they charged a hundred dollars for one," Cody said. "You can buy this one for twenty-five and sell it for fifty." Tate was stunned and immediately suggested trading for items that Cody might need. "Nope," Cody declined. "I need cash money. That's the only reason I would give away a rifle like this."

His interest spiked now, Tate asked, "What else have you got?" So Cody unpacked the rest of his acquired armory and was able to unload most of it because of the condition of the weapons and his low asking price. When he left Tate's Store, he had enough money to resupply his needs and cash to spend on other things. And because of that, he decided to buy himself some supper as soon as he got to town. "You be sure and come back when you've collected some more merchandise you need to get rid of," Tate said. He didn't ask Cody how he came about the items he had to sell, but he thought he could pretty well guess.

Cody was undecided what to do about his supper. There weren't many choices in the little town, especially for someone who appeared to be an Indian at first sight. His preference would be the Village Tavern because he liked the way Minnie cooked, and he knew she didn't mind his buckskins and moccasins. The trouble now, however, was they knew he was Cody Hunter and Morgan and Holt liked to eat there, too. And at this point, they thought he was long gone from there. Maybe it was time for him to return to the Triple-H. Now that there seemed to be no more trouble from the Double-K, there might be no further need for him to constantly watch them. There was also the dining room in the hotel. No one knew him there, but dressed as he was, he would not likely be welcomed in the hotel itself, much less the dining room. "I sure had a hankerin' for a good cup of coffee and a plate full of whatever Minnie cooked for supper tonight," he complained to Storm. "Well, I've got fresh deer meat and I reckon I'll just go pick up some coffee and other supplies and just fix my own supper." So he went down the street to Humphrey's Store, next to the hotel. He would have ordinarily bought his supplies at Stevensville Supplies, but they knew him there now, so he thought it best to go to Humphrey's where they didn't.

He bought the supplies he needed and was in the process of packing them on his packhorse when he noticed a wagon parked in front of the hotel that looked just like the Triple-H's wagon. While he was watching, a man who had been sitting in one of the rocking chairs on the hotel porch got up and walked over to meet three ladies coming out of the hotel. Cody had to look again to be sure, but it was Frank Strom. "What in the world . . ." Cody started to mutter but stopped short when he recognized one of the ladies as Edna Hunter, Morgan's wife. But the other two were strangers to him. Frank escorted the three ladies over to the wagon and helped them up into the wagon where they sat themselves on three pillows that had evidently been placed there for their comfort. Then Frank climbed up on the driver's seat and drove the wagon away from the hotel. It's awful late to be starting back to the ranch, Cody couldn't help thinking. Maybe they're staying in town somewhere, he thought and decided to follow them to be sure.

Frank drove the wagon out the end of the main street, then took the first side road he came to. There were several houses on the road and Cody stayed far enough back so he would not be noticed. Frank stopped the wagon at the third house and jumped down to help the two ladies with Edna out of the wagon. Edna got down as well, and after talking a few minutes to them, she climbed up and sat beside Frank in the driver's seat. When Frank turned the wagon around, Cody pulled Storm off the street and circled around the back of a house to come back to the street behind the wagon again. He continued to trail the wagon, since it was already beginning to get dark and he decided to follow them until he knew where they were going.

Frank drove the wagon back to the main street, then turned onto the road out of the south end of town. "They're headin' back to the ranch," Cody muttered as darkness began to set in in earnest. "Edna, have you lost your mind?" he mumbled. "It'll be two hours before you get home tonight." He imagined that poor Frank was frantic, so he decided to continue to tail them to make sure they got home all right. He was also on the lookout for Morgan with several riders coming to meet them. Cody was sure Morgan had to be on his way already. And as he expected, the wagon appeared to come to a stop a few minutes later and he made out the two horses coming out of the darkness. He couldn't help grinning, thinking that Edna was catching hell now and poor Frank was going to catch it later. He started to ride on up to defend Frank and remind Morgan that Frank couldn't bring himself to order the boss's wife around. Then he decided he would remain invisible. *I'd like to hear the conversation,* he thought when they remained standing there in the middle of the road, instead of just continuing on home.

Cody was right when he guessed that Frank Strom was frantic. The two riders had suddenly materialized out of the shadows beside the road to halt the wagon. "It's kinda late for you folks to be out here all by yourselves, ain't it?" Bo Dawson asked as he pulled up beside Edna. "Smoke, grab a-hold of that bridle so them horses don't decide to take off." Smoke Davis stopped his horse in front of the team hitched to the wagon and reached over to hold onto one of the bridles. "Where you folks headed, sweetheart? There ain't nothin' in this direction but the Triple-H, unless you're goin' past that to the Double-K."

"How 'bout you fellers just get along about your own business and leave us be," Frank said.

"You'll do well to set there and keep your mouth shut, old man," Bo told him. "I'm talkin' to Miss Honey Britches, here."

"You just watch your mouth," Edna responded. "I'm a married woman and the mother of two children. You two just ride on into town to find the women you're look-ing for."

"She's a feisty one, Bo," Smoke remarked.

"She sure is," Bo said. "Married with two young'uns, I'll bet she's married to one of them Hunters. Is that a fact, Honey Britches? I'll tell you what. I ain't real busy right now. I think I'll try a little bit of you on. And I'll pay you the same as I do the gals in town. So you ain't got nothin' to lose."

Still waiting in the darkness of the road maybe fifty yards away, Cody suddenly realized that they were taking an unusually long time to turn and head for home. It oc-curred to him that it was not Morgan at all. He didn't wait for another thought, threw the packhorse's reins over his head, pulled his six-gun and fired it in the air at the same time he slapped the packhorse on his rump. The startled packhorse took off down the road and Cody chased him, firing into the air for a short distance before swerving off beside the road. Startled as well, Bo and Smoke pulled their guns and started shooting at the charging packhorse, unaware of Cody galloping along the side of the road until Smoke was knocked out of his saddle and Bo caught a shot in his shoulder. Still confused, Bo didn't try to continue the fight and chose to flee into the darkness. Cody chased him for a little way before turning around to return to the wagon to check on Smoke.

Shocked to the point where they were not sure if they were about to die or they had been saved, Frank and Edna sat frozen on the wagon seat. "You're all right, Edna, you're safe now," Cody called out to her as he quickly checked to make sure Smoke was dead.

"Cody?" Edna questioned fearfully.

"Yes," he answered, "it's Cody."

"Cody!" Frank blurted out. "I thought we was dead for sure. Thank the Lord! Thank the Lord!"

"Cody, where did you come from?" Edna asked. "How did you know? Oh Lordy! I don't care. I ain't ever been so glad to see someone before."

"There ain't no doubt who they were," Frank said. "I'll bet they were a couple of that Double-K bunch of outlaws. I didn't think you was anywhere around here. How did you know where we were?"

"I saw you when you came out of the hotel and decided to follow you to make sure you got back to the ranch all right. I figured as late as it was that Morgan would most likely come lookin' for you. Matter of fact, I waited almost too long because I thought that was Morgan when you got stopped. Who were the two women you came out of the hotel with?"

"That was Norma Lawrence and her daughter Spring," Edna told him. "Spring is going to be your sister-in-law, and Frank brought me into town to talk about planning for the wedding."

"So Holt finally got up the nerve to ask her?" Cody asked. "Good for him. We'd best get you started back home again. Let me take care of the fellow lyin' in the road."

"I'll help ya," Frank said. "What are you gonna do with him?"

"Grab his boots," Cody said. "I'll take the other end and we'll just get him off the road. Strip him of anything of value and throw it in the wagon. I'll go round up his horse and see if I can find my packhorse. I hope they didn't hit him when they were shootin' at him." He left Frank to search Smoke's body while he went to look for his packhorse. He found it about forty yards farther down the road. Smoke's horse was standing beside him. A quick check told him the packhorse wasn't struck by any bullets, so Cody tied him and Smoke's horse to the back of the wagon and they started out for the Triple-H.

They had traveled little more than a mile and a half when they met a party of three riders coming to meet them. Cody was relieved to recognize his brothers, Morgan and Holt, along with Shorty Black. Seeing the wagon but confused by the extra horses and the rider beside the wagon, Morgan pulled his horse to a stop in the middle of the road, stopping the wagon. "Edna, are you all right?"

"I'm all right," she answered.

Then taking a closer look at the man on the horse beside the wagon, Morgan exclaimed, "Cody?"

"Evenin', Morgan, Holt," Cody replied.

"What in the world are you doing here?" Morgan asked. "What the hell is goin' on?" He looked back at Edna and said, "You shoulda been back two hours ago. What the hell were you doing all this time?" Then he turned his frustration upon Frank. "You shoulda known when to start back, Frank."

"Don't go jumping on Frank," Edna told him. "Blame it on me or Norma Lawrence. That woman hasn't any idea of how much time she wastes. You need to thank your lucky stars for your brother. If he hadn't come when he did, I don't know if Frank and I would be here or not."

"Who does the extra saddle horse belong to?" Holt asked.

"He belonged to that man we left back there beside the road," Frank volunteered. "He was with another feller that Cody shot, but he took off." He went on then to tell Morgan and Holt how they had been stopped by the two men and how Cody arrived, charging like the cavalry.

Morgan looked at his younger brother then. "I swear, Cody, I don't know how you always manage to show up when you're needed the most. But I wanna thank you, brother. Thank you for saving Edna and Frank. We weren't even sure you'd come back."

"I never left," Cody said. "And now I find out that Holt is gettin' married. Things happen mighty fast when you're not around to keep your eye on 'em."

"You shoulda known I'd be gettin' married," Holt japed. "The women in this county ain't gonna let an eligible bachelor like me stay single for very long."

They continued on back to the ranch, and Edna went to the main house where her children were waiting for her and their father's return while the men took care of the horses. Since Cody agreed to stay there that night, he had a little more to do in unpacking his packhorse and stowing his packs. So when he grabbed his saddlebags and came to the house, they were all waiting to give him a big welcome home. He expressed his surprise to find he still had a room when he took his saddlebags in. And he commented that the first thing he saw was his package of new clothes, tied with a string, sitting on the bed. "We're still waitin' to see how you look in 'em," Pansy said. She made a special effort to welcome him home and asked if there was anything he wanted to eat. He told her anything would do if he could get a cup of coffee with it. After they questioned him about where he had been camping and what he had been doing, he changed the topic of conversation to the upcoming wedding of Holt and Spring.

"Ain't much to say about it," Holt declared. "I asked her and she said yes. And that's all I know about it. Edna and Spring and her mother know all the rest. I just hope they don't forget to tell me when they're gonna have it."

"Well, I've got some more information on Holt's proposal to Spring," Edna said upon hearing his comment as she came back from putting the children to bed. She had been looking forward to telling what she had learned in town that day. "Norma and Spring told me in a little more detail about it when you asked Spring to marry you." She paused to make sure she had everyone's attention. "Remember, Holt said that two men tried to hold up the post office that day? He didn't tell us that he had walked in the post office right in the middle of the holdup. He had to shove a chair away from the door before he could even get in." She went on to tell them what had actually happened as related to her by Spring Lawrence. "Spring said Holt didn't try to stop the two gunmen until they started to take her with them. And then he took one of the robber's guns away from him and shot both of them." Then she described the actual proposal, which caused a round of applause from the group, led by Pansy Hutto, who seemed to enjoy it most of all.

"I expect you're gonna want me to vacate my room if Holt and Spring are gonna move into the house after they get married," Cody said. "They're gonna need lots of room for all their young'uns."

"Mr. Hunter and I have already been working on that," Pansy said. "Ain't that right, Mr. Hunter?"

"That's a fact," Duncan answered. "We decided that back hall where the bedrooms are needs a little bit of carpentry work to make it more like a separate house. So we're gonna move your room up to the front of the house in the study. We don't use the study, anyway. And we won't need the rosebush." He looked at Pansy and laughed when he said that.

When everyone but Duncan and Pansy looked puzzled by his last remark, Pansy explained. "I told him I was gonna plant a big rosebush under Cody's window to keep him from going out of it."

It was much later that night, in the early hours of the new day in fact, when Bo Dawson's weary buckskin gelding limped into the barnyard of the Double-K ranch and stopped at the back of the cookshack. Too exhausted to dismount, Bo just sat slumped in the saddle for a minute or two, the shoulder and sleeve of his shirt on his right side soaked with blood. Finally, when no one appeared to be awake, he started yelling, "Tater!"

And he kept yelling it until the back door of the cookshack flew open and an angry Tater Duggan demanded, "Who the hell is makin' that racket? What the hell do you want, you drunken fool?" He stood there blinking the sleep out of his eyes at Bo, slumped halfway over on the horse's neck.

"It's Bo, Tater," Otto Ross said, having been one of a couple of the men roused out of the bunkhouse by Bo's constant yelling of Tater's name. "What is it, Bo?" Otto asked.

"I've been shot, damn it," Bo complained. "Help me off this horse."

"He's been shot, Tater," Otto said.

"I know it," Tater barked. "I heard him. You men help him off his horse while I get my boots on." He went inside his kitchen and lit a lamp and put it on the table. Then he opened the front door of the cookshack. "Bring him in here and lay him down on the bench by the table." He looked at Bo's bloody shirt as they walked him over to the bench. "Hold on," he said and stopped them. "Just hold him up till I get his shirt off or we'll have blood all over my kitchen." When he got the shirt off, he walked over and dropped it outside the door. "Who shot you?" he asked when he came back.

"I ain't sure," Bo answered, "but I think it mighta been the Injun." That captured the attention of Otto and the other men there, and they moved in closer to hear.

"On Kincaid land?" one of them asked.

"No," Bo groaned. "It was between the Triple-H and town. He killed Smoke Davis. I was lucky to get away. I knew I couldn't do nothing left-handed and I was losin' so much blood I had to get away."

"That ain't gonna tickle Emmett when he finds out about this in the mornin'," Tater said. "I don't reckon I'm gonna be able to work on that shoulder on the bench. You're too blame big," he decided after seeing where the wound was. "We're gonna have to lay you on the table so I can have the shoulder flat."

Otto didn't care much for the picture that created in his mind. "Ain'cha got a piece of canvas or somethin' to put on the table?"

"Little blood ain't gonna hurt it," Tater said. "I'll splash it down good and scrub it with the broom when we're finished."

That didn't serve to improve the picture in Otto's mind. "I'll go take care of your horse for you, Bo," he said.

"'Preciate it, Otto," Bo said, then flinched when Tater picked at the wound with the tip of his kitchen knife.

"Yeah," Tater said, "that slug's in there pretty deep. It didn't come out your back. You want me to try to dig it outta there or just leave it in there?" When Bo seemed confused, Tater said the bullet was in a place where it didn't look like it would cause him much damage. "It's lodged in that heavy muscle and that muscle will just grow right around it. I can try to dig it outta there, but it's gonna take a lot of cuttin'. You'll heal up a lot quicker if you just leave it in there. And you wouldn't even know you was ever shot."

"I swear, I don't know, Tater." Bo hesitated. "It feels pretty bad, and I feel mighty weak."

"That's because you lost so much blood," Tater said. "You'll lose a lot more if I go to cuttin' on it. Best thing to do is slap a bandage on there and stop the bleedin'. Then you go to bed for the few hours you got left tonight. I'll put a sling on your arm in the mornin', and it'll start to heal up pretty quick." To help him make up his mind, Tater kept probing into the wound with his knife point until Bo said to just leave the bullet in there. "That's what I woulda done if it was me," Tater said and started stuffing some rags over the bullet hole to stop the bleeding. "After break-fast in the mornin', I'll change that bandage and fix you up in a sling."

It didn't take Tater long to tie a bandage around Bo's shoulder and send him to the bunkhouse to try to sleep. "It's gonna hurt for a spell. Can't do nothin' about that unless you've got some whiskey to help you. But that muscle will start to heal up right around that bullet and pretty soon you'll forget it's in there. The hardest part is gonna be tryin' to wipe your butt with your left hand. Now, get yourself to bed." He had really talked Bo into leaving the bullet in his shoulder for the simple reason he didn't want to spend the time it would likely take him to dig that bullet out, then patch it up. As it was, he had only a couple of hours left before time to get up to start preparing breakfast.

CHAPTER 17

Pansy Hutto pulled her big iron skillet off to the side of the stove after letting the potatoes finish browning up the way Duncan Hunter liked them. She reached into the cabinet beside the stove to fetch a warming pot to transfer the potatoes into. The pots and pans made so much noise in the process that she didn't hear the kitchen door open and was unaware of the man who walked in. He was almost upon her when she straightened up and turned around to confront the stranger, almost dropping the pot as she recoiled backward. "Cody!" she blurted out. "You scared the hell outta me!" She put the pot on the table. "You're lucky I didn't hit you with this pot."

"I'm sorry, Pansy, I didn't mean to scare you. I was just goin' to pour myself a cup of coffee. You looked like you were busy, so I didn't wanna bother you. You ain't usually that jumpy. Is everything all right?"

Hands on her hips, she stood tall and gave him a good looking over. "Yes, everything's all right. I just ain't used to havin' a stranger sneak up on me this early in the morning. You shoulda told me you were gonna put on your new clothes this morning."

"I thought everybody hated my buckskins so much that

I'd better wear my paleface clothes while I'm at the ranch, anyway. Can I get a cup of that coffee now?"

"You just shoulda given me some warning last night," she said. "Yes, you can have a cup of coffee. You can eat if you're ready. Just sit down at the table and I'll get it for you." She grinned at him and shook her head. "You really do look different. I can't wait to see your father's reaction."

As Pansy expected, his father and Holt both reacted in much the same fashion as she had, especially since she insisted that Cody sit down at the table with his back toward the kitchen door. They were both surprised to see a strange man seated at the table before they walked around the other side to discover who it was. "They fit pretty well," Duncan commented. "How do they feel?"

"They're kinda stiff, but they fit all right," Cody answered. "I don't know about the boots, though. I don't like the heel and they're so stiff they rub my skin. I might have to go back to my moccasins."

"Did you put on any socks?" Pansy asked.

"No," Cody answered. "I don't have any socks."

"Didn't Morgan get you any socks when you bought those clothes?" Holt asked.

"I reckon not," Cody answered. "There weren't any in that package I left on the bed when I opened it this mornin'."

"You can get him a pair of mine," Duncan said. "I've got plenty of 'em in my drawer."

Pansy decided to do it right away, so she went to Duncan's room and got a pair of socks and insisted that Cody put them on then and there. So while they watched, he took off the new boots and put the socks on. "That does make a difference," he said, but he still thought to himself that he would probably go back to his moccasins.

Once the issue of removing the savage appearance of the younger brother was resolved, the topic of conversation at the breakfast table reverted to the prior night's discussion.

According to what Edna had told them, John and Norma Lawrence wanted to have their daughter married in the little Methodist Church in Stevensville. Duncan was more in favor of having the wedding there on the Triple-H. His reason was simple. Everyone would want to attend Holt's wedding. But with the state of Triple-H's truce with the Double-K, Duncan was not comfortable having all the Hunter men gone from the ranch. The confrontation on the road to Stevensville the night before could only serve to aggravate the condition. Although there was no real proof that the two men who accosted Frank and Edna were part of the crew that rode for the Double-K, Frank felt that they were. To no one's surprise, Cody immediately volunteered to stay there at the ranch if the wedding had to be in town. He suggested that he should logically be the one who missed the wedding, since he had really been no part of the family's life for the past fifteen years. "We have some good men we can count on to be responsible," he named, "like Chris Scott, L. C. Pullen, and Shorty Black."

"We'll just have to see what we can work out with Holt's in-laws," Duncan said. "If John and Norma don't want to cooperate with us, you might have to ride in, snatch Spring up, and carry her off to the preacher."

"Hey, I think I like that plan best of all," Holt spoke up.

"Well, you can run that by them Sunday," Duncan said. He was referring to a visit to the ranch by John and Norma when the post office was closed. Holt, along with some of the Triple-H hands, would ride into town to escort their buggy to and from the ranch. It was a visit that Edna and Pansy were both excited about.

Like the Triple-H, breakfast time that morning came with much to discuss, although not of the joyous nature at the Double-K. Typically Bo Dawson made himself available early every morning in case Emmett wanted something done. It had been his role ever since Reese Walsh was shot down by the Injun. On this morning, however, Emmett had to go looking for Bo, and he was not happy to find him still abed in the bunkhouse. His first impulse was to grab Bo's feet and jerk him out of the bunk, thinking he must be sleeping off a drunk. He yanked the blanket off the sleeping man to discover the bloody bandage and the blood stains on the straw mattress. "What the hell happened to you?" Emmett demanded.

Having finally dropped into unconsciousness after trying to sleep for a couple of hours, Bo was snatched back after only about ten minutes. "Boss!" he blurted, confused. "I was just gittin' up to see if you needed anything."

"You were, were you?" Emmett responded. "Where did you get shot?"

"In the shoulder, Boss, but Tater said it oughta heal just fine."

"I can see you got shot in the shoulder, you damn fool. I wanna know where you were when you got shot."

"Me and Smoke Davis was ridin' into town to have a couple of drinks and we got jumped. Smoke didn't make it," Bo said. "And they hit me right off in my right shoulder. I couldn't even hold my pistol. I tried to help Smoke," he lied, "but he was dead. There weren't nothin' I could do, so I made a run for it."

"Smoke's dead?" Emmett asked, angered to hear he had lost another man. "Who was it? Who jumped you?"

"It was so dark on that road that it was hard to see, but I know for sure it was some of that Triple-H bunch, too many for me and Smoke to fight. And I think that damn Injun was with 'em."

Emmett didn't want to hear that. Disgusted, he said no more and turned around and strode angrily out of the bunkhouse. "Tater said I was gonna be good as new in a few days," Bo called out after him. Emmett didn't stop to talk to Tater about Bo's wound. He was fighting off an attack of frustration. He didn't know what Bo and Smoke had gotten into. Maybe it was with some of the Triple-H hands as he claimed. But it had cost the Double-K one more man, and they were already down to about half the crew they originally started out with. He and Ralph were committed to the plan they had finally agreed upon, to play dead as far as any plans to compete with Triple-H. All they needed was some time to attract a few more guns for hire, so they would be ready to launch an all-out war on Duncan Hunter and his two sons. He thought about what he was going to tell Ralph now, as he walked to the house.

"You don't look too happy this mornin', brother," Ralph Kincaid said when Emmett walked back into the kitchen. "Better pour him a cup of coffee, Sadie. I recognize that face. He's got some bad news to tell me." Sadie placed a cup of coffee on the table across from Ralph, having already poured it when she saw Emmett come in the back door.

"You talk like you're in a good mood," Emmett said. "Well, let me see if I can change that for you. We lost another man last night and another one got himself shot."

"Damn," Ralph swore. "You're right about that. Who did we lose?"

"Smoke Davis," Emmett said. "Him and Bo rode down to Stevensville last night and Bo claims they got jumped on the road into town. Bo got shot in the shoulder. He's layin' in his bunk down in the bunkhouse."

"Well, shoulder wound, that ain't too bad," Ralph said.

"It's in his right shoulder so he can't do much of anything with his left. I reckon he's kinda like you right now," Emmett joked cruelly. In response, Ralph tried to play like he was shooting at him with his withered arm.

"Who jumped them? Did he say?"

"He says it was a bunch from Triple-H. Said it was too dark to recognize any of 'em, but he says he's sure they were Triple-H. He even said he thinks one of 'em was the Injun. But if it was the Injun, I'd be damn surprised Bo woulda got away. That's what I think," Emmet said.

"I'd be inclined to agree," Ralph said. "How many was in the bunch that jumped 'em?"

"He didn't know exactly. But he said there was a lot of 'em."

"I don't know about you, but I think his story is full of holes," Ralph declared. "All I believe after what you've told me is that Bo and Smoke got themselves into some kinda mess they ain't too proud of and they got their butts kicked. And they've just caused us more problems. You think it's about time we sent a letter to Vargas Roach to see if he wants to do some business up this way?"

"I don't know," Emmett hesitated. "Roach's effective, but he's expensive as hell and once he gets started on something, he's hard to pull off."

"Think about it, though. Roach will go after every person who is responsible for running that ranch until there ain't anybody left who knows what to do. And then it would be a pretty easy thing to walk right in and take the reins of the outfit." Ralph slapped the table with his good hand. "Lock, stock, and barrel," he declared.

Emmett thought about it for a few moments before responding. "I swear, that is the truth. It would be a cake walk to move into Triple-H. But there's no controlling Vargas Roach. We'll still have to hire some more men, but we'll have some time anyway. Too bad Roach's headquarters ain't anywhere near a telegraph. One of us will have to go into Stevensville and mail him a letter, then wait for his reply."

"So are you in agreement that that's what we're gonna do?" Ralph asked.

"I reckon so," Emmett said. "Sadie, is there any more coffee in that pot? If there ain't, put on a new one. I think we've got something to celebrate."

So they spent the rest of the morning discussing their drastic plan for the takeover of the Triple-H ranch. The man whose services they planned to employ was not an ordinary gun for hire. He was a man who had a passion for killing, and the only way to reach him was through the mail. He kept a small cabin in an out-of-the way place in Wyoming called Burnt Hollow when he was not on the road. Ralph wrote the letter with instructions on how to find the Double-K and emphasized that the job was for several targets. He wanted him to know it was well worth a trip from Wyoming to the Bitterroot Valley. Ralph decided to ride into town that day to mail it. "You want to take one of the men with you?" Emmett asked.

"What the hell for?" Ralph replied. "Conversation?" He knew Emmett was suggesting someone to ride along for his protection since he only had one good arm. "As shorthanded as we are now, you'll need every man here."

"You ain't been to town in so long, I thought you mighta forgot how to get there," Emmett said. "How soon ya goin'?"

"I'm gettin' ready to go right now so I'll have time to get back for supper. And I'd appreciate it if you'd tell one of the men to saddle my horse for me."

"I'll saddle him, myself," Emmett said. "Which one you want?"

"The gray. I expect he needs the exercise more than the bay."

"I'll saddle the gray," Emmett confirmed. Ralph was right, neither one of his two favorite horses got enough exercise. Unbeknownst to Ralph, Emmett rode one of the two horses from time to time. So Emmett went down to the barn and sent Jimmy Todd to cut Ralph's gray out of the horse herd, and Emmett saddled him. In a little while, Ralph showed up wearing his business coat. "I swear, brother," Emmett japed, "you look like you're goin' into town to do some big business. You sure you don't want me to get Bo outta that bunk so he can ride into town with you. That'd give you two good hands if you needed 'em."

Ralph ignored him and took the reins. Using just his right hand on the saddle horn, he stepped up into the saddle. Tater walked out of the barn then, carrying a keg of molasses. "Goin' for a little ride, Boss?" he said to Ralph.

"That's right, Tater," Ralph answered. "I've gotta go to town to take care of some business. Take another look at that shoulder of Bo Dawson's. It'll help him to move around a little bit, instead of layin' around on that bunk."

"Yes, sir, I'll do that," Tater replied. "I was fixin' to put his arm in a sling this mornin'."

Emmett didn't make any comments about Bo. He was aware that Ralph was making a showing to remind Tater and Bo that he was a partner and equal to him in authority. He knew that it bothered Ralph that Emmett worked with the men every day, so they naturally thought he was the boss. "Have a good trip into town," Emmett told him. "I'll keep an eye on things till you get back." Ralph nodded to him in reply, then left the barnyard at a trot.

It had been a long time since Ralph had been into the town of Stevensville, and he could see that the little town had added quite a few stores and shops since his last visit. He couldn't help wondering if he and his brother had made a mistake in not spending some time creating a better relationship with the merchants of the town. It would certainly help if the Double-K had a reputation of fairness when the time came that war developed between them and the

Triple-H. *It's not too late,* he thought. *We'll start with the postmaster.* When he came to the post office, he pulled the gray gelding up at the hitching rail and dismounted. Then he reached into his saddlebag and pulled his letter out. Straightening out his coat collar, he stepped up onto the boardwalk and went inside the building.

"Good afternoon, sir," Stanley Thomas greeted him. "Can I help you?"

"Indeed you can," Ralph replied. "I have this letter here that I want to send and it's important that it arrives intact. But I'm afraid I didn't have anything to seal it with properly and I'm afraid it may come apart before it arrives at this little out of the way place in Wyoming." While he was talking to Stanley, he was watching an older man seated at a desk behind the young clerk.

"Let's take a look at it," Stanley said. He picked up the letter and examined the flap. "It's sealed pretty good, but we can put some more glue in the corners to make it stronger."

"I would appreciate that," Ralph said, "and of course I would be happy to pay you for any extra service." Stanley assured him there would be no extra charge and took the letter over to a side table to glue it. "I feel a little remiss," Ralph went on. "My brother and I operate a cattle ranch about twenty-five miles from here. And we've been meanin' to get to know the business owners of this pleasant little town for a couple of years now, and we just haven't gotten around to doin' it. I told my brother this mornin' that I would make it a point to meet some of the town's businessmen." Finally, he had said enough to kindle an interest in the older man at the desk, for he got up and came to the window.

"Excuse me, sir, my name's John Lawrence. I'm the postmaster. I couldn't help overhearing you talking to Stanley." He extended his hand through the window and

Ralph shook it. "I'm always happy to meet newcomers to our town."

"Ralph Kincaid," he answered. "My brother Emmett and I own the Double-K ranch in the south end of the valley." As soon as he said it, he felt the grip in the postmaster's hand go limp, so he released it.

"Your range runs right up against the Triple-H, right?" Lawrence asked. He had never heard anything good about the Double-K.

"That's right," Ralph replied and knew he'd better talk fast. "That ranch is owned by the Hunter family. I have to confess we're not on the friendly basis my brother and I attempted to establish with them. I admit, I can understand they look at us as competition. But there's plenty of room for both our ranches. We tried to contact Duncan Hunter and his sons, too. But they said they are not interested in any cooperation between our two ranches."

Now it was Ralph's turn to be surprised. "I have to tell you I'm really surprised to hear you say that about the Hunter family," Lawrence said. "I've always known the Hunter men to be fair-minded and easy to do business with. I was interested to hear what you just said about your dealings with them for a personal reason. You see, my daughter is engaged to marry Holt Hunter. My wife is working out the place and the date for the wedding now with the Hunter women. Edna, Morgan Hunter's wife, was in town yesterday to meet with my wife and daughter. She didn't start back until after dark. I was more than a little worried because she only had one man with her to drive the wagon. I surely hope they got home safely."

"Well, I hope I haven't caused you any doubt about your daughter's wedding," Ralph said. "The trouble my brother and I have had with the Hunters is no more than the trouble businessmen have with competitive businessmen. So I wouldn't think it would have anything to do with their families. And speakin' for me and my brother, I can tell you that anytime the Hunter men want to get together with us to better our relationship, we're ready to meet." He emphasized his sincerity with a strong nod of his head. "It was a pleasure talkin' to you, sir."

"Likewise," Lawrence replied, "and I hope things work out better between your ranch and the Triple-H." He stepped back to give Stanley room to show Ralph the envelope and charge him for the postage.

Ralph went out the door and closed it behind him before he took a moment to exhale a lung full of tension. *What a hell of a coincidence,* he thought. *His daughter's marrying Holt Hunter.* He stepped off the boardwalk and pulled himself up into the saddle. *If he believed half of what I said about the Hunters, I'll bet he's thinking some new thoughts about the upcoming wedding.* He turned the gray back up the street, trying to decide if he wanted anything to eat as he passed the shops. He decided he wasn't hungry, so he nudged the gray into a comfortable lope and guided him back to the wagon road toward the south end of the valley.

He rode only a few minutes down the road when he came to a spot where there was an excessive number of hoofprints facing each other and the dirt churned up right in the middle of the road. Then a thought struck him and he remembered Emmett telling him that Bo said he and Smoke were jumped on the road into town. Could this possibly be the place? Extremely interested now, he took time to look the road over closely. Whatever happened here, there was definitely a wagon involved in the incident. And the postmaster said that Morgan Hunter's wife left after dark in a wagon, down this road. If this was the place where Bo and Smoke were supposedly attacked, where was Smoke's body? Maybe someone came along earlier this morning and found it. Maybe not. Too interested to leave it at that, he decided to look for the body. So he looked at both sides of the road and decided to look first on the side that was mostly covered by scrub trees and brush. He walked the horse slowly for about a dozen yards before he came upon Smoke Davis staring up at him from a slight depression in the ground.

He turned the gray back to the road and began to try to fit all the scraps of information into one reasonable story. All those tracks in the middle of the road could fit right in with two men on horseback stopping the wagon with Edna Hunter and her driver in it. What happened after that was harder to guess. But Bo insisted it was they who were attacked, and by Triple-H men. And he was sure the Injun was with them. It might not be the exact story, but he felt he had enough to get the complete picture out of Bo.

He rode through the crude gate at the Double-K Ranch at just about suppertime and was still at the barn telling Jimmy Todd to unsaddle his horse and to make sure it was watered when Emmett rode in. "Yo, Ralph," Emmett called out to him, "I wasn't sure you'd be back this early." He pulled up beside him and stepped down from his horse. "How'd things go in town?"

"I went to the post office and got the letter mailed, and I talked a little while to John Lawrence," Ralph replied. When Emmett asked who that was, Ralph said, "He's the postmaster. We had an interesting talk. Come to find out his daughter's fixin' to marry Holt Hunter."

"Ha!" Emmett reacted. "You don't say. Reckon we'll get an invite to the weddin'?" He handed his reins to Jimmy who was standing there waiting. Emmett waited until the young boy led the horses away before commenting, "Maybe we oughta send word to Holt not to wait too long. She might be a mighty young widow."

"Where's Bo?" Ralph asked. "Is he still layin' around the bunkhouse?"

"I don't know. I just got back here, myself. I had some of the boys move part of the cattle to some new grazin' this mornin, which woulda been Bo's job. But Tater was gonna take another look at Bo's shoulder and put his arm in a sling. So he's around here somewhere. You wanna see if he's in the bunkhouse?"

"No," Ralph replied. "Let's go on up and eat supper. I ain't ate no dinner. I've got a little story I've been tryin' to put all the pieces together to see if it makes sense. Then we can tell it to Bo and see what he says about it." They started toward the house and Ralph made another comment. "I saw Smoke Davis on my way back home."

"You what?" Emmett responded.

"I said I saw Smoke Davis on my way back home. He was layin' on his back about a couple dozen yards off the road."

"Well, I'll be . . ." Emmett started. "So they were jumped on the road into town, like Bo says."

"Maybe," Ralph replied, "but there's a lot more to the story than that. I'll tell you what I've put together so far, and then we'll likely get the true story outta Bo."

CHAPTER 18

Sadie looked out the back window and saw them coming from the barn, so she filled a couple of plates and set them on the table. And she was pouring the coffee when they walked in the door. "I weren't sure what time you'd get back," she said to Ralph. "I figured I'd be sloppin' the hogs with your supper."

While they ate, Ralph went back over everything he had talked about with John Lawrence, especially the part about Edna Hunter going back home in a wagon after dark. He said Lawrence was concerned for the woman, and her only protection was the fellow driving the wagon. Then he talked about the tracks in the middle of the road and how they could have been made, and the fact that Smoke's body was found off the road at the same place. "Sounds to me like Smoke and Bo mighta seen that woman in the wagon and stopped her," Sadie interrupted to give her opinion. "They likely thought about takin' advantage of the woman, and what they didn't know was that Injun was watchin' out for her."

Emmett and Ralph both looked at her as if to remind her their discussion was none of her business. But then Ralph looked back at Emmett and said, "That's what it sounds like to me. So I think we've got enough of that story to get the rest of it outta Bo. What do you think?"

Emmett shrugged while he considered it. "I reckon you're right," he allowed. "What I don't understand is why do we give a damn if Bo and Smoke stopped the woman or not?"

"Because if Bo tells you the truth about it, you'll know it was the Hunter woman on that wagon and she had that damn Injun watchin' out for her," Sadie interrupted again. "So now you know you ain't got rid of that damn Injun after all."

"I swear," Ralph barked, "we're gonna have to go into the other room to talk about anything important." Back to Emmett then, he said, "She might be right, though. I was hopin' that damn Injun was gone for good."

"Let's finish eatin', and we'll go back down to the bunkhouse and get the full story outta Bo on this thing," Emmett whispered in an effort to keep Sadie from hearing it.

"Tell you what I think," Sadie offered. "I think you oughta go down to the bunkhouse and get the full story outta Bo."

"Have you got any more coffee in that damn pot?" Ralph demanded impatiently. "Do I have to get up and get it myself?"

"You've had quite a bit already," Sadie said. "Sometimes if you drink too much black coffee, it'll make you irritable. You sure you ain't had enough?"

"Maybe you're right," Ralph said. "Come on, Emmett, let's go down and talk to Bo." They got up from the table and walked out the back door. Just to be cautious, Ralph didn't say anything more until they were halfway down to the cookshack. "I swear, sometimes I wanna cut that woman's tongue out. If she wasn't right every time she opens her mouth, I swear I'd cut her tongue out tonight."

Tater was sitting on his stool by the corner of the cook-shack, scrubbing a pot when they walked up. "Howdy, bosses," he called out. "I've still got a little coffee left in the pot. You care for a cup?" They both declined immediately, having sampled Tater's coffee before.

"Where's Bo?" Emmett asked." Is he in the bunk-house?"

"I saw him go in the barn a little while ago," Tater said. "I didn't see him come back out."

"How's that wound?" Emmett asked. "I ain't talked to him today."

"It's comin' along just fine," Tater replied. "He's lucky that bullet caught him where it did. I fixed him up with a sling. The worst part of it is it's in his right shoulder and that takes some gettin' used to."

"I reckon so," Emmett said and he and Ralph walked on over to the barn. Inside, they saw Bo standing in an open stall feeding a portion of grain to a buckskin horse. "How's the wound?" Emmett asked as they walked back to join him.

"It's comin' along, I reckon," Bo said at once, feeling a little cautious upon seeing both of the owners coming to see him. "Tater says it's gonna be just like new. It's slowed me down a lot since it's my right shoulder."

"Were you gettin' ready to take that horse out?" Ralph asked.

Bo released a little chuckle. "No, sir," he said. "This is Chigger. He's the horse I rode last night and I was just lookin' him over to make sure he ain't hurtin' anywhere. I rode him pretty hard and I just wanna make sure he's all right."

"Speakin' about last night," Ralph said, "I saw Smoke

Davis today." He paused to let that sink in. "I went into town this mornin'."

Misunderstanding, Bo became excited, thinking Smoke was alive. "Where did you see him?"

"He was layin' in a briar patch where somebody had left him," Ralph said, "right opposite where the wagon was stopped in the middle of the road. You remember the wagon, don't you? And the woman?"

"It was too dark to see anything on that road, and they was chargin' up the middle of the road and some more of 'em on the side of the road. When the shootin' started, me and Smoke pulled our guns and started shootin' at the ones chargin' up the middle of the road. I couldn't tell if we hit any of 'em or not. They just kept comin'. Then some more of 'em started to shoot from off the side of the road and one of the first shots knocked Smoke down. Then I got hit in my right shoulder and dropped my gun. I didn't know how bad I was hit and I still couldn't see where they were all comin' from. I gave Chigger my heels and he didn't let me down. One of 'em came after me and chased me for a while before he turned around and went back to the others. I was just lucky to get away, and I'm sorry for Smoke's bad luck."

"Sounds to me like there wasn't much else you could do," Emmett said. "When I talked to you this mornin', you said you thought the Injun was one of 'em. If you couldn't see 'em in the darkness, how do you know that Injun was with 'em?"

"I don't know, Boss. Maybe I was wrong. I just thought the one that came after me looked like he was wearin' buckskins. I know he weren't wearin' no hat."

Ralph and Emmett looked at each other, needing no words to communicate their understanding of what had taken place on the road to Stevensville. It was obvious that Bo and Smoke had happened upon Edna Hunter and her driver on that dark road. And they stopped the wagon and no doubt intended to take advantage of the woman. And they were too dumb to realize Morgan Hunter wouldn't let his wife travel that distance at that time of night without proper protection. The question for Emmett and Ralph to be concerned with was whether or not the Triple-H protection riding with Edna Hunter knew that Smoke and Bo rode for the Double-K. If they did, then the Double-K could expect some form of punishment from the Hunters. This at a time when they were so short of men. With that thought in mind, Emmett asked Bo, "Did you tell that woman in the wagon that you and Smoke rode for the Double-K?"

"No, sir," Bo answered simply. "We didn't say who we were."

"Good," Emmett said. "That's good. You did the right thing." He looked at Ralph and sighed a gesture of relief. "Well, you'd best rest that shoulder up so you can get back to work," he said to Bo. He and Ralph turned and walked out of the barn, heading back to the house to talk about where they could go to pick up half a dozen good men. They would have a few weeks only to find them, depending upon how long it would take for that letter to be delivered.

While the Kincaid brothers were sweating out the coming weeks and the shortage of gun hands, the Hunter brothers were working late hours in an effort to change the back hallway of the main house into separate quarters for Holt and Spring. Cody had already moved into what was once the study, although he was still threatening to retreat to the woods. On this Sunday morning, however, he was accompanying his brother Holt and Chris Scott on a trip to Stevensville. The purpose of the trip was to escort John and Norma Lawrence and their daughter Spring on a visit to the Triple-H to meet their daughter's future in-laws. Edna and Pansy were planning a big Sunday dinner as well. So the three Triple-H men arrived early that morning at Roland's Stables with a team of horses where they rented Roland's biggest buggy. Although the Triple-H owned a buggy, it was a small one with just enough room for two people, so they were afraid it would be a little tight for the three of them.

"They're here, Norma," John Lawrence called out to his wife when the buggy rode up into their yard. He had been watching from the living room window to see what the accommodations for the two-hour trip might be. "Looks like they brought a buggy for me to drive." He was pleased to see the buggy because he halfway expected them to bring a wagon like the one Edna had come into town on. "You and Spring ready? Holt's coming to the door." He walked over to the front door and waited for Holt to knock before opening it. "Good morning, Holt, I believe we're all ready to go." He turned to call back, "Norma, Holt's here."

"Good mornin', Mr. Lawrence," Holt replied. "I hope we're not too early."

"No, indeed. The women are all ready to go." He turned to call again, "Norma, Spring."

"Goodness sakes, we're coming, John. Good morning, Holt," Norma greeted him.

"Good mornin'," Holt returned, although his eyes were on Spring as she followed her mother into the room carrying a couple of dusters for the trip. He led them out to the front yard and introduced them to Cody and Chris. "I brought this team of horses in with us," he told John. "They're a gentle pair that shouldn't give you any trouble." Then he helped Norma and Spring into the buggy, giving Spring's hand a little squeeze in the process, and receiving a sweet smile in return. "I put a canteen full of fresh water behind the seat in case you get thirsty," he said. Chris and Cody grinned at each other, enjoying Holt's polite performance.

They started out of the yard with the postmaster driving the team of horses and the escort of three positioned one on each side and one behind the buggy. John was happy to find the horses as easy to handle as Holt had said. Normally, he and his wife and daughter would attend church on Sunday, but he had told Reverend Talbot that they would not be there this Sunday. He couldn't help thinking about his conversation with Ralph Kincaid and his accusations against the Hunter men. He had heard about Holt's younger brother suddenly showing up after being separated from the family. He thought at first that Chris was the younger brother, but the more he looked at the young man introduced as Cody, the more he picked up the Hunter characteristics. He found it odd, however, that Cody wore no hat and instead of boots, he wore Indian-style moccasins. He might have studied him more, but Cody chose to ride behind the buggy while Holt and Chris rode along beside it and kept a conversation alive with the occupants of the buggy. Like Ralph Kincaid had before, Cody noticed all the signs still evident in the middle of the road where the wagon had been stopped days ago. He gave a silent offering of thanks to Man Above for giving him the opportunity to be there for his sister-in-law on this dark deserted road that night.

After a pleasant ride of just under two hours, they pulled into the entrance gate of the Triple-H Ranch. Holt led them up to the front door of the main house and Morgan and Edna came down the front steps to greet them. Duncan Hunter came out and waited on the porch to greet them and Pansy came out to stand with him. After Morgan and Edna welcomed them, Holt let Cody and

Chris take care of the horses and the buggy, and he went in the house with the guests.

Edna told Holt to show them the work being done on the house while she and Pansy got the dinner ready to go on the table. Duncan went with Holt when they took the Lawrences to see the renovation underway to convert the back part of the ranch house into a home for the newly-weds. "We thought we might build you a small kitchen just in case you and Holt want some privacy," Duncan told Spring. "But Pansy and Cody and I are kinda hopin' you'll just wanna share the big kitchen with us. Pansy likes to cook big meals."

"That's a fact," Holt said.

"That sounds like fun," Spring said, "but only if she'll let me help her."

Shortly, dinner was ready so they went into the dining room to a table filled with food. Duncan picked up his knife and fork, but then hesitated. "Would you wanna say the blessin', John?" Duncan asked. Pansy looked at Holt and grinned.

"Yes, sir," Lawrence said, "I could say a little word of thanks for these two families sharing this magnificent meal." He said a short blessing.

In a few minutes, Cody came in and sat down where there were two empty plates. When Duncan said he should have brought Chris back to eat with him, Cody said, "I told him that. I told him there would be an empty plate for him. But he said he rather eat with the rest of the men. He was afraid he might do something to embarrass himself if he ate with us." Not accustomed to sitting around the table when he had finished eating, Cody excused himself as soon as he was through.

"We'll leave here to go back to town at three o'clock," Holt told Cody when he got up from the table. "That way we'll get the Lawrences back home by five o'clock."

"Right," Cody replied. "I'll tell Chris." He left them to plan the wedding while he went down to the barn to see if he might be needed to help out anywhere.

Pansy was left with the job of cleaning up the dirty dishes until Spring stepped up to help her. "That's mighty nice of you," Pansy said, "but don't you wanna hear what they're plannin' to do for your wedding?"

"I can hear what they're talking about while I'm helping you," Spring told her. "You shouldn't have to do all the cooking and then have to clean everything up by yourself."

"Well, if you insist," Pansy said. "I appreciate it." Spring looked at Holt and winked. She knew she had already won Pansy over. He was well aware of just how smart that was.

By the time three o'clock rolled around, the date had been agreed upon, but John and Norma were set on having their daughter married in their church by their pastor, the Reverend Robert Talbot. And they wanted their friends in the church to attend the wedding. Duncan Hunter wanted the wedding to take place at the Triple-H primarily because he was not willing to risk leaving the ranch with all four Hunter men gone. It was true that the Double-K had apparently given up their quest to take over Triple-H. But he feared that if word got out that all of the Hunter men were in town for a wedding, the temptation to strike would be too much for the Kincaid brothers to resist. Since it was the bride's family who traditionally paid for the wedding, the Lawrences insisted it would be held at the church. This even after Duncan offered to pay for the whole wedding, including the cost to transport Reverend Talbot to the ranch.

Finally, Duncan yielded to the Lawrences' demands to have the wedding in town. But he would permit only Morgan and himself to attend. Morgan would have to go because Edna would be in the wedding. So that left Cody as the only Hunter to be left on the ranch. That suited

Cody because he didn't want to go to the wedding, anyway. Duncan had no idea how effective Cody would be in commanding a possible defense of the ranch. But he knew Cody was a fighter and fearless to boot. And the men knew that, as well. So the final plans were settled; the wedding would be in town. Duncan confessed to his son that he wished to hell he had snatched the young lady up and run off to the justice of the peace. Holt confessed that he wished he had, too.

When it was all settled, it was approaching the time of departure, so Cody went in search of Chris Scott. Then they hitched the horses up to the buggy and saddled their horses, then returned to the front yard where everyone was saying goodbye. The Lawrences climbed aboard the buggy and the party set out for town. After an uneventful trip back to Stevensville, the escort dropped their passengers off at home. Spring gave Holt a goodnight kiss and promised that after the ceremony was over it would only be the two of them and no parents. There was one more thing to take care of before they could ride back to the ranch and that was to return the buggy to Roland's Stable.

After Holt paid Roland, it occurred to him that it was going to be pretty late by the time they got back home. "And I'm gettin' a little hungry right now."

"So am I," Cody said, "and it wouldn't hurt to let these horses rest for a little while before we start back."

"Right," Holt said. "And I don't know about you two, but I've had a hard day with my in-laws. So I'm thinking about buyin' myself a little supper at the Village Tavern."

"That sounds right up my alley," Cody said. "Let's go do it."

"I think I'll pass on it, myself," Chris Scott commented. "I can watch the horses while you eat."

"You ain't hungry?" Holt asked, surprised.

"I didn't say that," Chris answered. "I'm broke."

"Well, for Pete's sake," Holt responded, "Cody and I will pay for it. Right, Cody?"

"That's right," Cody answered. So they turned their horses toward the Village Tavern, which looked to be doing a fair business that night. They tied their horses at the hitching rail, and as a precaution, pulled their rifles out to take inside with them.

"Well, if it ain't the Hunter boys," Ed Bates greeted them when they walked in. He knew Holt, and he had finally found out that Cody was a Hunter, so he assumed that Chris was one, too.

"Howdy, Ed," Holt replied. "We're lookin' for some supper." He looked the busy room over, then pointed to a table two men got up from and started for the door. "We'll set down over there if you'll tell Minnie we want three plates. And maybe you can pour three shots of whiskey to help our bellies get ready for the food."

"You just need two shots of whiskey," Cody said.

"Oh, that's right. I forgot you don't drink the stuff," Holt said. "Pour three shots anyway, Ed. I may need another shot."

"You mind if I stick your rifles under the end of the bar?" Ed asked. "Otis is tryin' to get more family business in here, so we're tryin' to keep the guns outta sight."

"No problem at all," Holt said. "We just didn't wanna leave them out there on our horses." They walked over and sat down at the table then and Ed brought the three shots over on his way to tell Minnie they wanted to eat supper.

In just a few moments, Ed came back out of the kitchen with Minnie right behind him. "Well, if it ain't Holt and Cody Hunter. Holt, ain't seen you in a while. And I almost didn't recognize you, Cody, dressed up in white man's clothes. And I don't know who this young feller is. I don't believe you've ever been in before, have you?"

"No, ma'am, I ain't ever been in before."

"This is Chris Scott," Holt said. "Chris, this is Minnie Mills, the best cook in the Bitterroot Valley."

"Pleased to meet you, Chris. It's always nice when Holt brings in the big, good lookin' boys like you. If my kitchen was a little more tidy right now, I'd invite you to eat in the kitchen." She grinned when she saw Chris blush. "You want a cup of coffee with your supper, Sweetie? I know they do."

"Yes, ma'am," Chris answered, so she did an about-face and went back to the kitchen.

She was back in a short time with three cups of coffee. "I've got a pan of biscuits coming outta the oven in about five minutes," she said. "You wanna wait for them before I serve up your plates? Or do you wanna go ahead and get started before the biscuits are done?"

"I'll wait for the hot biscuits," Holt said.

"Did you hear what I just heard?" Albert Cheney whispered to his two companions. Their table was only about five feet from the one Minnie just left. "She called them by name."

"I wasn't payin' her no attention," Otto Ross said. "I was more interested in workin' on these beans and rice."

"She called them by name," Cheney repeated. "Did you hear her, Deke?"

"Maybe they're regular customers," Deke Moore answered, his mouth full of food. "I didn't pay her no mind, neither. I had more important things to concentrate on. When she comes back with that coffeepot, you can tell her your name."

Cheney looked at both of them in disgust. "You two meatheads, the name she called two of 'em was Hunter," he whispered. They both stopped chewing and jerked their heads around to look in their direction. "Dammit, don't gawk at 'em. They don't know who we are." Although there was a standoff war going on between the two ranches, most of the men had never gotten close enough to become familiar with their faces. "She called one of 'em Holt." That stopped the chewing in both mouths simultaneously as they tried to stare sideways without turning their heads in that direction. Whereas they had never been close enough to identify Holt Hunter, they were very familiar with the name. "She called the other one something that sounded like Cody Hunter and I ain't never heard of that one."

"Well, they don't know we ride for the Double-K," Otto said. "Whaddaya reckon we oughta do about it? If we was to knock two of the Hunters down, it would be a big deal to Ralph and Emmett. Who do you reckon the other fellow is?"

"It don't matter," Cheney said. "He rides for the Triple-H. That would be one less of 'em to worry about. I ain't never heard of Cody Hunter neither."

"Don't turn your head to look," Deke said. "Just cut your eyes toward the floor under this side of their table." He paused to give them a minute to do so. "That one Minnie called Cody is wearin' moccasins. What if he's the Injun?" There was a long pause in the conversation before Deke asked the question again, "What are we gonna do?"

"I know what Emmett wants us to do," Cheney replied, "shoot the bastards down, settle up for some of our men they've killed. And it couldn't be a better setup for us. They don't know who we are. When they leave here, we'll get on their tails and it'll be three quick shots in the back and take the news to Emmett and Ralph." Otto and Deke nodded in agreement and all three enjoyed their supper even more than before.

CHAPTER 19

Always possessing a tendency to observe his surroundings, Cody became aware of the three men eating at a table several feet away from his. Watching out of the corner of his eye, it occurred to him that they appeared to be unusually interested in Holt, Chris, and himself. And he detected an obvious attempt to be discreet about it. He wondered if there was a possibility that they knew who Holt was. Maybe they had heard Minnie call him by name. They made no attempt to approach them, however, so he made no mention of it to Holt. He enjoyed the supper Minnie put on the table even though he was bothered slightly by a feeling of concern about the three strangers.

When he and Holt and Chris were finished and getting ready to leave, the three men at the nearby table finished a minute or two ahead of them and walked out. Holt started to get to his feet, but Cody stopped him. "Sit here for a few minutes until I get back. I need to confirm something." The mystery that had bothered him all through supper was suddenly solved as he watched the three men walking out. He had seen them before. He had seen two of them when they had ridden past a calf trapped in a hole in the river, a calf that he had rescued from the river when they ignored it. Holt was puzzled by Cody's request, but figured he had his reasons, so he sat back down while Cody went to the end of the bar to get his rifle. Then he walked into the kitchen, startling Minnie. "Pardon me," he said and walked through the kitchen and out the back door. He moved rapidly around the building to the front corner where he saw the three men getting on their horses. He watched as they rode down the street toward the road leading home. But instead of continuing out the road, they pulled around behind the corral at the stables.

Cody went back into the Village Tavern, through the front door where he found Holt and Chris waiting, having retrieved their rifles, as well. "What is it, Cody?" Holt asked as soon as he came in the door.

"The three men that were sittin' at that table over next to us ride for the Double-K. I saw two of 'em when they were ridin' the outer limits of their range. But it didn't hit me until they got up and walked out."

"I thought those fellows seemed mighty interested in what we were talkin' about," Chris commented.

"That's why I went out the back door so I could see where they were plannin' to ambush us, 'cause I'm pretty sure they know we're from the Triple-H."

"There's plenty of places on that road back to the ranch," Holt said. "Too bad we didn't know who they were before they walked out of here. We coulda taken care of 'em right here."

"It's just as well we didn't know," Cody said. "It seems like just about every time I eat here, I get into some kinda trouble. If we'da shot them down in here tonight, they probably wouldn't ever let me come in again."

"Are we goin' after 'em?" Chris asked.

"I expect that's the only polite thing to do," Holt said, "since they've gone to the trouble of settin' up an ambush."

"Well, I hope you won't be too disappointed to find out they ain't hidin' in the woods along that road," Cody said.

"They're so anxious, they didn't even get outta town. They rode around behind the corral down at the stables. So I'd suggest that we leave our horses here and walk behind the buildings till we find where they're hiding."

So they started walking along behind the buildings toward the stables. Before they got too close to the corral, Cody decided to cross over to the other side of the street. He figured they would be set up to catch them in a cross-fire when they rode down the street. Chris stayed with Holt, hoping to spot the horses, thinking that would be close to where the rider was hiding in ambush. The corral didn't really offer much cover so Holt was watching the corner posts and feeding troughs, anything that could offer protection in a shoot-out. Cody was slipping from shop to shop counting on the bushwhackers thinking they would catch their targets completely by surprise and consequently they wouldn't really need much protection. He could imagine their plan was to simply sit there in the corral and wait for the three of them to pass them by. Then they would walk out in the street behind them and shoot them in the back.

In fact, that was exactly what Otto Ross, Albert Cheney, and Deke Moore had in mind. So, it was not surprising that Cheney was startled when he heard Cody behind him, "Hey, Double-K?" In sheer panic, he spun around, squeezing the trigger that sent a bullet into the ground at his feet. Cody placed a shot in the helpless man's chest, then looked across the street to see Deke Moore collapse by the corral railing as he tried to catch his horse. Waiting in advance of Deke and Albert in case one or more of their victims made it that far, Otto froze when he heard Cody's shot. His first reaction upon seeing the two bodies collapse was to spring on his horse and gallop through the barn and out the back door. Both Cody and Chris ran out into the street to try to get a shot at the fleeing assassin but Otto kept the barn between him and the shooters until he was able to disappear into the trees behind the barn.

The three Triple-H men came together in the middle of the street to discuss the success of their counterattack on the ambush. "Well, it wasn't a hundred percent successful," Holt declared. "We didn't count on that one son of a gun parkin' himself that far ahead of the other two. But we did reduce the Kincaid brothers' crew by two more." He looked at Cody then and said, "If you hadn't remembered seein' those two ridin' scout that one time, the three of us might be layin' in the middle of the street. We'd best get back to the Tavern and get our horses."

Unfortunately, Tom Gordon, the town marshal, was in the street in front of the Village Tavern by the time they walked back to their horses. "Evenin' Holt, Cody," the marshal said when they walked up. He nodded to Chris, since he didn't know him. "I suppose you can tell me what the shootin' was about."

"Be glad to, Marshal," Holt replied. "Three fellows decided to set up an ambush to kill the three of us. Two of 'em are lyin' dead in the street by the corral. The other one got away."

Gordon thought about that for a few moments before asking, "I expect I'd be right if I was to guess the three were Double-K men?"

"As a matter of fact they were," Holt said.

"How did you know they was fixin' to ambush you fellows?" Gordon asked.

"We didn't know for sure, but we had a feelin' they might, so we decided it was a good idea not to go ridin' up that street until we saw there wasn't nobody waitin' for us. It turned out what we suspected really was a fact."

"It was a case of attempted murder by those three men, Marshal," Cody spoke up then. "We didn't know who those men were. If you talk to Ed or Minnie in the saloon, they can tell you that there were no words of any kind passed between us and those three fellows. We just ate our supper and minded our own business. And when we found them hidin' in the stable, waitin' to kill us, I even asked the fellow what was goin' on. He didn't answer me. He just turned and shot. So I had no choice."

"Well, I reckon that's the truth of it," Gordon said. "I'll take care of the bodies and the horses and you fellows are free to go." He had no desire to pursue it any further. He would send for the undertaker to pick up the bodies for their standard arrangement to split anything of value. And he would take possession of the two horses and saddles.

They climbed on their horses and trotted past the bodies lying in the street. Before reaching the road out of town, they discussed the possibility of the one surviving assassin setting up somewhere between there and the Triple-H in another ambush attack. But they decided it unlikely. The man ran scared. He didn't even attempt a shot, so he wasn't likely to try when his odds were three to one. So they took a leisurely ride back to the Triple-H.

Otto Ross had a much longer ride home and it was nowhere close to being as leisurely as the ride the three Triple-H men took. It was close to midnight when he rode into the barnyard and everyone had gone to bed. He took the saddle off his horse and turned it loose in the herd, took his saddle in the barn, then went into the bunkhouse. He took his boots off but didn't bother with his clothes, jumped into his bunk, and pulled the blanket up over his head. He prayed the trembling in his body would stop so he could go to sleep, knowing he was going to have to tell Emmett what happened in the morning. It took him quite a while before he finally drifted off to sleep to be awakened by the sounds of the other men getting up for breakfast.

"Damn, Otto," Earl Mathers commented when he saw him climb out of his blanket fully clothed. "What time did you boys get back last night?" When Otto didn't answer right away, Earl looked behind him to see Albert and Deke's bunks made up, so he figured they were already at the cookshack. "They musta been hungry."

"They didn't come back," Otto said and walked out of the bunkhouse with Mathers trailing him.

"How come they didn't come back?" Mathers asked. "Did you boys get in trouble in town?" His first thought was that they were in jail.

"They're dead," Otto said, "and I was damn lucky to get back here to tell it." He hurried into the cookshack, anxious to have a cup of Tater's vile coffee.

Mathers was one step behind him, and as soon as they were inside, he announced, "Deke and Albert are dead!" The four men already eating breakfast, as well as Tater Duggan, all became alert and looked at him for an explanation. "That's what Otto said. He was with 'em."

They all turned their attention to Otto then. "Who done it, Otto?" Sam Kilbourne asked. "Where did it happen?"

"In town," Otto answered. "It was three Triple-H men and two of 'em was Hunters. They caught us when we was riding outta town, killed Deke and Albert, I was lucky enough to get away." He gave them a simplified version of the deaths, preferring not to admit that it was a result of an ambush on their part that got turned upside down.

"I swear," Tater commented, "that ain't gonna be very good news to start Emmett's day off with. We keep losin' men and I might have to start workin' with you boys."

It was half an hour before Emmett showed up at the cookshack where he often talked over the assignments for the day if everyone was still sitting at the table. He glanced at the table this morning and asked, "Who's missin'? Is everybody out of the bunkhouse?" They all turned to look at Otto.

"Albert Cheney and Deke Moore are missin', Boss," Otto said.

"Where are they?" Emmett asked.

"They're dead, Boss," Otto answered. "They was shot by three Triple-H hands. We went to town yesterday and we were on our way back after supper. Didn't have no idea they was waitin' for us to ride out. When they started shootin', we took off. They got Deke and Albert, but I got away." Emmett didn't say anything, but it was obvious that he was smoldering inside to hear he had lost two more men. "One of 'em was Holt Hunter," Otto continued in an effort to make sure Emmett's wrath was concentrated in the right direction. "There was another Hunter, too, but I never heard his name before."

Emmett listened to what he was saying and decided he needed to go into greater detail. "All right," he finally spoke, "that's bad news about Deke and Albert, but we've still gotta take care of the cattle." He issued a few assignments to be worked on for the day. "But you and me need to talk some more about what happened in town, Otto. The rest of you go ahead and get started."

They all filed out of the cookshack, obviously disappointed not to hear the discussion between Boss and Otto. When they were gone, the first question Emmett asked was, "You said one of the men was Holt Hunter. How do you know that?"

"I heard somebody call him Holt," Otto replied.

"Where'd you hear that?" Emmett asked. "While they were chasin' you and shootin' at you?"

Otto paused then, realizing he had slipped up. "No, I musta forgot to tell you we was in the saloon eatin' supper and that's when I heard somebody call him Holt."

Emmett realized at once that Otto had not given him the complete story. "And you said there was another Hunter there. Was his name Morgan?"

"No, his name sounded like Cody Hunter." He remembered then and added, "He was wearin' moccasins like Injuns wear."

"He was wearin' buckskins?" Emmett asked, immediately interested.

"No, sir, he was wearin' regular cowhand britches and shirt, just wearin' Injun moccasins."

"How'd they know you boys were from the Double-K?" Emmett asked then.

"I don't know," Otto replied. "We didn't tell anybody in that place where we was from."

"They just decided they didn't like your looks, I reckon, and decided to shoot all three of ya," Emmett remarked facetiously. He suspected that he had the real picture of the whole incident. His three men must have heard the Hunters called by name, so they decided to kill them. He did not fault them for that. He wished they had been successful. Still, he was frustrated over their inability to do the job. Ordinarily, he might have been tempted to shoot Otto for his lack of guts when Holt and the other two men came after them. But his crew was so crippled at the present that he couldn't afford to lose one more man. So he told Otto that was all he needed to know about the killings and sent him to work with Sam Kilbourne on the south range. The decision he and Ralph had already made to hire a professional killer was going to cost them a hell of a lot of money, but Vargas Roach was quick and efficient. He got up from the bench he had been sitting on and walked out of the cookshack, giving Tater a nod as he went by him. He walked back up to the house to report the morning news to Ralph.

"You want coffee?" Sadie asked when he walked in the

back door. Ralph was still sitting at the table, so Emmett walked over and sat down across from him.

"You don't look too happy, brother," Ralph said to him. "Were the men missin'?" he japed.

"Just two of 'em," Emmett said. "Deke Moore and Albert Cheney. Both of 'em are dead. The two of 'em and Otto Ross went into town yesterday and got into it with Holt Hunter, one of their ranch hands, and another young fellow that Otto said is named something like Cody Hunter. Maybe he said Colt. You reckon they're twins? Holt and Colt?" Ralph simply shrugged his indifference to the question. He was already heating up upon hearing about the loss of the two men, so Emmett continued. "Well, I don't give a damn what his name is. Otto said he didn't wear boots. He said he was wearing Indian moccasins and he weren't wearin' a hat. I think he's that damn Injun."

Ralph slammed his good hand down hard on the table in frustration, causing coffee to splash out of the freshly poured cup Sadie had just placed before Emmett. She threw a big dishtowel on the table in front of him and told him to clean up the mess he made. He took the towel and mopped up most of the coffee without interrupting the rant he was in the middle of. "Where the hell are we goin' to find the kind of men we need to run this ranch? We can't spare neither one of us to ride back to Dodge City where we picked up most of the men we started out with. Right now, we're left with enough men to take care of the cattle, and that's all they can do. The best gun hand we had was Bo Dawson and damned if he ain't worth nothin' with his right shoulder in a sling."

"I know it ain't good," Emmett said. "We're just gonna have to stick to the plan we've already put into action. And that means we're gonna be workin' our cattle and minding our own business till we hear something from Vargas Roach. Then I might be able to take a short trip up to Missoula to

Gallagher's. That's where we hired Reese Walsh, one of our best gun hands. There might be several more like him hangin' around there."

"What you're sayin' will be just fine, if things stay like they are," Ralph said. "But what if the Triple-H ain't satisfied to let things run like they are now. This business in town last night, you said our men knew it was the Hunters that was in that saloon. You know damn well our men tried to ambush them. Maybe the Hunters know that it was Double-K men. And if they do, there ain't gonna be no stoppin' them from comin' after us, and maybe that one named Cody will put on his damn Injun suit and start pickin' off our men again."

"Otto swore they didn't have no idea him and the other two were Double-K men," Emmett assured him. "I pushed him pretty hard on that and he said there weren't no way they coulda known. He said they never spoke a word to any of the three of them. So I'm pretty sure they don't know who was tryin' to bushwhack 'em."

"I hope to hell you're right," Ralph said. "I still ain't sure you got all the truth out of Otto."

"Well, if we didn't, I reckon we'll find out in the next day or two. Won't we?" Emmett asked. "All we can do is tell the men to keep their eyes open for anything that don't look right."

The incident in town the night before was also being discussed at the Triple-H ranch that morning. Duncan and his three sons were sitting at the kitchen table talking over whether or not there should be more action taken against the Double-K. The Double-K men attempted an ambush, and they were punished for it with the loss of two of their men. The question the Hunter men were discussing was whether or not the attack was something the three foolhardy men decided to do on their own. Or were they sent into town specifically to murder Holt and Cody Hunter? There had been many days of peace between the two ranches. And now, with the loss of two more of their men, surely they should want to avoid any further conflict.

Also, of great concern, was the wedding day to be decided upon, hopefully one day this week. And this was another reason not to retaliate against the attempted attack by the three Double-K men. "I think it best to continue the peace we've enjoyed up until the incident last night," Duncan decided. "It looks to me like it was something those three decided to try on their own, and they didn't even know it was Holt and Cody before they went to that saloon. The Kincaid brothers don't have any reason to come after us for the boneheaded attempt those men made. If anything, I think they'll just be damn glad we don't come back at them for it." He paused to smile. "The most important thing we've got to do is get that wedding done before that little gal realizes what a mistake she's makin'."

CHAPTER 20

Vargas Roach pulled the bay gelding up to the hitching post in front of Conroy's Store in the tiny settlement of Burnt Hollow, Wyoming Territory. The store, located on the south fork of the Shoshone River, had survived many years as a trading post before Jake Conroy took it over when his father died. Now, Jake's son Pete was working in the store with his father, planning to one day own the store, himself. "Look comin' yonder, Pa." Pete walked to the front door and watched while Roach tied the bay to the hitching rail, a packhorse tied to a rope behind the bay. "It's been a while since he's been back." Roach was a good customer, but he was often gone for a long time before showing up again like today to buy supplies. He seldom brought things to trade, always had cash money, and sometimes he had mail.

The Burnt Hollow post office was temporarily located in one small room a little bigger than a closet with Jake Conroy the temporary postmaster. It was an arrangement with the US Postal Service that was originally established to operate only until the official post office was built in a town several miles up the river. The people who were going to build the town decided to delay construction temporarily but then decided to relocate the whole project. It was no disappointment to Jake because he was fearful that the development of a town would shortly dry up his little business. As for the postal business, it was no trouble at all. They only had three customers who ever received any mail, one of whom was walking up the steps to the porch right now.

"Well, well, if it ain't Vargas Roach," Jake gave him a lusty greeting. "Been a while since you've been in."

"Howdy, Jake, Pete," Roach greeted them both. "I expect it has been a while. And I need to buy some things I'm runnin' short of. I've 'bout wore out these britches, too. You think you got any more of these that'll fit me? I brung me a fresh deer hide I'd like to leave for that little Shoshone woman to make me a new shirt out of. Is she still here?"

"She sure is," Jake said. "Pete, go back to the kitchen and get Blue Doe."

He returned in a few seconds with the petite Indian woman right behind him. "You need a new shirt, Mr. Roach?" Blue Doe asked.

"Yes, ma'am," Roach replied. "I brought a new hide to leave with you. If you wanna take some measurements, I'll pay you for it now and I'll pick it up next time I'm here. You can make it just like you made this one."

"I'll go get my measuring rope," she said and hurried away.

"I got a letter for you that came the other day," Jake said. "I'll go get it while Pete is gettin' up your supplies." He walked over to the little room next to the store and unlocked the padlock on the door. Inside, he picked up a small box that held a few letters and picked Roach's letter out of it. "It's from a Mr. Ralph Kincaid in Montana Territory," he said as he handed it to him. He and Pete often speculated on who these people might be that Roach heard from occasionally. They couldn't imagine what business he could be in. From all appearances, he looked like a trapper who lived in the mountains.

Roach opened his letter and read it right away. When he finished it, he stood there a few seconds, building a map in his mind, speculating the route he must take and how long it would take him to get there. "I need to add a few things to my order," he told Jake. Then he told Blue Doe there was no need to hurry with her sewing, for it might be quite a while before he returned for it. He called out a few more things he needed, some of it additional ammunition. Then he paid Jake for the order and paid Blue Doe for his shirt after getting the deer skin out of his pack for her.

Jake thanked him for the order, then he and Pete stood on the porch of the store and watched him as he rode up the path to the river road. They started their game of speculation on what the man could possibly do to always have money. It had to be some form of crime, but he looked too peaceful to be involved in violent crime. "And he looks like he spends all his time in the mountains, huntin' and trappin'," Pete commented.

"He sure rides well-armed, though," Jake said. "He wears a Colt .45 and carries a Winchester 73."

"You think he might be holdin' up stagecoaches or trains?" Pete asked. "He sure don't look like he would. He don't look like he'd hurt a flea."

As he rode away, Roach was thinking about the one time he had been to Missoula. Two years before, that had been a long trip, too. But he had started out from Great Falls in Montana Territory and he could follow the Mullan Road. This time, starting from Wyoming Territory, there was no direct route he could figure out and there were several mountain ranges he would have to get past. Consequently, he wasn't sure how long it was going to take him to reach the Double-K Ranch. He could only guess it was going to be anywhere between eleven and fourteen days. Kincaid said in his letter that there was a telegraph in Stevensville and he would check it every three days for a reply to his letter. So when he reached a town big enough to have a telegraph, he could at least let Kincaid know he had accepted the offer and was on his way. He figured that town would be Bozeman. He had made the ride from Burnt Hollow to Bozeman before. He would start out in the morning, so he headed back to his camp by the river. He wondered what day tomorrow would be. If he had thought about it before, he would have asked Jake Conroy what day it was.

Holt Hunter knew what day it was. It was Wednesday, his last day as a free man. On Thursday he was scheduled to appear before the preacher to be sentenced to life in wedlock. He only hoped he had done the right thing in proposing the union. He had gone to a great deal of trouble to ask Spring to marry him because at the time he was sure he couldn't live without her. But after the ceremony, what if Spring ripped the mask off her face and revealed the face under it that looked just like the face of her mother? "What?" he heard himself ask.

"I said I'll bet I know where your mind was," Pansy Hutto said. "You were off in dreamland, thinkin' about marryin' your beautiful bride tomorrow, weren't you?"

"Yeah," he answered. "That's where I was. I'll just be glad when that ceremony is over and we're back here at home."

"You'd better get the hell outta my kitchen and go find yourself something useful to do," Pansy told him. "If you don't, you're gonna be a nervous wreck by the time you get to that church tomorrow."

"I reckon you're right," he admitted. "Maybe I'll go

saddle a horse and go make sure everybody else is workin', and not sittin' around bitin' their fingernails like I am."

Pansy couldn't help laughing when she realized this was the first time she could remember ever having seen Holt's true feelings so openly exposed. He had never been with a woman before. Always the bold confident one when it came to handling any situation, he had now come to face a helpless situation. "You'd best go saddle that horse and go help the men like you usually do. Work you up a good sweat and you get your body wore out. Then you won't worry about what happens tomorrow night when you two are alone. Spring's a smart little gal. She'll handle everything, and you'll do fine. But after you do all that work you're talking about, then you take yourself a bar of soap and a wash rag and you scrub yourself clean.

"Did you and Spring decide to rent a room in the hotel tomorrow, instead of driving all the way back here after the weddin'?" Pansy asked then.

"We talked about it, but Pa didn't want us to do it," Holt answered. "He's still worried about this business with the Double-K, even though we ain't had no trouble with them in weeks now. Unless you wanna count that ambush three of their men tried at the corral. I think Morgan was against the hotel room, too. Hell, we're havin' the weddin' early enough in the day that I don't see any reason we need to stay in the hotel tomorrow night. Besides, I'd rather have the weddin' supper back here." He got up from the table then. "At least I know I'll like the food here."

"That's right," she said as he headed for the door. "And don't forget to take that bath and wear clean underwear."

"Uh-oh, condemned man comin'," Shorty Black called out from the hayloft when Holt walked into the barn. He threw a pitchfork's load of hay down to land on the barn floor. "There you go Holt, you might wanna stuff that in your mattress tonight so it'll be nice and soft tomorrow."

"Maybe it wouldn't hurt if you ate a little bit of that hay," Patch McGee cracked. "Ain't that what you're supposed to feed stud horses?"

"I reckon you boys ain't heard the latest news," Holt remarked. "We called the weddin' off. She decided she don't wanna live on a ranch, and I don't wanna work for her daddy in the post office. So we called it off." He picked up his saddle and walked out of the barn.

Shorty and Patch both chuckled for a few moments before Patch said, "You don't think he was serious, do ya?"

"Nah," Shorty said, "he was just japin' us." Nothing more was said for another moment or two before he commented, "He weren't laughin' when he said that, though."

"He sounded like he was dead serious," Patch said. "He got his saddle. I wonder where he's goin'. You reckon one of us oughta go with him? You don't reckon he's gonna do somethin' crazy, do ya? I'm gonna go ask Sully if Holt said anythin' to him."

He went out of the barn and went into the cookshack where Sully Price was peeling potatoes. "Say, Sully, have you talked to Holt this mornin'?"

"Nope," Sully answered, "not this mornin'. Why?"

"He just came in the barn to get his saddle and he told me and Shorty that they called the weddin' off tomorrow."

"The hell you say," Sully responded. "How come?"

"He said somethin' 'bout that gal not wantin' to live out here on the ranch."

"Well, I'll be . . . Where'd she think they was gonna live in the first place?" Sully asked.

"In town, I reckon," Patch said. "I think she was wantin' him to work for her daddy in the post office 'cause he said he didn't wanna work in the post office."

"That's the craziest thing I ever heard of. That little gal acted like she had more sense than that," Sully said. "And when they was out here at the ranch on that Sunday and Holt brought her around to meet everybody, she acted like she was tickled to death to meet us. I reckon this is hurtin' Holt real bad, but it's better for him to find out what kinda female she really is before he married her." He got up from the stool he had been sitting on peeling his potatoes and walked over to the door. He stood there for a few minutes looking out past the barnyard. "You didn't see which way he headed out of here?"

"No, I didn't," Patch said. "I didn't think about that. Maybe Shorty did. He was up in the hayloft."

"I just hope he didn't ride out toward town," Sully said. "I wish I'da had a chance to talk to him before he rode outta here."

"You reckon we oughta go tell Morgan about this?"

"I don't think so," Sully said. "That's family business we ought not be stickin' our noses in. I expect he already knows about it, anyway."

Seeing Sully standing in the cookshack door, L. C. Pullen called out to him. "Hey, Sully, you seen Holt?"

"He just rode outta here a little while ago," Sully answered.

"Dang," L.C. snorted. "I reckon he forgot."

"Forgot what?" Sully asked.

"He told me yesterday he'd go with me today to see if we couldn't run all them strays that have been bunchin' up in that dry bottom east of the creek. We was gonna drive 'em back to this side of the creek. I told him yesterday that I was havin' a helluva time gittin' 'em outta there by myself. I wish to hell I knew where he was."

"Maybe you better just leave him be today, L.C.," Sully advised. "He's got some other things on his mind."

"What other things?" L.C. asked. "Whaddaya talkin' about?"

"It ain't none of our business, but they've called the

weddin' off tomorrow and it looks like poor Holt is takin' it pretty hard. So I expect it's best to leave him alone."

"I swear, that is sorry news. I hate to hear that. She looked like a sweet little gal, too. Why are they callin' it off?"

"Don't know for sure," Sully replied, "but I think she didn't like the looks of the Triple-H, and she don't wanna live out here."

"Well, I'll swear, Holt deserves better'n that." He shifted his weight in the saddle and thought a minute. "I reckon I'll ride on over the creek and try to get some of them cows outta that dry bottom by myself again." He wheeled his horse away from the cookshack and rode off toward the east.

It was obvious to Holt why L.C. needed help getting the strays out of the dry bottom, an area about an acre in size that remained dry for most of the year. But in rainy seasons the creek filled so high that the water ran off into the normally dry area of scrub brush and stunted trees. There had recently been rain enough to flood the dry bottom, turning it into a muddy bottom. The cows were prone to getting themselves trapped in low spots containing enough water to turn the mud to slush. It required a lot of roping to help some of the cows to escape. He was in the process of extracting one of the cattle that had managed to wander into a hole it couldn't back out of when he heard the voice behind him. "I don't know if I can get you and the cow out of that mess." Holt looked back over his shoulder to discover Cody watching him from the bank of the creek.

"Well, thank goodness they sent me a real cowhand with a rope. We'll get these strays out of here now," Holt japed, knowing Cody wasn't as skilled as the average cowhand working for the Triple-H.

"I've been practicing my roping so I can someday get a

job with a real bunch of cowhands," Cody replied. "I'm still convinced that my Crow father taught me the proper way to rope a cow or a horse. If you want to rope a cow, walk up to the cow and place the rope around its neck. That way, the cow does not run all over the place tryin' to avoid the rope."

Holt laughed, then backed his horse up to pull the cow out of the mud. He led it across the creek then, before he let it go. Coiling his rope then, he asked, "What are you doin' over on this part of the range?"

"Just lookin' around," Cody answered. "I haven't spent much time on the eastern side of the range. So I thought with me being left in charge of the ranch while Pa and Morgan are in town at your weddin', I at least oughta know what's over this way."

"Then I reckon you found out there's plenty of trees and mountains but not a whole lot of good grazin' land."

"That's about right," Cody agreed. They were distracted then by the sudden appearance of a rider approaching in the distance. "Looks like you've got more company."

They watched for a short while and then Holt said, "It's L.C. I told him yesterday I'd help him find these strays out here today. I thought he musta forgot."

"I declare, Holt, I didn't expect to find you out here," L.C. said when he pulled up beside them. "Sully said you left there, but he didn't know where you was headin'. He didn't say Cody was with you, either."

"He wasn't," Holt said. "He just showed up, just like you. So now I reckon we can drive the rest of the dumb cows outta this mudhole."

"Whatever you say, Holt," L.C. replied. "If that's what you feel like doin'. If you don't, though, me and Cody can do the job. Ain't that right, Cody?"

Cody and Holt both looked at L.C. like he'd suddenly

lost his mind. "Hell, no," Cody said. "We can do it a whole lot quicker if we all three get after these cows."

L.C. looked confused. He wanted to express his sympathy to Holt for the cancelation of his wedding. But Holt was obviously trying to hide his sorrow and he was doing a good job of it. Evidently Cody didn't know the wedding had been called off. And if Holt didn't want his own brother to know about it then L.C. decided it was best if he pretended not to know as well. Getting the job done here might be the best thing for Holt right now, so L.C. sang out, "All right, then, let's get after these cows!" He gave his horse a kick and galloped away after a couple of strays that were heading for the same hole Holt just pulled the cow from.

"What the hell?" Holt exclaimed to Cody. "Is he drunk?"

"Maybe so," Cody said with a chuckle. "But if he keeps it up, we're gonna be through here in no time a-tall." They both moved out to join him.

As it turned out, the three of them cleared the dry bottom of stray cows in short order, then drove the little herd of some thirty-six cows back to join the main herd. When that was done, Holt surprised L.C. and Cody with an announcement that he was going to take advantage of the creek. "I brought some soap and a towel and I'm gonna jump in the creek and give myself a good scrubbing."

"Well, I suppose that's a good idea after playin' in the mud with the cows," Cody said, "but don't expect me to jump in the creek with you." He was pretty sure he knew why Holt wanted to scrub himself clean.

"I wasn't gonna ask you to join me in the creek," Holt said. "I much prefer my privacy. You two just ride on in to the ranch. I'll be a little while."

"All right," Cody said. "Right now, I need a cup of coffee more than I need a bath. Come on, L.C., let's head for the barn."

They rode away and left him there by the creek where he sought to take Pansy's advice to him. Cody and L.C. rode in silence for a little while before L.C. could stand it no longer. He had to find out if Cody knew or not. "I swear," he started, "danged if Holt didn't handle it pretty good."

"Handle what?" Cody asked.

"You know, the weddin'," L.C. replied.

"What about the weddin'?"

"I swear," L.C. said, "you really don't know. He's your brother, and he didn't tell you?"

"Tell me what, L.C.?"

"That the weddin' was called off," L.C. said. "They ain't gettin' married tomorrow. And it's because that little gal won't come to the ranch to live."

"Where the hell did you get an idea like that?" Cody demanded. "Of course they're gettin' married tomorrow."

"It ain't my idea. Everybody back at the house knows it. Hell, Holt told Patch and Shorty, himself. They was workin' in the barn when he came to get his saddle. Sully's the one who told me about it."

"That's crazy talk," Cody said. "If there was any truth in it at all, don't you think he woulda told me about it when we were back there with the cattle?"

"I don't know. Sully told me Holt was takin' it pretty hard and he didn't wanna talk about it to anybody."

"That's crazy talk," Cody repeated. He pressed his heels for a little more speed and Storm responded with a comfortable lope.

When they reached the ranch house, Cody found out that L.C. was right. Everybody knew about the cancelation of the wedding and Cody's response to each question he was asked about it was, "Don't you believe it."

It was much later when Holt finally showed up at the barn and unsaddled his horse. He found it curious that most of the men were waiting around outside the cookshack. And he sensed an undercurrent of conversation as they all seemed to be watching his every move. "What the hell's goin' on?" he finally demanded.

Frank Strom, being one of the older men, volunteered to speak on behalf of the crew. "Holt," he said. "I just want you to know all the men are behind you in your time of grief. We know it had to hit you pretty hard."

At once thinking his father may have died, he panicked, "What happened? Is it my father? Where's Morgan?" He started to run for the house, but Frank grabbed his arm to stop him.

"Your father's all right. We're talkin' about them callin' your weddin' off. Shorty and Patch told us what you said in the barn today."

Holt couldn't believe it. He looked around the group until he located the two. Closing his eyes and releasing a weary sigh, he said, "There'll be a weddin' tomorrow, boys." He shook his head then and walked off toward the house.

CHAPTER 21

Because the post office was open six days a week, the wedding was scheduled to be held at two o'clock on Sunday afternoon at the Methodist Church. That gave the guests time to attend Reverend Talbot's Sunday service with plenty of time for dinner at the hotel dining room before returning to the church for the wedding. After the wedding, the Hunters and a few of the Lawrences' close friends, as well as the newlyweds would go to the Lawrences' home for a brief reception before the newlyweds returned to the Triple-H. The Hunter party would have preferred to go back to the ranch as soon as the couple was pronounced man and wife. But John and Norma Lawrence were insistent upon keeping the schedule they had prepared for the whole wedding. "Hell," Duncan Hunter swore, "I don't see why we have to go to that thing at their house. After Holt and Spring are married, they can go where they want, and we oughta go back home so our folks can celebrate a little."

A couple of the men hitched a team of horses up to the wagon and another horse to the buggy, which had to be cleaned up and checked out to make sure it was in good running condition. It had been a good while since anyone had driven it. A little before noon, Johnny Becker and

Chris Scott drove the wagon and the buggy up to the front porch of the house and tied them to the porch posts. The wedding party got up from the table and filed out the front door. Pansy stepped in front of Holt to inspect him before he followed the others outside to the porch. She straightened his collar and took a step backward to look at him at arm's length. "You look just fine," she said. "You did a good job with your bath. I think she'll be mighty pleased." She stepped aside then and smiled proudly. "We'll see you tonight."

"Thanks, Pansy, I appreciate your help." He followed the others out the door.

They loaded up the wagon and the two-seater buggy. Holt insisted on driving the wagon into town so Morgan and Edna could drive the buggy in. Then after the wedding, Holt and Spring would drive home in the buggy and Morgan and Edna could take the wagon. "Well, that's a helluva note," Duncan protested. "I have to ride in the wagon both ways."

"Well, I reckon you and Spring could ride back in the buggy," Holt joked, "and Edna, Morgan, and I can come back in the wagon."

"Suits me," Duncan said, and they all laughed.

As they untied the horses from the porch posts, Cody rode up to see them off. "Good luck, Holt," he said. "I hope you don't get into town and find out she's called off the weddin' again."

Holt chuckled and replied, "When she sees me all cleaned up after that bath I took in the creek last night, there ain't a chance she'll back out."

"You mighta made a big mistake takin' that bath," Cody said. "She might want you to take one every day now."

"Then I'll be the one callin' it off this time," Holt said and popped the reins over the horses' rumps and followed the buggy toward the front gate. Cody rode along beside them until they reached the gate. Then he reined Storm to a halt and remained there watching them for a few minutes before turning back to the barn. It occurred to him that he was the only Hunter left on the Hunter ranch. It struck him at once that he didn't like the feeling.

It was a very pleasant afternoon for the usual two-hour ride to town, and Edna commented to Morgan that it was a good sign for Holt and Spring's wedding. Morgan reached into his pocket and pulled out his watch. "Yep," he said, "and it looks like we're gonna get to the church in plenty of time for the ceremony." They rolled into town to find it typically dead for a Sunday afternoon. The only sign of activity were the few horses tied at the hitching rails in front of the Valley Tavern and Bannerman's Saloon down the street.

As they passed in front of the Valley Tavern, Edna couldn't resist saying, "It's too bad we've got to go straight to the church. I imagine you'd like to stop in and say hello to Minnie Mills while we're in town."

"Oh, is that her name?" Morgan responded.

"Like you don't know," Edna came back. "And every time you come to town for supplies, you have to eat dinner at the Village Tavern. Minnie Mills, best cook in the valley, right?"

Damn, he thought, *I'm going to have to learn to keep my mouth shut.* "I reckon she's a fair cook when you're talking about a saloon cook. I ain't ate in all the other saloons in the valley, so I can't say if she's the best in the valley or not."

They arrived at the church a little before two o'clock to find the Lawrences already there, so they drove the horses around to the back of the church where a couple of buggies were parked. Then they walked back around to the front door. Just inside the door, they were greeted by John and Norma Lawrence who were talking to three couples who were close friends of theirs. Holt saw Spring sitting on a bench against the opposite wall, so he went straight over to her, instead of waiting for John and Norma to introduce him to their friends. "Hey, good-lookin', you still wanna do this thing?"

"I'm here, aren't I?" she answered. "I wasn't sure you'd show up." She paused then and looked toward her parents who were frantically signaling her. She understood then. "They want you to take off your gun before you go into the church."

"Oh, I didn't think about that. Where can I put it?" He looked around with no intention of taking it outside and leaving it in the wagon. Then he saw a big flowerpot just inside the door with a large plant of some kind in it. So he unbuckled his gun belt and quickly walked over and pushed it down in the pot, only to find another gun belt in it. Surprised, he looked back at the door where Morgan and Edna were talking to the Lawrences' friends and saw Morgan watching him. When he caught Morgan's eye, Morgan just gave him a big shrug of his shoulders and a guilty smile. So he dropped his gun on top of his brother's. No sooner had he gotten rid of his weapon than the Reverend Talbot came into the church through a door in the back.

"If everybody's here," Reverend Talbot said, "we might as well get these two young folks married." Evidently in as much a hurry to get it over with as the bride and groom, he starting giving directions to everyone. When he had everyone seated and John Lawrence ready to walk his daughter down the aisle, he said, "All right, we're ready. When my wife starts playing the organ, you can walk your lovely daughter down to join the groom." When Duncan came down to stand as Holt's best man, the preacher joked, "Which one's the groom?"

Just as quickly, Duncan replied, "Let her pick."

Talbot responded with a hearty chuckle and looked over at his wife sitting at the organ. "All right, Grace," he said, and she immediately aggravated the organ to howl the wedding march. Taking her father's arm, Spring walked down the aisle while her mother sobbed. When they reached the altar, her father stepped back, and Holt took her hand. Reverend Talbot went through the ceremony very quickly. Past the "I do's," he pronounced them man and wife. "You may now kiss the bride," Talbot finished. Grace abused the organ again, and the small group in attendance applauded. Holt and Spring headed for the front door. Before they reached it, however, they were stopped by a large man wearing a bandanna over his face and holding two six-guns aimed at them.

At the other end of the church, a second masked man came in behind the preacher. He yelled at Grace Talbot, "Shut up that damn noise! And get over here with the rest of 'em. You!" he yelled at John Lawrence. "Pick up that collection plate and put it on that table there. Now, me and my partner wanna see you empty every damn cent you've got into that plate. The first one that tries to hide his money gets shot. Lem, bring them two lovebirds over with the rest of 'em. I know they's wantin' to donate."

"Where the hell you think you're goin'?" Lem blurted at Holt, who had been slowly backing Spring and himself closer to the wall by the door, his hands behind his back.

"Just tryin' to stay outta the way," Holt said when he felt his hand on the flowerpot. "I don't wanna cause no trouble." He dropped his hand in the flowerpot, grasping for anything until he felt the handle of his six-gun.

The man his partner called Lem cast an evil eye upon Spring, who was trembling uncontrollably. When his partner repeated for him to bring the bride and groom over with the rest of them, Lem said, "In a minute. I'm gonna kiss the bride." He scoffed at Holt. "Ain't that right, Bud? How 'bout I give your bride a little kiss?"

"How 'bout you kiss my ass, instead," Holt replied and whipped his hand out from behind him to pump a shot into Lem's midsection just below his ribcage. He stepped in front of Spring to protect her from the shot he expected from Lem's partner while he cocked his six-gun again. But Lem's partner was startled by Holt's shot. So much so that his shot went through the ceiling when Morgan slammed into him, forcing his arm straight up. They went to the floor with Morgan on top, still forcing his arm straight up until Duncan wrestled the gun out of his hand. Duncan took the gun then and used it to give the robber a blow beside his head that ended his struggles. Up at the front of the church, Lem was sitting on the floor in a stupor as he held his hand over the hole just below his breastbone. Holt had picked up both of Lem's guns when he dropped them on the floor. With both robbers incapacitated, Holt went outside the church where he found two horses tied up to the wagon. He grabbed a coil of rope from each saddle and went back inside where they tied the one robber hand and foot but couldn't decide if it was necessary to tie Lem or not.

"I'll go see if I can find the town marshal," Holt said. "He mighta heard the two shots but didn't think they coulda come from the church." So he went in search of Tom Gordon and found him coming out of Bannerman's Saloon. "Marshal Gordon," Holt called out, "I reckon you heard the two shots."

"Holt Hunter," the marshal replied, looking somewhat amazed. "I shoulda known they were a signal that you were in town. What is it this time?"

"It wasn't nothin' that we were in town for. We've got

a couple of robbers at the church that we need to turn over to you. We're just in town for a wedding and these two fellows tried to rob everybody at the wedding. One of 'em's tied up, the other one's shot, and I don't know if he needs a doctor or an undertaker. Preacher Talbot and his wife can tell you exactly what happened."

"Who got married?" Gordon asked.

"I did," Holt answered.

"Congratulations," the marshal said, "maybe you won't be comin' to town that much anymore."

They walked back to the church where they found the two captives just as Holt had left them, although Lem's partner was beginning to make some motions of coming consciousness. The marshal jerked the bandannas off their faces. "Lemuel Packer and Dwayne Goodman," he said. "Lemuel don't look too good. I expect this is the first time he's ever gone to church on a Sunday." Addressing the wounded man directly then, Gordon asked, "How bad are you hurt? Are you gonna make it?" Lem didn't answer but continued sitting in an upright position on the floor, as if afraid if he laid down flat he might never get up again. "I reckon I'll have to root Dr. Taylor out to take a look at him, and that ain't easy on a Sunday." He looked over at the wedding guests now gathered together around the preacher, obviously horrified. "I expect it'll be easy to remember this weddin', won't it folks? I'm gonna have to get some help movin' these two down to the jail, and my deputy's outta town today."

"We'll help you get 'em outta here," Morgan said. "We can load 'em in the back of the wagon and haul 'em down there."

"I was fixin' to ask you if I could use your wagon. 'Preciate it. Gimme a hand, and we'll throw Dwayne in first." Morgan took the securely bound man by the shoulders and Holt grabbed his feet. They picked him up and carried him out to the wagon while the marshal held the door open for them. Lemuel and Dwayne's horses were already tied to the back of the wagon, so they just left them tied. Transporting Lemuel required more help, since he appeared to be stuck in the sitting position. It took the additional help of the postmaster and the husband of one of the couples who came to witness the Lawrences' daughter's wedding to help Morgan and Holt lift Lemuel without changing his position. They laid him on his side in the wagon. "'Preciate your help," the marshal said again as he watched the transfer.

Ready to leave the church then, Edna and Spring didn't want to go to the jail with the prisoners, so they accepted an invitation to ride with the other guests to the reception at the Lawrences' home. Marshal Gordon walked along beside the wagon for the short trip to the jail. When they got there, he unlocked the door, and since they needed help to carry Lemuel into the cell room, he decided to untie Dwayne so he could help. "I expect I'd best keep you covered in case you take a crazy notion to run," Gordon said. He drew his gun then and stepped back. Dwayne helped the three Hunter men struggle with the reluctant Lemuel. With Duncan and Dwayne holding Lemuel's feet and Holt and Morgan at his shoulders, they managed to get him inside on a cot. Lemuel's constantly blinking eyes were the only sign that he was alive. And he maintained his sitting position, deathly afraid if he straightened out flat, he might pass away.

Outside, Morgan and Holt untied the reins of the two robbers' horses from the wagon and retied them at the hitching rail. "I expect we'd better get goin' before he comes out and sends us to the stable with their horses," Holt suggested as he climbed in the buggy. "Then he can take a rest after all the work he did." Gordon stepped out the door just as they turned to go back up the street.

"Thanks again, boys. 'Preciate the help," he called after them. They waved back. "Dang," he mumbled, "they coulda took these horses to the stable. Now, I gotta go find Doc."

When they reached the upper part of the street, Holt pulled up beside them. "One thing you have to say about Marshal Gordon," he said, "he don't mind jumpin' right in and doin' the hard work."

"That's a sure enough fact," Morgan replied. "Well, we've got one more job to do before we can go home. You ready to go to the reception at the Lawrences' house?"

"I say to hell with that," Duncan objected. "We got done what we came to do. Holt and Spring are married. We don't have to go and socialize with 'em if we don't want to. Let's just go home."

Morgan and Holt exchanged a look of astonishment. "Holt and I kinda wanted to go to the reception," Morgan said to their father.

"What in the world for?" Duncan responded. "I guarantee you, you'll enjoy whatever Pansy's cooked up for supper."

"We'd both kinda like to bring our wives back with us," Morgan said.

"Oh, right," Duncan confessed, "I reckon I forgot about that." He chuckled, then said, "Just wait till you boys get to be my age."

Holt smacked the gray on its rump with the reins and the buggy led off to the postmaster's house. When they arrived at the house, they pulled up in the yard and started toward the house. Spring heard them arrive and went out the door to meet them. No longer concerned about appearances, she went straight to greet Holt and threw her arms around his neck, almost backing him off the porch. "Let's get in that buggy and go home right now," she whispered in his ear.

"You're the second one who's wanted to skip the party

here after our wedding," he said, thinking of his father. "And now, I reckon I make number three." He planted a big kiss on her then, which she returned with equal enthusiasm. When they finally broke to take a breath, he said, "Maybe we'd better go inside before somebody comes out here to throw a bucket of cold water on us." She gave him a great big smile as she backed away. Still holding his hand, she led him inside the house where he was met with faces still reflecting the wedding ceremony. They looked to be faces of people who had been witnesses to a barn burning instead of a wedding.

John Lawrence was troubled with doubts about his son-in-law after his performance at the church. On the day Holt came to the post office to propose to Spring, he not only prevented a robbery of the mail, but he put two men out of action when they attempted to kidnap his daughter. After that performance, he was impressed with Holt's ability to defend his daughter against all threats. But in the church today, he looked almost casual when he pulled a gun and shot a man. It was enough to make Lawrence wonder if he lived a life of violence, and he confided that thought to his wife on the way home from the church. Norma's answer was brief. "Really, John, had you rather had him let that man put his hands on Spring?"

The Hunter family stayed only long enough at the house to be polite until Edna gave the signal that it was all right to take their leave. Then they said their farewells and Holt and Morgan loaded all Spring's belongings into the wagon while Spring was saying a tearful goodbye to her father and mother. Away at last, they made one stop to water the horses before arriving at the Triple-H. Pansy was in the process of preparing a tremendous supper for the wedding party. Almost all the cowhands went up to the front of the main house when word got out that the buggy and the wagon were sighted. Pansy had taken a part of her day to bake two huge cakes in honor of the occasion, which she took to the cookshack for the ranch hands. Consequently, they gave Holt and his bride a rousing cheer when they pulled up in the buggy. Then for the hell of it, they gave Morgan and Edna a cheer as well when Morgan helped her down from the wagon. There was plenty of help unloading Spring's belongings onto the porch and volunteers to take care of the horses, wagon, and buggy. Spring was overjoyed to feel so welcomed. Holt thanked them all for the reception and when he was asked how the wedding ceremony went, he answered that it was just another routine wedding ceremony. Edna looked straight up in the sky, threw her hands up in a gesture of surrender, turned around, and went into the house. "Main thing is, we got back in time for supper," Holt said, "so we better get to it before Pansy throws a fit." He picked up a couple of Spring's suitcases and followed her inside. She hurried down the hallway, anxious to see their living quarters since it had been finished. "Hold on," Holt called after her. "Wait right there." She stopped and when he caught up, he put her suitcases down and opened the door. Then he picked her up and carried her across the threshold. "It's official now," he said.

CHAPTER 22

"Howdy, Mr. Kincaid," Jeffrey Murphy greeted Ralph when he walked into the telegraph office in Stevensville. "That wire you've been expecting came in yesterday." He went over to a series of boxes on the wall, reached into one of them, and looked through a small stack. "Here we are. Wire's from V. Roach, Bozeman, Montana." He handed it to Ralph and walked over to stand by his desk while Ralph opened it. The gesture was intended to give him privacy to read his message, as if he didn't know what it said. *I accept,* the simple message said, *start today.* Ralph didn't say anything more, turned around, and walked out of the office. "Sociable son of a gun," Jeffrey mumbled.

Ralph was not concerned with being sociable that day. He had the word from Vargas Roach, he was on his way. He decided that called for a little celebration in the form of a drink of whiskey, something he rarely did on a trip to town. He decided that the people in Bannerman's Saloon were less likely to know who he was, so he went there. It was still early in the day, but there were a couple of card games going on. The two tables were relatively close to each other so there was talk going back and forth between the two. "Can I help ya?" Benny, the bartender, asked.

"I'll take a bottle of rye whiskey, if you've got one that

ain't got the seal broken, and a glass," Ralph said. He intended to sit down at a table and have a couple of drinks. Then he'd have another with Emmett when he got back to the Double-K.

Benny got a new bottle from under the counter and showed it to him so he could see that the seal wasn't broken. He placed it on the counter then and placed a glass beside it. "Ain't seen you in here before," he said when Ralph paid him.

"That's right, you ain't," Ralph replied and turned away from the bar and went over and sat down at a small table. He poured himself a drink and thought, *Here's to the first step in taking over all the cattle business in the Bitterroot Valley.* Then he tossed it back and paused to enjoy the burn before he poured his second shot. The talk at the two card tables suddenly got louder.

"Hell, yes," Ralph heard one of them say. "Lem Packer's dead. He died in the jail last night from a gunshot in his gut. Him and Dwayne Goodman tried to hold up the church and Dwayne's still in the jail." Ralph couldn't hear the other man's question but he heard the first man's answer. "You ain't heard about that? They had a weddin' Sunday. One of the Hunter brothers married the postmaster's daughter, and it turned out to be a real bang-up weddin'. Dwayne and Lem tried to hold up the whole weddin' party and the groom shot Lem in the gut. And the old man and the other brother took Dwayne down and tied him up."

Well, I'll be damned, Ralph thought, *I reckon I'll drink this next one to the bride and groom and hope the bride's gonna like being a widow real soon.* After downing the second drink, he picked up his bottle and headed for the door, looking forward to telling Emmett all the news he had learned in town.

He started figuring in his head, trying to estimate the

time it would take Roach to get there. "He sent that wire yesterday," he started, then stopped when he realized that he had no idea how far Bozeman was from Stevensville. Over two hundred miles maybe," he thought. . Six days or maybe more, but that gives Emmett time to take a ride over to Missoula to Gallagher's to look for some more men. He scowled then, irritated by the fact that he had to let his brother make contact with the type of men they sought to hire. All due to the fact that it was difficult for any roughneck outlaw to take him seriously because of his withered arm. He would like to go with Emmett when he goes to Gallagher's, but they could not take the chance to leave the ranch in the hands of the idiots they were left with. He let those frustrations eat away at him for a while before he brought his mind back to the plan for the taking over of the Triple-H. It might seem unnecessary to pay Vargas Roach's price for killing a man, but Cody Hunter was no ordinary man. And Ralph and Emmett were convinced now that Cody Hunter was in fact the killer they had dubbed "the Injun." But Vargas Roach was as much an Injun as Cody Hunter was. He was as much at home in the wilds of the mountains as any Indian born. Ralph was convinced that the outbreak of war between the two ranches would immediately send Cody Hunter back to his role as the Injun. And he would disappear into the mountains again. So with the thought that "It takes one to catch one," this is where the real value of Vargas Roach would be appreciated.

Roach was too expensive, so that was why their plan called for the final settling up with him to be a bullet in the back. Although Roach had a reputation for never discussing who he might be working for, there was no need to risk his admission that he worked for the Double-K. These were the thoughts Ralph was still thinking through when he rode back into the ranch that afternoon. He looked for

Emmett immediately to tell him about the telegraph that came from Vargas Roach. "Roach is on his way," he told his brother. "So you need to get on over to Gallagher's and see if there are any prospects for some new men."

"How much time have we got before he'll get here?" Emmett asked.

"I don't know exactly," Ralph told him. "He was in Bozeman yesterday, and I ain't exactly sure how far away that is, but I'd guess less than a week. So why don't you make sure you're back here in a week."

"I reckon I could do that," Emmett said, thinking about the days he would be enjoying the time spent at Gallagher's hog ranch. "You'll have to take charge of the men, though. I'll tell you what, I'll put Sam Kilbourne in charge. He's older than most of the men, and he's got a little more sense than all of 'em put together."

"That sounds like a good idea," Ralph said. "And tell him he needs to report to me every day so I'll know what's goin' on."

"I'll tell him that," Emmett said.

"I found out one more thing while I was in town," Ralph said. "So I stopped in the saloon and bought this." He reached into his saddlebag and pulled out the bottle of whiskey. "I thought we might want to drink a toast to Mr. and Mrs. Holt Hunter. They got married Sunday."

"Is that a fact?" Emmett responded. "Well, I hope she's gonna be an awful young widow."

"They started off with a bang," Ralph said, then told him the accounting of the wedding that he had overheard someone in the saloon telling someone else.

Emmett was thoroughly entertained by the story. "Let's go to the house and have that drink," he said as Jimmy Todd came to take Ralph's horse to the barn.

"You got back in plenty of time for supper," Sadie

Springer said when they walked in the kitchen door. "It ain't gonna be ready for another half hour yet."

"That's all right," Ralph said. "We're gonna take a little drink of likker first."

"Is that so?" Sadie asked. "What are we celebratin'?"

"Holt Hunter married the postmaster's daughter," Ralph replied.

"Well, in that case, I think we all oughta have a drink," Sadie said and got three glasses out of the dish cabinet. "How come we weren't invited?"

"It sounded like your kind of weddin'," Emmett said. "Tell her about it, Ralph."

Ralph repeated the story and when he was finished, she said, "I swear, I'da give anything if I coulda been at that weddin'. That's the kind of weddin' you'll always remember." They continued hitting the bottle with Sadie doing the pouring until it was empty. "Now, you two have took up enough of my time. Get outta here and let me finish makin' supper."

Vargas Roach rode into the settlement of Butte, hoping to find some place to buy something to eat along with a drink of whiskey. The only place that looked as if it might be able to satisfy his needs was a saloon called the Silver Dollar. The sign advertised food and drink. So he tied his horses at the hitching rail with several others. He drew his Winchester 73 from his saddle sling and went inside, pausing there at the door to look the room over. Then he walked over to stand in front of the bartender, who seemed oblivious to his presence until he spoke. "Excuse me, sir, can I get something to eat and a drink of whiskey here?"

The bartender tilted his head to one side as if evaluating the mild little man dressed in a well-worn buckskin shirt that covered his woolen trousers almost all the way down to the tops of his boots. On his head, he wore a hat often worn by pilgrims. On his face, he wore a short black beard. The bartender, Henry Cripps, having already formed an opinion of the little man, answered his question. "You can get a drink and some dinner here if you've got the money to pay for it. We don't give no handouts." He expected he might try to sell him the rifle he had acquired from somewhere.

"Very well," Roach said. "How much do you charge?"

Surprised that he asked the price, Henry said, "Two bits for the dinner, two bits for the shot of whiskey, and five cents for the coffee."

"I think I can make that," Roach said and dug inside his heavy buckskin shirt to fetch his purse. He fished around inside the purse, picking out the exact change, which he laid on the bar.

Henry raked the change off the bar and dropped it in the till, thinking that maybe he might have taken the man's last cent. "Just set yourself down at one of the tables in the back and I'll go tell the cook." Roach didn't move, so Henry poured his whiskey and put it on the bar. Roach took it then and walked to the back of the room to sit down. He picked a table closest to the kitchen door and propped his rifle against the wall behind him.

In a few minutes, a sweating, heavy-set woman came out of the kitchen carrying a plate of food and a cup of coffee. "You the one ordered dinner?" she asked, although there was no one else in the back of the room.

"Yes, ma'am, I am," he answered politely. She put the plate down in front of him and set the cup down hard enough to spill part of it on the table. Making no effort to apologize or take the rag from her apron to wipe some of the coffee off the table, she did an about-face and returned to the kitchen.

"Damned if he ain't somethin'," Bill Yates said to his friend, Gus White.

"Who?" Gus asked, having been watching Margie Day working a customer at a table across the room.

"That little mouse that just sat down back by the kitchen," Yates said. "He looks like he mighta crawled out from under a log."

"Yeah, I reckon so," Gus said. "But I've got my eye on somethin' else I'd a whole lot druther look at than a mouse." Like Roach, the two drifters were just passing through Butte on their way to nowhere in particular. They had already decided that the little settlement had nothing to offer them

Yates continued to stare at Roach, who was busy eating the dinner he had just been served. "He's goin' after that damn hash that woman cooked up like he ain't ate in a coon's age." He noticed something else then. "Look propped up against the wall behind him, Gus. That looks like a Winchester rifle. I wonder where that little mouse stole that rifle. He don't look like he knows what to do with a rifle like that. You know he must have stole it from somewhere. And he brought it in here to keep somebody from stealin' it from him."

Taking an interest in the odd-looking little man at that point, himself, Gus stared hard at Roach, watching as Rena came from the kitchen with the coffeepot. She went at first to a couple of men eating at another table to fill their cups. As an afterthought, she stopped on her way back to the kitchen to take a look at Roach's cup. "You want more?" she asked when she saw that he hadn't drank more than a sip or two since she first poured it. "Somethin' wrong with it?"

"No, ma'am," he was quick to respond. "I was just lettin' it cool off a little bit so's I don't burn my lip."

"Want me to blow on it for you?" she asked sarcastically.

"Oh, no, ma'am," he replied, "but thank you, anyway." She went back to the kitchen.

Impatient to move on, since the town didn't seem to offer any opportunity for an easy score, Gus said, "Come on, let's get to hell outta this town."

"Just hold on a minute," Yates told him. "We mighta been handed an easy payday here. I wonder where he got that rifle, and I wonder what else that little mouse has got. I'd like to take a look and relieve him of some of it."

Gus shrugged. "What the hell, you may be right. We might as well see if he's collected anything else. Right now, the little pimple looks like he's doin' better than we are, and that's a fact."

They decided to have one more shot of whiskey and wait the little man out at the table, so Yates walked up to the bar and paid Henry for two more shots and carried them back over to the table. Roach took his time finishing his dinner. When he was through, his plate cleaned and his cup emptied, he got up from the table and walked out of the saloon. Gus and Bill got up from their table as soon as Roach went out the front door. When they got to the door, however, they stopped to watch Roach replace the Winchester in his saddle scabbard. "Look at that," Yates whispered, "two packhorses and they're both loaded down. There ain't no tellin' what he's packin'. We damn-sure need to take a look in them packs." They waited until Roach climbed on his horse and started out the north end of town. "Good," Bill Yates declared, "he's passin' right on outta town. The farther, the better."

They both agreed that it was best to be patient in doing what they were planning to do. If they tried to catch up with him right away, he might scare too easily and try to make a run for it. And that would make it pretty hard to explain why they chased after him. The best way, and by far the easiest to accomplish what they wanted, was to remain out of sight and tail him until he stopped to rest his horses. Then they could just join him while they rested theirs. And judging by his appearance, he was not likely to put up much of a fight to resist their inspection of his packs. So with that in mind, they climbed on their horses and rode up to the north end of the street where they stopped to make sure he had continued on the road toward Deer Lodge. It appeared to be a sign that everything was going in their favor when it turned out that Roach was heading in the same direction as they were. They wouldn't have to follow him fifteen or twenty miles, then turn around and come back to Butte. So they waited until he was out of sight before they started out after him, satisfied that he would pick the first place to stop to rest his horses.

With only occasional glimpses of him when they would have to drop back to keep from being spotted, they continued on for about twenty miles. They almost passed by him when they came to a wide stream and heard an inquisitive call from one of his horses. Pulling up at once, they looked upstream and down until they sighted a weak line of smoke drifting up through the trees upstream. Yates looked at Gus and smiled as he turned his horse toward the column of smoke. He pulled his horse to a stop when he was about halfway into the camp that Roach was in the process of making. "Hello, the camp!" Yates called out. "We come in peace. Mind if we come in?"

"If you come in peace, you're welcome," Roach called back to him. Yates winked at Gus, and they rode on into a small clearing where they saw the short, chubby-looking man kneeling by the beginnings of a campfire. He was holding the Winchester rifle across his knee.

"We didn't know there was somebody camped in here, so we almost rode right in on you. Me and my partner have camped here before because it's about the right distance from Butte to rest the horses. But if it cramps you a little bit, we can keep going a little farther till we get to some more water."

"There's no need for you to do that," Roach told him. "I've got no right to hog the whole stream. You can go upstream or downstream, or you can stay right here in this clearin' if you want to. There's plenty of room."

"Are you sure we won't bother you?" Gus asked. "The way you're holdin' that rifle across your knee, it looks like you'd druther not have us make camp here."

"Oh, I'm sorry about that," Roach said. "It's not loaded. I was gonna clean it and load it after I got my fire started good. But when I heard your horses coming through the bushes, I picked it up so it would look like I was ready in case it was somebody bad comin' in."

"Well, that was a good one 'cause it sure fooled me. How 'bout you, Bill?" Gus asked and they both chuckled. They both climbed down from their saddles then. Roach remained kneeling by the fire.

"That's a nice lookin' Winchester. Ain't that a 73?" Yates asked.

"Yes, sir," Roach answered. "It sure is, and it's just like new."

"How'd you happen to come by it?" Gus asked.

"I got it from a fellow who didn't have any use for it anymore," Roach said. They didn't ask why the fellow didn't need it anymore, and Roach didn't volunteer the reason. "I saw you two fellows back in Butte," Roach said then, "in the Silver Dollar saloon."

"You did?" Yates replied. "Well, I'll be . . . You was in the Silver Dollar?"

"Is there some reason you're following me?" Roach asked.

"Why, of course not," Yates responded at once. "He thinks we was followin' him, Gus. Why would we be following you?"

"I don't know, other than your interest in this Winchester rifle," Roach said, "and maybe you might think there are other things of interest in my packs. So I'll just save you some time and tell you there's nothing you two would be interested in in my packs. Even if there was, I wouldn't give them to you. So maybe the best thing for you two would be to go on and find you another place to camp tonight. What do you think?"

"I'll tell you what I think," Yates said, surprised by the little man's sudden change of attitude. "I think you're too damn dumb to know there ain't nothin' keeping us from shootin' you down right now if we take a notion." He drew his six-gun and leveled it at Roach, who was still kneeling by the fire. Gus drew his pistol as well and held it on Roach. "Now," Yates said, "hand me that fancy Winchester." Making no show of resistance, Roach lifted the rifle off his thigh, using one hand around the trigger guard and extended it up for Yates to take. When Yates reached for it, the rifle went off, striking him in the face and dropping him to the ground instantly. Stunned, Gus could not react fast enough to beat the shot that came out of the broken tree branch lying next to Roach's boot and triggered by his left hand. He staggered backward several steps before he collapsed.

Roach pulled the two-shot Derringer out from under the tree branch and put it in his pocket. Then he picked up the tree branch and held it up to look at it before he threw it on the fire. He was pleased with the results of his trap for the two would-be murderers. "The world is better off without these two worthless gunmen," he said for the benefit of his horses. "One was killed by an empty gun, the other by a tree branch." He got up on his feet then and walked over to check on Gus, who was lying in agony, knowing he was dying from the bullet in his heart. "I won't bother to check on your partner," Roach said to the dying man. "That .45

went right through his head. So he's already on his way to hell. Would you like it if I speeded you up a little so you can catch him? Or do you want to live as long as you can? Makes no difference to me. I'd be glad to help you." Gus was unable to speak as he fought for every breath. "Can't make up your mind, right? I think you'd be better off to go ahead and try to catch your partner." He pinched Gus's nose shut and clamped his other hand tightly over his mouth. Then he held on for what seemed like an extraordinarily long time, Gus's arms flailing, his legs shuffling insanely. "Look at him go," Roach chuckled. "I believe he'll catch up to his partner."

When both corpses were finally still, he used one of the dead men's horses to drag them out of his camp. Killing always made him hungry, whether it was a rabbit, a deer, or a contract killing. But he decided he would take an inventory of the two dead men's belongings first to see if there was anything of value. He didn't expect much, but he hoped to show a profit for his endeavor. They did come with a couple of decent horses with saddles, but there was nothing to brag about when it came to their packhorses. Their weapons were reliable but nothing outstanding, little wonder they were so fascinated by the Winchester 73. And they hadn't even seen the Colt .45 he was wearing under his buckskin shirt.

Next, he opened all of their packs to compare their cooking utensils to his and promptly decided they didn't compare to his own. Spare articles of clothing were of no use to him because they were all too large, so they were discarded along with the cooking utensils. Lastly, he opened the packs containing food supplies and decided the two men were on the verge of starvation. There was some bacon that was still good, so he kept that. But there was nothing to cook with, like flour or saleratus, molasses, sugar, salt. They lived like dogs, he thought. But at least they had coffee. Through with his inventory now, he went to the creek to fill his coffeepot with water and got his coffee working while he cut thick slices of bacon to fry and provide plenty of grease for his fried beans and hard tack.

That night, he slept well. The day had started well and ended even better. He knew that Ralph and Emmett Kincaid were anxious to see him arrive at the Double-K. But there were no towns of any size from where he started out that morning until he reached the town of Missoula. So he decided to take some time to hunt for a deer to supply him with food for that distance. He was making better time so far, anyway, so he could afford to take a day to replenish his fresh meat. He planned to unload his newly acquired horses in Missoula.

CHAPTER 23

Emmett Kincaid rode up to the large two-story building a mile and a half north of the town of Missoula. Built by a man named Dylan Gallagher, back when the army established a fort in the town, it started as a typical hog ranch. Enjoying instant success, it was expected to decline when the army closed the fort down and moved the troops to another station. To the contrary, however, the establishment maintained its success especially as an attraction to the lawless class of the population. "Business must be good," Emmett declared aloud when he noticed the freshly painted sign that boldly introduced itself as Gallagher's Retreat. "Retreat, hell!" Emmett chuckled. "Full speed ahead!" He stepped down from the saddle and tied his horse to the hitching rail, anxious to get started with his primary reasons for being there. Contrary to what he had convinced his brother Ralph, his primary reason for being there was not to hire gunmen. That was secondary. His primary reason had to do with issues that arose because there was no Mrs. Emmett Kincaid, that and a need to get away from Ralph's constant complaining for a spell. In the short time he had to be there, it would be extremely lucky to find a few men willing to risk their necks when the time came.

He crossed the long narrow porch and walked in the front door to the main saloon. It was approaching suppertime and business in the saloon was fairly brisk already. So he paused there just inside the door to look the room over. There were men dressed in cowhand gear as well as clerks and businessmen. He walked up to the bar and said, "Mr. Moon, if I recall."

The bartender searched his face, trying to remember. "Yes, sir, it's been a while since you've been in to see us. What can I pour you?"

"I'll have a double shot of rye to start out with. My name's Emmett Kincaid, and it has been a while."

"Yes, sir, I remember it now, Mr. Kincaid. Glad to see you again." He poured the whiskey. "You gonna be stayin' with us?"

"Not as long as I'd like, unfortunately," Emmett replied, "but I'll need a room for two nights."

"Yes, sir, let me call Thelma over here and she oughta be able to take care of that." Moon put his hand up and waved it back and forth until Thelma Rich noticed it and started immediately toward the bar. "Thelma, you remember Mr. Kincaid. He's gonna need a room for a couple of nights. Can you fix him up?"

"I certainly do remember Mr. Kincaid," Thelma lied. "It's been too long since you've been back to see us. You want to walk upstairs and I'll show you what's available right now?"

"Might as well," Emmett said and tossed back his second shot of whiskey. He left some money on the bar and followed Thelma toward the stairs.

At the top of the stairs, Thelma unlocked a small closet that doubled as a room register and took two keys out of a cabinet. "All the way to the back of the hall," she said as she led the way. She unlocked the doors to the last two rooms and waited while Emmett went in to inspect each room. When he took his pick, she gave him the key to the room and put the other key back in the cabinet. Like everything in this fancy hotel, the room rate was paid in advance, so he gave her four dollars for the two nights. "I hope you enjoy your stay with us," she said. "The dining room will be open for supper in thirty minutes."

"That oughta give me enough time to take my horse around back to the stable," Emmett said. They walked back downstairs and he went out the front door to take his horse to the stable where he paid the attendant in advance, then took his saddlebags back to leave in his room. With all that taken care of, he still had about ten minutes before the dining room opened. So he walked across the barroom and opened the door to the card room. There were three tables in use out of ten available. He didn't expect to see any of the caliber of men he was looking for in there playing cards. He was just curious. The men he was looking for would be hanging around the barroom spending the last few dollars they had on alcohol and a woman. So he walked back over to the end of the bar and bought another shot of whiskey before going to supper.

"Who are those two fellows arguin' down at the other end of the bar?" Emmett asked Moon. "You know 'em?"

"I know one of 'em," Moon said, "the smaller one wearin' the black shirt. His name's Peyton. He's got himself a little reputation goin' as a fast gun. I don't know the big fellow he's arguin' with. He just came in here for the first time today. But I'll tell you one thing, I don't know what they're arguin' about, but if that big fellow don't give up pretty quick, he's liable to find himself outside facing Peyton with a six-gun. It's happened before."

"Is that a fact?" Emmett asked. "Maybe I oughta see if I can save that big fellow's life. You can go tell him to take off, if I get Peyton's attention. All right?" Moon nodded even though he wasn't sure what Emmett was talking about.

He was startled then when Emmett yelled, "Hey, Peyton, get your butt down here. I wanna talk to you!" Peyton was the next to be startled, then he turned at once to see who had the guts to yell at him like that. "Don't just stand there lookin' like a prairie dog. Get down here," Emmett yelled again.

Dumbfounded, Peyton wasn't sure how to react to being ordered around like that. He wasn't sure if he should tell the man to go to hell, or if he should go down to the end of the bar and tell him to go to hell. Emmett stood there watching him and tapping his fingers on the bar impatiently. Finally, Peyton stormed down to the end of the bar to confront him. "Who the hell do you think you are?" he demanded.

"The dining room just opened for supper," Emmett said, ignoring Peyton's question. "Are you gonna eat in there?"

"Hell, no, I ain't gonna eat in there. What do you care? Are you crazy or somethin'?"

"You can't afford to drink whiskey and eat supper, too, right?" Emmett asked.

"Why, you son of a . . ." he started, but Emmett interrupted.

"I'll buy your supper, if you ain't afraid to eat with me," Emmett said.

"I ain't afraid of anythin'," Peyton claimed.

"Well, come on, then. Let's go eat. I'm hungry." Emmett stepped away from the bar, then stopped when Peyton failed to move. "I thought you said you ain't afraid of anything," Emmett said.

"I ain't."

"Then let's eat," Emmett said again and waited until Peyton started walking toward the dining room door. When they walked inside, they were met by the host who took the price of two meals from Emmett, who then picked out the table of his choice.

Peyton, still confused by what was going on, followed him to the table, trying to figure out what Emmett's motive was. There was only one thing that came to his mind and as soon as they sat down, he warned Emmett. "I ain't gonna pass up a free meal in this place. But I'm gonna tell you you're wastin' your time if you're one of them priests from that abbey up in the mountains. You can talk your head off about walkin' the path of righteousness and it ain't gonna do you no good. I'm goin' straight to hell and I'm gonna enjoy it all the way."

"Have you got any steady work somewhere?" Emmett asked.

"Not right now, I ain't, but I expect I could get work if I wanted it."

"Doin' what?" Emmett asked.

"Whatever needed doin', I reckon."

"You ever work cattle?" Emmett asked.

"Some," Peyton answered, "but I didn't care that much for it." He grinned then. "Is that what this is about? Are you tryin' to hire cowhands?"

Emmett paused while a young girl placed their plates before them, then went for their coffee. "My name's Emmett Kincaid. My brother and I own one of the two biggest cattle ranches in the valley. We're short some cowhands but I ain't lookin' for no ordinary cowhand. The cowhands I'm lookin' for are good with a gun and not afraid to use it. For that reason, we pay close to double what a regular cowhand gets. And I'm lookin' for a few more hands because we're fixin' to have a war with that other ranch. There's already been some blood spilled, so there ain't no doubt there's gonna be more. If you're tired of hangin' around here, pickin' fights with sodbusters and store clerks, you might wanna take about a fifty mile ride with me down the Bitterroot Valley." He could see that he had definitely captured Peyton's attention. "You can think about it for a while. I'm gonna stay here tonight and tomorrow night, so if you decide you wanna go back with me, be here for breakfast Wednesday mornin' at six o'clock, ready for a long day's ride."

"I'll sure think about it, Mr. Kincaid. Yes, sir, I sure will," Peyton said. Their conversation downgraded to little more than comments about the food after that. And when they finished eating, they went back to the barroom but Peyton decided to take his leave, saying he was needing a good night's sleep. "I 'preciate the supper," he said upon leaving.

Emmett watched him until he went out the door. *He's gonna give it some heavy thought,* he told himself, *but I think he'll be goin' back with me.* He turned and headed for the door that led to a room behind the saloon, where four musicians were providing the music for those who wanted to dance with the women lolling around on several couches in the back of the room. "Good evenin', ladies," he said when he approached the couch he favored over the others.

There were three women sitting on the couch. Two of them returned his greeting with nothing more than a bored expression. The other one, the plainest of the three, smiled at him and returned his greeting. "Evenin', sweetheart, are you wantin' to dance?" she asked sweetly. "We have to charge you if you do, a dime a dance."

"No, I reckon not," Emmett said. "I ain't much of a dancer. I've got a room upstairs and I'm lookin' for a woman who'd like to come up and visit for a while. Whaddaya charge for that?"

"If you're talkin' about how much for a ride, that's two dollars," she said. "If you're talkin' about all evenin', that's five dollars."

"I was thinkin' about a nice friendly visit till I get ready to go to sleep and that's about eleven o'clock. I'd give you ten dollars for that," he proposed. It was enough to spark an interest in both of the other two women on the couch.

"You know you can pick any of us for that price," one of them said.

"I reckon I'll pick you," he said to the plain one. "What's your name?"

"Ruth Ann," she answered, beaming in response.

"Are you ready to go?" he asked.

"I would like to freshen up first," she said. "Then I'll be right up. What's your room number?"

"I'm in room number four, down at the end of the hall. I'm gonna stop by the bar on my way upstairs to pick up a bottle of whiskey."

Emmett woke up a little later than usual the next morning. He blamed it on the amount of whiskey he had consumed the night before. He also blamed his desperate need for a cup of coffee on the alcohol as well. So he dressed right away and went downstairs to the dining room for breakfast. While he sat at a small table near the back of the room, he thought of Ruth Ann and realized she was so thankful that he picked her instead of her more-attractive competition. This was the reason she had showed up at his room in a new dress, some fresh makeup, and her hair combed. It had been a long time since he had spent any time alone with a woman, so he had purposely picked the plain-looking woman. He figured she would be happy to find it had been too long for him to be too demanding of her. As a consequence, most of the evening was spent in casual drinking and conversation. He confessed that he was really most interested to find out if that part of his life had passed him by. And he admitted that it evidently had and thanked her for the evening they had spent visiting. She was happy that he had taken one short ride and the rest of the evening was taken up with friendly conversation.

Now, his mind was back to what his purpose was supposed to be at Gallagher's. And that was to find men who were not afraid to kill when faced with the opportunity. He would hang around the place to see if there were other prospects to go back with him and Peyton. Tuesday proved to be about as busy as Monday at Gallagher's, but Emmett didn't see any likely prospects to ride for the Double-K until late in the afternoon when a hard-looking rider walked into the saloon and asked Moon the price of supper. Moon told him and the man put his small amount of change on the bar. He divided the price of supper from the change on the bar, then asked the price for a bottle of whiskey. Moon told him that and when he couldn't count out enough change for the bottle, he asked how much for a shot of whiskey. "Two bits," Moon said.

The man counted the rest of his change, then said, "I reckon I'll have three shots after I eat supper."

"You have to pay the fellow in the dinin' room for your supper," Moon told him. "You want your whiskey now?"

"I'll take one shot of whiskey before I eat supper, and take a couple of shots after I eat," the man said.

"Whaddaya gonna do tomorrow?" Emmett asked.

The man looked at him for a few seconds before responding. "Whadda you wanna know for?"

"I just wanna know what you're gonna do tomorrow if you're fixin' to spend every cent you've got tonight," Emmett said. "You gonna quit eatin' tomorrow?"

The stranger looked him up and down before he answered. "I don't know what I'm gonna do tomorrow, old man, but I won't go hungry. It's always easy to find some old fool that ain't as smart as he thinks he is."

"Somebody like me?" Emmett asked. "Maybe I ain't as

old as you think I am. Maybe I'm a little faster than you think I am, too."

The stranger smiled, confident. "We can find out easy enough," the stranger said, still smiling. He pulled his coat tail back to clear his Colt .45 Peacemaker and stepped back away from the bar. Then, keeping his eyes on Emmett, he said to Moon, "You saw that he called me out, right?" Moon didn't answer, not sure that Emmett meant to do that.

Emmett smiled back at the stranger, confident he had judged him correctly. "I ain't callin' you out, I'm invitin' you to supper with me," he said. "You can spend the rest of your money for whiskey."

Like Peyton had been the night before, the stranger was confused by the unexpected supper invitation. "What are you talking about?" He looked at Moon then for an explanation.

"He's serious," Moon said, still thinking Emmett was crazy.

"I want to talk to you about a job you might be interested in," Emmett said. "And like I said, I'll pay for your supper. What have you got to lose?"

"Nothin', I reckon," he said and shrugged. "Let's go eat, then."

"What's your name?" Emmett asked as they walked to the dining room.

"Clute Bledsoe," the stranger said. "What's your'n?"

They went into the dining room and Emmett gave him the same story he had gone through with Peyton the night before. Like Peyton, Clute started out as a ranch hand before he turned to cattle rustling, but he served time in a Kansas prison before he killed a guard and escaped. Unlike Peyton, however, Clute needed no time to think it over. He accepted the job offer on the spot.

"All right, then," Emmett said. "We've got a long ride

tomorrow and I wanna make it in one day. This dinin'
room don't open till six o'clock in the mornin'. I'd like to
get started back much earlier than that, but we need to eat
breakfast before we go. I didn't even bring a packhorse
with me on the trip over here. There's a couple of places
between here and Stevensville where we can get something to eat, and that'll hold us till we get to the Double-K.
So meet me here at the dinin' room at six in the mornin'.
All right?"

"I'll be here," Clute said. "I'm gonna go celebrate my
new job with a drink of whiskey now. I'll invite you to
have one with me, since I've got enough to pay for it."

"I'll take you up on that," Emmett said, so they walked
back to the bar where Clute ordered two shots of whiskey.
Astonished, Moon poured the drinks and took Clute's
money.

Emmett watched Clute go out the front door, satisfied
that he had managed to find two good men who were bound
to help the Double-K's situation. He said goodnight to
Moon and turned toward the stairs to find Ruth Ann waiting
at the foot of the stairs. "Howdy, Ruth Ann," he said when
he approached her. "What kinda day did you have?"

"About like every other day," she said. "If you're goin'
upstairs, I thought I'd come and keep you company for a
little while. You were so generous to pay me for last night,
I figured I owed you some time, if you want company."

"Why, that's mighty thoughtful of you," he said. "I enjoyed your company last night, and I'd like to visit with
you tonight." He took her by the arm and helped her up the
stairs now that she no longer tried to hide her crippled leg
from him.

They enjoyed another casual evening together and
Ruth Ann was disappointed to hear that he would be leaving in the morning with two men he had hired to work at

his ranch. When he was ready to retire for the night, she crawled into the bed beside him, instead of returning to her room. He awoke at five-thirty the next morning to find her still in his bed and still fast asleep. So he made it a point not to wake her while he got dressed and packed his personal items back into his saddlebags. Then he peeled another ten dollar bill off the money roll in his pocket and stuck it in her shoe and slipped quietly out the door. It had not been quite the same as prior experiences with women at hog ranches, and it had served to show him that he might be getting soft. It's time to go to war with Duncan Hunter and take over that ranch before it's too late, he told himself.

Putting the plain little woman out of his mind for good, he went to the stable to get his horse. He found it open, but there was no one inside. So he walked down the stalls until he found the black Morgan gelding and his saddle in one of them. He saddled his horse and rode him around to the front of the saloon where he was pleased to find two saddle horses tied at the rail, each with a packhorse attached. Past the bar, which was not open this early, he saw Peyton and Clute standing by the dining room door. "Mornin'," he said as he walked up to join them.

"Mornin," they both returned simultaneously.

"You two met each other?" Emmett asked. When they said they hadn't, he just introduced them as Peyton and Clute, and they shook hands. "They open the door yet?" He tried the knob and found it still locked. "It's gotta be gettin' close to six." They made no conversation at all for a few minutes before they heard the bolt slide back and Emmett opened the door, startling the woman who unlocked it.

"Gracious sakes," she said, "you boys must be hungry."

"Good mornin'," Emmett said. "We've just got a long way to go, so we're in a hurry to get started."

"Well, set yourself down and we'll get you going," she said and went to get their coffee.

They made short work of the breakfast, especially the first batch of biscuits that came out of the oven, and gulped the last of their coffee, instead of lingering over it. Emmett paid the woman for it, and they were soon in the saddle.

For much of the trip, Emmett alternated the pace of the horses between a fast walk and a gentle lope in an effort to shorten the time it would take to reach the Double-K. Even at that pace, however, they were not going to reach the ranch until well after Tater had thrown any leftover chuck to the hogs. So he decided to stop for supper at the Village Tavern when they reached Stevensville. "I can guarantee you, you'll get a good supper here," Emmett said. And Minnie Mills didn't disappoint.

It was close to nine o'clock when they pulled their weary horses into the barnyard of the Double-K ranch. Some of the crew had already gone to bed and to those still sitting around the cookshack, Emmett introduced Clute and Peyton as two new hands. They pulled the saddles off their horses, turned them out to graze, and took their saddles and their packs in the barn. Then Emmett took them into the bunkhouse so they could pick out a bunk. He introduced them to Tater and told him that they would be riding for the Double-K now. "Tomorrow after breakfast I'll get you set up with what you'll be doin'."

He went up to the house then to tell Ralph he had brought two new men back with him. And he was confident that both of them were good gun hands. "Two men, huh?" Ralph asked. "Not that many hangin' around that hog farm?"

"Nope," Emmett answered. "But, like I said, I think I got two good ones. Even though it took three days and two nights to do it. But, hell, there wasn't anything else to do," he said, thinking of Ruth Ann.

CHAPTER 24

Vargas Roach took a strip of fresh venison from over his campfire and blew on it a couple of times before he took a bite to test it. A little bit longer, he thought, and stuck it back over the fire. While he waited for the deer meat to get a little more done, he walked over to his horse, drinking from the stream, and got Ralph Kincaid's letter out of his saddlebag. On the back of one of the sheets of paper, Kincaid had drawn a map telling him how to get from Stevensville to the Double-K ranch. He took the map back to the fire and sat down to look at it again. When he thought his venison should be done enough, he put his map on the ground beside him. Then he placed a rock on the map to make sure the wind didn't blow it in the fire when he removed the meat from the fire again. Perfect, he thought, when he took a bite of the meat. He studied the simple map while he chewed the hot venison, his main interest now to get a general idea of how much farther he had to go. He estimated a distance of eight or ten miles. He could have pushed his horses on to the ranch, but that would put him there between dinner and supper. And he was hungry, and his horses were tired, so he decided to wait to arrive there closer to suppertime.

The road to the ranch seemed to be fairly easy to

follow. He could see the river just on the other side of the trees the entire way, and the road appeared to follow it. And according to Kincaid's map, the turn off the road onto the trail to the Double-K ranch house would be easy to see. So he finished his dinner of fresh venison while he waited for his horses to rest. And when he was ready, he climbed back into the saddle and continued to follow the road down the valley. He rode for close to an hour before he came to an obviously well-used trail turning off to the east. Half an hour later, he approached the Double-K ranch house and went straight to the front door.

"Who the hell is that?" Otto Ross remarked when he saw the stranger ride up to the house.

"Where?" Earl Mathers asked.

"Yonder," Otto answered. "Look up at the front of the house. Looks like he just crawled outta the woods somewhere, and he's goin' right up to the front door."

"He's liable to get his butt booted right off the porch," Earl said. "Reckon we oughta go up there and see what he wants?"

"Nah," Tater said, having heard their comments. "Sadie will be out there in a minute to boot him right out in the yard."

They continued to watch from the barnyard, but the odd little man was still waiting on the front porch. Growing impatient, he started walking along the front porch, banging on the windows and back to the front door again. "What the hell was that?" Ralph suddenly erupted when they heard what sounded like someone knocking down the door. Having been sitting at the kitchen table, drinking coffee with Sadie, both Ralph and Emmett jumped up and ran out the kitchen door. Emmett pulled his six-gun as they ran up the hallway. Ralph wasn't wearing one. When he realized it, he stepped aside and let Emmett open the door.

They had both seen Vargas Roach, but it had been a

long time ago, so it was a shock to both brothers when they saw the little man standing on the porch. "Vargas?" Ralph questioned, not certain at first.

"In the flesh," Roach said. "I thought for a minute there weren't nobody home."

"Vargas," Emmett said then. "Sorry for ignorin' you but we were back in the kitchen and didn't know you were out here."

"You ain't fixin' to shoot me for bangin' on the house like that are you?" Roach asked.

Emmett looked down at his hand, just then remembering he was still holding the gun. "I forgot I had it out," he said as he quickly put it away. "Come on in the house. I'll call one of the boys up to take care of your horses."

"No need to do that," Roach said at once. "I 'preciate the offer, but I'll take care of my horses. That's what they're used to."

"Well, can we help you carry your things in the house?" Ralph asked.

"Oh, no thanks," Roach replied. "I 'preciate the invitation, but I won't be stayin' in the house. I don't never stay in the house. I stay outside with my horses."

"Whatever you say," Emmett commented. "What about supper? Can we invite you in the house for supper?"

"You sure can," Roach said. "I really enjoy a good meal, cooked by a woman every once in a while. Either one of you boys married?"

Ralph laughed. "No, but we've got a genuine woman cook. Come on back and we'll let her know she's gonna need to cook a little extra for supper tonight. Then we can talk about what we called you way out here for."

They led him into the house, then down the hall to the kitchen. Sadie spun around when she heard them coming down the hall, curious to know the cause of the banging noise. Then she took a step backward when she saw the almost dwarf-like Roach follow them into the kitchen. "Roach, this is Sadie Springer," Ralph said. "Sadie, this is Vargas Roach, he'll be staying for supper."

"Well, I guess I'd best get started on it," Sadie declared. "Tell me, Mr. Roach, do you prefer cornbread or biscuits?"

"Why, thank you ma'am, whichever one you was fixin' to bake. I'm partial to both of 'em," Roach declared.

"We can go into the study now and talk about what our plans are for you now while Sadie is fixin' supper," Ralph said. "You need to look after your horses before we get started?"

"Nope," Roach answered. "They're all right."

As soon as they went into the study, Ralph started, "Vargas, we're about to go to war with another cattle ranch. And we need to have you eliminate the old man and his three sons so we can take it over. But one of them is the most dangerous because he's more like you than his two brothers. He fights like an Indian and he's already killed too many of our men."

"How can I get a look at him, so I know which one to go after first?" Roach asked. "Is there any place where he goes away from his ranch?"

"That is gonna be a problem," Emmett said. "I don't think he ever goes much off that ranch. Maybe he goes to town sometimes. I reckon you'd have to hang around town and hope to get a chance to see him."

"There ain't no tellin' how long that would take," Roach said. "I expect the best thing to do would be for me to just ride on into that ranch and get a look at him. What did you say his name was?"

"Cody," Ralph said, "Cody Hunter, and he ain't one to be took lightly."

"Oh, I never would," Roach assured him. "But I expect I might as well visit that ranch and see if I can't get a look at every one of them Hunter boys and the old man, too.

I don't see no other way to get the job done in a hurry, like you'd want."

Ralph and Emmett exchanged questioning glances, both thinking that Roach would prefer not to be seen by a potential victim. "You're the expert," Ralph said. "So I reckon you'll do it the way you want. We'll show you the shortest way to get to the Triple-H from here."

"Just tell me how to get there after supper and I'll make my camp tonight on your range and ride on into the Triple-H in the mornin'," Roach suggested. With that settled, they went into discussion about the payment for his services to be paid in full as soon as the job was completed. He said he would plan on eliminating the father and the three sons, but he could not guarantee the death of the old man because he might never leave the house, once his sons started dropping. Emmett and Ralph agreed to that because, without the three sons, they didn't think there was anybody capable of knowing what to do. To show their good faith, Ralph asked if he needed an advance on his fee. Roach asked for an advance of only a couple hundred dollars, since he had already had some expenses. Ralph graciously gave him the two hundred, since their plan was to settle with him after the total job was done, and it wouldn't cost them another dime.

When business was all done, they sealed their contract with a drink of whiskey while they waited for Sadie to make supper. When it was ready, she called them into the kitchen to eat. After seeing the unimpressive little man with a mop of shaggy hair hanging from under his battered hat, she was not inclined to go to the trouble to serve supper in the dining room. When the three men filed in to sit at the table, Roach politely removed his hat to expose the top of his shiny hairless head. Sadie turned quickly toward the stove to catch herself from laughing. Then she placed the food bowls on the table as well as a platter with biscuits fresh out of the oven. Roach looked as childlike as a kid at Christmas as he attacked his supper. When he finished he thanked Sadie graciously. "I expect I'd best get about my business now," he said to Ralph, "if you'll just point me in the direction of the Triple-H."

"I'll go down to the cookshack and get one of the boys to saddle a horse and ride out with you to a stream that runs into a creek we call boundary creek," Emmett said, "When you cross that, you're on Hunter range."

"Send Sam Kilbourne," Ralph said, "he's your acting foreman now, ain't he?"

"I'll see if he's back," Emmett replied. "He's been ridin' our boundaries with the two new men, Peyton and Clute." He went out the kitchen door while Ralph went back out to the front yard with Roach.

When he got down to the cookshack, Emmett found some of the crew sitting around outside. "Sam and the new men back yet?" he asked Otto.

"They just got back," Otto said. "They're in the cook-shack eatin'. Who's that little feller in the buckskin shirt?"

"I'll let you go meet him," Emmett said. "Throw a saddle on a horse and ride up to that stream that runs into boundary creek, so he can follow it over to Triple-H range."

"What's he wanna go there for?" Otto asked.

"He's just lost," Emmett told him. "And he's a little bit crazy to boot."

"Well, I'll swear," Otto asked, "he ain't dangerous, is he?"

"No, he's harmless," Emmett said. *As long as nobody's put a contract out on you.* "Just go take him out to that stream, so he can follow it to the boundary." Otto went to saddle a horse and Emmett couldn't help thinking, *Two great minds together. They oughta get along just fine.*

When he got back to the front yard, Emmett found Roach and Ralph admiring Roach's seven-year-old bay

gelding, and Roach was telling him what a fine horse he
was. "He came to me when he was a three-year-old, and
he got to be like family to me. He stands beside me when
I sleep at night and he don't let nobody bother me."

"What's his name?" Ralph asked, not really caring, just
giving the little man something to talk about until Emmett
got back.

"I ain't thought of a good one yet," Roach replied, "and
he deserves a good one."

"Right," Ralph agreed. "And you ain't had him but four
years." He was finding it harder and harder to carry on an
adult conversation with the vicious contract killer. So he
was happy to see Emmett arrive. "Where's Sam?"

"He's still eatin' in the cookshack with Clute and
Peyton. Otto's comin' up. He's saddling a horse right now."
In a few minutes Otto showed up, and Emmett introduced
them while Otto openly gawked at Roach. Roach thanked
Otto for taking him to the stream.

Ralph and Emmett stood there watching as they rode
out the front gate. Then Ralph turned and said to his
brother, "I don't know if that man is sane enough to do
what we hired him to do or not. I'm beginning to think his
line of work has gotten to his mind."

"I don't think we have anything to worry about," Emmett
said. "If he ever says we hired him to kill somebody, anybody can see he's crazy as hell."

Vargas Roach woke early in his camp by the boundary
creek. He revived his campfire from the night before, and
once it was going well he went down to the creek to fill his
coffeepot. With the last of his fresh deer meat gone, he
untied some of the smoked meat from his packs. When
he ate his fill of that, he killed his fire, saddled his horses,
and continued on toward the Triple-H. He was not in any

particular hurry to reach the headquarters of the ranch, so he took his time, figuring he might be more likely to find most of the hands there at dinnertime. So it was a little past high noon when he saw the gathering of buildings come into view. As he had hoped, there appeared to be quite a few hands that had ridden in to eat at the cookshack. He continued on into the barnyard before anybody took notice of the odd-looking little man leading the two packhorses. Then it seemed that everyone saw him at once. It was not an unheard of thing for a drifter to occasionally ride in, looking for a meal. It was unusual for one as odd-looking as Vargas Roach to ride in, however.

"Something we can help you with, partner?" L. C. Pullen walked up to Roach's horse.

"Howdy," Roach said. "I reckon I got myself turned around here a little bit. I weren't expectin' to come up on a cattle ranch here. I thought I was near 'bout to a town called Stevensville that's supposed to be up this way."

"Where did you come from," L.C. asked, "to be headin' north to go to Stevensville?"

"I came up south of this valley from the Beaverhead Mountains, headin' toward Missoula," Roach said.

"Well, you ain't so far off as you thought," Shorty Black said. "Stevensville ain't but a couple hours farther up the valley."

"Dad-blame-it," Roach exclaimed. "I knew I shouldn'ta skipped breakfast this morning, but I figured I'd eat in a regular saloon or something at dinnertime. I hate to wait two more hours. You reckon your cook would sell me some dinner?"

"I don't know, I'll ask him," Shorty said. "Hey, Sully," he yelled then, "feller out here, headin' north, wants to know if you'll sell him some dinner. He's willin' to pay for it."

Sully stuck his head out the door. "What the hell are you talkin' about? What feller?" Then he saw Roach sitting there on his horse. "I don't sell no food to anybody." He figured he'd better say that because one of the owners was sitting in the cookshack eating dinner.

"Tell the man to come on in and you'll give him something to eat."

Sully stuck his head back out the door again. "Cody said to tell him to come on in and we'd feed him."

Roach couldn't believe his luck. He was prepared to go through any amount of questioning to try to get even a clue that might identify Cody Hunter. But instead, it was to be handed to him as a gift. He quickly slid off his horse and dropped his reins on the ground in an effort to get inside the cookshack in a hurry, in case Cody might be leaving. "Boy, he musta been starvin'," Shorty said when Roach disappeared through the door.

Cody was sitting down at the end of the table. He had finished eating but was still enjoying another cup of coffee and talking to Sully. He couldn't suppress a smile when he saw the comical-looking figure of Vargas Roach appear in the doorway. "I hope I'm not drinkin' the last of the coffee in that pot," he said to Sully.

"No, there's more in there," Sully said. "It's gettin' old, but it ain't gone."

Roach didn't say anything at once, but he had a smile matching Cody's. The reason was because he still couldn't believe his luck had been so good. Not only was Cody eating in the cookshack with the men, there was no one else in there with him. So he would not have to determine which one was Cody. He wanted to laugh when he noticed that he was wearing Indian moccasins, instead of boots. And he remembered Emmett and Ralph saying Cody was like a wild Indian. "So, I reckon you must be Cody Hunter," he said. "It's mighty kind of you to share your food with me."

"I'm glad Sully had food left over," Cody said. "I don't

like to see anybody goin' hungry." He watched while Sully dished out a plate of food for Roach. "So, are you goin' into Stevensville when you leave here, or are you headin' straight to Missoula?"

"Oh, I guess I'll head straight to Missoula," Roach said.

"Well, I hope you have a good trip," Cody said as he got up from the table and walked out of the cookshack. "Sully," he said as he went out the door.

"Cody," Sully returned.

As soon as Cody walked out of the cookshack, he spoke briefly with Shorty and L.C., then he hustled over to the barn, picked up his saddle, and threw it on Storm's back. He wasn't sure he wasn't overreacting but he had a strange feeling about the odd-looking little man who just happened to wander into the barnyard. What bothered him was that no one but Sully had said his name, and he only said it once. Yet this stranger, who said he was just passing through said, "I reckon you must be Cody Hunter." And nobody had called the name Hunter. It was enough to make him feel like he had just been identified and now he might be a target. With that in mind, he thought it would be a good idea to tail this little man until he really headed straight toward Missoula.

He led his horse to the barn door and tied him just inside. Then he stood behind the open door where he could watch the man's horse. In a very short time, the little man came out of the cookshack and climbed on his horse. With not a word for anyone, he turned the bay horse toward the front gate and loped out to the wagon road. Cody climbed up in the saddle, rode out of the barn, and guided Storm over beside the cookshack door where he reined the horse to a stop and called, "Sully." When Sully came to the door, Cody asked, "Did that little rooster eat much?"

"No, that son of a gun," Sully replied. "He didn't eat much of anything, just took his fork and messed it up a little. Then he said thanks and walked out. I guess he don't like my cookin' very much."

"Trust me, it ain't your cookin'," Cody said. "He wasn't hungry in the first place." He turned to watch the man ride through the gate, then he turned Storm away from the cookshack and followed him. Cody had no idea what Vargas Roach was going to try to do to ambush him. Vargas surely wouldn't wait for him to ride out the gate sometime. The only thing that made sense would be to scout the ranch and watch for him to ride out to work with some of the men on the range. To do that, he would have to find a place close enough to the barn to see him ride out. And then the shot would be at a distance. Right now, Cody could confirm this plan of execution if he followed Vargas to a place close by and the man made camp there. That would pretty much confirm it in Cody's mind that Vargas was here to kill him and nothing else. And if he succeeded, then which brother was next?

Everything pointed to the accuracy of his thinking. Everything pointed to a paid assassin. The fact that he was a harmless looking little individual had nothing to do with it, for evil came in all sizes. "I'd best not lose him," he decided and pushed Storm into a lope until he reached the gate. He pulled up short then when he got a glimpse of the man turning off the trail only a couple hundred yards ahead of him. Obviously he was planning to circle back through the trees to find a spot where he could see the comings and goings from the barnyard. There was no doubt in Cody's mind now that his suspicion was fact.

Vargas Roach wound his way through the heavy growth of evergreens that covered the slopes of the low ridge that bordered the Triple-H Ranch. It was an ideal place to keep watch on the ranch headquarters. The ridge was close enough to the barn that he could see the men coming and going without the need for his field glass. There was no sign of Cody Hunter, so he figured he must have gone up to the main house for something and he would no doubt show up soon. He would have considered taking the shot when Cody came back to the barn, but at the distance he now stood from the barn, it might be pushing his Winchester's accuracy. And it was important that he got a kill shot. He would earn no money if he only wounded his target. So he would have to content himself to wait for Cody to ride out somewhere, either alone or with a work crew. Then he could work in closer to a more certain range before sending Cody Hunter to hell. After that, he figured the two other brothers would be easier to spot and kill. The old man may not be necessary. He would leave that decision up to the Kincaid brothers. There was nothing to do now but wait for Cody Hunter's reappearance. Then he froze when he heard the voice behind him.

"Lay the rifle down on the ground." Roach hesitated. "Lay the rifle on the ground or I'll shoot you down now."

Realizing he had a chance or he would have already been dead, Roach said, "I'm puttin' it down." He very carefully laid the Winchester down on the ground and started to turn around.

"Don't turn around or you're dead," Cody warned.

"Right!" Roach exclaimed. "I ain't turnin' around. I think you've got the wrong idea. I wasn't here to do you no harm."

"Unbuckle that gun belt and let it drop to the ground," Cody ordered.

"Right," Roach replied, then opened his buckskin shirt and unbuckled his gun belt and let it fall to the ground. "Can I turn around now?"

"Yeah, you can turn around slowly," Cody said.

Roach turned slowly until halfway around and then he spun quickly the rest of the way, his two-shot Derringer in his hand, only to be doubled over by the shot from Cody's rifle. He grimaced with shock and pain as he tried to aim the pocket pistol but was stopped cold when Cody cranked a second shot in his chest. Cody stood looking at the body for a few moments while he reloaded his rifle. "I guess we'd better return you to your owner," he told the corpse. "First let's see if you've got enough to cover your travel expenses." He went through Roach's pockets and found close to two hundred and fifty dollars. He figured the money and his rifle and gun belt was enough to cover the cost of taking him home. Then on second thought, he looked in his saddlebags and discovered the odd little man was carrying twelve-hundred dollars. "Looks can sure as hell be deceiving," he said in surprise. "I'm glad I looked."

He tied Roach's horse to a tree while he struggled to lift the body up into the saddle, fighting to hold it in a sitting position until he tied his feet in the stirrups. Then he tied the rope around his waist and secured that to the saddle horn. The body flopped around, and back and forth when the horse moved, but it remained seated in the saddle. "That was a helluva lotta work," he decided, "but I was well paid for it."

He left Roach's horses tied up at the edge of the trees while he rode back into the barn. Chris Scott was working in the barn, so Cody gave him Roach's weapons and told him to take them and the money to Holt and to tell him that he would not be back until late that night.

"Where are you goin'?" Chris wanted to know. "'Cause you know Holt will ask me."

"Tell him I've got to return some of the Kincaids' property to 'em. I'll explain when I get back."

"Did it have anything to do with those two shots I heard a little while ago?" Chris asked.

"It might have," Cody answered as he rode away. It was going to take a while to ride out to the Double-K and he was in a hurry to get started.

When he left the Triple-H, Cody took the most direct route to his destination that he could, alternating between a walk and a lope to make the best time possible until he got to the line between Triple-H and Double-K. Once he reached Kincaid property he had to avoid being spotted so he was much more cautious. It was beginning to get dark by then, so that helped. And by the time he could see the ranch house in the distance, it was almost twilight. He looped Roach's reins around the saddle horn and gave the horse a slap on the rump. The bay and the packhorses ran for a few yards then stopped. Cody pulled his six-gun and fired a couple of shots up in the air behind the horses and that sent them galloping toward the barn, and Cody galloping in the opposite direction.

CHAPTER 25

"What the hell!" Sam Kilbourne blurted when he heard the gunshots. He jumped up from the wooden box he was sitting on at the same time Willy Vick and Otto Ross ran out of the bunkhouse with their guns drawn. Then they heard the horses charging toward the barn, thinking at first they were under attack until they realized it was one rider and two packhorses. In the dim light, it appeared that the rider was gyrating wildly back and forth and from side to side.

"It's that peculiar feller that was up at the house to see Emmett and Ralph yesterday," Otto said. "Ate supper with 'em. Looks like he's drunk as a fool."

"He ain't drunk," Sam said, "he's dead. Get hold of that horse. I better go get Boss." He hustled up to the house to knock on the kitchen door, knowing that's where Emmett would likely be. When Sadie opened the door, Sam said, "I need to see Boss."

Sadie swung the door open wide so Emmett could see him standing on the top step. Emmett was sitting at the table with Ralph, drinking coffee. "What is it, Sam?"

"Don't wanna bother you, but that little feller that came to see you yesterday just came ridin' up in the yard deader'n hell," Sam said, still standing on the top step, since he hadn't been invited in.

"What?" Emmett and Ralph reacted almost at the same time, both on their feet a second later. They didn't take time to ask any questions but filed past Sam and ran down to the barnyard where Otto was holding the horses.

"This ol' boy got hisself in a real mess, Boss," Otto said when Emmett ran up beside him. "I wonder how he managed to wind up back here again. He's got two bullet holes in him and then whoever done it tied him up so he could set in the saddle."

Emmett and Ralph exchanged meaningful glances. They knew with no doubt who was responsible for sending them the message. Their expert assassin had been delivered back to them like so much meat. Finally, Ralph said, "Get him off the horse." By this time, most of the men were aware of what was going on, so they were all interested spectators. They untied him and laid him on the ground, but they couldn't straighten him out. It made a search of his pockets much more difficult, but Ralph persevered. Finding nothing, he whispered to Emmett, "Two hundred dollars gone, those son of a bitches."

"There ain't no tellin' who he got into it with," Emmett said for the benefit of the men. "Couple of you men carry his body away from here. Bury him or take him for a long ride. I don't care which, long as I can't smell him in the mornin'. Unload those packhorses, turn the horses in with the other horses. The man was crazy, anyway. I don't have any idea why he came to see us. We fed him a good supper and sent him on his way. Didn't expect to see him again."

"Whaddaya reckon them two gunshots were we heard just before that horse came runnin' in here?" Sam asked.

Emmett didn't answer right away, although he knew what it was. It was that damn Injun, he thought. "I don't know," he answered, "I didn't hear any gunshots. Come on, Ralph, tomorrow's a workday." He turned and went back to the house. Ralph followed him.

When they walked back into the house and closed the door behind them, Emmett picked up a kitchen chair and threw it against the wall as hard as he could. Sadie flinched slightly but otherwise showed no emotion. "As bad as that, huh?" He looked at her accusingly.

"It was Vargas Roach, all right," Ralph told her, before Emmett decided to blame her for it. "Evidently, he found Cody Hunter, just like he said he would. Roach had the reputation as the best assassin in the business, but Cody Hunter beat him at his own game. And that left us holding the bag. Roach was the key to our plan. We were counting on him to take out the decision-makers of the Triple-H."

"Will you shut up with that trash?" Emmett interrupted him. "You're talking like you're ready to go to Duncan Hunter and tell him you wanna surrender. The whole valley's yours."

"No, what I'm sayin' is we're going to have to do the key assassinations ourselves, instead of payin' a fortune to a little man who looks like a dwarf to do them," Ralph answered him. "The more I think about it, the more convinced I am that you and I will do a better job of it than Vargas would have."

"Now you're talkin'," Sadie sang out. "There ain't nobody smarter than you two, and you just keep hirin' men to work for you who ain't got a grain of sense."

Emmett started cooling down considerably after hearing Ralph's comments as well as Sadie's. "I reckon we really ain't got much choice anymore, have we? We thought we were striking the first blow in this war. And it ended up with the Hunters gettin' in the first lick. So I reckon it's our turn again. And the most important step is still to take Cody Hunter down. We kill him and we kill half their killin' power. And I don't care what anybody says, when a man gets married, he thinks about takin' less dangerous chances, and Holt Hunter has a brand-new bride. She's most likely already talkin' to him about taking less chances."

"Maybe we oughta start concentratin' on findin' somebody for Cody Hunter to marry," Sadie suggested.

The planning went on in earnest for a good part of the night. "I know I'm damn tired of waitin' for some luck to come our way," Emmett said. "I say it's time to take the fight to them. I think I picked up two men who ain't afraid of fightin'. I think Peyton and Clute are the men we were waitin' for. I'll tell you something else I think," he went on. "Back down in this valley, nobody knows nor cares what's goin' on between these two big cattle outfits. One of us could eat the other one up and nobody would know it."

It was late when Cody returned to the Triple-H. He rode into the deserted barnyard and pulled up at the barn, unsaddled Storm, and gave the tired horse a portion of grain before putting him in a stall for the night. When he walked up to the house, he noticed that a lamp was burning in his bedroom and when he went inside, he found Holt and Morgan waiting for him. They stopped talking when he walked in, waiting for him to report. "It looks like the war's back on again," Cody said.

"I reckon that money, the Winchester rifle, and the Colt handgun you sent me musta belonged to that strange little fellow that Shorty said showed up here today," Holt said. "What happened to him?"

"I think he showed up here to try to identify us Hunter brothers," Cody answered. "If you had seen him, I think you would have thought the last thing he was was a paid assassin." He proceeded to tell them what caused him to become suspicious of him, suspicious enough to follow him back to an ambush spot from where he could watch the ranch. He was interrupted at that point by a light tap on the door. "Come in," he said.

The door opened and Pansy, dressed in her nightgown and bed robe, walked in the room carrying a tray with a plate of biscuits and cold ham on it. "I know you didn't get any supper, so I brought you a little something in case you're hungry. I don't have any coffee, but it's too late for that now, so I brought you a glass of water."

"Well, bless your heart," Cody said. "You're right, I'm starvin'. Thank you, Pansy."

"All right, well goodnight then," she said, put the tray on the table by his bed, and left the room.

"All the time I've lived here, she never did that for me," Holt said.

"That's because you never missed supper," Morgan said, then back to Cody, he said, "so you found him watching the barnyard with his rifle out."

"I don't know why I didn't just shoot him when I first found him, but it turned out he didn't give me any choice, anyway, when he tried to get me with that pocket pistol."

"It sounds to me like you were the one they sent him after," Morgan said. "They wanted to get the Injun out of the way to begin with. Then it would be Holt and me next."

"I just want to be sure that this little episode with this hired killer today is enough to keep you two from gettin' careless," Cody said. "We need to alert all the men to always be aware of what's goin' on around 'em. But if they know who we are, they'll go after us for sure. I'm thinkin' I can do us more good, if I go back to being Crazy Wolf."

"You're liable to get yourself killed," Morgan said.

"Well, what are we gonna do?" Holt asked. "You know damn well Pa ain't gonna like it if we're the ones who go after them."

"That's true," Morgan said, "but they attacked us when they sent that killer after Cody. So anything we do right now is in defense, and if we don't counterattack, it'll just get worse for us." If they could have known what Emmett Kincaid was planning to do, there would have been little worry about any action they took against the Double-K. "We'll talk about the best thing to do in the mornin'. It's gettin' late, and I need to go to bed." He grinned and added, "And I know Holt is anxious to get to bed."

John Bostic, one of the older hands at the Triple-H was almost always the first man at the cookshack in the mornings. He not only provided company for Sully while he was cooking breakfast, he would often go to the pump outside the cookshack to refill Sully's bucket for the second pot of coffee. Such was the case on this morning. "I'll fill your bucket for you," Bostic joked, "but only if I get the biggest slice of that bacon."

"If you don't fill that bucket, I ain't gonna give you no bacon at all this mornin'," Sully came back at him.

Bostic laughed and picked up the bucket. "Mornin', Shorty," he greeted Shorty Black on his way to breakfast.

"Sully got you doin' kitchen duty again?" Shorty japed.

"That's right," Bostic answered. "You might not get any breakfast, if it weren't for me helpin' out." He walked to the corner of the cookhouse and started priming the pump till he got a steady flow as several of the other men came out of the bunkhouse. The sharp crack of the rifle shot rang out to split the heavy morning air. Bostic stopped pumping and took two steps forward to fall against the pump before falling to the ground. Three more shots came in quick succession as the shooter tried to hit the men running wildly to find cover.

With only a general idea where the shots came from, some of the men ran back inside the bunkhouse to get their weapons. Then, led by Shorty Black and Chris Scott, they ran across the pasture to the clump of trees the shots seemed to have come from. The shooter was gone, but there was evidence of his having been there. All three Hunter brothers were at the bunkhouse where John Bostic had been carried. The bullet had struck him right between his shoulder blades, and he was clearly not going to make it. So they could only try to make him as comfortable as a man could be whose life was rapidly draining out of his body. When he finally let go, his last words were, "Tell Sully I'm sorry about the water . . ."

Cody saddled Storm and rode out to the sniper's position. He didn't get off his horse because the tracks left by the shooter were so obvious in his attempt to get away fast. Cody held Storm to an easy lope still easily following the tracks as he passed within a dozen yards of the spot where Vargas Roach had waited for him. But then the tracks blended in with all the many other tracks on the road, and he knew he couldn't separate them. "Not even an Indian," he mumbled to himself. He knew then he was going to have to return to being Crazy Wolf and wait for the next sniper. He turned his horse around and loped back to the barn.

When he went back in the house, Pansy greeted him with, "You better be real glad you got back here when you did. You already passed up my supper last night."

"Yeah, but those biscuits and ham, I woulda hated to miss those," Cody replied.

"Holt said you rode off to see if you could follow the shooter's tracks," his father said.

"Yes, sir, I did, but once he got to the road, I couldn't tell which tracks were his," Cody said. "We know who's responsible for the shooting, we just don't know which one of 'em pulled the trigger. I would have liked to have found the one that shot poor Bostic though." Back to Pansy then, he said, "Don't plan on me for breakfast in the mornin'. I'll be leavin' way before breakfast time, and I might not be back for a while."

"You're going Injun again, ain't you?" Pansy asked."

"Just partway," he said. "We can't have those snipers from Double-K showin' up here every mornin' to pick our men off."

Otto Ross got back to the Double-K headquarters in the middle of the morning. He was pumped up with pride for what he had accomplished. He pulled his horse to a stop in front of the barn and slid off the saddle and hit the ground grinning. "Did you get a shot?" Sam Kilbourne asked.

"Like pickin' cherries," Otto answered. "I got the cook. He was at the pump fillin' a bucket, and I placed a shot right between his shoulder blades. I threw three more shots at 'em, but they was runnin' all over the place by then, so I couldn't hit another one. Then a bunch of 'em grabbed their guns and started after me. So I had to leave." He couldn't get the grin off his face. "Where's the boss?"

"He's in the barn," Sam said, then followed him inside.

"Well, look who's back," Emmett said when Otto walked in. "Did you get one?"

"I sure did, Boss. I was settin' right there in the bushes when they was gittin' ready to eat breakfast. Only I ain't sure they ever got any 'cause I think I mighta shot the cook. He come outta the cookshack and went to the pump and started fillin' a bucket. And I popped him right between the shoulder blades. The rest of 'em scattered."

"So you took off then?" Emmett asked.

"Not before I threw three more shots at 'em." He gloated.

"Then I reckon you can ride with me and Clute and Peyton and Sam, up where the shootin's gonna be goin' on. You can ride with us, instead of back there with Willy and Mathers and the boys moving the cows we're gonna cut outta their range."

"Good, that's where I wanna be, where the shootin's goin' on," Otto said.

"Me and Sam are gonna be ridin' today to pick the cattle we're gonna take tomorrow," Emmett said. "Then after we take 'em, we're gonna kill anybody who tries to take 'em from us."

Cody got up the next morning well before daylight. He put his cowhand clothes aside and climbed into his old buckskins. Being careful not to wake anyone, he slipped out of the house by way of the front door, carrying his rifle with him. He figured if there was a sniper again this morning, he would be concentrating on the barnyard as before and not the house. That is, even if he was in position yet, which Cody doubted. But if he was, Cody thought it better to go to the ridge on foot and there would be less chance of being seen.

Once he reached the cover of the trees, he moved to the best place he could find that would give him a clear shot of anyone going to the cookshack. He sat there in the dark then, watching and listening. He thought it unlikely that a sniper would return two days in a row, but he felt he had to guard against it. So he remained there until the first rays of the sun splashed across the barnyard before he went back to the barn to saddle his horse. Sully was fixing breakfast by that time, so he went in the cookshack to have breakfast before he rode out to do a little scouting over near the Double-K range. "Mornin', Cody," Sully said, after turning around expecting John Bostic. He said as much.

"Hey, little brother," Morgan Hunter called out a short time later when he saw Cody leaving the cookshack. "I see you got back into your buckskins. What you plan on doin'?" He was afraid Cody was planning to do something dangerous.

"I'm just gonna do a little scoutin'," Cody said. "With Double-K startin' to send snipers in close to the ranch to shoot at us, I think it might be a good idea to keep an eye on 'em. I just feel a little more comfortable in my old buckskins."

"You be careful," Morgan said. "We've gotten used to havin' you around."

"Well, that's good to know. I ain't plannin' to go anywhere." He nodded to his brother and rode off toward the Double-K range. He wasn't sure what he was looking for, just anything that didn't look right. So he rode up the Triple-H eastern range where most of their herd was grazing at this time.

After about a mile, he decided to ride down into Double-K range. He had not gone far when he caught sight of a couple of riders coming his way. So he pulled his horse up behind a thicket. When the riders passed by him, he was surprised to see that one of the riders was Emmett Kincaid. The thought crossed his mind that he should shoot him and probably solve most of their problems at once. Then it occurred to him that they were riding onto Triple-H range. So he turned around and followed them to see what they had in mind, and it became obvious what their intentions were. They were going to steal Triple-H cattle again, and not just a few. It was also obvious they were planning the easiest route to move the largest number of cattle onto Double-K range. It was evidently the end of the peaceful respite from cattle rustling. The question to be answered first was when was Kincaid planning his raid. And surely he would expect Triple-H to respond, which meant for some reason, Kincaid was confident he would succeed this time. To begin with, Cody decided he needed to know how Emmett planned to drive their cattle to their range. So he continued to follow Emmett and the other rider as they selected the easiest and the fastest way to drive the cattle.

Emmett and Sam were forced to hide in a gulley once when L. C. Pullen rode by the herd. Cody hid in the same gulley some forty yards behind them. Then they continued on until Cody knew the general route they planned to drive their cattle. He knew where he would place men to turn the cattle back toward the Triple-H. He thought of Chris Scott and Shorty Black to turn that herd. When Emmett was apparently satisfied his man knew exactly what to do, they headed back to the Double-K. Cody continued to follow them until they were well onto their range and obviously heading straight back to the ranch house. Then he headed back to Triple-H headquarters to meet with Morgan and Holt and ready themselves for their defense.

CHAPTER 26

As soon as he got back to the ranch, Cody went in search of Holt and Morgan. When he realized it was dinnertime, he went to the house to see if Holt was there. He found that he was and that Spring had helped Pansy cook dinner. When Cody walked into the house, Pansy's first words to him were, "That Indian's back."

When Cody saw Holt there, he said, "I'll be right back," and he went back out the door. He went next door to Morgan's house to tell him to come to the main house when he had finished eating because they had to get ready for a raid.

After dinner, they were joined by Morgan, and they adjourned to Duncan Hunter's room. "They're plannin' to steal a large part of our herd, and I think they're comin' prepared to fight for 'em," Cody said, and he went on to tell them what he had seen that morning.

"Emmett Kincaid right on our doorstep," Morgan remarked. "He ain't come outta his hole since he almost got shot at the boundary creek. I reckon since his plan to kill all the Hunter men by a paid assassin fell through, he's decided he's gonna do it himself."

"He must have hired some more men," Holt said, "and

from the sounds of it, some guns or he wouldn't be in such a hurry to try it again."

"If what you say is true, and I expect that it is," Duncan said, "I'm afraid it's come to the point where we have to fight to survive."

"I'm afraid you're right, Pa, and I don't know if our crew has got what it takes to fight it out with the likes of those outlaws," Morgan said. "Our men are cowhands. How many of them have ever killed a man? I suspect none of them. I suspect the real fightin' is gonna have to be done by me and Holt, and Crazy Wolf over there. I'm just hopin' we can count on the rest of the men to control those cows while all the shootin's goin' on."

"My concern is our families," Holt said. "We've got to somehow make sure the war stays out there on the range."

"They're gonna have to go through me to get to the family," Duncan said.

"I count on that, Pa, but I wanna stop it short of that," Morgan said.

"I'm afraid we don't have much time," Cody said. "After following them all around this mornin', I think they're gettin' ready to move tomorrow. We need to get the men together this afternoon and give 'em the story. Then it would be to our advantage if we could get them in place tonight so if they come tonight, they'll find us waiting for 'em."

"That don't leave us much choice," Morgan said. "We'll have to get the men together this afternoon and tell them how things are. Those who don't wanna participate in the fightin', maybe they'll volunteer to help protect the families."

They left the house and went down to the cookshack where they gathered most of the men for a meeting. Several of the men had already ridden back out to work so they would have to get the word to them later somehow. Much to the three Hunter brothers' surprise, no one opted out of the fight. Even Frank Strom, one of the older men, said that it was high time we settled with that gang of outlaws. His comments got a hearty backing from the others. So Morgan laid out the plan so that everybody knew what they were going to try to accomplish and why they were going out tonight to be in position. When they figured they had covered everything, Morgan told them to get everything they needed ready that afternoon. Then after they ate supper they would ride out, and he would put them in position to receive their guests. After the meeting was over, Morgan asked Holt, "Whaddaya think?"

"I think we're gonna give 'em a helluva fight," Holt said.

"How 'bout you, Big Chief Crazy Wolf?"

"What he said," Cody answered.

Cody spent most of the time before supper cleaning his Henry rifle and his Colt six-gun, then making sure he had plenty of ammunition for them. He examined his bow and his big-game arrows to make sure they were all in good condition. Last, but by no means least, he gave Storm some attention to make sure the big dun was rested enough and ready to go.

He ate supper with the men, as did Holt and Morgan, and when they were finished, they climbed into their saddles, and the Triple-H fighting men followed the Hunters out of the barnyard toward the east range. When they reached the herd of cattle, Cody took over the placement of the men. The first place was where Emmett had indicated to Sam Kilbourne that the cattle would be turned down a shallow draw and headed back toward the Double-K. This was where Cody stationed Shorty Black and Chris Scott along with two other men with instructions to turn the cows to the east. They proceeded on toward the probable place where the Double-K gang would enter into Triple-H land, dropping a couple of men along the way.

When they got to the end of their battle line, Holt and Morgan dismounted and picked their defensive positions. Cody went a little farther toward the Double-K to effect more of a crossfire. There was nothing left to do but wait to see if Kincaid and his gang would arrive that night.

Emmett Kincaid walked out of the kitchen after telling Ralph that the Triple-H would never know what hit them. He walked down to the barn to make sure everyone was ready to ride. They had a long ride to get to the eastern part of the Triple-H range, which was actually a long pasture protected by a low wooded ridge. It was close to the ranch headquarters and consequently not as closely watched as the ranch's open pastures in the valley. The Double-K was still short of men, but they had enough for this cattle theft, and the guns to protect it. So while there was still daylight, they would ride up the valley to the ridge that separated Double-K from Triple-H and wait there until dark. Then they would ride over the ridge and move the cows out that shallow draw back toward their ranch.

When the sun finally set, but the moon had not risen yet, this was the time Emmett favored for rustling cattle so he ordered, "Mount up boys! It's time to move some beef!" He rode toward the ridge with Peyton and Clute on either side of him, and Otto and Sam behind them. Coming down the other side of the ridge, approaching the pasture, Sam suddenly cried out in pain when he was struck in the side with an arrow. A few moments later Clute let out a roar when an arrow pierced halfway through his thigh before the bone turned it.

"Injuns!" one of the men behind Otto and Sam cried out, and their little formation scattered as everybody looked for a target.

Sam strained to pull the arrow from his side, but it was in too deep. "Boss," he gasped, "I'm hurt bad. I'm hurt bad."

"I can't do nothin' for you, just hold on," Emmett told him. "Clute, you ain't hurt bad. You can still ride."

"The hell you say," Clute responded painfully. "That damn Injun broke the bone in my leg."

Then it occurred to Emmett that there had only been two arrows. "It ain't Injuns. It's that damn Cody Hunter! He's out here by hisself, and now he's tryin' to get back to warn 'em! So let's get up there and get those cows movin' before he gets back to the ranch!" He gave his horse a kick and charged into the pasture, but suddenly, the darkness of the pasture was lit up by the muzzle blasts of the three Hunter brothers' rifles in a rapid fire of hell. Peyton and Mathers were knocked out of their saddles. Emmett was hit in the shoulder but managed to stay on his horse. He dropped over on the horse's neck and wheeled him away into the trees. A couple of the men broke to their left and tried to escape the blistering rifle fire only to be cut down by Chris and Shorty. They and the two men with them were already busy holding the cows in the pasture after all the gunfire stirred them up.

Lost momentarily in the middle of the bodies and rider-less horses, Otto Ross crawled on his hands and knees toward a bank of bushes about fifty feet away. He was not wounded, but he felt it best to drop off his horse while those around him were dropping from wounds. He was suddenly stopped when he was grabbed by the collar. "You goin' somewhere?" Holt lifted him to his feet by his collar. With his rifle barrel stuck in his back and the one hand still on his collar, Holt walked him over to sit on the ground with three of his fellow rustlers. Morgan walked over to the group, now under guard by Steve Smith and all wounded except Otto Ross.

"You know why you got shot, I reckon," Morgan said.

"You came on private property to steal cattle and that's against the law. When you break the law on our land, then we're the law. I'm gonna let you go this time to take care of your wounds, but we've had all the trouble we're gonna stand for from the Double-K. You can get up from there and find your horses and get offa Hunter land. If you're smart, you'll find you somewhere else to work. Which one of you was the sniper that was brave enough to ride in close and make that perfect rifle shot yesterday?" All three wounded men looked at Otto. Following their glances, Morgan asked, "Did you make that shot?"

Otto couldn't bring himself to deny the compliment. "Yessir, I made that shot."

Morgan drew his pistol and shot him. "John Bostic was a damn good man. The rest of you get the hell off this land." He looked around him then and asked, "Where's Cody?" No one knew.

In his panic to escape, Emmett drove his horse hard toward the point where he had intended to turn the herd of cattle. He saw Chris Scott and Shorty Black rise up from their hiding places, so he swerved in the only direction open to him and that was into the midst of the herd. With his shoulder bloody, he continued to hug his horse's neck and he realized the only choice to escape was in the direction of the Triple-H headquarters. After he worked his way through the nervous cattle, he found there were no Triple-H riders on the other side of the herd. He was in the clear. When that struck him, his fear lessened to the extent where his anger could take over. He sat up in the saddle again and began to feel the pain of having his entire crew of men wiped out with no reserves back at his ranch but his useless brother.

The farther he rode in that direction, the more angry he became. If he didn't turn soon, he would ride right into the Triple-H headquarters, the home of the people who had ruined him in one single night. In the darkness of the night, it occurred to him that he had not met another rider on the trail to the ranch. Thoughts of revenge and retaliation took possession of his mind then, so he decided to keep going to see if there was anyone left to protect the Hunter family. When he approached the ranch house, he pulled up, but saw no one in the barnyard at all. That's good, he thought, and rode past the circle of light provided by the lantern hanging by the barn door. He pulled his horse to a stop in the darkness while he considered the large house and the smaller house next to it. He decided the smaller house was most likely the home of Morgan, the eldest of the brothers, and the ranch manager. What revenge could be sweeter than to have Morgan Hunter return home tonight to find his wife's body gutted and his children's throats cut?

Inside the house, Edna started when she heard the sound of a shoulder against the front door. Without thinking, she came out of the kitchen to investigate, only to stop in horror when she met the looming figure of Emmett Kincaid standing in her hallway. She backed slowly toward the kitchen and the gun she should have taken with her. He advanced step-by-step with her. "Good evenin', Mrs. Hunter. I must apologize for gettin' blood on your front door. It came from the bullet hole your husband put in my shoulder." He pulled a long skinning knife from a sheath on his belt. "You wanna make a try for that pistol on the edge of the cabinet?" He stepped between her and the pistol just as both four-year-old Mason and two-year-old Louise ran in from their bedrooms, thinking their father was home.

In the main house next door, they were alerted only when they heard the screams of Edna and the children. Pansy grabbed her Colt .45 and ran for the front door, a good bit ahead of Duncan. On the way, she told Spring to get back in her room and lock the door. Seeing the horses in front of Morgan's house, she feared she was too late. But she charged in, anyway, to collide with a big body in the dark hallway. "Pansy! Don't shoot!" Cody blurted. She moved over against the side of the hallway to give him room to drag Emmett's body out the front door. "Hold that door open, will you, Pa?" Duncan held the door and Cody dragged the body out and laid it on the porch. Duncan noticed it still had nothing but the handle of a knife protruding from up under the ribs. He and Pansy went back in the kitchen to see what kind of shape Edna was in while Cody pulled the knife out of Emmett's chest. He wiped the blade clean on Emmett's shirt, which was already bloody from the shoulder. After returning the knife to its sheath, Cody picked up the body and laid it across the saddle. He wasn't sure what Morgan and Holt would want to do with it. But he thought that maybe they should return it to his brother, since he was the part owner. He decided he'd better make sure everybody was all right now before he rode back out to check with his brothers.

Edna was in the midst of telling Duncan and Pansy her terrifying tale when Cody walked back in the kitchen. She immediately interrupted herself, walked up to him, and threw her arms around him. "Thank you for me and my children," she said.

"I'm just glad I was here in time," he said.

"Why didn't you just shoot him?" Duncan asked.

"I reckon I didn't have time to decide," Cody said.

"You don't understand," Edna said. "When Cody ran in, that devil had me backed in that corner over there, standing over me with that knife raised in the air, I closed my eyes when I saw it already coming down to kill me. I heard him grunt and fall away. I didn't know what happened."

"I was just lucky," Cody said. "She's right, he was fixin' to kill her. He was already coming down with that knife. I just had enough time to grab his arm and help him find a better place to put that blade."

He left them then, thinking he'd better let Morgan and Holt know what had happened to him. Then they could decide what to do with Emmett's body. When he got back to the herd, everything had calmed down. Morgan saw him ride, up and he asked, "Where'd you find that?"

Cody couldn't resist. "In your kitchen," he said.

"What are you talkin' about?" Morgan asked. "Who is it?"

"Mr. Emmett Kincaid," Cody replied. "I saw him cuttin' through the herd and headin' toward the ranch. I figured he had some bad intentions, so I went after him." He went on to tell him the whole story. Morgan was as thankful as Edna was.

"That's one more thing to celebrate," Morgan said. "I don't know what I would have done, if you hadn't been there. But doggone it, you're always where you're needed." He motioned around himself, then at the bodies. "I swear, I think we won our war tonight. And we didn't lose a man. It was a total ambush. I sent three wounded men home. Another one, big one that you shot in the leg with an arrow, he said he's movin' on, said he just signed on a couple days ago and it was a mistake. So I think it would be a good idea if we take a ride out to the Double-K day after tomorrow and have a talk with Ralph Kincaid to see what his plans are. Give him a day to think about it."

"You think we oughta take ol' Emmett, here, with us?" Cody wondered.

"Probably not," Morgan said. "We'll tell Ralph we buried him with his gallant men."

Just to be safe, Morgan and Cody rode down to the Double-K two days later, taking Chris Scott and Shorty Black with them. When they arrived, they found the three wounded men still there as well as Tater Duggan, the cookshack cook, and Sadie Springer, who was drunk as could be. They couldn't say what Ralph Kincaid's plans were, since he took off the day before and said he wouldn't be back. The three wounded men, Tater, and Sadie planned to stay until all the food and whiskey supplies were used up, and then they were leaving. "We don't know what the cows are gonna do, and we don't give a flip," Sadie said.

"I know Emmett Kincaid would be plumb happy to contribute his holdings to the Hunter boys," Morgan said, "especially the 'Injun.' Whaddaya say, Crazy Wolf? You finally ready to hang up your bow and arrows?"

"Guess I'd better be," Cody answered. "Looks like this is a job that calls for all the Hunters." He paused to give him a smile. "As long as you don't go gettin' any ideas about my moccasins."

TURN THE PAGE FOR AN EXCITING PREVIEW!

**Orphaned in a massacre. Raised by Crow Indians.
Destined to become a powerful hunter, a legendary
scout, and a true American hero . . .**

THEY CALLED HIM CRAZY WOLF

As a widower with three young boys, Duncan Hunter
dreamed of a new life for his sons in the heart of
Washington Territory. But the journey was doomed from
the start. Before reaching Hell Gate, their wagon train
was attacked by Blackfoot Indians. Most of the pioneers
were viciously murdered. But Hunter's son Cody
survived—taken in by Crow Indians and raised
as one of their own. They called the boy Crazy Wolf.
This is his story . . .

From hunting and tracking on the American frontier to
leading patrols on covert missions for the US Army,
Cody Hunter would become one of the most valued
scouts in the nation. But a part of him would always be
Crazy Wolf—a man of two worlds, as wild and free as
the land itself. And every bit as dangerous . . .

**First in a blazing new series
by Spur Award–winning author**

CHARLES G. WEST

**The Hunters
TO HELL AND GONE**

"Rarely has an author painted the great American West
in strokes so bold, vivid, and true."
—Ralph Compton

On sale wherever Pinnacle Books are sold.

Visit us at www.kensingtonbooks.com

CHAPTER 1

"I reckon there ain't no use to try talking you out of it, no more," John Hunter said, making one final attempt to change his brother Duncan's mind about leaving. "We've always managed to get by so far, one way or another, ain't we?"

"I appreciate what you're saying, John, but you know, just like I know, this farm ain't big enough to support two families like yours and mine. We gave it a helluva try, but every winter after that has just gotten worse."

There was not much John could say to refute that. The winter of 1862–1863 was an unusually harsh one on animals and crops alike. But the cruelest blow it struck was taking the life of Louise Hunter, Duncan's frail wife, with a fatal bout of pneumonia. Twelve years ago, Duncan had brought Louise to live with John and Louise's sister, Mildred, on a ninety acre farm in northern Montana. Although not a sturdy woman, Louise gave Duncan three strong sons. "With three strong appetites," Duncan always said.

"There's a wagon train leavin' Fort Benton to take that new road the army built, that Mullan Road that goes to Walla Walla, Washington Territory. Me and the boys are gonna be on it."

"I swear, I just hate to see you go, Duncan. It ain't gonna be the same with you gone."

"I'm gonna miss you and Mildred, too," Duncan said, "but it'll make life a whole lot easier on you, and especially Mildred. I woulda gone a long time before this, but Louise didn't want to leave her sister. Mildred's got enough on her hands takin' care of her own young'uns. It wouldn't be fair to add my three to her chores." He gave his brother a big smile then and said, "Hell, my boys are raring to go. When we file a claim on a good piece of land out in Washington, you might wanna come out there, too."

"Maybe so," John said. "I don't know if Mildred is up to a trip like that or not. Right off hand, I'd say she ain't, seeing as how she comes from the same stock as Louise. Ain't you worried about Indians and things like that?"

"Not a whole bunch," Duncan replied. "They say there's not much danger if you've got a pretty good number of wagons in the train. They say the folks in the wagons usually have better weapons than the Indians attackin' 'em. Morgan ain't but ten, but he's already a pretty good shot with a rifle."

John just shook his head, still doubtful when he thought of his brother trying to drive his wagon and protect his three sons, Morgan, ten, Holt, seven, and Cody, five. "Duncan, for God's sake, be careful."

"You know I'll do my best," Duncan said. "I've spent dang-nigh every cent I've got, equipping my wagon for the trip, so I can't change my mind about goin'. We'll say goodbye tonight after supper 'cause we're pullin' outta here for Fort Benton in the mornin' before breakfast."

Mildred insisted on fixing one final big supper for them before a tearful goodbye and Godspeed, knowing in all likelihood, she would never see them again.

* * *

Arriving at Fort Benton, Duncan was to find only two other wagons waiting on the appointed date. He found the wagon master he had corresponded with at one of the wagons, a man named Luther Thomas. Duncan asked where the rest of the wagons were parked. There were supposed to be eighteen making up the train. Luther said all but Duncan and the other two wagons had joined a train that left a week earlier.

"I'm sorry about that," Luther said. "It sure caught me by surprise. You can talk to Mr. Frasier there in the other wagon. He's trying to make up his mind what he's gonna do. It's already after the first of May, so if you're gonna get through the mountains before the first snowfall, you gotta go now."

"What are you gonna do?" Duncan asked Luther.

"Me? Hell, I'm goin' to Walla Walla first thing in the mornin', even if I'm by myself. The army built that road, and I know it's in good shape 'cause I already took one party out there. There ain't been nothin' about no Injun problems reported back here to Fort Benton. So I'm goin'. How 'bout you, Mr. Hunter? I don't blame you one bit if you feel like it's too risky for you and your boys."

"I ain't got nothin' to go back to, so I'll go with you," Duncan answered.

"Good man," Luther said. "We're glad to have the company. We'll see what Frasier decides to do, now that he's got more company."

When they went to Frasier's wagon to get his decision, he said, "I'll see what my wife says," and went back into the wagon.

Luther looked at Duncan and cracked, "Wise man. Might as well get it from the boss."

Frasier returned with his wife.

"Howdy," she said and went straight to Duncan. "I wanted to welcome somebody as crazy as Robert and me."

She looked around behind him before continuing. "I'm Rose Frasier. I wanted to meet your wife."

"I'm very sorry, ma'am. My wife has passed away. But I'm pleased to meet you. My name is Duncan Hunter. These towheads are Morgan, Holt, and Cody. Say howdy to Mrs. Frasier boys."

They all did in one polite "howdy."

"Outstanding young men," Rose said. "I know they'll be respectful around my two girls and friends with my two sons."

"My four are around here somewhere," Luther said. "Looks like we ain't gonna run short of young'uns on the trip. Why don't we all have supper together tonight, then everybody can get to know everybody else," he suggested. "And tomorrow we'll start day one of our trip."

And so the journey began.

Leaving Fort Benton, they started out west on the Mullan Road. Passing north of Great Falls, the road then dropped south to cross the continental divide west of Helena, following a path through Mullan Pass, driving for the Clark Fork River.

Tragedy struck the little three-wagon train just as darkness began to fall one evening. Coming out of the Mullan Pass, Frasier's right front wheel was struck by a small boulder that had come tumbling down the slope above the wagons. Unknown to them, the boulder had been set in motion by a large war party of Blackfoot Indians, and it smashed the spokes of the wheel, stopping the wagon.

Ahead of the doomed wagon, Duncan and Luther grabbed their rifles and tried to return fire, but they could not identify targets to shoot at. The Blackfoot snipers were too well hidden in the slopes above the pass. Frasier's fourteen-year-old son, Tim, started firing his rifle at anything he thought might be a target until a Blackfoot bullet slammed him in the chest. Luther's wife, Flo, called all the younger children to run and take cover in their wagon, which was the lead wagon and farthest away from the deadly ambush. Morgan Hunter, Duncan's ten-year-old, remained with his father to return fire, using his squirrel rifle.

"Duncan!" Luther yelled. "We've gotta get these wagons outta here!"

Duncan could see that. They had to move out of the deadly killing passage. But first, he had to jump down from his wagon to help Rose and Robert Frasier when he saw them running from their wagon. Morgan jumped down to help, too, only to provide better targets for the Blackfoot snipers. In a steady hail of rifle slugs, they retreated toward the wagon. From his wagon ahead of them, Luther could only watch as one of the families he was guiding ended their aspirations of starting a new life on the fertile plains of the far west right there in Mullan Pass.

"There," Spotted Pony said, pointing down a rocky ravine where they could see the glow of flames in the darkness of the mountains. "They have found something to attack." He and his Crow brothers had been avoiding the Blackfoot war party since first discovering their camp that afternoon. Judging by the sign left at their campsite, the war party was fairly large and surely outnumbered Spotted Pony and his five companions.

"That fire is too big to be a campfire," Walks Fast said. "Maybe they found a wagon on that white man road."

"Let's go see," Gray Wolf urged.

They made their way down from the top of the pass, descending carefully in the darkness to avoid creating any rockslides until reaching a flat ledge near the bottom. From there they saw that it was indeed a wagon burning.

"I smell meat," Gray Wolf said. "What are they cooking? I don't see anyone around."

"The horses," Spotted Pony said. "They are still tied to the wagon. There's no one here. The Blackfeet have gone."

They moved down off the ledge and looked around the burning wagon at the bodies lying there. All of them were mutilated and scalped. Suddenly, there was a rustling in a bank of low bushes, and all five of the Crow hunters were immediately alert to an attack, aiming their weapons at the spot where the leaves were shaking.

"Come out!" Spotted Pony ordered, but no one did. He moved carefully toward the bush, his rifle ready to shoot. With the barrel of the weapon, he pulled a heavy branch aside and immediately recoiled, surprised to see a wolf lying beneath the bushes. "Wolf!" he cried, alerting the others as he took a cautious step back to look all around him. For where there was one wolf, there were usually many. But there was no sign of any other wolves.

"Maybe he is wounded," Two Moons said. "Be careful."

Spotted Pony slowly pulled the branch aside again, his finger on the trigger of his rifle, ready to shoot if the wolf attacked. The wolf did not attack or run at once, as Spotted Pony expected, so he continued to hold the branch aside. The wolf continued to look at him but made no sign of aggression.

"Be careful," Two Moons cautioned again. "I think the wolf is crazy."

Since the wolf showed no signs of attacking, Spotted Pony continued to hold the branch aside while he reached down with his other hand and pulled some lower branches aside as well. He recoiled, startled, for he saw a small boy lying on the other side of the wolf, his body pressed tightly against the wolf's.

Seeing Spotted Pony suddenly recoil, the other Crows prepared to fire their weapons.

"Wait!" Spotted Pony exclaimed when a whimper and a slight movement of the hand told him that the boy was alive. Not until he reached into the bush to pull the boy out from under its branches did the wolf suddenly bolt away into the darkness. "This boy's been shot in the back," Spotted Pony told his companions. "He has not been scalped. He must have crawled up under the bush to hide when the Blackfeet shot the others."

Spotted Pony rolled the body over on its back and pressed his ear to the boy's chest. After a minute, he sat up and said, "He is not dead. His heart still beats."

"I think the wolf was keeping him alive until we could find him," Gray Wolf said. "It shook the bushes to get your attention, but it did not flee until you took the boy."

"I think you are right," Spotted Pony said. "I will take him back to our camp and see if he will live or die. I think that is what the wolf wanted me to do. Look around you. Everyone else is dead. There is a reason the wolf was sent to keep this boy safe."

"I think we missed a chance to have some fresh meat," Walks Fast complained. "You were so close to it, you could have killed it with your knife, instead of grabbing the boy."

"Maybe that is so," Spotted Pony said. "But I think the wolf's spirit was keeping the boy alive. If we killed the wolf, then maybe we kill the boy."

"He looks pretty bad," Walks Fast said. "I think he's going to die, anyway, and we could have had fresh meat."

"That wolf had to be crazy. If it wasn't, it would have eaten the boy, instead of guarding him," Spotted Pony said. "If you had eaten the wolf you might have died."

Spotted Pony was right. The boy did not die, and he was given the name Crazy Wolf and raised by Spotted Pony to be a strong young Crow warrior.

CHAPTER 2

Sergeant Arthur Kelly walked over to the campfire to report the return of the Crow scouts to Lieutenant Preston Ainsworth. "Scouts are back, Lieutenant."

"Bring 'em on over here, Kelly," Ainsworth said. "Did they find that war party?"

"Yes, sir. I think they did." He signaled the scouts to come on over to the lieutenant's fire. Ainsworth was new in assignment to Fort Keogh, and consequently not familiar with the Crow scouts as yet. This, in fact, was his first scouting patrol. Aware of this, Sergeant Kelly told him the scouts were Crazy Wolf and Bloody Axe.

"Thank you, Sergeant," Ainsworth said. He watched them as they approached, one of them a head taller than his companion. The shorter of the two Indians seemed to hang back a little, so Ainsworth addressed the tall one. "Bloody Axe?"

"No, sir. I'm Crazy Wolf. You wanna talk to Bloody Axe?" He stopped and stepped aside for his companion.

Ainsworth shrugged indifferently. He didn't really care which of the scouts he talked to. He had just been guessing at the names, and in his mind's eye, he thought the tall one looked more apt to be Bloody Axe. "The sergeant tells me you found the Sioux war party."

Bloody Axe nodded rapidly. "We find Lakota. Better you talk Crazy Wolf."

"Oh?" Ainsworth replied and turned to look at the other scout again.

Crazy Wolf stepped forward. "We found the Lakota camp. As near as we could count, there are about seventeen of them. They're camped by a stream about four miles from here. Hard to tell how many of them have rifles, but we saw at least eight of them carrying them."

Ainsworth was surprised by the report. "Very well, Crazy Wolf. By the way, your English is very good."

"Thank you, sir, I try."

Ainsworth didn't say anything more for a few moments while he studied the young man standing before him. His clothes were similar to those Bloody Axe was wearing and his hair was worn in two long braids, but he was different. Then he realized his tanned face was not that of an Indian. "You're not Crow, are you?"

Crazy Wolf smiled. "Well, I am and I ain't. I was born in a white family, but I was raised as a Crow since I was five years old. So I forgot what it's like to be white. My Crow father, Spotted Pony, taught me everything I needed to know to live in this world."

Ainsworth was fascinated by his story. "But your English," he said. "If you have been a Crow since the age of five, I would think you would have forgotten English."

"Well, I reckon part of that is because when Spotted Pony found me, I made a promise to myself to never forget my mother and father and my two brothers, and that I wasn't an Injun. I didn't know there were good Indians and bad Indians, just like white folks. But most of the reason is because of a Jesuit priest at Fort Laramie when our village wintered there two years in a row. He even taught me to read and write a little bit. I think he spent so much extra time with me because he realized I was born a white child."

"You mention a mother and father and two brothers. What happened to them?"

"My mother got sick and died. My father and brothers were killed by Blackfoot warriors. I was left for dead with a bullet in my back, but I hid till Spotted Pony found me and took me home with him. And now, I'm scouting for the US Army with my brother, Bloody Axe." He could have told the lieutenant that he and Bloody Axe were the same as brothers, for it was Bloody Axe's father who'd carried Crazy Wolf away from that field of massacre when he was five and took him in as a son. It was an act of compassion that could have caused a jealous rivalry between the two young boys, instead of the close friendship that resulted.

"Him talk good white man talk," Bloody Axe offered, a wide grin on his face.

"Yes, he does, and you're not bad, yourself," the lieutenant said. Back to Crazy Wolf, he asked, "Do you remember your name when you were five?"

"Yes, I do. My name is Cody Hunter. My father was Duncan Hunter, my brothers were Morgan and Holt. I'll catch up with them when it's my time to go."

"Well, I hope it's not on this patrol," Ainsworth said. "That's quite a story." He took a look at his pocket watch and said, "We still need to wait about thirty minutes and then we're gonna move on that Sioux war party. You think your horses will be rested enough?"

"Yes, sir. They'll be all right. Like I said, it's not but four miles to their camp, so they ain't worked very hard up to now."

"There's probably a couple cups of coffee left in that pot on the fire there," Kelly said, pointing to one of two pots sitting in the edge of the fire. "If you want a cup, help yourself."

"Thank you, Sergeant," Crazy Wolf said. "Bloody Axe and I appreciate it." He turned to relay the message to Bloody Axe in the Crow language, and they went to get their cups out of their saddlebags.

When they left, Sergeant Kelly said, "I reckon I shoulda told you about Crazy Wolf really being a white man, but I didn't know whether you already knew it or not. Him and Bloody Axe used to scout for Lieutenant Ira McCall, D Troop of the Second Cavalry, when they were temporarily assigned here. When the whole Second Regiment was sent to Fort Ellis, Lieutenant McCall wanted to take Crazy Wolf and Bloody Axe with him. But they had been signed up here at Fort Keogh and the colonel said he couldn't approve their transfer. Between you and me, sir, that's what he said, but the real reason was because Crazy Wolf and Bloody Axe are the two best scouts in the whole regiment. And Colonel Miles wanted to keep 'em right here."

"Well, that's good to know, Sergeant," Ainsworth said. "I'm glad you told me."

When the horses were rested, Lieutenant Ainsworth gave the order to mount up. The fifteen-man patrol moved out to attack the Sioux war party that had raided a Crow camp two nights before, killing several and wounding several more. There had been an increase in the number of such attacks upon Crow camps within their reservation ever since Custer's devastating defeat at the Little Bighorn. The Sioux victory over Custer was a stinging defeat for the Crows as well as the US Army because the battle was fought on Crow territory against a combined force of Lakota Sioux, Northern Cheyenne, and Arapaho. After the battle the combined Indian forces scattered. But the Sioux continued their attacks on Crow villages in the Crow reservation. It was time for the US to finally come down hard on the Sioux, and the man they relied on to end the Sioux aggression was Colonel Nelson A. Miles. Operating out of Fort Keogh on the Yellowstone River, Miles conducted raids on the scattered bands of Sioux warriors, either capturing them or causing them to flee to Canada.

After they had ridden about three miles farther south, Crazy Wolf rode back to confer with Lieutenant Ainsworth. In English, Crazy Wolf said, "You see that ridge yonder? There's a healthy stream on the other side of it. You can see the tree line running up to it. The Sioux are camped by that stream on the other side of the ridge. If they've got somebody on top of that ridge as a lookout, they'll see us comin' so you might wanna wait till dark to go any farther. When we found them earlier, they were just makin' camp to rest their horses, I suppose. They didn't seem too worried about anybody botherin' them. They didn't send a lookout up on that ridge the whole time Bloody Axe and I were watchin' 'em." Noticing Ainsworth looked confused, Crazy Wolf added, "If you wanna take a risk that they didn't post a lookout on top of that ridge, we can ride right up to their camp, then catch 'em in a crossfire from both ends of the ridge. Oughta make quick work of 'em, if there ain't no lookout."

Ainsworth thought it over for a minute. The chance of making quick work of it was very important to him at that particular point. When they had left on patrol, they had rations for fifteen days. Already out fourteen days chasing that band, and still two full days away from the fort, he said, "Let's see if we can move on them now."

He turned to Sergeant Kelly. "Sergeant, tell the men to rig for silence. We'll divide the patrol in half. You take half and find a position at the east end of that ridge. I'll take the other half and take the west. Hold your position until I order them to throw down their arms and surrender, then at the first sign of resistance, open fire. You understand? I'll give 'em a chance to surrender, but I'm not going to wait long for their decision."

"Yes, sir," Kelly said. "I'll take one of the scouts with me."

"Right," Ainsworth said. "I'll take Crazy Wolf with me."

Continuing their advance upon the ridge at a slow walk, all eyes scanned the top of the ridge for any sign of a lookout, or an ambush. Crazy Wolf wasn't overly worried about either. Scouting the camp earlier, he'd seen no signs of caution and believed the Sioux had no idea they were being tracked.

Ainsworth reminded Sergeant Kelly he would demand a surrender before opening fire, and possibly that would drive the Sioux warriors back toward him and his men. "If you hold your fire for a brief time, you should be able to take a toll on the warriors if they choose to fight."

Kelly understood what the lieutenant was planning and conveyed it to his men.

"Let's try not to shoot each other," Ainsworth said in conclusion.

When they reached the base of the ridge, they split up and rode to opposite ends of it and dismounted. One man was left to guard the horses. At the western end of the ridge, Ainsworth designated Private Cary Fitzgerald as the horse guard, since he was the youngest and least experienced trooper in his company.

Crazy Wolf led Ainsworth and six troopers cautiously around the end of the ridge and down into the trees beside the stream where they stopped to look the situation over. The ridge was approximately one hundred yards in length, but the Sioux campfire looked to be closer to the western end. Kneeling in the trees by the stream, they could see the Indians, apparently at their leisure.

"They haven't got any idea," Ainsworth whispered. He looked around at his men. "Everybody ready?" He received all affirmative nods. He stepped out from behind the tree he planned to use for cover and yelled to a startled camp of Sioux. "Throw down your weapons! You are to be taken back to your reservation."

A cry of surprise went up from the startled warriors and they sprang up from their blankets to grab their weapons. Ainsworth ducked back behind his tree as the first shots came his way. His men didn't wait for an order to fire but cut down on the exposed Indians, killing three in the first volley. As Ainsworth had predicted, the other warriors backed up rapidly toward the opposite end of the ridge, only to engage the fire from Sergeant Kelly's men and suffer more casualties. Ainsworth's men advanced to new positions, pinning the Sioux down on the creek bank as they returned fire at targets they were still having trouble clearly defining. As their casualties gradually increased, and their already meager supply of ammunition steadily decreased, it became clear they had little chance of surviving. The survivors raised their voices in cries of surrender, all except one.

Black Dog, the leader of the Sioux war party, dropped into a gully that ran down from the top of the ridge. Only a few feet deep, it nevertheless offered him enough protection to crawl up it without being seen. Reaching the top of the ridge, he raised his head high enough to see out of the gully.

Sure no one had seen his escape, he slid his body out of the gully, onto the top of the ridge, and rolled a few feet over the other side. Then he looked back down at his Sioux brothers with their hands held up over their heads. He knew the soldiers must have left their horses at the base of the ridge. He ran along the length of the ridge, weaving his way through the shoulder-high bushes that covered the slope, until he saw the horses.

Young Private Cary Fitzgerald held his rifle tightly in his hands as he heard the gunfire from the other side of the ridge. He knew why the lieutenant had picked him to take care of the horses, but he was just as glad not to be shot at by a bloodthirsty Indian. He had never killed a man, Indian or soldier, and he wondered if he could if the time came. Suddenly, he realized the shooting had stopped. What if the Sioux had won the battle? Would they come looking for the horses right away? How would he know who won until somebody came for the horses? He realized how hard he was squeezing his rifle, and released his desperate grip from the stock and wiped the sweat from his palm.

He turned toward the ridge and froze, his eyes locked on those of the savage, Black Dog, several feet above him. His war axe was drawn back in his hand prepared to strike. Cary's whole body recoiled from the shock of the rifle shot behind him that slammed the fierce warrior in the chest, sitting him down to drop the war axe on the ground beside him.

"Are you all right, soldier?"

Cary turned around to find the scout, Crazy Wolf, ejecting the spent cartridge from the Henry rifle he carried. He reached down and picked up the brass cartridge, a practice he had learned since working for the army. "I figured it'd be a good idea to make sure none of those Sioux back there slipped over the ridge and got to the horses." Realizing the blood had not yet returned to the startled young man's brain, he thought to ease his pride. "I hope you ain't mad 'cause I jumped your shot. I saw that you were gettin' ready to shoot, but I was already aimin' at him, so I went ahead and shot."

Finding his voice again, Cary swallowed hard and took a step back from the fierce-looking body that had rolled down at his boots. "No, I-I ain't mad," he stammered. "Don't make no difference which one of us killed him."

"That's a fact," Crazy Wolf said. "I thought you'd feel that way about it. We might as well take the horses around to the other side where the rest of the men are gettin' the prisoners ready to ride. Gimme a hand, and we'll throw this ugly devil on one of the horses and take him back with the other dead Sioux."

They put their rifles aside and picked up Black Dog and laid him across the saddle on one of the horses.

Recovered from his recent fright, and grateful Crazy Wolf had chosen not to ridicule his inability to act, Cary studied the Crow scout. He was inspired to comment, "You know, you don't talk like an Indian a-tall."

Crazy Wolf laughed. "Just when I'm talking to the likes of you—soldiers and such. I do when I'm talkin' to Indians."

The eight surviving warriors of the raiding party were stripped of all weapons, placed on their horses, with their hands tied behind them. Under guard at all times, including the night when they tried to sleep, the horses were led to Fort Keogh, a journey of two days.

They made it back to the fort in time for the five o'clock mess call, and after turning the Sioux prisoners over to the stockade sergeant, the mess hall is where they headed. Crazy Wolf and Bloody Axe ate with the other Indian scouts in a special section of the enlisted men's mess hall.

Beans, beef, and bread was simple fare, but it was especially good, since there had been nothing to eat but a couple of strips of jerky for all of the day before. They washed it down with the mess hall's version of fresh coffee. Talking with some of the other scouts at the table, Crazy Wolf paid no attention to B Company first sergeant when he came into the mess hall and stood scanning the scout section until he spotted the man he was looking for.

He walked directly over to Crazy Wolf and Bloody Axe. "Crazy Wolf," he began. "I'm Johnny Douglas, first sergeant of B Company. Captain Boyd, my company commander, would like to have a word with you if you don't mind."

Surprised, Crazy Wolf looked past Sergeant Douglas, expecting to see Captain Boyd behind him somewhere. He knew who Captain Boyd was, but he had never scouted for him before.

"Right now?"

"When you finish eatin' your supper," Sergeant Douglas said. "He's in the officers' mess right now, and when he's done eatin', he's goin' back to the orderly room. He'd like you to come there. You know where the B Company orderly room is, don't you?"

"Yep, I know where it is. What's he wanna talk about?"

"I'll let him tell you. He's hopin' you'll do him a favor," Douglas replied. "After you finish eatin'. B Company orderly room, right?" he repeated and waited for Crazy Wolf's answer.

"Right."

"What you think?" Bloody Axe asked when Douglas walked away. "Maybe he's going to give you Freeman's job. Make you chief of the scouts."

"I don't think so," Crazy Wolf answered in the Crow tongue. "He said the captain just wants a favor." He grinned at Bloody Axe and joked, "Anyway, I don't want Cliff Freeman's job, and have to deal with crazy people like you."

When they had finished their supper, Bloody Axe said he would see him at the camp the Crow scouts had made by the river, and Crazy Wolf walked across the parade ground to the long building that housed the different company headquarters. He went in the door with COMPANY B painted above it.

Company Clerk, Private George Cousins, looked up from his desk, surprised to be confronted by a wild Indian. Thinking the man must be lost, Cousins said, "This is B Company. What are you trying to find?"

"I found it. I am Crazy Wolf. Sergeant Douglas said your captain wants to see me."

"He does? Well, he didn't say anything to me about it. What was it about?"

"The sergeant didn't say. Just said he wants to see me."

The captain hadn't said anything about wanting to see one of the Crow scouts, and Cousins was not inclined to have him surprised by a wild Indian when he got back from supper. He was about to tell Crazy Wolf the captain was gone for the evening when the door opened and Captain Boyd walked in.

"Crazy Wolf, right?" Boyd asked.

The scout nodded.

"Thanks for dropping by," Boyd continued. "Cliff Freeman tells me you're actually a white man."

That remark caused Cousins to raise his eyebrows in shock.

"It's true I was born to a white woman," Crazy Wolf said, "but I was raised by the Crows since I was five. I reckon I feel more Crow than white."

"Come on into my office and I'll tell you why I asked you to come talk to me," Boyd said. "You come highly recommended by Lieutenant Ainsworth. As you know Ainsworth is fairly new to this post, as am I. He thinks you are head and shoulders above every other scout in the regiment, and we've got some pretty good scouts."

"I appreciate that, but I don't know why he would think that," Crazy Wolf replied honestly. "Everything I know, I was taught by my Crow brothers."

"Ainsworth said it was you that found that Sioux war party he brought in tonight," Boyd said.

"It was Bloody Axe and me. We both tracked that war party."

"Ainsworth said it was you," Boyd insisted. "But never mind that. I want you to go with a patrol tomorrow, a patrol that is very important to me personally. It's not against a Sioux war party. In fact, I don't expect contact with any Indians. This is an escort assignment. You see, I was posted at Fort Abraham Lincoln for several years before I was transferred to this post. I was attached to the Seventh Cavalry, but they were moved out of Fort Lincoln after Custer's tragic defeat. I've been a widower for seventeen years." He paused to ask, "Do you know what a widower is?"

"It means your wife died. Like my mother did."

"That's right," Boyd continued. "My wife died giving birth to our only child, a daughter we named Amy. My daughter is seventeen now. She is the only family I have, and I am the only family she has. She's never known her mother. She was raised by nursemaids and the US Army. When I was transferred from Fort Lincoln, there were no quarters here for family, so I have had to wait until they were built before I could send for her. Now, thanks to Colonel Miles, I have my private quarters, so my daughter can come live with me."

Crazy Wolf began to understand what the job was. "You want me to go get her?"

"No," Boyd said. "I've already sent a detail of six troopers and a wagon driver to escort her safely back here with all her belongings and our furniture. It's about one-hundred-and-seventy-five miles from here to Fort Lincoln. I had Corporal Tyree wire me from Lincoln the day they arrived and again on the day they departed to return here. I can pretty well guess about how much longer it will take them to arrive. Because of the recent increase in the number of Sioux raiding parties, I'm sending a couple more cavalry men to meet them about halfway back, and I think it would be helpful if they took a scout along. I want you to be that scout. Do you have any problems with that?"

"Nope. You're payin' my wages. Whatever way you wanna use me is all right with me, as long as it ain't scrubbin' out the latrines."

Boyd chuckled. "I'll keep that in mind. And I should have said so in the beginning, but Lieutenant Ainsworth is fine with my wanting to steal you for this personal job. In fact he recommended you."

"About how far do you figure we'll ride before we meet your escort party?"

"As I said, I instructed Corporal Tyree to wire me to let me know the day he left Fort Lincoln. According to my calculations, if you leave in the morning, you can ride two good days and meet them about halfway. The two men you'll be riding with already know about this and they've drawn rations for all three of you. They'll be here in front of the orderly room ready to go right after breakfast to-morrow morning. Eat a good breakfast before you start." Boyd watched Crazy Wolf for his reactions, then asked, "You have any questions or concerns?"

"No, sir. I think I pretty much understand how concerned you are to get your daughter here safely. I'll do what I can to help." Although he didn't express it, Crazy Wolf was somewhat puzzled the captain wanted him specifically. From what he'd just heard of the mission, there didn't seem any need for scouting, and would be no tracking involved, since the escort party was supposedly taking the common wagon road from Fort Lincoln. He also wondered why Boyd chose to send two men and a scout to meet the escort party. If he had concern for his daughter's safety, why not send a fifteen-man patrol? But Crazy Wolf had learned long ago soldiers often did things that didn't make sense to him so he didn't ask any questions.

Reading some skepticism in the scout's expression, the captain explained. "You wonder why I'm sending only the three of you. Right? It's not so much in the form of reinforcements with just two men and a scout. Actually, it's because of the recent increase in reports of Sioux raiding parties up that way. I'm counting on you three to pick up any signs of potential trouble between here and that escort party so the escort could be warned in advance."

Crazy Wolf nodded. "I reckon that makes sense. Like I said, you're payin' my wages, so I would do what you told me to, even if it didn't make sense to me. I will be ready to ride first thing in the morning."

Visit our website at
KensingtonBooks.com
to sign up for our newsletters, read
more from your favorite authors, see
books by series, view reading group
guides, and more!

BOOK CLUB
BETWEEN THE **CHAPTERS**

Become a Part of Our
Between the Chapters Book Club
Community and Join the Conversation

Betweenthechapters.net